Thursdays at Eight

Dear Friends,

Most people skip this page unless there's a chance they'll stumble across their own name. I hope you won't because what I have to tell you is pretty amazing. About six years ago, I felt the need to connect with other businesswomen. I'd recently moved my office out of my home and rented space in a commercial building, which is a bit unusual for a writer. I loved having my work life separate from home and family.

Even in my small hometown, it didn't take me long to meet other women who face the same struggles I do. After one luncheon date with Lillian Schauer, in which we both ended up in tears, I realized how often it's necessary to hide our emotions. I suggested we develop a support group for one another, and Lillian agreed. That was how my own Thursday morning breakfast group was started.

For the last five years I've met with five incredible women—Betty, Lillian, Karla, Stephanie and Diana. We've been through a great deal together—weddings, births, celebrations, crises and death. Last year, we lost our own Stephanie to ovarian cancer.

We continue to gather together to learn from each other, to share our challenges and seek advice, to talk about books we've read, our children, grandchildren… You name it and we've talked about it. We talk, we listen, we laugh, we cry, but mostly we support and encourage one another. We are a bank president, an attorney and business owners, but more importantly we're women who share one of the strongest of female bonds: friendship.

So here's *Thursdays at Eight*, which is dedicated to each member of my Thursday morning breakfast group (although I did not, of course, use actual events or real people in my story). Thank you for being a part of my life, for listening to my frustrations and helping me laugh at myself. I love you all.

Debbie Macomber

P.S. I enjoy hearing from my readers. Feel free to write me at P.O. Box 1458, Port Orchard, WA 98366, or visit my Web site at www.debbiemacomber.com.

DEBBIE MACOMBER

Thursdays at Eight

ISBN 1-55166-811-4

THURSDAYS AT EIGHT

Visit us at www.mirabooks.com

Printed in U.S.A.

First Printing: June 2001
10 9 8 7 6 5 4 3 2 1

This story is dedicated to:
Lillian Schauer, Diana Letson, Betty Roper and Karla Cain

The wonderful, wise and fascinating women of my
Thursday morning breakfast group.

For
Stephanie Cordall
March 13, 1948–
November 12, 2000
We shall miss you,
my friend

"It's the good girls who keep the diaries; the bad girls never have the time."

—Tallulah Bankhead

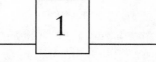

CHAPTER

CLARE CRAIG

January 1st

A promise to myself: this year is a new beginning for me. A fresh start, in more ways than one. I'm determined to put the divorce behind me. About time, too, since it's been final for over a year. Okay, thirteen months and six days to be exact, not that I'm counting...well, maybe I am, but that's going to stop as of *today*.

Michael has his new life and I have mine. I've heard that living well is the best revenge. Good, because that's what I intend to do. I'm going to live my life as a successful, happy (or at least, contented) single woman and mother. This is my vow. I will no longer expect another person to provide me with a sense of worth. I don't need a husband to make me feel complete. It's been a struggle to let go of the marriage, but holding on to all that pain and anger is getting me nowhere. I'm sick of the pettiness, sick of fighting and sick to death of the resentment, the bitterness. I just never thought anything like this could possibly happen to Michael and me.

I saw divorce mow down marriages all around us, but I somehow thought we were safe....

It didn't help any that I ran into Marilyn Cody over the Christmas holidays. She hadn't heard about the divorce, and when I told her my husband had left me for a twenty-year-old—*correction,* my ex-husband (I still have trouble remembering that)—I could see how shocked she was. Then, apparently thinking she was giving me good advice, Marilyn suggested I find myself a boy toy (or is it toy boy?) to get my confidence back. She was actually serious, as though going to bed with a man only a few years older than my own children would make me feel better. Marilyn is a good example of why I can't remain friends with the people Michael and I once associated with.

Losing Marilyn as a friend is no great loss, anyway. I read the pitying look in her eyes, and I didn't miss her innuendo that I could've kept my husband if I hadn't let myself go. It was all I could do not to get in her face and defend myself—as though *that* would prove anything. As a matter of fact, I happen to weigh within fifteen pounds of what I did at twenty-five, and damn it all, I take care of myself. If anyone's suffering from middle-age spread, it's Michael. The audacity of Marilyn to imply that Michael's affair is somehow *my* fault!

How the hell was I supposed to compete with a girl barely out of her teens? I couldn't. I didn't. Every time I think about the two of them together, I feel sick to my stomach.

The journal-writing class has helped. So did meeting Liz, Julia and Karen. They're my friends, and part of my new life. Forming a solid relationship with each of these women is one of the positive changes I've made. As the saying goes, "Out with the old and in with the new." I'm glad the four of us have decided to continue seeing each other, even though the class isn't being offered again. Thursdays for breakfast was an inspired idea.

Writing down my thoughts is the only way I got through the last six months. This should be a good time in my life. Instead, I've been forced to start over—not my choice and not my fault! Okay, fine. I can deal with it. I *am* dealing with it, each and every day. I hate it. I hate Michael, although I'm trying not to. The best I can say at this point is that I'm coping.

I will admit one thing. Michael's affair has taught me a lot about my-self. I hadn't realized I could truly hate anyone. Now I know how deep my anger can cut...and I wish to hell I didn't.

My mistake—and I made a few—was in delaying the divorce as long as I did. Eternal optimist that I am, I clung to the belief that, given time, Michael would come to his senses. I was convinced that eventually he'd see how much he was hurting me and the boys. An affair with a twenty-year-old was sheer madness. Surely he'd wake up one morning and re-alize he'd destroyed his entire life—and for what? Good sex? I doubt she's *that* incredible in the sack.

In retrospect, I could kick myself for waiting so many months to see an attorney. I merely postponed the inevitable, because I was so sure he'd admit what he was doing and put an end to it. How I prayed, how I longed for the opportunity to save my marriage. If only Michael would come home again. If only he'd give us another chance. Little did I understand that his actions had utterly destroyed the foundation of our lives together. The minute he told me he'd fallen in love with Miranda (sure he had!), I should've hightailed it into a lawyer's office and set the divorce in motion. Doing that would have saved me a lot of grief.

At a particularly low point, when I was feeling absolutely desperate, I signed up for counseling. The irony didn't escape me, even then. *I* wasn't the one defiling our wedding vows, yet I was the one making appoint-ments with a shrink!

Then, on a particular Thursday morning about a year and a half ago, I got up after another restless, miserable, lonely night. I remember lean-ing against the bathroom sink in such emotional pain I couldn't even stand upright. I looked at myself in the mirror and barely recognized my own face. Something *happened* in those moments. Nothing I can precisely identify, but the experience changed me. The victim disappeared and there I stood, straight and tall, glaring back at my reflection, determined to survive. Michael might want to kill our marriage, but he wouldn't kill *me* in the process. In retrospect, I realize that was when I'd reached my limit.

I got dressed and marched myself right down to Lillian Case's office. If there's anything to smile about regarding this ugly divorce, it's the mis-ery Lillian put Michael through. Michael repeatedly claimed he wanted a friendly divorce, but as Lillian said, it was far too late for that.

The boys still aren't speaking to him. I'm not sure Mick ever will. Alex was always close to his father, and I know he misses Michael. We don't talk about him. I wish we could, but nothing I can say is going to take away the pain of having their father walk out the door. What Michael failed to understand was that in leaving me, he abandoned his children, too. He didn't just betray *me*. He broke faith with us all.

I probably should have figured out what was happening—that was what Marilyn seemed to insinuate. I *did* suspect something was wrong, but never, ever would I have guessed *this*. I thought maybe a midlife crisis or boredom with our marriage. Maybe that was how he felt; maybe it's why he did what he did. But he should've been honest with me about his feelings—not had an affair. Bad enough that my husband screwed another woman, but a friend's daughter?

I can only imagine what Carl would think if he were alive. It's all so crazy. Just a few years ago, Michael and I attended the party Kathy and Carl threw for Miranda's high-school graduation. Our top car salesman keels over from a heart attack and Michael, being a caring friend and business-owner, helps the grieving widow with the funeral arrangements and the insurance paperwork. Even crazier is the fact that I actually suggested it.

My one concern at the time was that Michael might be getting too close to the widow. Only it wasn't Kathy keeping my husband entertained all those nights. It was her twenty-year-old daughter. I don't think Kathy or I will ever get over the shock of it.

Michael still doesn't fully appreciate the consequences of what he's done. He sincerely believed that once we were divorced, everything would return to normal between him and his sons. Mick set him straight on that score. Alex, too. I know Michael hasn't stopped trying, but the boys won't be so easily won over. I've done my best to stay out of it. Nothing will ever change the fact that he's their father; how they choose to deal with him is up to them. I refuse to encourage either boy to forgive and forget, but I won't hold them back from a relationship with Michael, either. The choice is theirs.

Twenty-three years of marriage and I never looked at another man. Damn it all, I was a faithful, loving wife. I could have tolerated an affair if he'd given it up and returned to our marriage. But, no, he—

Okay, enough. I don't need to keep repeating the same gory details. As I said, this is a fresh start, the first day of a new year. I'm giving myself permission to move on, as my psycho-babbling counselor used to put it.

Part of moving on is belonging to the breakfast group—and continuing to write in my journal. Liz suggested we each pick a word for the year. A word. I haven't quite figured out why, let alone which word would best suit me. We're all supposed to have our words chosen before we meet next Thursday morning at Mocha Moments.

I've toyed with the idea of *beginnings,* as in new beginnings, but I don't want to carry that theme around with me for the next twelve months. At some point, beginnings have to become middles and potential has to be realized. I guess I'm afraid I won't be as successful as I want to be.

What I really need to do is discover who I am, now that I'm single again. For twenty-three years my identity was linked to Michael. We were a team, complementing each other's strengths and weaknesses. I was always better with finances and Michael was the people person. He took a part-time job selling cars the first year we were married in order to supplement our budget, and quickly became the top salesman. His degree was in ecology and he had a day job at the town planning office but made three times the money selling cars. Soon he was working full-time at the dealership and I was stretching every dollar he made, creating a small nest-egg.

Then we had the chance to buy the Chevrolet dealership—the opportunity of a lifetime. We scraped together every penny we could. By the time the paperwork was finished, we didn't have a cent between us, but we were happy. That was when we—

I can't write about that, don't want to dwell on how happy we were in those early years. Whenever I think about it, I feel overwhelmed by the pain of loss and regret. So much regret...

Word. I need a word. Not memories. I can't tie my new identity to the past and to who I was; I've got to look toward the future. So I need a word that fits who I am today, the woman I'm becoming. The woman I want to be.

Just a minute here. Just a damn minute! *Who I was, who I want to be.* Why do *I* have to change? There's nothing wrong with me! I wasn't the one who ripped the heart out of this family. I was a good wife, a good mother. I was faithful...

FAITHFUL.

That's it. My word. Not *beginnings,* not *discovery,* but *faithful.* From the moment I spoke my vows I was faithful to my husband, my marriage, my family. All these years I've been faithful to myself; I've never acted dishonestly and I've always put my family responsibilities above my own desires. I don't need to *find* myself. I found out who I am a long time ago and frankly I happen to like that person. I wasn't the one who changed; Michael did.

This feels good. The burden isn't on my shoulders to prove one damn thing. I'll remain faithful to *me.*

Happy New Year, Clare Craig. You're going to have a wonderful year. No financial worries, thanks to Lillian Case and a judge who's seen far too many men mess up their family's lives. Michael will be spending twenty very long years paying off my share of the dealership. Plus interest. I have the house, a new car every year, health insurance, the boys' college expenses and enough money to live comfortably.

I don't have anything to worry about. I can do whatever I want. I certainly don't have to work if I don't feel like it.

Hey! Maybe getting a job wouldn't be a bad idea. Maybe I should put my two decades of experience back into play. Didn't I recently hear that Murphy Motors was advertising for a general manager? With my experience, I could work any hours I chose. News of my taking that job would really get Michael. It's what he deserves. Turnabout is fair play (another of those handy sayings). Oh God, it's awful of me, but I love it.

This is what I've been waiting for. It's taken a long time to feel anything but horrendous, crushing pain. I'm smiling now, just thinking about the look on Michael's face when he learns I've been hired by his largest competitor.

Marilyn Cody was wrong, but then so was I. Living well isn't going to teach Michael a thing, is it? Knowing that he's lying awake at night, worrying about me sharing all his insider secrets with the Ford dealership—now, *that* will go a long way toward helping me find some satisfaction. And once I'm satisfied, I'll start to concentrate on living well.

* * *

"Mom, can we talk?"

Clare Craig glanced up from her desk to find her seventeen-year-old son standing in the doorway of the family room. They'd spent the morning taking down the Christmas decorations, as they always did on January sixth—Epiphany, Twelfth Night—and getting Mick ready to return to college. How like Michael he looked, she thought with a twinge of sorrow. Michael twenty-five years ago, athletic, handsome, fit. Her heart cramped at the memory.

"I'm not interrupting anything, am I?" Alex stepped inside, dressed in his soccer uniform. The holiday break was already over; school had begun earlier in the week. Mick had left that morning for college in San Francisco.

Clare capped the end of her fountain pen and set aside the checkbook and bills in order to give her younger son her full attention. "What can I do for you?"

Alex avoided her gaze. "We haven't been talking as much as we used to," he mumbled, walking slowly toward her desk.

"I've been busy." The Christmas tree had only come down that morning, but she realized he wasn't referring to the last few days; he meant over the past year.

"I know," he said with a shrug, his eyes darting around the room. "It's just that..."

"Is there something you wanted to tell me?"

He raised his head and their eyes briefly met. Reading her younger son had never been a problem for Clare.

"How about if we talk in the kitchen?" she suggested. "You thirsty?"

The hopeful look on his face convinced her to abandon paying the bills. She'd get back to all that later.

"Sure." He led the way through the large family room and into the kitchen.

Clare loved her expansive kitchen with its double ovens and large butcher-block island. Shining copper pots and kettles dangled from the rack above, the California sunlight reflected in their shine. Clare had designed the kitchen herself and spent countless hours reviewing every detail, every drawer placement, every cupboard. She'd taken pride in her home, in her skill as a cook and homemaker.

These days it was unusual for her to prepare a meal. Alex had a part-time job at a computer store, and if he wasn't at school or work, he was with his friends or on the soccer field. Cooking for one person hardly seemed worth the effort, and more and more often she ordered out. Or didn't bother at all.

"I'll get us a Coke," Alex said, already reaching for the refrigerator handle. Clare automatically took two glasses from the cupboard.

Alex placed the cans on the round oak table. Many a night, unable to sleep, the two of them had sat here while Clare sobbed in pain and frustration. Alex had wept, too. It hadn't been easy for a teenage boy to expose his emotions like that. If Clare didn't already hate Michael for what he'd done to her self-esteem, then she'd hate him for the pain he'd brought into their children's lives.

"Mick and I had a long talk last night."

Clare had surmised as much. She'd heard them in Alex's bedroom sometime after midnight, deep in conversation. Their raised voices were followed by heated whispers. Whatever they were discussing was between them and she was determined to keep out of it. They needed to settle their own differences.

"He's upset with me."

"Mick is? What for?"

Alex shrugged. He seemed to do that a lot these days.

"Brother stuff?" It was what he generally said when he didn't want to give her a full explanation.

"Something like that." He waited a moment before pulling back the tab on his soda can and taking a long swallow, ignoring the glass she'd set in front of him.

"Does this have to do with Kellie?" Alex and the girl across the street had been dating for a couple of months. Mick had dated her last summer and Clare wondered if the neighbor girl was causing a problem between her sons.

"Ah, Mom, we're just friends."

"If you and your brother had a falling-out, why don't you just tell me instead of expecting me to guess?"

He lowered his eyes. "Because I'm afraid you're going to react the same way Mick did."

"Oh? And how's that?"

Alex took another drink of his Coke. Clare recognized a delaying tactic when she saw one. "Alex?"

"All right," he said brusquely and sat up, his shoulders squared. "I've been talking to Dad."

Clare swallowed hard, but a small shocked sound still managed to escape. She felt as though she'd taken a punch to the solar plexus.

"Are you mad?" Alex asked, watching her anxiously.

"It shouldn't matter what I think."

"But it does! I don't want you to feel like I've betrayed you, too."

"I..."

"That's what Mick said I was doing. First Dad and now me. Mom, I swear to you, it isn't like that."

"Michael is your father," she said, her mind whirling as she struggled with her conflicting emotions. Alex would never intentionally do anything to hurt her. As much as possible, Clare had tried not to entangle her sons in this divorce. When Michael moved out of the family home and in with his under-age sweetheart, the two boys had rallied around her as if they could protect her from further pain. It didn't work, but she'd cherished them for their show of sympathy and support.

"He called... Dad did."

"When?" Now she was the one avoiding eye contact. She distracted herself by opening the can of Coke and pouring it carefully into her glass.

"Last week at Softline."

"He phoned you at work?" She shouldn't have been surprised; Michael was too much of a coward to risk having her answer the phone here at the house. Naturally he'd taken the low road.

"He invited me to dinner."

"And you're going?"

Clare felt her son's scrutiny. "I don't know yet. Mick doesn't think I should."

"But you want to, right?"

Alex stood and paced the area in front of the table. "That's the crazy part, Mom. I do and I don't. I haven't talked to Dad in over a year—well, other than to say I wasn't going to talk to him."

"He *is* your father," Clare said, to remind herself as much as her son.

"That's what Kellie said."

Sure Kellie said that, Clare mused darkly. She hadn't seen *her* mother betrayed and then dumped like last week's garbage. Kellie had two loving parents. She couldn't even imagine what divorce did to a person's soul or how it tore a family apart.

"I told Mick and I'm telling you. If my seeing Dad hurts you, then I won't do it."

Clare forced a smile but wasn't sure what to say.

"Kellie thinks I should be talking to Dad," he said, studying her closely, as though the neighbor girl's opinion would influence her. Clare wasn't particularly interested in what Kellie thought, but she knew how difficult the last two years had been for Alex, knew how badly he missed Michael.

"Kellie's right," she said briskly. "You and your father should be communicating."

"You don't mind?"

His obvious relief was painful to hear. She swallowed and said, "Alex, you're my son, but you're also your father's."

"I can't forgive him for what he did."

"I know," Clare whispered. She sipped her Coke in order to hide the trembling in her voice, although she was fairly certain Alex had noticed.

Her son glanced at his watch, did a startled double-take and bolted out of the chair. "I'm late for soccer practice."

"Go on," she said, waving toward the door.

"Dad said he might start coming to my games," Alex said, the words rushed as he hurried to the back door.

"Alex—"

"Sorry, Mom, gotta go."

Oh, great! Now she had to worry about running into her ex at their son's soccer games. And what about his girlfriend—was she going, too? If Alex chose to have a relationship with his father, that was one thing, but Clare couldn't, *wouldn't,* be anywhere in Michael's vicinity when he was with Miranda.

The anger inside her remained deep and real, and Clare didn't trust herself to control it. But under no circumstances would she embarrass her teenage son, and if that meant not attending the games, then so be it. Almost immediately, the resentment sprang up, as strong as the day Michael had left her. He'd already taken so much! How dared he steal the pleasure she derived from watching Alex play soccer? How dared he!

For a long time she sat mulling over her conversation with Alex. She knew how relieved he was to have this out in the open. Alex had been on edge for a while now, and she'd attributed his tension to the upcoming SATs. But it wasn't the tests that were bothering him, or his relationship with his girlfriend or even his part-time job. It was Michael. Clare was positive of that.

Once again her ex-husband had gone behind her back.

* * *

January 15th

I got the job! There was never any doubt I'd be hired. Dan Murphy nearly leaped across the desk when he realized what he had. He gave me everything I wanted, including the part-time hours I requested. He'll go ahead and hire a full-time manager and I'll be more of a consultant.

Damn, it feels good. I've never experienced this kind of spiteful satisfaction before—and I do recognize it for what it is. Until these last two years, I had no idea I could be so vindictive. I don't like this part of me, but I can't seem to help myself.

> "The teeth are smiling, but is the heart?"
>
> —Congolese proverb

CHAPTER

LIZ KENYON

January 1st

For the first time in my fifty-seven years I spent New Year's Eve alone. I ordered in Chinese, ate my chicken hot-sauce noodles in front of the television and watched a 1940s movie starring Douglas Fairbanks, Jr. They sure don't make films like that anymore. Then at midnight, I brought in the New Year sipping champagne all by myself. I was in bed a few minutes after twelve, my thoughts full of Steve.

After six years the memories aren't as painful as they were in the beginning. What continues to haunt me are the last minutes of my husband's life. I wonder what went through his mind when he realized the huge semi had crossed the yellow line and was headed straight toward him. I wonder obsessively if his last thoughts were of the children or me, or if in those split seconds there'd been time to feel anything but panic and fear. I keep imagining his absolute terror when he knew he was about to be hit. Witnesses said he'd done everything possible to avoid the collision. At the last second, he must have faced the gut-wrenching horror of knowing there was nothing he could do. I've lived through my husband's final minutes a thousand times. The sound of the impact—crunching metal and shattering glass—the screeching tires, his scream.

I thank God he died instantly.

As I lay in bed, I remembered our last morning together, as clearly as if it had happened yesterday instead of six years ago. April twentieth was an ordinary day, like so many others. We both got up and dressed for work. He helped me fasten my necklace and took the opportunity to slip his hand beneath my sweater. While I made breakfast, Steve shaved. We sat across from one another and chatted about the morning news, then he kissed me goodbye as I left for the hospital. I remember he said he had a staff meeting that afternoon and might be late for dinner.

An hour later my high-school sweetheart and husband of thirty-one years was dead. My life hasn't been the same since; it'll never be the same again. I'm still trying to accept the fact that Steve won't come bursting through the front door wearing his sexy grin. Even now, I sleep on the far right side of the bed. Steve's half remains undisturbed.

The last three months have been hard. I knew when Amy phoned to tell me Jack had been transferred to Tulsa that being separated from my daughter and grandchildren was going to be difficult. What I didn't realize was *how* difficult. Spending time with Andrew and Annie was what kept me sane after losing Steve. I miss them so much! And then, as if my daughter and her family moving to another state wasn't bad enough, Brian had to go and move out on his own. My son always did display impeccable timing.

He got a great job offer and I don't begrudge his taking it for a minute. And yet I have to admit I wish it hadn't happened quite so soon. It was hard to let him go and keep a smile on my face. I'm glad he's happy, though, and adjusting to life in Orange County. At the same time, I'm sorry he's living so far from Willow Grove. A couple of hours doesn't sound like much, but I know my son and he's far more interested in his social life than in visiting his widowed mother. That's the way it should be, I suppose, only I can't help feeling abandoned. First Amy, Jack and the grandkids, then Brian—and all at once I'm alone. Really alone.

I understand why I went to bed with thoughts of Steve. All my distractions have moved away. Even with the champagne, I couldn't sleep. After an hour I gave up trying. I sat in the dark with an afghan wrapped around my legs and contemplated my future. During the holidays I put on a brave front, acting as though I'm okay about being alone. I didn't want the kids to know how wretched I was feeling. Brian was here for Christmas, but he has friends he wanted to see and there's a new girl in his life. I wonder if that son of mine is ever going to settle down. I guess he's one step closer now, living on his own; at least that's what I tell myself. Amy and I talked, but she phoned me and I know that with a single income and a large mortgage, they're on a tight budget, so the conversation was short. Normally I would've called back but it sounded so hectic there with the kids opening their gifts and all the craziness of Christmas morning. I put phoning off until later and then just didn't.

As for New Year's Eve, spending it alone was my choice. Sean Jamison casually suggested we get together for dinner. The problem with this doctor is that outside of his work, everything's casual with him. I'm not going to make the mistake of getting involved with a man who has a reputation as a womanizer (although I readily admit his interest flatters my ego). Besides, I'm older than he is. Not by much, six years, maybe seven, just enough to make me a little uncomfortable...not that I'd seriously consider dating him, anyway. My major complaint, in addition to the age difference, is that he's the exact opposite of Steve, who was genuine and unassuming. The good doctor is stuck on himself.

Still, he's obviously an interesting man. I wouldn't mind talking to him on a strictly-friends basis. Nothing romantic or sexual. Just conversation, maybe over coffee or a drink. After all, everyone can use another friend.

Speaking of friends, when Clare, Julia, Karen and I met after our last journal-writing class, we decided to continue the friendship by meeting for breakfast every Thursday. I came up with the suggestion that we should each take a word for the year. A word to live by, to help us focus our thoughts. A word to reflect what's happening in our lives and what we want to do and be. I'm not sure where that idea came from, probably some article I read, but it struck a chord with me.

Karen loved the idea, but then Karen's young and enthusiastic about everything. That's what makes her so much fun and why she fits in so nicely with the rest of us. We each bring something individual to the group, and yet we connect....

Last night, I started thinking about my word, considering various possibilitie. I still hadn't found the *right* word. It's like trying on dresses at Nordstrom's for a special occasion. I only need one and I want it to be perfect. It has to fit properly, look wonderful and feel great. My thoughts went around and around—Steve, my job, Amy and Brian. My word for the year—*love? Change?* Something else? Strangely, unexpectedly, I found myself remembering Lauren. Lauren. My baby daughter, whom I never had a chance to know. The baby I held in my arms so briefly. Born too soon, she died during the first week of her life, nearly thirty-six years ago. Every year on the date of her birth, Steve would bring me a bouquet of daisies, to let me know he hadn't forgotten her or the pain we endured as young parents, losing our first child. I'm really not sure why I started thinking about Lauren just then.

. Determined to dwell on the present and not the past, I turned my attention to searching out a suitable word for the year. It took a while but I found one that feels right for me. As I sat in the shadows, unable to sleep, listening to the grandfather clock tick away the minutes, my word came to me.

TIME.

I'm fifty-seven. In three years I'll be sixty. *Sixty.* I don't feel close to sixty and I don't think I act it. Still, it's the truth, whether I choose to face it or not. There always seemed to be so much time to do all the things I'd planned. For instance, I always thought that someday I'd climb a mountain. I don't know exactly why, just because it sounded like such a huge accomplishment, I guess. Now I know I won't be doing any mountain-climbing, especially at this stage of my life. It all comes down to choices, I guess. Besides, I've got other mountains to climb these days.

At one point, when we were in our twenties, Steve and I wrote a list of all the exciting things we were going to do and the exotic vacations we planned to take. The years slipped away and we were caught up with raising our family and living our lives. Those dreams and plans got pushed into an indefinite future. We assumed there'd always be time. Someday or next year, or the year after that. This is a mistake I don't intend to repeat and why the word *time* is appropriate for me. I want to be aware of every moment of my life. And I want to choose the right plans and dreams to fulfill in the years that are left to me. As soon as I settled on my word, I was instantly tired and fell promptly asleep.

Because I didn't go to sleep until after two, I slept late. I didn't make breakfast until past noon. I had the television on for company, but football's never interested me. That was Steve's game, though, and I found it oddly comforting to keep the channel on the Rose Bowl. For a few hours I could pretend that my husband was with me. The house didn't feel quite as big or as empty.

The house...that's something else I have to consider. I should make a decision about continuing to live here. I don't need three thousand square feet, but this was the home Steve and I bought together, where we raised our family. With the way real-estate prices have escalated, I'm sitting on a lot of money that could well be invested elsewhere.

It's silly to hold on to this place. The house was perfect when Andrew and Annie came to spend the weekend. Two rambunctious grandchildren need all the space they can get. It didn't bother me then or when Brian lived at home. We needed a big house in order to stay out of each other's hair, but for just me... Actually it's the thought of getting it ready to sell—sorting through all the stuff that's tucked in every nook and cranny, then packing up fifty-seven years of accumulated junk—that's giving me pause.

After Steve died, my friends advised me to delay any major decisions for twelve months. That's good advice to remember now. What I'm experiencing is a second loss. The loss of my children. I'm the only Kenyon left in Willow Grove.

I'm not entirely alone, however. My friends are here—those I've known all my married life, although it seems we've drifted apart since Steve died. My new friends live here, too—the women I met in the journal-writing class. I'm grateful to Sandy O'Dell for recommending I enroll. It was exactly what I needed, and I've learned a lot about myself through the process of writing down my thoughts every day. I wish now that I'd kept a diary when I was younger. Perhaps then I'd have found it easier to understand and express my own feelings.

Our teacher, Suzanne Morrissey, was an English professor assigned to the class at the last minute. Unfortunately, she didn't have any idea where to start, although she gave it a good try. Mostly, she had us read and critique literary journals, which was interesting but not all that useful. Still, I suppose keeping a journal isn't really something that can be taught. It's something you do.

What came out as I wrote in my journal was this deep sense of loss and abandonment I've felt since Steve's death. I'd assumed that after six years I'd dealt with all that, but coupled with Amy and Jack's move to the mid-West, followed by Brian's moving out...well, it's too much.

Amazing, isn't it, that I can cope with one crisis after another in my job at the hospital yet feel so defeated by the events in my own life?

Clare and I have been spending quite a bit of time together. That's probably natural, her being recently divorced and me a widow. Clare's situation is similar to mine a few years back when I realized, to my dismay, that my friends came in couples. Most of them are matched sets. Like me, Clare has come to recognize that she lost not only her husband but the framework of her social world, which crumpled right along with the marriage. Although her circumstances are different from mine, the outcome has been the same. The dinners, card-playing, even something as uncomplicated as a night at the movies—it all seems to be done in pairs.

Within a few months of Steve's death, I found myself drifting away from the very people I'd once considered our dearest friends. We have so little in common anymore that I couldn't see the point.

It was awkward, too. People didn't know what to say after the accident. In fact, I didn't want anyone to say anything. What I needed was someone to listen. Few of my friends understood that.

Clare's had a hard time adjusting to the divorce. Losing the people she once considered her friends is a bitter pill after everything she's been through with Michael. Maybe she should have taken it up with the attorney: custody of the friends. Who gets to stay friends with whom?

Really, it's odd that Clare and I should have bonded at all. We're very different kinds of people; in our previous lives, we probably wouldn't have felt the slightest interest in knowing each other. Right now, Clare's angry and bitter and struggling not to be. I still have my share of anger, too, yet I'm more accepting of the events that led me to this point (but then, my husband didn't leave me for another woman). I enjoy Julia and Karen, too, but it's Clare I identify with most. Perhaps it's the loneliness. That's something we both understand. Something people can't truly appreciate until they've experienced it themselves.

Time. This should be the best time of my life. I have a fabulous career. When I started out at Willow Grove Memorial, I never dreamed that one day I'd end up as the hospital administrator. My children have grown into responsible adults. I had a wonderful marriage and I've got lots of memories to sustain me. Yes, this *should* be a good time, and it will be—once I learn how to live contentedly by myself.

* * *

Liz stared at the phone on her desk, dreading its ring. Her Monday had begun badly, and already she could see that this first week of the new year was going to be a repeat of December, with many of the same problems she'd faced then. The hospital was no closer to a new contract with the nurses' union, and the state health inspectors were scheduled for Wednesday afternoon. In addition, she'd had several hot flashes and been downing Chai tea with soy milk all morning. This was not a good start to the year, she thought gloomily.

She got up and removed her jacket, placing it on a hanger. Then she unfastened the top button of her white silk blouse and rolled the long sleeves past her elbows. Picking up a piece of paper from the desk, she fanned her flushed face and paused to look out the sixth-floor window to the parking lot below.

"I can see I've cornered you at a good moment." It was a deep male voice, one Liz immediately identified.

"Dr. Jamison," she said in a crisp, professional tone. He was rarely at Willow Grove Memorial. Most of his patients were admitted to Laurelhurst Children's Hospital, where he worked primarily with premature infants. Sean Jamison was an excellent pediatrician but he had a well-deserved reputation for being demanding, impatient and arrogant—an arrogance that found expression in his womanizing behaviour. Liz couldn't fault his medical skills, but when it came to dealing with staff, he could use a few lessons in emotional maturity.

"Come now," he said, his voice seductive, "we know each other well enough for you to call me Sean."

Liz stepped behind her desk and resumed her seat, motioning for him to sit down, too. "How can I help you?"

"This is more of a social visit." He claimed the closest chair and struck a casual pose, crossing his legs and balancing one ankle on the opposite knee. He relaxed, leaning back as if he was settling in for a long visit. "I stopped by to see how you're doing."

"I'm busy," she said quickly, thinking he might have time for chitchat but she didn't.

He ignored her lack of welcome. "How was your New Year's Eve?"

So that was it. He'd asked her out—well, sort of. What he'd done was propose that they get together, the invitation flavored with sexual innuendo, and she'd promptly refused. Although she'd been a widow for six years, Liz rarely dated. Opportunities were available, had she been interested. For the most part, she wasn't.

"I had a lovely night. What about you?" From Sean's reaction she'd realized it wasn't often a woman turned him down. Liz had certainly heard all the rumors about Dr. Jamison. He was tall, sandy-haired and craggy-faced, with an undeniable presence; comparisons to Harrison Ford were regularly made—by women from twenty to sixty. Sean possessed the ageless appeal of a man who was smart, handsome, wealthy and single. The hospital was full of gossip about him, and more than one of the female nurses had fallen under his spell. Divorced for ten years, Sean Jamison seemed to consider himself a prize to be caught. He never dated anyone for long and Liz disliked his arrogant approach in romance as much as she deplored his indifference to staff relations.

Liz and Steve had met in high school, and other than the normal ups and downs that were part of any longstanding relationship, they'd had a good, solid marriage. She wasn't interested in a fling, no matter how handsome or wealthy the man.

Sean's attention confused her, although she'd never allow him to see that. From what she understood, he generally went out with women several years younger than he was. While Liz kept fit and watched her diet, she wasn't a trim thirty-year-old. With loving humor, Steve had suggested that her hourglass figure had begun to show an hour and ten minutes. She still smiled whenever she thought of that.

"Stayed home New Year's, didn't you?"

"Yes," she admitted, and crossed her arms, letting him know she wasn't open to a discussion involving her private life, "but as I said, I had a perfectly lovely evening."

"All alone?"

"I happen to enjoy my own company." Standing, she braced both hands on the edge of her cherrywood desk. "I'm sorry to cut this short, but I have a meeting in ten minutes."

"I'm willing to give you another chance to go out with me."

"No, thanks."

He grinned, dismissing her rejection as though it was her loss, not his. Then he stood and turned away, ambling toward the door.

"Sean," she said, shocking herself just a little.

His smile firmly in place, he raised his eyebrows. "Change your mind?"

"As a matter of fact, no," she said, knowing that for some reason she didn't want this conversation to end the same way the others had.

"No?" He arched his eyebrows again, affecting a look of mild surprise.

"This is the second time you've stopped by my office to ask me out."

He didn't comment.

"I've turned you down both times," she reminded him. "And I'm wondering if you've asked yourself why."

"It's self-explanatory," he murmured. "You're afraid."

"It's more than that."

He shrugged carelessly, and she could practically read his response. *No big deal.* Plenty of women willing to take him up on his offer.

"It's your attitude."

For the first time in their lengthy association, Sean appeared to be at a loss for words.

"I'm not some bimbo you can schmooze into bed. This might come as news to you, but there's more to a relationship than what happens between a man and a woman in the bedroom."

He stared at her, as if daring her to continue. "I happen to think you're one of the finest pediatricians in this state," she went on. "I respect your diagnostic and medical skills, and I've seen the way you are with the children. My regard for your professional abilities is immense. But your manner with most people in this hospital leaves a lot to be desired, and frankly I'm not impressed."

"Is this the long version of why you're not interested in dating me?" he asked with barely disguised disdain.

"Actually...I'd like to get to know you."

His look implied that he wasn't sure he should believe her. "You have an odd way of saying so."

Despite his apparent indifference, she knew this couldn't be easy on his ego. "I suspect there's more to you than meets the eye."

"Great. Your place or mine?"

Liz wanted to groan out loud. He hadn't heard a word she'd said! "Neither." She held the door for him and added soberly, "When you're ready to see me as an intelligent, mature woman whose professional interests are compatible with yours, let me know." She leaned against the open door. "Otherwise you're wasting your time."

"I doubt that," he said as he stepped past and paused to touch his lips to her cheek. "Give me a call when *you're* ready for some excitement in your life."

Liz rolled her eyes. *Forget it, Doctor. I have enough excitement just dealing with all the staff complaints against you.*

Some people never learned.

> "The thing that makes you exceptional, if you are at all, is inevitably that which must also make you lonely."
> —Lorraine Hansberry

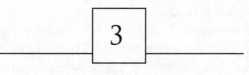

CHAPTER

KAREN CURTIS

January 1st

I woke at noon, nursed a tall, half-caff/decaff, double-sweet mocha latte for breakfast. Nichole phoned and wanted to hang out at the mall so we did. I ran into Jeff, who's working at Body and Spirit Gym, and we talked for a while. He's wasting his life teaching Tae-Bo classes to a bunch of overweight business executives who don't care about anything beyond their corporate image. I found it really hard to hold my tongue. Jeff is letting his talent go down the drain and it upsets me.

Jeff and I made a vow to one another in high-school drama class that we wouldn't give up the dream. It was all I could do not to grab him by the shoulders and remind him. *It's too soon to throw away the future*, I wanted to tell him. Although I kept my mouth shut, I could see that Jeff was eager to make his escape. Hanging with me made him uncomfortable; it forced him to face what he's doing.

What bothers me most is knowing Jeff isn't the only one who's given up; Angie and Burt did, too. Last I heard, Sydney and Leslee had regular nine-to-five jobs. So did Brad. Out of the seven of us who made up the acting ensemble, there's only me left. I refuse to surrender to the mundane. I refuse to take second-best. I am an actor. Currently a starving one, but that's beside the point.

All right, I'll step down from my soapbox. God forbid, my biggest fear is about to become a reality. I'm beginning to sound like my mother, the Woman Who Always Knows Best. Now there's a thought to send me screaming into the night.

She and Dad insisted I get a college education. I disagreed, stood my ground, fought the good fight, but then—during a period of below-poverty-level existence—I caved. Hey! They might've won the battle, but the war's all mine. Since the day I was born, my domineering mother has attempted to run my life. From the moment I enrolled in college, she's demanded I be a teacher. A lifelong occupation, she said. A good job for a woman. Give me a break!

Well, I have that precious degree, but it's in history with a minor in education. I have no intention of using it, except where it'll aid my acting career. Fortunately I've found a way in which to do that. Oddly enough, it also means my mother's kind of getting what she wants. But that's just a by-product. The important thing is I'm getting what *I* want.

You see, I'm a substitute teacher. Temporary and part-time. Due to the severe teacher shortage currently happening in southern California, anyone with a college degree—and it doesn't matter in what—can be hired as a substitute teacher. Isn't that incredible? I can have a degree in basket-weaving and qualify as a teacher for a whopping two-hundred-and-fifty bucks a day. Now, I don't mind telling you that's good money for part-time work. What's so fantastic is this: I can pick and choose the days I want to teach.

If I can fit subbing into my schedule, I spend two or three days a week in a classroom. Three at the most. That way, I still make enough money to support myself. On the days I don't work, I can audition for whatever's available.

Before the holiday break, my agent sent me out to audition for a TV commercial for a new kind of toilet brush. The district called first thing that morning and without fear of losing my job and without so much as a twinge of guilt, I said I had other plans. No problem; they simply went to the next name on the list. I headed out the door, knowing there'll be a job for me another day, if I want it. Sadly, I didn't get the commercial, but rejection's the name of the acting game.

As soon as school starts up after the holidays, I'll be ready to go back to substitute teaching. With so many days off, I have to admit I'm experiencing a bit of a cash-flow problem. Christmas didn't help, and neither did the cost of the one-day acting workshop last week. In fact, Jeff bought my latte for me today. But never mind, I'll survive. I always do, despite my mother's dire predictions.

I know I'm an embarrassment to her. She can't brag about me to all her society friends the way she does Victoria. My sister had the good judgment to marry an up-and-coming attorney who raised our family's social standing an entire notch. As far as I'm concerned, Roger is a twit, but no one's asking for my opinion. Good thing, too, because I'm not afraid to give it.

One positive aspect of Victoria's brilliant marriage is that Mom and Dad's attention is now focused on my sister and her first child instead of on me (although I do have to admit my nephew's a real cutie!). Basically Mom's been leaving me alone. Thank God.

I once heard a psychology professor say that the females in his class should take a good look at their mothers because in all likelihood we'll be just like them as we mature. Heaven help me—say it ain't so!

Mother means well. I can't fault her there. It's just that I'm such a bitter disappointment to her. Mom's so...so sterile. So predictable. There's no passion in her soul. I'm nothing like her, so I don't know how Professor Gordon could categorically state that in a few years I'll resemble her.

If anyone's like Mom, it's Victoria. To her, what people think and say is of ultimate importance. Social standing. Appearances. Money. None of that interests me. Well, maybe the money part, but only enough to get by. Unless I earn it doing what I love, and that's acting. I guess I'm a woman who needs an audience. As a kid, my first word wasn't Mom or Dad but *look*.

When Mom heard I'd tried out for a role in a toilet-brush commercial, she freaked. The very thought of her daughter appearing on national television and admitting she cleaned toilets would have mortified her. However, I was thrilled with the part and devastated when I learned it'd gone to someone else. But that's all part of the business... And as Dad keeps saying, I've got a university degree to "fall back on."

Liz, Clare and Julia are three surprises that came out of me finishing my credits to get my degree. I love these guys and I'm thrilled we've decided to keep meeting, just the four of us. Me and three smart, professional women. I don't know what exactly I offer the group. My guess is comic relief.

The only reason I took that journal-writing class was because I needed an easy credit, and from the course description this was a simple way to raise my GPA. From the time I was a kid, I've kept a journal. There must be twenty spiral-bound notebooks tucked away in my bedroom closet, and they document my entire life. I signed up for the class, convinced I'd be bored out of my mind, and became friends with three of the most fascinating women I've ever met.

The English professor who taught the class was a real ditz. I knew more about keeping a journal than she did. But I didn't miss a single session, and that's only because of Liz and the others. They've kind of adopted me and I'm grateful. What I like is the perspective they give me, being older and all. Liz is the sort of person I wish my mother could be. Hey, if my mother wants to change me, then I should be granted the same privilege. If I'm a disappointment to her as a daughter, then she should know she's not my picture of the ideal parent, either.

Unlike Mom, Liz has been nothing but encouraging about my acting career. I know what the chances are of actually making it, but I can't allow unfavorable odds to dissuade me from trying. This is my dream. My life's ambition. If I don't go after it now, I never will. I honestly don't understand why my mother can't support my choices.

Enough already. This entire journal is turning out to be about my mother instead of me. I'd prefer not to deal with her today, or any day. Besides, Liz gave us an assignment.

I need a word before we meet next Thursday. We're all selecting a personal word. It's supposed to have special significance in our lives. Maybe I should use this as an acting exercise, do some free association.

Actually, I rather like that idea. Let's see. Acting. Goal. Audition. Wouldn't it be great to audition for a TV show like *Friends*? Friends. New friends. Liz, Clare and Julia. What I love about them is that they're so accepting of me. I love that they laugh at my jokes and make me feel a real part of the group. If only my mother were half as accepting...

That's it. I've got it! *Acceptance.* I want my parents to accept me for the person I am. I might not have turned out the way they envisioned, but I'm a good, decent, honest person. That should count for something. If my parents can welcome a twit like Roger into the family, they should be able to cope with a daughter who wants to act. And no, Mother, I don't think performing in a toilet-brush commercial is beneath me. I was emotionally wiped out for a week when someone else got the role.

ACCEPTANCE. *I've got to be me.* Ol' Blue Eyes really knew what he was talking about. Acceptance. I like it. My hope is that one day my mother will accept me for who I am and be just as proud of me as she is of Victoria.

* * *

Fresh from her first audition of the year, Karen excitedly wrote in her journal, sitting at her usual window table at Mocha Moments. The upscale coffee shop was bustling as customers moved in and out. She'd been the one to recommend the place to the breakfast group and felt good about the way they'd applauded her suggestion. Two summers ago she'd stood behind that counter, concocting lattes and serving up fiber-filled bran muffins. Despite being fired for repeated absences, she maintained a friendly relationship with the manager and often stopped by. She did almost all her journal-writing at this very table.

She was about to leave when Jeff slid into the chair across from her. "Whatssup?" he asked.

"Hey, Jeff." It was great to see him. One advantage of teaching those fitness classes was that he looked positively buff. His shoulders were muscular and his chest had filled out. He wore a winter tan so rich, it must have come out of a booth.

"Thought I'd find you in here," he said, flashing a smile. Oh, yeah, he was the California poster boy, all right, with his gorgeous white teeth, whiter than ever against the tan, and his sun-streaked blond hair.

"You were looking for me?" Her ego wasn't immune to having this hunk seek her out, especially here, where everyone knew her. They'd been together some in high school, but nothing serious. Her mother's generation called it dating, but all Karen and Jeff had really done was hang out together. They were part of the acting ensemble, and their commitment had been to that, which left little time for anything social.

"I've been thinking about what you said." Jeff leaned back in his chair and crossed his arms. "I'm impressed with your determination. You believe in yourself."

"Jeff, you've got as much talent as I do. You can make it, I know you can."

"Yeah, I know, but it takes more than talent."

Talent was cheap, Karen knew that; she ran into it everywhere. And as Jeff said, it wasn't enough. What made the difference was drive, determination and plain old-fashioned stubbornness.

A slim strawberry blonde with her hair tied back in a ponytail came into the coffee shop and walked up to the counter, where she placed her order. Jeff's attention drifted from Karen to the blonde. She wore navy-blue spandex and a matching sports bra, her face glistening with sweat. It was obvious that she'd recently been at the gym.

"You know her?" Karen asked.

"She's in one of my classes, along with her sugar daddy."

Karen stared. It couldn't be, could it? She'd once been at the mall with Clare, meeting for lunch, when a pert blond woman, younger than Karen, had emerged from Victoria's Secret. Clare had pointed her out. Could this be the woman Clare's husband had dumped her for? Miranda Something? Nah. The world got smaller all the time, but it wasn't *that* small. "What's the name?" she asked.

"Miranda."

"No kidding! What about the sugar daddy?"

Jeff frowned as he mulled over the question. "I don't remember."

"It isn't Michael, is it?"

His eyes widened. "I think it might be. Yeah, I think it is. You know him?"

"Of him," she muttered, checking out the other woman. So this was Miranda. Clare had told her a bit of the story; Liz had told her more, and over the last few months, Karen had picked up a few of the nastier details.

"He dumped his family for her."

Jeff's attention went back to Miranda. "She's not bad-looking," he said thoughtfully.

"What's Michael like?"

Jeff frowned again. "You interested in him?"

"No." She wanted to clobber him for being so stupid. "He was married to a friend of mine. Tell me about him."

Jeff seemed to be at a loss. "I don't know." He shrugged. "Personality-wise he seems all right, but he's not much of an athlete. He had trouble keeping up with the class. Must've dropped out because I haven't seen him around lately."

"But you've seen Miranda?"

"Oh yeah, she's there."

"Really?" Karen's gaze narrowed as she studied the other woman more closely. "What do you think she sees in him?" she asked Jeff.

"The sugar daddy?" Jeff said. "What they all see. He's got money to burn."

Karen shook her head. "There's got to be more than that."

"Why do you care?"

"I don't. I told you, it's just that I know his ex-wife and I'm curious."

Jeff raised his eyebrows skeptically. "Miranda's okay, I guess. I don't know why she hooked up with this older guy, but as far as I'm concerned, to each his—or her—own. It's not exactly unusual, Karen. I see this sort of thing at the gym. The older men come in and hit on the younger women all the time. It's part of life in the fast lane."

"That doesn't bother you?"

"Me?" Jeff laughed. "Hey, I get more attention than I can handle. I'm happy to share the wealth."

"I wonder where *he* is this afternoon." Karen wondered aloud.

"Michael? Either she completely exhausted him and he's still too weak to get out of bed, or he's hard at work, keeping Miranda in the style to which she's become accustomed."

Karen doubted that. Clare's attorneys had taken her ex to the car wash. If Michael Craig was hard at work, the pennies weren't being spent on

Miranda. Looking at the other woman, Karen felt a pang of something approaching pity. There had to be a real lack in this girl's life, or she wouldn't have hooked up with a man old enough to be her father.

* * *

January 16th

The first few times I filled in as a substitute were fun, but lately it's gotten to be like real work. Maybe it's because I've been with a group of junior-high kids all week. They wear me out fast. Makes me wonder if I was that energetic at their age.

Today I got smart. Instead of standing at the front of the class all day yelling at kids who have no intention of listening, I brought in a huge bag of mini-chocolate bars. That got their interest. Why did it take me so long to figure out that a little thing like bribery would tame the savage beasts? (Yes, I know I'm misquoting!)

Mom phoned. It's the first I've heard from her since Christmas. She wants to take me to lunch on Saturday. I agreed before I learned that Victoria was coming, too. Mom did that on purpose. She knows how I feel about Victoria. We don't get along. Why should we, seeing that we don't have a thing in common? Mom dotes on her precious Victoria. My entire childhood, I was treated like an outcast because I wasn't like my perfect-in-every-way older sister. Apparently, all that's changed since I started teaching. Now that I'm respectably employed (even if it's only part-time) Mom's free to brag about me to her friends, too.

As soon as I learned Victoria would be at lunch, I should've found an excuse to get out of it, especially when Mother told me we'd be going to the Yacht Club. But with my current cash-flow difficulties, I'm not above accepting a free lunch.

Jeff's been interesting lately. He seems to be fired up about acting again and asked if I'd recommend my agent. I was happy to pass on Gwen's phone number and apparently they're talking. I don't know if she'll take him on or not; that's not my decision. Jeff took me to dinner to thank me. There's a great Mexican place close to the gym. It was good to see him and talk shop, to recharge my own enthusiasm. Focus, that's what it's all about. No one else is going to do this for me.

I'm still bummed about not getting the toilet-brush commercial, but Gwen said the feedback from the director was positive. She's planning to send me for another audition with the same guy, although she warned me this next one involves a dog. She didn't say what kind, and asked if I liked puppies. Who doesn't? But let's not forget what W. C. Fields said about working with kids and dogs.... Anyway, the director liked me, but didn't think I was right for the role of fastidious housewife. I guess he must've taken a look at my apartment. Cleanliness and order aren't exactly my forte. If God had meant women to do housework, He wouldn't have created men first.

"Parenthood: that state of being better chaperoned than you were before marriage."

—Madeline Cox

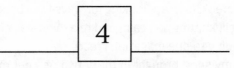

CHAPTER

JULIA MURCHISON

January 1st

This leather-bound journal is a Christmas gift from my husband and I've been waiting until today to make my first entry. My hope is that every morning I'll be filling the crisp, clean pages, writing out my thoughts, my concerns, my doubts, discovering who I am, one day at a time. That's something I learned in the journal class, along with a whole lot more. Taking that class was one of the best things I've done for myself in ages.

It's funny—here I am waxing poetic about this lovely journal that I've been waiting all week to start, and now that I have, I don't know what to write.

I'll begin with the kids, I guess. Adam and Zoe are growing up before my very eyes. It seems like only yesterday that they were babies. Now they're both in their teens, and before Peter and I know it, they'll be in college. It doesn't seem possible that Adam will be driving this year! He's champing at the bit to get behind the wheel. He's ready, but I'm not sure Peter and I are.

Zoe at thirteen is turning into a real beauty. I look at her, so innocent and lovely, and can hardly believe my baby is already a young woman.

The Wool Station is a year old now. I've always loved crafts, and opening my own small knit shop was a risky venture. I thought about it for quite a while before making the commitment. Peter's encouragement was all I really needed and he gave it to me. The store's been wonderful for us both, bringing us together. And business has been good. The recent articles about all the celebrities knitting these days certainly didn't hurt! More and more women are looking for ways to express themselves creatively; as well, knitting can calm and relax you—as effectively as meditation, according to one magazine I read.

Last year my shop brought in thirty-two percent more than my projected gross income. (Peter's calculations, not mine. I'm hopeless with numbers.) At this point, we're putting all the profit back into the business, boosting the inventory at every opportunity. I'm not making enough of a profit to draw a salary yet, but it won't be long. A year, two at the most. I just wish I was feeling better physically. Lately—ever since the flu bug hit me before Thanksgiving—I've been under the weather. I didn't bounce back nearly as fast as I thought I would. Being thrust into the holiday season right afterward wasn't any help. I barely had a week to regroup when it was time for the big yarn sale. Then the shop was crazy all through December. Added to that were the usual Christmas obligations—buying gifts, wrapping them, sending cards, entertaining, etc. When I think about everything I've had to do, it's no wonder I haven't been feeling well.

Peter's mother flew in for Christmas Day. She had a meeting in the area and combined business with pleasure. I'm writing this with my teeth gritted. I don't enjoy dealing with my mother-in-law, who in my opinion never should have been a mother. She's cold and self-important and all she seems to care about is her career and her volunteer projects. Naturally, I'm grateful she had Peter, otherwise I wouldn't have my husband, but I swear the woman doesn't possess a single maternal instinct. Peter was left with a succession of nannies and baby-sitters most of his childhood while his mother climbed the corporate ladder and sat on one volunteer board after another. I don't disparage her commitment, just where it's been directed for the past forty years. It irks me no end that she can fly halfway across the United States for her causes, but practically ignores her only son and her grandchildren. Okay, enough. I've already written copious pages about my relationship with my mother-in-law.

Onto a far more pleasant subject, and that's the Thursday Morning Breakfast Club. We're each supposed to choose a word for the year. I've been giving it some thought, but my mind was made up almost from the minute Liz mentioned the idea. I wanted to wait to be sure this is truly *my* word. Experience tells me my first instinct is often the best. Still, I've taken this week between Christmas and New Years to mull it over, and I think I'm going to go with *GRATITUDE*.

I want to practice gratitude. I know that sounds hokey, but instead of concentrating on the negative, I want to look at the positive side of life. After that horrible flu, I'm grateful for my health, and yes, I can even find reasons to be grateful for my mother-in-law. (She must have done *something* right, considering how Peter turned out.)

I've decided to start every journal entry with five things for which I'm thankful. I'm calling it my *List of Blessings*. That way I can begin my day on a positive note.

I feel the breakfast club has become my own personal support group. Every Thursday at 8—what a treat! And to think that I never would have enrolled in the journal-writing class if not for Georgia. Leave it to my cousin to con me into something I didn't want to do, because *she* refused to go alone. Sure enough, I sign up for the class and three weeks later Georgia drops out. But I didn't feel abandoned since I'd met Liz and Clare and Karen by then and we'd bonded like super glue. I stayed in the class so I could be with them.

It began with the four of us meeting after class. We'd go to the Denny's restaurant near the college for coffee. Then when the session was over, Liz suggested we continue meeting. She's the one with all the good ideas. It made sense that we get together at the same time as the original class, but with teenagers at home it's difficult for me to take one night a week out of my already heavy schedule; doing that was hard enough while the course was in session. Trying to find a mutually agreeable time proved to be the biggest challenge. I suggested we meet for breakfast, and everyone leaped on that. Sometimes the obvious solution isn't immediately noticeable.

Georgia's sorry she dropped out of the class. I haven't invited her to join our breakfast group. Perhaps it's selfish of me to keep my newfound friends to myself, but I need this. I need them. The things we talk about, the things we share, are not always for Georgia's ears. She might be my best friend and my cousin, but I wouldn't want any part of the group's conversation to be repeated. Georgia, God love her, couldn't keep a secret if her life depended on it.

Peter and I didn't do anything all that exciting to bring in the New Year. The kids were with friends at church for an all-night youth program. We went out to dinner with the Bergmans. It's tradition now that we spend New Year's Eve together, but I wasn't really up to it this year. I would have preferred a night with just the two of us, but I didn't want to disappoint either Peter or our friends. We played cards and at the stroke of midnight, Peter opened a bottle of the best champagne we could afford and we toasted the New Year.

I didn't mean to get sidetracked. My word is *GRATITUDE,* and the first thing I'm going to do is write my List of Blessings just so I'll remember to keep counting them. Then, seeing that the house is quiet for once, I'm going to take a long nap.

COUNTING MY BLESSINGS
1. New beginnings.
2. My husband and his mother. God bless her!
3. Good friends like the Bergmans.
4. The sound of Adam's laughter and the sweet beauty of my daughter.
5. Sleeping for ten uninterrupted hours.

* * *

"Hi, Mom." Zoe walked into the kitchen not more than ten minutes after Julia woke up from her afternoon snooze. New Year's was always a lazy day around their house. Her thirteen-year-old daughter fell into the seat across from her, landing clumsily in the chair. Zoe laid her head on the patchwork place mat and yawned. Her arms dangled loosely at her sides.

"Did you have a good time last night?" Julia asked.

"Yeah," Zoe murmured with no real enthusiasm.

Julia knew that the church youth leaders had kept the kids active with swimming and roller-skating, plus a number of games that included basketball and volleyball. The night ended with a huge breakfast at 5:00 a.m., and from there everyone went home. Peter had picked up Adam and Zoe at the church, and Julia had assumed they'd sleep for much of the day. She was wrong.

"Did you and Dad have fun without us?" Zoe asked, as though she expected Julia to announce that the evening had been intolerably boring without their daughter to liven things up.

"We had a wonderful, romantic evening," she said, wanting Zoe to realize that she and Peter had a life beyond that of being parents.

Zoe frowned. Yawning again, she stood and made her way back to her bedroom.

"What was that all about?" Peter asked, coming in from the family room where the television was tuned to one of the interminable New Year's Day football games.

"Haven't a clue," Julia said, secretly amused.

"Come sit with me," Peter invited, holding out his hand.

A dozen objections ran through her mind. The kitchen was a mess and she was behind with the laundry, but she couldn't refuse him.

They snuggled up on the leather couch with Julia's head on his shoulder and his arm around her. It was peaceful; the only sound came from the television, the volume kept purposely low.

"I saw you writing in your new journal," he mentioned absently, his gaze on the TV.

"It's perfect," Julia said, cuddling close and expelling her breath in a long sigh.

Peter turned to study her. "What's wrong?"

"Nothing." He seemed to accept that, but Julia decided to confide in him about her gratitude plan. "Do I complain too much?" she asked, not certain she was going to like the answer. "The reason I ask is that I want to make an effort to be more appreciative."

"Really." Peter's gaze wandered back to the screen.

"I'm making a list."

"Good for you."

Julia doubted he'd even heard her. Still, she continued. "I want to work on me this year."

"That's nice, sweetheart."

Julia stifled a groan. "The kids are growing up and before long it'll be just the two of us."

"Hey, I'm in no rush," he joked.

"I'm not, either, but it's inevitable. Adam will get his driver's license this year and we'll be lucky to see either him or the car after that." Their son was a responsible boy and it would help Julia immeasurably not to be transporting him to and from track practice, which was an irony of its own. Driving him to the track so he could run.

"Zoe's going to be in high school soon," Peter added.

It seemed just the other day that their daughter was seven and missing two front teeth.

Peter slipped his hand inside Julia's blouse and cupped her breast. "I like the way we christened the New Year." His mouth nibbled at her neck with a series of kisses that grew in length and intensity. Julia straightened, and their lips met in a kiss they normally reserved for special nights.

"There *are* advantages to one's children growing up," Peter whispered, as his hands grew bolder with her breasts.

"Oh?"

"They seem to stay in their rooms a great deal more."

"That they do," Julia agreed, twining her arms around his neck and luxuriating in his kiss.

"Mom. Dad." Adam walked into the family room, his face clouded with sleep.

Peter quickly removed his hand and an embarrassed Julia tucked in her blouse.

Their son took one look at them and frowned darkly. "What's going on?"

"Ah...nothing," Julia mumbled, glancing away.

Adam wandered into the kitchen and made himself a cup of hot chocolate.

"I thought you two would be over the mushy stuff by now," he muttered disgustedly as he returned. "It's embarrassing to catch your parents in a lip lock."

"You just wait," Peter told his son. "When you're forty, you'll see things very differently."

Adam gave them an odd grimace, then carried his cup back toward his room. "I'm going online," he announced as he disappeared down the hallway.

"Where were we?" Peter asked and reached for Julia again.

"Advice is what we ask for when we already know the answer but wish we didn't."

—Erica Jong

5

CHAPTER

CLARE CRAIG

"This is so nice," Liz Kenyon said, sliding into the booth across from Clare in the Victorian Tea Room on Friday afternoon. Clare dredged up a smile, although the year wasn't beginning well. Barely two weeks into January, and the issues with Michael were once again staring her right in the face.

Clare was pleased—no, she was *relieved*— to see her friend, even though they'd had breakfast with the others just the day before. There were things she needed to talk about that she wasn't comfortable saying in front of the whole group. Liz was the person who'd understand. Who might even have some practical advice or at least encouragement.

The restaurant was close to Willow Grove Memorial where Liz worked as administrator, which made it convenient for both of them.

A decisive woman, Liz picked up her menu, looked at it for no more than a minute, then set it aside.

Clare required much longer to make her selection, but only because she found it difficult to concentrate. Her head reeled, and making the simplest choice seemed beyond her at the moment. Spinach salad or a Monte Carlo sandwich? It wasn't a life-and-death decision but it took more effort than she was able to muster. There didn't seem to be a dish appropriate for spilling out one's heart to a friend.

When she finally closed her menu, Clare glanced up to see that Liz was watching her. "Are you okay?" Liz asked quietly.

With anyone else, Clare would have plastered on a phony smile and offered reassurances. She didn't think she could fool Liz. Nor did she want to.

Just as she was about to explain, the waitress arrived to take their orders, and looked to Liz first.

"I'll have the seafood sauté salad," Liz said and handed her the menu.

The woman nodded. "Good choice," she murmured.

She turned to Clare, but by then neither the spinach salad nor the sandwich sounded appetizing. "I'll have the same thing."

"Very good," the waitress said in the same approving tone she'd used earlier.

Liz waited until the woman was out of earshot. "I thought you didn't like seafood."

"I don't."

"Then why'd you order the seafood sauté salad?"

Clare wasn't aware of what she'd ordered; furthermore she didn't really care. She hadn't planned this lunch so she could eat. She needed support and advice, not food. "Oh, well," she muttered.

"Clare, what is it?" Liz studied her, staring hard. "Something to do with Michael, no doubt?"

Clare nodded and chewed at her lower lip. "Alex and Michael have been meeting behind my back," she said bluntly. "I knew they were talking—Alex admitted as much shortly after the first of the year. Then on Tuesday, Alex said he wouldn't be home for dinner because he was working late. It was a lie. I phoned the computer store and learned that Alex had left before five."

"You asked him about it?"

Clare nodded. "He'd gone to dinner with his father. He didn't mention Miranda, but I suspect she was there, too." The knot in her stomach tightened at the thought of her son dining with her ex-husband and his live-in lover. The pain never seemed to go away. Whenever Clare felt she was making progress, some new crisis would emerge. Some emotional stumbling block—like this one. She just hadn't expected it to involve her youngest son.

"It bothers you that Alex is seeing his father?" Liz asked.

"No." Well, she didn't really *like* it, but she was committed to her sons' right to communicate with their father. In any event, that part wasn't nearly as troubling as the lie. "I don't want to stand in the way of the boys having a relationship with Michael. Our differences don't have anything to do with Mick or Alex."

"Is that lip service or do you really mean it?" Liz had a way of cutting straight to the heart of the matter.

"I mean it—at least I think I do. Sometimes it's hard to know. I'm just so angry with Alex."

"Alex, not Michael?"

"Michael, too, because it seems to me that Alex is imitating his father's tactics. He didn't want to admit he was having dinner with Michael, so he did it without telling me."

"But he *did* tell you he'd been in contact with his dad."

That was true enough. "Alex said Michael had *phoned* him. Well, this is a lot more than a simple phone call. What I object to most is the secrecy. As if my not knowing was somehow supposed to protect me."

"What did Alex say when you confronted him?"

By the time her son had walked into the house, Clare had been so angry she'd barely been able to speak to him. To his credit, Alex didn't deny seeing Michael. He calmly told her where he'd gone, then he went to his room, leaving Clare to deal with impotent rage. She was convinced this was Michael's revenge for her taking the job at Murphy Motors.

"Alex lied to me, and I think Michael encouraged him."

"You don't know that."

"I know my ex," she snapped.

"Clare," Liz said softly. "I'm on your side, remember?"

"I know...I know. Part of me is relieved that the ice between Alex and Michael is broken. I mean, I realize how difficult our divorce has been on Alex. He was always so close to his father." She felt herself tense as she thought of the pain her ex-husband had inflicted on their family. Poor Alex had been put in an impossible position. He loved both his parents and yearned to please Michael as well as her. *That* she could understand, but not the lie. Surely he knew what his dishonesty would do to Clare when she found out.

It wasn't only his relationship with her that Michael had destroyed. Mick and Alex weren't getting along, and Michael was the source of that trouble, too. He'd managed to drive a wedge between the two brothers, and Clare feared that was about to happen between Alex and her, too.

"On his way out the door recently, Alex oh-so-casually said that Michael might be attending the soccer games. Now I find out he'll be there tomorrow afternoon."

"And you won't be there if your ex is?"

"Can you blame me?" She scowled. "At least Miranda's not coming. Alex told me that much, anyway."

"No, I don't blame you." Liz patted her arm. "It's perfectly understandable," she said. "I wouldn't go under those circumstances, either."

Clare instantly felt better. "What am I supposed to do now?"

"What do you mean?"

Michael had already taken so much from her, and Clare couldn't tolerate his stealing more. "I enjoy watching Alex play. I'm the one who drove him to and from soccer practice for the last twelve years. I'm the soccer mom who treated the team to ice cream and slumber parties. The other parents are my friends."

"And not Michael's?"

"No," she said so loudly that it attracted the attention of several people dining nearby. "No," she repeated, more softly this time. "It'll be awkward for everyone if Michael shows up. Not just me, but the other parents, too. His presence will be a distraction. Besides, I'm scheduled to work the concession stand."

"I see," Liz murmured with a darkening frown. "But I—"

The arrival of their meal interrupted whatever Liz was about to say. The waitress brought two huge Caesar salads piled high with sautéed shrimp, clams, scallops and an assortment of other seafood delicacies. Clare studied the salad for several minutes before she could produce enough enthusiasm to reach for her fork.

"Oh, Clare, you don't know what you're missing." Liz eagerly stabbed a fat shrimp.

Clare shook her head. "I'm not hungry," she said. Pushing aside a mound of seafood until she uncovered the lettuce, she managed a mouthful of that.

"Back to your dilemma," Liz said, looking thoughtful. "I think I have a solution."

Clare glanced up hopefully. "Tell me."

"You're going to contact Michael yourself."

"What?" The fork slipped from Clare's fingers and fell to the table. She retrieved it, glaring at her friend. "You must be joking."

"Not at all."

"I have no intention of *ever* speaking to Michael again."

Without a pause Liz sprinkled some pepper on her meal. "Don't you think that's a bit drastic?"

"There's no reason on this earth important enough for me to contact Michael Craig."

"What about your sons? Aren't Mick and Alex important enough?"

"Well, yes...but it's been over a year—"

"Does it matter how long it's been?"

"No, but..." Clare returned, growing frustrated. Liz made it sound like a foregone conclusion that she'd sort this out with her ex-husband in a calm and reasonable fashion—when reasonable was the last thing she felt. "Let me get this straight. You're suggesting I phone Michael and the two of us would decide which games each of us will attend."

"Correct." Liz beamed her an encouraging smile.

"Why do I have to be the one who calls him? Can't Michael understand this is awkward for me—for all the parents?"

"It's unlikely. Men don't think that far ahead."

Clare hesitated, doubting she could swallow another bite. The knot in her stomach had doubled in size. She'd come to Liz looking for suggestions and sympathy. Her friend had offered a little of both, but Clare didn't think she could follow her advice. "I—I can't do it," she admitted, her voice faltering.

"You can and you will."

"I don't think so...."

It'd been almost thirteen months since she'd heard Michael's voice. Clare wasn't sure she could trust herself not to respond to him in anger. Liz couldn't understand that, couldn't know. If her friends had any idea of the rage she still battled, it would frighten them. In fact, the intensity of her own anger terrified Clare.

"I'm not saying you should ask him to a picnic lunch."

Despite herself, Clare smiled.

"All you need to do is make a phone call. Suggest you split the games up. He attends half and you attend the other half. It'll save you both a lot of angst."

"Couldn't I write him instead?"

"Sure. Just as long as you communicate with him."

"I prefer that we not speak." Clare wondered why she hadn't thought of that sooner. A written explanation wouldn't leave room for any misunderstanding. She'd be clear, succinct and to the point. Michael believed in brevity—he was always quoting that line from *Hamlet* about "the soul of wit." Well, then he'd find her message very witty, indeed.

"Whatever's most comfortable for you," Liz said.

"I wouldn't even need to write a letter," Clare went on, feeling inspired. "I could take the schedule and underline the games he can attend and tell him to stay away from the ones I've selected." She wouldn't mention the dinner. That was between Alex and his father—but ultimately she blamed Michael. He'd lived a lie for several months before confessing to the affair, and apparently her son had learned that kind of deception.

"You could mail him the schedule," Liz agreed without much enthusiasm. "When's the next game?"

"Tomorrow." As she answered, Clare realized that even with overnight delivery service, Michael wouldn't get the schedule in time for the upcoming game. Okay, so she'd skip this game and make arrangements for someone to replace her at the concession stand. No big deal—only it was. It was a very big deal.

"Clare?"

Clare looked up.

"You didn't hear me, did you?"

"Hear what?" Her friend was right; she'd been so caught up in her own thoughts she hadn't heard a word in the last few minutes.

"I said your heart will tell you the best thing to do."

Now that was an interesting concept. If she'd listened to her heart, Michael would have died an agonizing death two years ago.

And she'd be making license plates in a federal pen.

> "You may be disappointed if you fail, but you are doomed if you don't try."
>
> —Beverly Sills

CHAPTER

LIZ KENYON

January 19th

Here it is Friday night, and I'm nestled in front of the television watching *Seinfeld* reruns and munching on popcorn while writing in my journal. I'm almost tempted to feel sorry for myself. Even Tinkerbell is showing signs of sympathy by sitting in my lap. Steve never did understand my affection for cats, but he liked Tinkerbell.

Work this week was dreadful. I hardly had a chance to deal with one crisis before I was hit with another. I don't even want to *think* about the nurses going out on strike. I didn't get home before seven once this entire week, so it's no wonder that all I want to do is hibernate in front of the TV tonight!

The weekend's already arrived, which means an entire week has vanished. It makes my word for the year, *time,* all the more significant. I'm feeling a sense of panic—a sense that if I don't do something *now,* the weeks and months will slip through my fingers. Spring will be here, and then autumn and I won't have accomplished any of what I've planned so carefully—travel, catching up on the books stacked by my bed, doing some charitable work, learning a new skill.

At the Soroptimist meeting last week, before everything at the hospital went to hell in a handbasket, Ruth Howe, the head librarian, talked about a program at the juvenile detention center. The librarians are taking turns reading the Harry Potter books over the loudspeaker system each night. There are only three librarians, and Ruth came to the meeting hoping to find more volunteers.

It seems she read about such a program in Grand Rapids, Michigan. She spoke of the difference this had made in the young people's lives. When she first proposed the idea here, the detention center told her there was little they could do to control noise. She was welcome to come in, but the staff couldn't guarantee that anyone would listen.

Ruth and the other librarians weren't dissuaded. As expected, their reception was lukewarm in the beginning, but they faithfully showed up every night, despite the hoots and hollers of protest. Apparently the disruptions didn't last long. According to Ruth, the reading period is the only hour of the day or night when the facility is absolutely quiet. For many of the teenagers, this is the first time in their lives anyone has ever read to them.

I knew right away that it was something I'd like to do. Ruth got a couple of volunteers at the meeting, and I was tempted to sign up right then, but I hesitated....

A while back, I read something smart. The exact wording escapes me now, but I remember the meaning: I need to stop and consider my options before volunteering for something. If I say yes, then I need to think about what I'm saying no to first. In other words, if I were a volunteer reader at the detention center tonight, what *wouldn't* I be doing? The answer is obvious—sitting in front of the TV watching reruns, writing in my journal and fighting Tinkerbell for the last of the popcorn.

Where would I rather be?

But after a work week like this, would I feel like trekking all the way to Charleston Street to read a chapter or two aloud. I don't know how good I'd be. Reading to my grandchildren is vastly different from trying to entertain adolescent felons. Still, it appeals to me and is something I'm going to consider.

I'm afraid this whole year will speed by, and I won't have achieved anything. I'm determined to make *some* kind of contribution to society.

When I volunteer for an activity, I'm going to do so wholeheartedly and with absolute commitment. That means I have to pick the right one....

> "If you think you can, you can. And if you think you can't,
> you're right."
>
> —Mary Kay Ash

7

CHAPTER

CLARE CRAIG

At noon on Saturday, Clare checked her e-mail messages for the sixth time that day. It hadn't occurred to her until after her lunch with Liz that she could contact Michael without speaking to him *or* sending a letter. E-mail. She hardly ever used it herself, since she considered it a time-waster. But she remembered that Michael, who was enthralled with anything high-tech, did much of his correspondence by e-mail.

Her message had been short.

Michael:
Unless you want an
embarrassing scene, I suggest

you stay away from Alex's
soccer match this afternoon.
Next Tuesday's game is all
yours.
You will receive a schedule
of which games I'm attending.
You're free to attend the other half.
It's up to you.
Hugs and kisses.
Not!
Clare

It'd taken her most of an hour to write those few words. She hoped the small touch of humor would help.

By one o'clock, her stomach was so queasy she couldn't even manage a cup of tea. She hadn't asked him to e-mail her back but had assumed he would, if for no other reason than to confirm that he'd read her message. Clare needed his assurance that he'd do nothing to embarrass her in front of her friends. That was all she wanted; she should have known better than to expect cooperation from Michael.

At two, just an hour before she had to leave for the game, Clare found herself so agitated, she actually broke into a cold sweat. Her queasiness had developed into full-blown nausea. When she couldn't bear it another minute, she reached for the phone.

She hadn't called the dealership in a very long time, but the telephone number was still on her speed-dial. She punched the button.

"Craig Chevrolet," the receptionist answered in a light, pleasant voice. "How may I direct your call?"

"I'd like to speak to Hollie Hurst," Clare said. No reason to talk to Michael when his secretary knew his schedule.

"One minute, please."

She was put on hold while an easy-listening radio station played in the background. The receptionist was new. Clare hadn't recognized her voice and wondered briefly what had happened to Janet Harris. She wanted to think the young mother had quit in protest when she learned of the divorce, but that wasn't likely. Everyone at the dealership had stayed on. Being rational, she had to suppose it wasn't a question of personal loyalties. Michael, after all, signed the checks.

"Michael Craig."

"What happened to Hollie?" Clare demanded before she thought to slam down the receiver without identifying herself.

There was a short, shocked pause, followed by, "Clare?"

"I asked to speak to Hollie."

"She has the weekends off."

Clare should have remembered that. Recovering quickly, she lowered her voice. She hadn't expected him to pick up the phone, but she wasn't about to let him know the effect he'd had on her. "Well, hello, Michael."

"What's the matter, did the support check bounce?" He didn't bother to disguise his sarcasm.

Clare smiled. Thanks to Lillian, Michael was required to send her a hefty check each month. He had to be feeling the pinch.

"I guess you haven't read your e-mail?" she asked.

"Should I have?" He snorted. "I've been busy, you know. Making money I don't get to keep. You sent me an e-mail? What for?"

"I'd hoped to avoid this," she muttered.

He sighed as though bored with the conversation. "Instead of exchanging useless banter, get to the point, would you?"

"It's about Alex—"

"I have a right to see my son," Michael snarled, not giving her a chance to explain.

"Did I say otherwise?" she returned in like tones. "Whether Alex sees you or not is his decision. Not yours and certainly not mine."

"I agree," he said, but his voice still held an edge.

"See? We can agree on some things," she said with exaggerated sweetness.

"Is there a legitimate purpose for this call?"

"Yes." She made herself sound calm and businesslike. "I understand you're planning to attend Alex's soccer games."

Clare could feel Michael's tension through the phone line. "Do I need to call my attorney? Is that what you're saying?"

Clare laughed softly. "I can't believe you want to tangle with Lillian Case again."

"I'll do whatever is necessary if you try to keep me away from my son."

"Michael, really!" Her aggrieved tone was convincing, she thought. She was a better actress than she'd realized. Hell, Karen should take lessons from *her.*

"Do you enjoy this? Do you get some kind of sick thrill out of making my life miserable?"

Clare could almost see his face getting red. She could feel his anger—and she loved it. The exhilaration she experienced now made up for the months of strained, angry silence. Had she known the sense of triumph, of satisfaction, this would give her, she'd have phoned him much sooner.

"I didn't say anything about preventing you from seeing his games, did I?" she asked, again maintaining a cool, even voice. "If you want to go to Alex's soccer matches, that's perfectly fine with me."

"You're damn straight I have a right to see Alex play!"

If he'd shut up long enough, he'd learn she had no objection to his being there. "Michael, listen," she said, trying to keep the smile out of her voice.

"No, *you* listen! If I need to have my attorney call yours, then so be it."

"Michael—"

"I'm warning you, Clare, I've had all I can take of your bullshit."

"I didn't phone to start an argument."

"The hell you didn't."

"No, really. All I wanted was to set up some sort of schedule. For Alex's sake." She waited for him to react.

"What do you mean?"

"Alex's soccer games. I was hoping we could be civilized about this. The last thing I want is to get the courts involved. Not again."

"I don't relish the idea myself."

She'd just bet he didn't. "You have to know how difficult it was for me to call you."

Silence.

"We haven't spoken in more than a year. I've put up with the situation, got on with my life. It isn't like I've made a pest of myself, is it?"

"Just say what you have to say."

"You want to attend Alex's soccer matches. So do I. He's my son, too. But I think it'd be best all the way around for us not to show up at the same time. That way Alex can concentrate on his game instead of what's happening off-field between his parents."

"All right," Michael said, sounding guarded.

"I tried to avoid this. If you'd read your e-mail, we could have solved everything without all this...unpleasantness."

"I assumed Alex told you I was planning to be there."

"Originally, all he said was that you might start coming to the games. Thursday night, he dropped the news—he said you were coming to *this* game. But that's not enough notice for me. Keith's mother asked me to help her at the concession stand and it would be irresponsible to cancel at the last minute. If you'd gotten back to me, I might have been able to find a replacement. I can't now."

"In other words, you don't want me there this afternoon."

"Exactly."

He hesitated. "All right, but I'm going to next Tuesday's game."

"And I won't," she said sweetly. "Now, was that so hard?"

"No," he admitted grudgingly.

"Goodbye, Michael," she said and replaced the receiver. Slumping in the chair, she buried her face in her hands. It shocked her to realize how badly she was trembling.

She'd talked to her ex-husband. During their conversation, she'd felt rage, exhilaration and a sense of bitter victory.

What she felt now was despair.

"The worst part of success is to try finding someone who is happy for you."

—Bette Midler

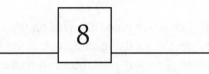

CHAPTER

KAREN CURTIS

This lunch was destined to be even worse than Karen had imagined. As she stood in the foyer of the yacht club restaurant, she saw her mother pull up to the valet attendant and step out of her Lexus. Catherine Curtis wore a pastel-blue linen dress with a huge wide-brimmed matching hat and white gloves. Victoria looked like her twin, only she had on a tailored blue suit with a white collar. Apparently, three-year-old Bryce was spending the day with his father. Karen was disappointed; she'd looked forward to seeing her nephew. It went without saying that her mother and sister weren't going to approve of her jean overalls from Old Navy.

"Hi, Mom," Karen said, standing when they entered the yacht club.

Her mother's expression spoke volumes. "Karen." She leaned forward and presented her cheek for Karen to kiss.

"You're early," was her sister's sole greeting.

"My car's on the fritz, so I took the bus." Actually, Karen had made a day of it, shopping in Willow Grove that morning, then catching the bus out to the marina. She'd read the current *Vanity Fair* during the forty-minute ride, which had been relaxing and enjoyable, calming her before the inevitable confrontation.

Her mother and Victoria exchanged glances.

"Don't worry," Karen said in a stage whisper. "No one saw me get off the bus. Certainly no one who'd connect me with the two of you."

"Shall we have the hostess seat us," her mother said, ignoring the comment.

"Yes, let's," her sister piped in with phony enthusiasm. The two headed in the direction of the restaurant, leaving Karen to trail behind. The temptation to slip away was almost overwhelming, but the consequences wouldn't be worth it. So, like an obedient child, she followed them.

The hostess directed them to a window table and handed them menus before she left. Karen sat across from her mother and sister and gazed out at the marina for several minutes. The water sparkled in the January sun, and boats of every size lined the long dock. Everything from the simplest sailboat to yachts with price tags that ran into the millions.

"What looks good to you?" Victoria asked Catherine. Karen observed, not for the first time, that Victoria rarely made a decision without consulting their mother.

"The crab and shrimp quesadillas, perhaps. With a small avocado salad."

"That's exactly what I was thinking," Victoria said, closing her menu. "What about you?" she asked Karen.

"I'll have the crab Louis."

"Excellent idea," Catherine said approvingly.

At least Karen had enough ordering savvy to please her mother.

Catherine set aside her menu and focused her attention on Victoria. "How's Roger?"

Karen frowned. She'd hoped all conversation regarding the twit would be over by now. They'd probably spent the entire drive out to the club admiring Roger and then discussing Karen—her lack of direction, her fanciful dreams, her multiple shortcomings.

Victoria smiled benignly at her mother. "Busy, as always."

Wishing now that she'd taken the time to change out of her jean overalls and into her new skirt, Karen leaned sideways, searching for the shopping bag. She'd purchased the skirt in a close-out sale, so the price was affordable. It would be the perfect thing to wear on the days she subbed for the school district; in fact, it was the most respectable thing she'd bought in years. She could hurry into the ladies' room and make a quick change. That way, she'd definitely gain a few points with her mother. Easy points.

Pretending to be enthralled by the witless conversation taking place, Karen edged the shopping bag closer with her foot. She reached for it without success, so she had no option but to lean down, peek under the table and grab it.

All at once her mother turned and glared at her accusingly. "What exactly are you doing?" she demanded.

Caught in the act, Karen flashed a brilliant smile. "What do you mean?"

"You're squirming around like a two-year-old in church."

"Oh," she said innocently. "I was getting my bag."

"Your bag? Whatever for?"

"I thought I'd change into my new skirt."

Her mother nearly leapt out of her seat, then regained control. Tight-lipped, she spoke in a slow, stiff voice. "This is neither the time nor the place for you to be changing your clothes."

"I intended to put it on in the ladies' room," Karen told her.

"At the Yacht Club? Karen, do I need explain that the facilities here are not dressing rooms?"

"Mom, don't get all worked up. I should've changed earlier. I meant to...." She hadn't, but then how could she know that her mother and sister would arrive looking like they expected to have lunch with the Queen of England?

"Please." Her mother was breathing hard. "Don't embarrass me any further."

"Embarrass you?" Karen asked in a puzzled voice. She'd had good intentions, and for her efforts she was rewarded with a hard, cutting look.

"Shall we order?" Victoria said, her voice slightly raised as the waitress approached the table.

Both her mother and sister ordered the shrimp and crab quesadillas, plus avocado salads as planned, and Karen asked for the crab Louis. As soon as the waitress left, the three went quiet.

Victoria was the first to speak, asking Catherine about her bridge club. It wasn't long before the two of them were involved in a meandering conversation about people who were of little or no interest to Karen.

She tried to comment once, but was cut off when their lunch arrived. The discussion continued with Karen feeling more and more out of place. It was just as bad as she'd feared. Worse.

Suddenly her mother turned her attention entirely on Karen. "You haven't contributed to the conversation once."

There was a very good reason for that; she couldn't get a word in edgewise. "What would you like to know?" she asked carefully.

Catherine raised her eyebrows. "You could tell me about school. I always knew you'd end up teaching. You're so good with children."

Karen felt gratified by the unexpected praise.

Victoria stared at her with more enthusiasm than necessary, obviously taking their mother's cue. "Mom's right," she announced. "You'd make a wonderful teacher. You're enjoying it, aren't you?"

"Well, *enjoying* isn't exactly the word I'd use. It's, um, a challenge."

"All children are a challenge," her mother said pointedly.

"How many days a week are you working?" Victoria asked.

"No more than three. Two's better, but that's pushing it financially. Teaching is exhausting and the little darlings couldn't care less, especially when they've got a substitute."

"Personally, I think teachers are grossly underpaid," Victoria said.

Her sympathy didn't go unappreciated, and Karen found herself warming to her sister. "Me, too. What I'm really hoping for is a part in a commercial. I'm trying out for another spot next week. The director liked me the last time and wants to see me again."

Her mother's eyes narrowed and she put down her fork.

"Naturally, I'd love a role in a weekly series," Karen added. "But according to my agent I need a few credits first. She thinks I should get my feet wet doing commercials. Plus, the pay isn't bad, and there are residuals. Then she wants me to audition for a part in a situation comedy."

With great deliberateness, her mother smeared a dollop of sour cream on the quesadilla, and Karen saw that her hand shook as she did so.

"Even if you got a part in a commercial, you'd go back to substitute teaching, wouldn't you?" Catherine asked.

"Well, yes, I suppose, but teaching is only a means to an end for me. I—"

"I thought you were finally putting your college degree to good use. Your father and I paid a great deal of money for your education. You can't imagine how much it distressed us to hear that you're more interested in...in cleaning toilets than in making something worthwhile of your life."

"It wasn't exactly a housecleaning job," Karen muttered. "Not that there's—" She stopped abruptly, forcing herself to swallow the rest of her retort. "I deeply appreciate my education, Mom." Which was true, but only because it allowed her to support herself while trying out for acting roles.

"Are you seeing anyone?" Victoria asked, once again diverting the conversation to a different subject.

"Jeff and I went out the other night."

"Jeff Hansen?" her mother asked. "Isn't he the boy from your high-school drama group?"

"Yes, he's teaching aerobics classes at Body and Spirit Gymnasium, and wants to get back into acting. I hooked him up with my agent."

"Oh, dear," Catherine murmured. "I play bridge with his mother.... She was so pleased when Jeff got a real job, and now this."

"Why do you think acting is such a horrible career?" Karen burst out. "Can you explain that to me once and for all?"

Her mother sighed as though the answer should be obvious. "You mean you don't know? Just look at the class of people who become professional actors! They're all involved with drugs and not a one of them stays married. These women get pregnant and most don't even bother to marry the child's father. They have babies by a bunch of different men. They take their clothes off for the whole world to see. They have absolutely no morals, Karen—and everyone knows the successful ones sleep with their casting directors. The unsuccessful ones are just unemployed."

"That's so unfair," Karen cried, not caring that she'd attracted attention to herself. "You're judging me by what's in the tabloids. There's more to being an actress than what those headlines scream and furthermore, you can't believe everything you read!" The only true thing her mother had said was that remark about unemployment, which Karen chose to ignore. "Besides," she added, "not all actors use drugs."

"I've read about those Hollywood parties with the drugs and sex and God knows what else. I don't want my daughter mixing with that kind of crowd."

"Mom, you don't know what you're talking about!"

"I do. They'll lure you in. Weird cults and casting couches..."

"I'm not doing drugs," Karen insisted. "I've never come across a cult, weird or otherwise. And I've never even *seen* a casting couch, let alone done anything on one."

"What about this director? He wants you to audition for another commercial?"

Karen sighed. "It's for a dog-food commercial. He told my agent he liked my style and—"

"I'll just bet he did," her mother said, lips pinched tight. "Exactly what are you going to have to do for that role?"

Enough was enough. As politely as possible, Karen placed the pink linen napkin on the table and picked up her purse. "I think it'd be best if I left." She kept her voice expressionless.

"Sit down right now!" her mother ordered. "I won't have you making a scene by leaving before we've finished our lunch."

Karen reached down for her shopping bag and held onto it with both hands. "If you're worried about creating a scene, then I suggest that the next time we meet, you refrain from insulting me."

"All I said was—"

"Thank you for lunch." Karen did her best to hide her anger—and disappointment. She should've known better. Whenever she saw her mother, they always played out some version of this encounter. The simple truth was that her family didn't respect her and had no confidence in her talent or, apparently, her judgment. And that hurt.

"Karen, wait," Victoria pleaded, rising to her feet.

Karen shook her head, fearing that if she stayed she'd end up saying something she'd regret.

"What a wonderful life I've had! I only wish I'd realized it sooner."
—Colette

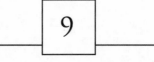

CHAPTER

JULIA MURCHISON

January 25th

List of Blessings
1. The security of order. Everything neatly in its place. Yarn arranged by color to form a rainbow effect in the store.
2. The welcome feel of my mattress after a long day on my feet.
3. Music and the way it nurtures me.
4. Zoe's snit fits when everything doesn't go exactly as she wants it to. Could this daughter of mine be taking after me? Never!
5. My customers, eager to create something lasting and beautiful.

I haven't been feeling well for weeks, and with my newfound determination to take care of myself physically, I've made an appointment to see Dr. Snyder, even though it means I'll have to leave the Thursday breakfast group early. The last time I saw Dr. Snyder was November when I had that dreadful flu bug and was flat on my back for an entire week.

I guess I haven't fully recovered from that virus. I assumed I'd feel better after the holidays, but I don't. In fact, I seem to be more tired now than ever. I can't seem to get enough sleep. Twice last week, I went to bed before Adam and Zoe did.

Peter, who almost never complains, mentioned it at breakfast this morning. But this is more than exhaustion. I'm constantly running to the bathroom. Could be I've developed a bladder infection. I certainly hope not.

My whole system is out of whack. Even my period is late. I'll be forty this year, but I didn't expect menopause to hit me this early. If it did, though, I wouldn't complain.

Reading this, it almost sounds like I'm pregnant. It's been so many years since I had the kids, I didn't put it together until just this minute. But that's impossible. I've been on the pill for years, and with the flu and the busyness of the season, Peter and I haven't been that active sexually.

After Zoe was born, Peter intended to have a vasectomy, but because we were both so young, the doctor advised us to hold off making that decision for a few years. We talked it over and agreed to wait. I went on the pill once I'd finished nursing, and all concern vanished from our minds. Five years later, Peter made an appointment for the vasectomy; I can't remember why he didn't go through with it. He'd gone in for his preliminary exam, but after discussing it with the specialist, he decided he wanted to think this through more carefully. So I continued taking the pill. Which is ninety-nine percent effective...

I'm *not* pregnant. I couldn't be. I'm methodical about my vitamins and my birth control pill. I don't miss. Ever. I refuse to think like this. A pregnancy now would be a disaster. I'm finished with the baby stage and couldn't imagine going back.

No need to borrow trouble when a baby simply isn't a possibility. Besides, I'd know if I was pregnant. I did with Adam and Zoe. Both times, within ten days of conception, I sensed the changes in my body. It felt as though everything inside me had welcomed this new life taking shape. There's no celebration happening now.

I'm ending this right here because I can't deal with what I'm thinking. *I am not pregnant.* I don't want to be pregnant and I refuse to torment myself with something that has only a one-percent chance of being true.

* * *

"I don't need a urine test," Julia insisted, meeting Dr. Lucy Snyder's unyielding gaze. "I already told you a pregnancy just isn't possible."

Dr. Snyder rolled the stool closer to the examination table where Julia sat, clutching the paper gown to her stomach, her bare feet dangling.

"The pelvic exam suggests otherwise," Doc Snyder said quietly.

"I *can't* be pregnant." Julia didn't know why she felt the need to argue when a pregnancy was now almost a certainty. The queasy feeling in the pit of her stomach had nothing to do with morning sickness and everything to do with her state of mind.

"With the pill, there's always that slight risk," the doctor murmured.

Julia adamantly shook her head.

"You say you never missed a pill? Not even once?"

"Not even once!" Julia cried, fighting back emotion so negative her voice actually shook.

Dr. Snyder read the chart. "What about when you had that flu virus?"

"I took my pills," Julia said.

"You kept them down?"

"Down? What do you mean down?" Julia asked.

"According to the chart, you suffered projectile vomiting for three days."

Julia's forehead broke into a sweat. "Yes... And I didn't eat solids for a full seven days." Her stomach hadn't tolerated anything other than weak tea and a few sips of chicken broth.

"I'd like you to have a urine test," the doctor said. "Just to be sure, one way or the other."

Numbness was spreading through Julia's arms and legs as she nodded. Dr. Snyder patted her shoulder and quietly slipped out of the room.

If she *was* pregnant, Julia could pinpoint the night it happened— after the tremendous success of her first yarn sale. She'd been incredibly happy. Adam and Zoe had spent the night with her sister, and

Julia and Peter had celebrated with a rare evening out, followed by an incredible night of lovemaking.

After providing the nurse with the necessary sample, Julia slowly dressed. Her fingers trembled as she fastened the buttons of her blouse. She'd just finished when Dr. Snyder came into the cubicle with the results.

Their eyes met, and in that instant Julia knew the awful truth. It was what she'd dreaded most. She was pregnant. Whatever Dr. Snyder said after that was a complete blur. She walked out of the office in a stupor and toward the parking garage.

The next thing Julia knew, she was at Benjamin Franklin Elementary, the grade school where Peter had been principal for the last four years.

"Mrs. Murchison, this is a pleasant surprise," the school secretary said warmly.

For the life of her, Julia couldn't recall the older woman's name, although she'd been working with Peter as long as he'd been at Ben Franklin. Linda Dooley, she remembered. It was Linda.

"Is Peter available?" Managing the question demanded full concentration on Julia's part. Her head continued to buzz, her mind skipping from one irrational thought to another. She'd left Dr. Snyder's not knowing where she was driving or what she was going to say or do once she got there. Obviously, she'd made a subconscious dedision that Peter, her calm and reasonable husband, would supply the answers.

"You go on in." A look of concern came over Linda. "Is everything all right, Mrs. Murchison?"

Julia shook her head. Nothing was right. Her entire life was off-kilter. She didn't want this baby, didn't want to deal with this pregnancy. Churchgoing, God-fearing woman that she was, her reaction would have shocked all who knew her.

"Julia?" Peter stood when he saw her. "What's wrong?" He left his desk and placed an arm around her shoulders, then gently guided her to a chair.

Julia sank down gratefully. Her legs had lost all feeling, and she felt on the verge of collapse.

Peter appeared to sense the gravity of the situation without her having to say a word. "What is it?" he asked. "Your mother?"

Julia shook her head again.

"Sweetheart, tell me."

Her eyes and throat burned with the need to cry, but she refused to allow it.

"You saw Dr. Snyder?" her husband prompted.

She nodded wildly. "The flu..." she managed, willing herself not to weep. Tears humiliated her. She wasn't like some women who used tears for effect. Nor did she look particularly fetching with red-rimmed eyes and a runny nose.

Peter's hands clasped hers. "It was more than the flu?"

Julia whispered, "Yes..."

"It isn't...cancer, is it?" Her husband had gone pale at the very word.

"No, you idiot!" she shouted, knowing even as she spoke how unreasonable she was being. "I'm pregnant!"

Peter stared at her blankly as though he hadn't heard or, like her, didn't *want* to hear.

"Don't look at me like this is a surprise or anything," Julia snapped. He was to blame, dammit! If he'd gone ahead with the vasectomy, they wouldn't be facing this situation now.

"Ah..." Peter straightened and buried his hands in his pockets. "Were we planning on having a third child?" If this was an attempt at humor, she wasn't laughing.

"This is all your fault...."

His frown slowly evaporated into a soft, teasing smile. "You're joking, aren't you?"

"Do I look like I'm joking?"

"No..." He hesitated, confusion in his eyes. "You're really pregnant?"

Julia swore to herself that if he dared to smile, she'd slap the grin off his face.

"But how?" He shook his head as if he wanted to withdraw the question. "Not how, but when? I thought you were on the pill."

"I am on the pill."

"And you still got pregnant?"

"Yes...apparently I threw up the birth control pills when I had the flu a couple of months back."

"I see." His expression remained sober and concerned, but Julia knew her husband well enough to see that his reaction to the news in no way matched her own. Peter started to chuckle, but she cut him off abruptly.

"Don't laugh!" She wasn't kidding, either. A pregnancy wasn't a laughing matter. Not at this stage of her life. She was through with being a stay-at-home mother. She didn't regret any of it, but that phase was over now. There wasn't a single committee or volunteer job she hadn't done in the twelve years she'd been home with Adam and Zoe. She'd served as the Parent-Teacher Association president, been a Cub Scout leader for Adam, a Brownie leader for Zoe, an assistant soccer coach, Sunday School teacher, room mother and all the rest of it. She was still actively involved in her children's lives, but as teenagers they were less dependent, required less of her time. Finally, it was *her* turn, and she was unwilling and unable to go back and retrace her steps.

"You find this amusing, do you?" she yelled. "We have two teenage children, Peter. Can you imagine what a baby would do to our family?"

"Julia," her husband said, his eyes filled with sympathy. "A pregnancy isn't the end of the world."

"Oh sure, *you* can say that, but it isn't you who'll be getting up in the middle of the night! And what about Adam and Zoe? What about our friends? No one has a child at our age."

"It happens all the time."

"Not to us. Peter, you actually seem happy about this. I can't believe it!"

"I'm surprised, and obviously you are, too, but there are worse things. We'll adjust."

"You might, but I won't. I don't want this child." There, she'd said it, those dreadful words, but God help her, they were the truth.

Peter gazed at her as though he hadn't heard. "Give yourself time," he advised, as though all she needed was a few minutes to get over the shock.

"Time for what? Do you think that'll change my mind? Do you seriously believe that once I get used to the idea of being pregnant I'll feel differently?"

"Julia..."

"Why do you think our children's names start with A and Z? A boy, a girl. A to Z, and I was finished."

"Apparently not."

Julia jerked her purse strap over her shoulder and bounced out of the cushioned seat. "I can see that talking to you isn't any help at all."

"Julia..." Peter followed her outside his office and down the long empty corridor. "Listen, Julia. It's not so bad. Having another baby will be kind of exciting...."

Her husband didn't understand. Nor did her physician. As soon as she'd delivered the news—news Julia didn't want to hear—Dr. Snyder had distanced herself emotionally. Julia sensed it, felt it.

And Peter—sure, he'd been surprised, but he apparently shared none of her qualms. If anything, he seemed pleased. Thrilled, even. Excited.

Everything Julia wasn't.

"Nobody has ever measured, even poets, how much the heart can hold."

—Zelda Fitzgerald

10

CHAPTER

LIZ KENYON

January 28th

I'm feeling depressed, and I'm not sure I want to analyze the reasons. Perhaps it's just this time in my life. I'm fifty-seven and alone. Never in a million years did I think such a thing would happen.

Not to me.

The alarm wasn't set since it's Sunday, but I woke at six anyway. After tossing for a half hour, I decided I wasn't going to sleep any longer, no matter how much I wanted to. So I got up and showered. When the mirror cleared, I stared at my reflection and what I saw made me feel like weeping.

When did those crow's feet appear? I don't remember noticing them before. It isn't only my eyes, either; there are lines at my mouth and neck that I swear weren't there a week ago. I looked old and beaten, and I'm feeling every day of my fifty-seven years.

Until recently—until I started a journal, in fact—I hadn't given much thought to age. Fifty-seven is still young. This morning, studying my reflection, I was forced to confront the truth. Fifty-seven *isn't* that young.

All at once it hit me.

As though losing Steve and having the children move away isn't bad enough, now I'm facing yet another loss, this one as devastating as the others. My youth. Oh, I don't mean that I thought I was still in my twenties or anything so foolish—just that I saw my life (and, admittedly, my looks) continuing into the future unchanged. And I know now it isn't true. There are supposed to be compensations for these losses...of beauty, health and endless possibility. Compensations like grandchildren, wisdom, insight. But as far as I'm concerned the trade hasn't been a fair one. My grandchildren are far away, and I'm definitely lacking in wisdom. All I feel is the loss and none of what I'm supposed to have gained.

Oh dear, I'm sinking to a new low. Self-pity. No. I won't allow it. I *refuse* to feel sorry for myself. Action must be taken and quickly.

To complicate matters, I'm convinced that Sean Jamison is partly responsible for this unwelcome and unappreciated epiphany. Rumor has it he's dating the new physical therapist.

I couldn't care less.

Obviously that's a lie—I do care—otherwise I wouldn't be writing about it. Nor has it escaped my notice that the woman is twenty years his junior and nearly thirty years mine. Naturally Sean finds her attractive. What man wouldn't? She's young, pretty and probably defers to him. I, on the other hand, am older (though maybe not wiser) and I have wrinkles. No contest there. Not that I'm interested in competing for Sean.

Really, it doesn't even make sense that I care. He isn't seeking what you'd call a meaningful relationship. He's attracted to me; he's made that plain and I have to admit I'm flattered. Truth be known, I'm attracted to him, too. I wish I wasn't, because it's clear that this is destined to be a dead-end relationship—if a relationship at all. Sean just wants me to blindly fall into bed with him.

Unfortunately I can't do that and be comfortable with myself. There's only been one man in my life and after thirty-one years with Steve, I can't get involved with a man who's looking for a bout of casual sex. To me, it has to mean more than a few hours of pleasure. I can't change the woman I am, even for Sean Jamison.

I shouldn't feel this disappointed. To his credit, Sean has been forthright about what he wants, but I'd hoped for something different from him. I've always believed there was real depth to the man. Apparently I was wrong.

In an effort to boost my spirits, I phoned Amy after breakfast. My Sunday-morning chats with my daughter and grandchildren are often the highlight of the weekend for me.

As always, the conversation made me feel better. I told her I'd decided to be a volunteer reader at the Juvenile Detention Center and Amy applauded my decision. Getting out and doing something positive for the community is bound to improve my frame of mind.

Amy asked about the breakfast group and I was able to give her an update on everyone. She hasn't met any of these women who've become my friends, but she likes to hear about them whenever we talk. I think Amy wishes she could be part of such a group.

After I'd chatted with Andrew and Annie, I thought about my Thursday-morning friends. They're more than that, of course; it's just a quick way to distinguish them from my other friends. We're each at a completely different point in our lives, and yet there are similarities, too. I see myself in Clare's anger and grief, in Karen's passion, in Julia's sense of domesticity and order. And do they see their future selves in me? I think they must. I also think these friendships have become the truest and deepest I have.

I'm so thankful I met Clare, Karen and Julia. I need my friends, and never more than now.

"The only thing that seems eternal and natural in motherhood is ambivalence."

—Jane Lazarre

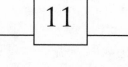

CHAPTER

JULIA MURCHISON

January 26th

> *List of Blessings*
> 1. A clean kitchen.
> 2. A bathroom close to the bed.
> 3. Truth…whether I want to face it or not.
> 4. Dark clouds that match my mood.
> 5. My family.

Last night, I didn't come home until after ten. By that time Peter and the kids were worried sick. The minute I walked into the house, Adam flew into the kitchen and demanded to know where I'd been. He sounded like an outraged parent. Talk about role reversal. Zoe was next; she burst into tears, stormed back into her room and slammed the door. Then Peter laid into me—only he didn't utter a word. He simply looked at me, and his expression said it all. He was furious with me for having worried them. He stomped out, leaving me alone in the kitchen.

I sat there for another hour. Had any of my family come in to listen, I would've told them exactly what I'd been doing. Driving around. After closing the shop, I left the strip mall and drove through town. I followed long, winding streets with no destination in mind, and then headed out to the highway. I went as far as McDonalds, where I had milk and a muffin, and turned back.

Peter was as upset as the children, but surely he of all people could understand why I did what I did. I couldn't look my children in the eye knowing I'm pregnant.

While I was driving around, I found myself at the cemetery for some oddball reason. My grandparents are buried there, but I barely remember them so I don't feel any deep connection. It probably had more to do with the way I was feeling. As if my life, the one I've been so careful to plan and nurture, is over. Corny symbolism, I know, but that's how depressed I felt.

Options are available to me. I'm well aware of what they are. I only wish I was the kind of woman who could walk into a clinic and be done with it, get rid of the burden. I never dreamed I'd even consider such a possibility. At first, the appeal of it was strong. No one need ever find out. Peter, of course. He wouldn't like it, would try to change my mind, but I know my husband and he wouldn't stop me. I thought about it, I really did. Even now, when I can be completely and totally honest, I can't make myself write the word.

An easy solution is what it sounds like, and for some women it might be the answer, but not me. I know myself too well. I hate that I'm pregnant, but I won't undo what's already been done.

Adam and Zoe realized something was wrong, but they seemed to think Peter and I had had a disagreement. I'm always home for them in the evenings. They're accustomed to having dinner on the table and me there to help with homework and to chat. Both of them were upset with me. Peter was, too. Later, when he'd cooled down, he asked if I'd eaten dinner and I told him yes. He said he'd ordered pizza for the kids. I went to bed and Peter came and asked if there was anything he could do. I told him no.

I thought of calling Georgia, but didn't. Much as I love her, I just don't know how to tell her about this. She's been married four times, twice to the same man, and she's childless. How could she understand what I'm feeling?

I could talk to the women in the breakfast group—except that I'm not ready. I'll tell them in a few weeks.

I wonder if the baby senses how much I don't want to be pregnant. Adam and Zoe were gifts; not this baby.

Is it wrong to hope I miscarry? The fact that I'm almost forty might mean the baby's at risk. There's a far higher chance of birth defects. Oh, God, I can't think about that now.

I feel so guilty and ashamed. Mostly I feel miserable.

* * *

Julia sat in her rocking chair, knitting by rote as her mind rapidly spun its thoughts. Thankfully, business had been slow all afternoon. The success of her shop was largely a result of the personal service she gave her customers, many of whom had become friends. Women—and a few men—visited her store; they trusted her advice and sought her opinion concerning their creative efforts.

Today, though, the quality of her service wasn't exactly what it should have been.

Preoccupied as she was, Julia found herself prone to mistakes. Irene Waldmann had certainly pointed that out. The older woman was a regular customer, and earlier that day Julia had made an error in calculating how much yarn she needed for her latest project. Mrs. Waldmann had noticed and complained at length. The woman's gruff personality made her hard to please, anyway, and she wasn't the type who would tolerate mistakes. Luckily, it'd been discovered early.

A car pulled into the parking space in front of her shop window and Julia glanced up to see Peter. They'd barely spoken that morning. Her husband and children had tiptoed around her as if they weren't sure what to expect.

As soon as they were out the door, Julia's stomach went queasy and the little coffee she'd managed to down was lost in a quick dash to the bathroom. This morning sickness was far worse than she'd experienced during the previous two pregnancies.

Maybe it was the baby's revenge for being unwanted.

When he walked into the store, Peter presented her with a bouquet of yellow daisies, her favorite flowers.

"To what do I owe this?" she asked, hating the edge in her voice but unable to hide it.

"I came to see how you're feeling."

She jerked on the yarn, pulling it unnecessarily hard. "Just great."

Peter took the empty rocker next to hers. If he'd tried to talk, forced her into a conversation, she might have been able to maintain her ugly mood. Instead he sat with her, gently matching his rocking motion to hers, the flowers in his lap, and said nothing. Not a word.

"This is God's big joke, you know," Julia whispered after a moment. "My word, I mean."

"Your word," he repeated. "What are you talking about?"

"My word for the year," she snapped, thinking it was obvious. He knew everyone in the breakfast club had chosen a word.

"Oh, you're talking about your friends from the journal-writing class. You told me what your word was, but I've forgotten."

Fearing she was about to break into tears, she just shook her head, not trusting herself to speak.

"Was it *surprise?*" he asked.

This was his idiotic attempt at humor, she assumed. Another time, she might have found him amusing, but not in her current mood.

"Gratitude," she managed.

"Gratitude," he said slowly.

"Funny, isn't it?"

He stopped rocking and placed his hand on her forearm. Julia continued knitting, afraid that if she stopped now she'd crumble completely.

"I'm sorry, honey," he said. "You're right, this is my fault."

"And mine... I should have— I don't know. Oh, Peter, I feel so awful, so guilty and ashamed."

"What did you do that's so terrible?" he asked, and rubbed his hand down her arm.

"I don't want this baby! I can't even think of it as a baby. Every child deserves to come into a loving home."

"I love the baby," he said.

He might have thought he was comforting her, but he wasn't. "Fine, you go ahead and love the baby. I don't. Maybe you should waltz on down to The Baby Emporium and stroll through the aisles and be happy. I'm not! And hearing you tell me how pleased you are isn't helping a damn bit." Her voice rose until she was close to yelling.

"Sorry," he said and raised both hands. "You're right. I won't say anything more."

"What are we going to do?" she wailed. "How will we cope?" She hoped he had some answers because she was completely out.

"I don't know," he answered.

"Neither do I."

They rocked a few more minutes while Julia knit, periodically tugging at the yarn, her fingers moving with confidence. She was working on a mohair sweater to display in the store. Maybe it should've been booties or a little blanket, she thought darkly, but even looking at the baby yarn was beyond her.

"Do you think we should tell the kids?" he asked.

Julia couldn't believe he'd pose such a question. "Absolutely not!"

He didn't respond for a long moment. "The only reason I ask is because they were both so worried about you last night," he finally said. "You should have phoned."

"I know." She did feel bad about upsetting her family.

"Adam and Zoe are old enough to recognize when something's wrong. I think we should tell them. They have a right to know."

In other circumstances she would have agreed with him, but not now. "I don't think it's a good idea."

"Why not?"

"What if I miscarry? I could, you know. I'm going to be forty soon...and when you're older, the risk of a miscarriage is much higher."

"I realize that, but the baby might be perfectly okay, too. There's at least an equal chance of that."

"Still, this pregnancy isn't a sure thing, so we shouldn't say anything yet," she said, holding onto her one hope of escape. She wouldn't do anything to terminate the pregnancy, but if nature should take its course...

"I'm sorry you're so unhappy about all this," Peter murmured.

"I'm sorry, too," and Julia was, more than she cared to admit.

"Don't worry, sweetheart, everything will work out. Somehow or other."

"Somehow or other," Julia echoed. She wished she could feel differently about this baby. Her husband loved children. If it'd been his decision alone, they would have had a houseful of kids.

Peter glanced at his watch. "I'll head home and get dinner started." Julia nodded.

"Don't worry, honey," he said, bending down to kiss her on the cheek.

A moment later, the door shut behind him. Julia tossed a ball of yarn at it.

Just as she was ready to close for the day, Georgia strolled in, sparking with her usual energy. They were cousins and best friends and about as opposite as any two women could be. In high school, Julia was the student-body president and class brain. Georgia was the flighty cheerleader with more beauty than common sense. She flitted in and out of marriage every few years, the way some people bought a new car. But despite their differences Georgia was the one person Julia knew she could trust.

"So. What's going on?" Georgia asked loudly, arms spread wide, bracelets clanking. Her cousin always made an entrance. It was her trademark. Everyone expected it of her.

"What—what do you mean?" Julia couldn't imagine how Georgia had heard her news.

"I haven't talked to you all week." Her cousin stood before her, hands now resting on her hips. "Must be *something* happening." Georgia's long blond hair was artfully arranged atop her head, with tendrils dangling down in all the right places. She was dressed in loose black clothes and heavy silver jewelry and looked stunning.

"I'm pregnant," Julia blurted out. She couldn't tell her mother, her sister or her own children, but felt no such compunction when it came to Georgia.

Georgia responded by sinking into the rocker recently vacated by Peter.

"Pregnant?" she repeated as though it was a foreign word whose meaning she wasn't quite sure of. "As in baby?"

Julia covered her face with both hands and burst into tears.

"Oh, Julia, you're not joking, are you?" Georgia got to her feet and grabbed her purse, spilling half the contents. Makeup, a hairbrush and loose change rolled across the table. "Damn, I need a cigarette."

"I thought you quit."

"I did, I'm down to five a day." She found what she was looking for, placed the low-tar low-nicotine cigarette between her lips and flicked her lighter. Stepping to the door, she took one deep puff, aiming a stream of smoke outside, then frowned at the cigarette. "I swear these things are giving me a hernia."

"It was an accident," Julia explained.

"All pregnancies are accidents," Georgia insisted. "What did Peter say?"

"He's thrilled."

"Naturally," she snorted and inhaled deeply on the cigarette. Leaning against the doorjamb, she waved her free hand toward the bouquet of daisies lying on the counter. "Peter?"

Julia nodded.

"I should've known."

Reaching for a tissue, Julia loudly blew her nose. "I haven't told anyone else—other than Peter."

"I was pregnant once," Georgia said.

"When?" They'd been close all these years, and this was the first she'd ever heard of it.

"Hell, I was just a kid."

"What did you do?"

"Not a damn thing. I lost the baby shortly after I married Ernie. I never would've married him otherwise."

Ernie was Georgia's first husband. The marriage lasted all of two years, if that. Georgia had still been a teenager and Ernie was only a few years older.

"I always liked Ernie," she said with some regret. "But neither of us was cut out to be a parent."

Georgia rarely talked about her marriages, but Julia knew that Ernie had broken her heart. He'd managed a restaurant and apparently had something sweet going on the side with the pastry chef. The minute Georgia found out, the marriage was over. She'd married on the rebound—a mechanic, who had an affinity for the bottle. That marriage had turned into a love-hate relationship. When they were getting along, it was very good, and when they were on the outs, it was a free-for-all. They'd married and divorced twice before Georgia met her third and current husband. She and Maurice had been married a year and Julia hadn't seen him even once since the ceremony. She didn't know much about him, but Georgia appeared to be happy and that was all that mattered.

When she'd finished dabbing the moisture from her eyes, Julia glanced up and was stunned to see the tears trailing down Georgia's cheeks.

"Damn, I need a cigarette," she sniffled. She tended to punctuate her conversation with that remark.

"You have one in your hand."

"A real cigarette," Georgia said. "These aren't worth shit." Leave it to her cousin to make her smile. Julia started to laugh then, and soon Georgia was laughing, too. Without a pause, they were both weeping again, the border between laughter and tears invisible.

"Unbosom yourself," said Wimsey. "Trouble shared is trouble halved."

—Dorothy Sayers

CHAPTER

THURSDAY MORNING BREAKFAST CLUB

Everyone had already arrived by the time Julia showed up for the weekly breakfast meeting on the first Thursday of February. Liz had ordered her usual coffee and croissant and looked wonderful in her pinstriped power suit. Her dark hair was stylishly short and utterly feminine. Julia knew her friend's life was much easier now that the nurses' strike had been averted. Liz's name had turned up in the local newspaper often in the past few weeks, and she'd played no small role in the ultimate resolution.

Clare had her double-shot espresso and currant scone, and sat next to Liz at the table for four. She looked less harried now than she had when they'd first met, Julia noted; still, the recent contact with her ex had thrown her, and her resentment and anger had quickly surfaced.

She seemed to be rebounding, though, and that was good for everyone involved—especially her sons. Julia didn't mean to be judg-
mental or critical; Clare had reason to feel the way she did. To Clare's
credit, she'd made a gallant effort to get on with her life. She worked
part-time and seemed less obsessive over the breakup of her marriage.
Julia believed the group had been a good sounding board for her, and
more than that, a real support.

Karen was there, too, with her multi-mix latte, a different flavor
combination each week. Last week it'd been a coconut cream concoction and the aroma had made Julia nauseous. She hadn't told them
about the pregnancy yet, wanting to delay it until she knew if there'd
actually *be* a pregnancy.

Her three friends greeted her with welcoming smiles as she joined
them. She ordered herbal tea and a blueberry muffin at the counter
and carried them to the table where the others waited.

"Morning," she said, sitting next to Karen. "How's everyone this
week?"

A chorus of "goods" followed. It was almost always like this. They
started off slowly, each talking a little about the week that had passed,
then gradually gaining momentum. Their lives were full of commitments, family obligations and stress. Outside of Thursdays, they rarely
saw one another, but that had started to change. Liz and Clare got together occasionally; they seemed to have formed a close bond. And last
Sunday afternoon, they'd all attended a movie.

Liz spread strawberry preserves across half her croissant as Karen
animatedly described a recent audition for a dog food commercial.
Apparently, the cocker spaniel had taken an instant dislike to her and
growled every time she'd attempted to say her lines. Not surprisingly,
she didn't get the part, but the way she told the story had them all
laughing and offering sympathy.

"This director likes me, though," she concluded, "and Gwen, my
agent, said she'd bring up my name the next time he's casting." She
finished with a heavy theatrical sigh. "It seems my entire career rests
on 'next time.' It really irritates me, too, because I love dogs and until
the audition they've always loved me. You can bet I'll never own a
cocker spaniel."

As they continued to talk about Karen's audition, Julia noticed that Liz had grown quiet. She wondered if her friend's lack of enthusiasm had anything to do with the recent troubles at the hospital. But the strike had been averted. Perhaps it was that doctor she'd mentioned a couple of times. Julia had caught on right away; Liz's offhand manner when she'd told the group about him had instantly signalled that there was more to the situation.

"Have you heard anything more from your doctor friend?" she asked.

Liz shook her head. It was obvious from the way she shifted in her chair and stared off into the distance that she didn't want to talk about Dr. Jamison.

"Is he bothering you?" Clare demanded. Her aggressiveness on Liz's behalf made Julia smile a little. Clare seemed ready to roll up her sleeves and do battle with Dr. Jamison.

"He's not exactly bothering me," Liz said, but Julia could tell she didn't like being put in the position of defending him.

Karen leaned across the table. "You're interested in him, aren't you? I thought you were when you first mentioned his name, and now I'm sure of it."

"I'm not," Liz insisted, but she didn't sound convincing.

"Who do you think you're kidding?" Clare said with a deep-throated laugh. "Somehow or other, the good doctor turns up in our conversation practically every week."

"Are you going to dinner with him? He asked you out again, didn't he?"

"As a matter of fact, he didn't and even if he did, the answer's the same. Really, I'm *not* interested."

"Yeah, right," Karen said good-naturedly. She propped her elbows on the table, clearly expecting Liz to supply more details.

Liz ignored her, paying careful attention to her croissant. "He hasn't stopped by the office in weeks, and from what I hear, he's seeing one of the physical therapists, which is perfectly fine with me."

"Is it?" Clare asked.

"Yes. I told you before I'm too old for him."

"Don't be ridiculous," Clare scoffed. "Besides, if he's as brilliant as you say, he'll soon figure out what he's missing."

"Valentine's Day is coming up," Karen said, raising her finely shaped eyebrows.

"Guys, I'm serious! I doubt I'd go out with him even if he did ask."

"You'll know when the time comes," Karen said confidently.

"Just be careful," Clare inserted. "Guard your heart." She dropped her voice on the last word, not meeting anyone's eyes.

"What about you, Clare?" Julia asked her. "How's the situation between Mick and Alex?"

A pained look came over Clare's face. "Mick isn't speaking to his brother yet, but I'm sure that eventually they'll settle this."

"You hate seeing your boys fighting about their father, don't you?"

Clare twisted her mouth. "Does anyone mind if we don't talk about Michael? I was just starting to get my appetite back."

They all grinned.

Clare relaxed, and Julia realized anew how hard her friend was struggling to keep the resentment out of her life.

"On a different subject, I'm thinking about selling the house once Alex graduates this summer," Clare said next. "I spent all week sorting through twenty years of junk, trying to decide what to do. I want to think positive, but it's damned difficult. When Michael and I built the house, it was with the intention of living there for the rest of our lives. That's why the master bedroom is on the main floor. We were looking to the future and didn't want to worry about climbing stairs when we hit our senior years."

"Then live there," Karen said. "No one's saying you have to move."

"No," Clare agreed, "but I'm not sure I can after Alex is gone. The house represents so much of what my marriage was to me, and now it's over. Everything I'd planned for the future is meaningless now."

"You'll make other plans," Julia assured her.

"I know," Clare said, sipping her espresso. "It just takes time."

"Have you talked to your mother lately?" Liz asked Karen.

Karen's reaction was immediate. She stiffened. "Not a word."

"What about your sister?" Clare asked.

Karen shook her head.

"I thought you said Victoria called you recently."

"She did," Karen admitted. "That's twice within the last month, which has to be something of a record. Generally I'm fortunate if I hear from her on my birthday."

"Any reason she's calling you more frequently?"

"None that I can figure out, except..."

"Yes?" Liz urged.

Again Karen shook her head. "I'm beginning to wonder if my sister's as happy as she leads everyone to believe."

"What makes you say that?"

"First, she hardly ever has people over. Second, I hardly ever see her and Roger together. Plus that last time she called, it sounded like she'd been crying."

"Did you ask her about it?"

"Sure I did," Karen replied, a bit indignantly. "She said she'd caught a bad cold." She rolled her eyes. "It wouldn't shock me, you know, if she's not Ms. Perfect, after all. But it *would* shock Mom."

"Maybe that's why she's calling you," Clare suggested.

"Maybe."

"What's her husband like?" Julia asked.

"He's a twit. He's a lot like my mother, only he's a man." Karen grimaced. "I can't imagine *anyone* marrying Roger."

"Your sister loves him," Liz reminded her.

"I know. In my humble opinion that means there's something wrong with her." Karen took a deep sip of her flavored drink; Julia thought it smelled like a cherry-vanilla combination. "Victoria and I were never close...."

"But she seems to be reaching out to you now," Julia said.

"Maybe she's hoping you'll reach back," Clare added.

Karen held the straw between her lips. "You think?"

Everyone nodded. There was silence for a minute or two.

"Have you heard anything from Jeff lately?" Liz asked suddenly.

"He's out of the picture. Looks like I'm going to be dateless on Valentine's Day. It won't be the first time and it probably won't be the last."

"What happened?"

She shrugged. "My agent decided not to take him on. He's got talent but no drive. He expected me to smooth the way for him, lead him by the hand. I've got enough trouble managing my own career. I can't baby-sit his. Once he figured that out, we had a parting of the ways. Trust me, it's no great loss."

"What about the guy you were telling us about a little while ago?" Clare asked.

"What guy?"

"George Somebody."

"I mentioned Glen?" She seemed surprised by this.

"I thought it was George," Clare said to Liz.

Liz smiled. "Apparently not."

"It's Glen."

"Tell us more," Liz said. "We're living vicariously through you."

Karen grinned and flipped a long strand of brown hair over her shoulder. "Sorry, there's nothing to tell. He's a high-school chemistry teacher. We met briefly in a parking lot across from the school where I was subbing. He's not my type."

"Damn," Liz muttered, and they all laughed.

"Just a minute," Clare said, turning to Julia. "What about you? Everyone else has been doing all the talking. How's your week been?"

Julia stared down at her hands. She hadn't planned to tell her friends about the pregnancy until March, when she reached the twelve-week point, but she wanted to confide in them now, wanted it so much.

"Julia?" Liz asked, sounding concerned.

"What's wrong?" Clare asked with a gentleness Julia hadn't seen in her before. This show of compassion gave her a hint of what the other woman had been like before the divorce.

"You can tell us, whatever it is," Karen insisted.

"I don't know how," she whispered, fighting back the desperation that always seemed to hover.

"It's Peter, isn't it?" Clare cried, outraged and angry now. "He's found someone else."

"No." Julia shook her head, wanting to laugh because that idea was so incredibly ridiculous. "No," she said again, sighing deeply. "I'm pregnant."

The other three stared at her as if they weren't sure they should believe her.

"You're joking, right?" Karen said, looking from one to the other for a sign that she'd missed something earlier.

"I'm afraid not." If there was a joke, it'd been on her. "In case you haven't guessed, I'm not particularly pleased."

"Oh, Julia," Liz said, her eyes warm with sympathy.

"What are you going to do?" Clare asked next.

"Do," she repeated. "What *can* I do? I'll have this baby." *And resent it the rest of my life.* "I keep thinking this is God's sense of humor. Here I am trying to be so grateful, listing five blessings each and every morning—and now this? A pregnancy at age forty is one blessing I could've done without."

"Hey," Karen said, "we didn't talk about our word this week."

"Screw the word," Clare said fiercely. "We have more important things to deal with right now."

"What does Peter say?" Liz asked.

"Peter?" Julia said and laughed humorlessly, "is positively delighted."

"Figures," Clare groaned.

"He loves children...he's always wanted more. I was the one who insisted we stop at two." Her husband wasn't the only person who was thrilled with this news, either. Julia's mother had been overcome with excitement. "My own mother—" she threw back her head, eyes closed "—said the baby's a blessing in disguise."

"It's a mother thing," Liz said. "She's happy about adding another grandchild to her brag book."

"Have you told anyone else?" Karen asked.

"My mom and sister know, and my cousin Georgia."

"How'd they react?"

"Janice *laughed.* She said she couldn't help it. I'm the one who so carefully planned her life—always so organized and methodical—while Janice just kind of...improvises. And look at me now! Which is why she finds the situation hilarious." Julia exhaled softly. "When I told Georgia, she smoked an entire pack of cigarettes in thirty minutes. Then we sat and had a good cry together."

"That sounds like Georgia."

Julia reached nervously for her tea. Ever since learning of the pregnancy, Georgia had made a habit of visiting the shop every afternoon.

Just yesterday, she'd brought Julia a bottle of vitamins that were large enough to choke a crocodile. With the vitamins had come a lengthy lecture on proper diet and the importance of exercise. It was Georgia's contention that Julia should get away from the shop more often; she insisted the two of them take up mall-walking. With that in mind, she'd purchased identical purple and hot-pink nylon running outfits. Julia declined, but Georgia had been relentless. Later, under pressure, Julia agreed to exercise, but only when she was feeling better.

"What about the kids?" Liz asked. "How did they react?"

"We haven't told them yet." Julia dreaded the thought. Her children were typical teenagers—meaning self-involved—and their entire world focused on their own needs. Peter had a blind spot when it came to his children; he sincerely believed they'd be just as delighted as he was. Julia doubted it.

"You have to adjust to it yourself first," Liz said and patted her hand.

"What about The Wool Station? Are you going to close it while you're on maternity leave?"

"I don't know," she said helplessly. So many questions remained unanswered. Peter was full of vague reassurances; he kept insisting they'd make it work.

Everyone was quiet for a while, as though they required a moment to absorb the news.

"If you need anything, you holler," Karen said. "I don't know much about babies, but I'll do what I can."

"I will, too," Clare assured her. "You have my complete support."

"And mine," Liz promised.

"Thank you," Julia whispered, grateful for these three dear friends. She had the feeling she was going to be calling upon them often in the months to come.

> "Life is under no obligation to give us what we expect."
> —Margaret Mitchell

13
CHAPTER

CLARE CRAIG

February 4th

I can't believe what happened yesterday. I saw Michael for the first time—outside a courtroom—since the divorce became final. Not by choice, mind you. Alex was in a soccer tournament in Fresno this weekend, and I assumed Michael wouldn't be there. My mistake. Michael's worked weekends for years and Fresno's a long drive. Needless to say, I took it for granted that he wouldn't show up.

Seeing my ex-husband was a shock. He's thinner now than when we were together, and what he wore—khakis and a Gap sweatshirt—reflected the change he's made in his life. If he's going to live with a twenty-year-old, I guess it's not surprising that he'd dress like one. As though he could fool anyone. It's pathetic.

What astonished me most was the pain I felt when I saw him. And not only pain but anger and resentment. I thought I was past this! It's disheartening to realize how far I have yet to go.

To be fair, I have to admit Michael didn't mingle with the other parents. He stood at the far end of the field, away from everyone else. In fact, he was there a good hour before I noticed him, which happened when Alex ran off the field to talk to him. Then, and only then, did I see that the stranger near the goalpost was Michael. From that point onward, the entire tournament was ruined for me.

Alex knew how upset I was and did his best to explain once we were alone. He told me he was surprised to see Michael at the Fresno game, too. I could tell he was pleased and didn't want to squelch his joy, but I was furious with Michael. He should have had the decency to let me know.

I've been depressed ever since last night. Alex isn't here right now; he's been gone a lot lately, busy with his job, soccer, school and friends. It wouldn't be appropriate to discuss my feelings with him, anyway. Usually when something like this comes up, I go to Liz. I suppose it's because she's older and she's been through the grief of losing her husband, but she always has a sensible perspective on things. I've been going to her a lot lately, relying on her too much, and I feel it's time I dealt with these problems on my own.

I spent last night wallowing in self-pity. I was exhausted after the long drive home, but I sat in the living room until the wee hours of the morning, thinking about all the times Michael and I attended the boys' games together. He missed some of the Saturday morning games, but for the most part we were there as a couple. I found myself crying again—all this heartache— and then I simply decided I couldn't let one man destroy me like this.

Easier said than done.

Sometimes I wonder if this pain will ever end. Michael's lost at least thirty pounds. So he's looking lean and craggy (very much his age, in my opinion). But he dresses in a style better suited to one of his sons. Miranda's obviously responsible for that. She's probably worn him to a frazzle with all her sexual demands. Good, maybe he'll die young and miserable. I've done my part to make sure he dies broke.

* * *

"Mom." Alex's raised voice rang over the telephone line. "I need a favor."

"What's up?" Clare had been busy working off her unhappiness over the soccer fiasco by scrubbing the shower stall in the master bedroom. She was determined to regain control of her emotions, and since it was Monday, didn't have the distraction of work. Her hours at Murphy Motors were Tuesdays and Thursdays.

"I need to write a makeup test this afternoon."

"English or algebra?

"Algebra."

Because of the soccer tournament, Alex had missed two important tests. Algebra was her son's poorest subject, and he resembled his father there, far more than he did her.

"What about the English midterm?"

"Mrs. Ford was cool about that. She said I could write it any time this week."

"Not so with Mr. Lawrence?"

"No. In fact, he said if I didn't take the test this afternoon, he'll give me a zero. And if I get a zero, you can kiss my chances of getting into Berkeley goodbye."

"Did you study?"

"Of course I did. I'll ace it if—"

"If what?"

"Mom," he said, then hesitated. "You know I wouldn't ask if there was any other way."

"What?" Clare demanded, growing impatient. Intuition told her she wasn't going to like this. Alex was generally straightforward when he wanted something; there had to be a reason he was being so indirect.

"I told Dad I'd pick him up at the hospital, and now I can't."

Clare's anger was immediate. "You're asking *me* to chauffeur your father around?"

"Yes." Alex's voice sounded small. "I know you and Dad are divorced, but that doesn't mean you can't be civilized."

Clare gritted her teeth and waited for the anger to pass. "I'm civilized, Alex. Are you suggesting I'm not?"

"No, Mom, please... I don't want to get into this with you. I wouldn't have asked if it wasn't important."

"What about his...friend?" Clare asked. Surely Miranda could pick him up.

"She can't just take off from work, you know."

Clare hadn't realized nail technicians were on such tight schedules.

"Can't he get a taxi?" If there was a way out of this, Clare planned to find it.

"Yeah, I guess, only I told him I'd be there and you always said it's important for us to keep our commitments."

Hmm. Moral righteousness. He was bringing out the heavy artillery.

Something wasn't logical here. A thought occurred to her that hadn't earlier. "Why can't he drive himself?"

"Mom, I'm between classes and I don't have time to discuss this, but apparently Dad's having some tests done at the hospital. He's not supposed to drive."

"Oh." She paused. "What kind of tests?"

"I'm not...sure." It was his turn to pause. "Will you do it or not?" he asked more sharply.

She desperately wanted to tell Alex that Michael could find his own damn way home. But deep down, Clare knew that if she refused, Alex would skip the exam and take the zero in order to fulfill his obligation to his father.

"Will you?" he repeated.

"All right," she muttered with ill grace, angry for allowing herself to be maneuvered into something she didn't want to do.

Alex quickly gave her the necessary information, then said, "Thanks, Mom. I knew I could count on you."

The line was disconnected before she had a chance to respond.

Dreadful though the situation was, it did give her an opportunity to speak to Michael about the next soccer tournament, scheduled for March. Look on the bright side, Clare! They'd agreed to alternate attending the games. This afternoon would be a perfect chance to sort out the details and make sure there wasn't a repeat of last weekend.

Clare suspected that Alex was secretly hoping his parents would reunite. What a joke. As far as she was concerned, Michael had proven himself completely untrustworthy. But according to the books she'd read and what she'd heard in her support group, this was a common fantasy for children of divorce—regardless of age.

It worried her a little that Alex felt this responsibility toward his father. He was only a kid; he shouldn't have to ferry Michael around or be involved with his problems. Yet Alex had accepted the burden as if it were his own.

As the time approached to leave for the hospital, Clare dressed in her best business suit. Staring at her reflection in the bedroom mirror, she stripped it off. Too formal, she decided. She was striving for a look of casual elegance.

No. That might give him the impression that she was living a life of leisure. Whatever she chose to wear had to convey how terribly happy she was, how terribly busy. Her goal was to make Michael believe she was extremely inconvenienced by having her day interrupted. At the same time, her graciousness and generosity in coming for him would clearly state that she was the bigger person, capable of putting bygones aside.

Best of all, Michael had no idea she was picking him up. According to Alex, it was impossible to get a message to him, letting him know the arrangements had changed. That being the case, Michael would be caught off guard when she arrived. Good—he could suffer the same shock Clare had last Saturday. Not only that, *she* was prepared, and her carefully contrived demeanor would remind him of what he'd thrown away. A mature, classy, compassionate and capable woman.

Yes. She had it all figured out.

Life's unpleasant surprises did come with compensations.

After emptying almost her entire closet, Clare finally chose a canary-yellow pantsuit. It suggested cheeriness and optimism; even better, Michael had always liked it on her. Whenever she wore it, he'd sing "You Are My Sunshine," and he'd— Enough of that! She planned to swing into the hospital like a...like a ray of sunshine. Cordial but not overly so. Michael would be in her debt, and she preferred that to owing *him* anything.

The hospital. Apparently Michael's current lifestyle had taken its toll on his health. Poor boy, he just couldn't keep pace with a youngster. She'd be sure to reveal exactly the right amount of sympathy, with just a hint of contempt.

On the drive to Willow Grove Memorial, she repeatedly played through the scenario in her mind, imagining Michael's reactions and rehearsing her own.

Michael was supposed to be waiting for her in the hospital foyer. All that was required of her, according to Alex, was to drive up to the front doors.

She tried that, but when Michael didn't show up, she circled the block a couple of times. When he still didn't appear, she parked the car in the first available slot, and strode purposefully toward the hospital entrance.

Her mood darkened.

Searching for Michael was *not* part of the deal. It ruined the way she'd envisioned their meeting, completely spoiling the little script she'd created. If he wasn't inside where she'd been told he'd be, Michael could damn well find his own ride home.

No sooner had she walked into the marble-floored foyer than she heard someone call her name.

"Clare," Liz said, hurrying toward her. "What are you doing here?"

This was embarrassing. Being seen by her friend wasn't part of the deal, either. "Ah..." A lie would be convenient, but unaccustomed to prevarication, she couldn't think of one fast enough.

"Everything's all right, isn't it?" Liz pressed.

"Oh, sure..." She sighed. "I'm here to pick up Michael."

Liz's eyes widened, but she said nothing.

Reluctantly Clare explained Alex's predicament and hers, ending with Michael's non-appearance at the appointed place. "I guess I'll wait a few more minutes," she said.

Liz's expression was sympathetic. "Are you sure you're up to this?"

Clare's answer was a shrug. "I'm about to find out, aren't I?"

"Yes, you are." She glanced past Clare's shoulder. "Is that him over there?"

It was, and he looked dreadful. Pale and gaunt. Seeing him close-up, she realized he'd lost more weight than she'd noticed on Saturday; he was downright thin.

He stopped abruptly when he saw her.

"Where's Alex?" he asked, gazing around.

"Taking an algebra midterm," she replied stiffly, staggered by the differences she saw in him. She nodded toward Liz. "This is my friend Liz Kenyon, the hospital administrator."

Michael inclined his head, acknowledging the introduction with a brief smile. "Do you mind if we leave now?"

"I'll see you Thursday," Clare said, turning toward the doors.

"Okay." As Clare began to walk away, Liz squeezed her hand.

Outside the hospital, Michael paused. "Where's the car?"

"In the east parking lot." She pointed.

He nodded and started walking in that direction.

Clare followed more slowly behind him. She should have pursued her question about the tests. Alex probably knew *something* and she should've insisted he tell her. In her eagerness to wear the perfect outfit, to show him how completely she'd recovered from their divorce, she hadn't given it much thought. Whatever the tests were for, they must've been hellish.

Neither spoke as they walked toward the parking lot. By the time they reached the car, Michael's breathing was labored. She pretended not to notice.

Once inside the vehicle, Michael closed his eyes and leaned against the headrest. He'd broken into a sweat. She struggled not to react with pity or fear. Struggled not to react as a wife would.

Clare started the engine and backed out of the space.

"I appreciate this, Clare," he said, his voice barely audible.

"I won't pretend it was convenient," she said, keeping her voice cool, refusing to allow herself to feel anything, and hating it that she did. "I wouldn't be here if it wasn't for Alex."

"I know."

She waited until they'd merged with the flow of traffic before she broached the subject of their son and the remaining soccer matches.

"I thought we'd agreed to split up Alex's games," she said in as reasonable a tone as she could manage. "If you wanted to attend the tournament, you should've let me know."

Michael didn't answer, and when she turned to look at him, he was staring out the side window.

So he intended to give her the silent treatment. Okay, fine. But she wasn't conceding defeat. She—

"I'm sorry."

Again she had to strain to hear him. In an odd way, she was almost disappointed by his apology. It sabotaged her anger.

"Sorry?" The least he could do was explain himself.

"Stop the car." His voice was harsh. Urgent. He pointed to a side street and added. "Hurry...please."

"Stop the car?" she repeated. Even as she said the words, she switched to the outside lane and pulled off the main street, onto the road he'd indicated. The second she eased to a stop at the curb, the passenger door flew open. Michael half fell out of the car, bent over and vomited on the sidewalk.

Clare remembered Julia's horrible case of flu last November. That must be what Michael had, although even worse. Doubled over, he heaved until there was nothing left.

When he'd finished, he leaned weakly against the side of the SUV.

Without a word, Clare opened the back and found a bottle of spring water and uncapped it. Next, she gave him a tissue from her purse, which he used to wipe his mouth. She handed him the water bottle.

Michael took it from her, rinsed his mouth, then used what remained to wash off the sidewalk.

He climbed back into the car, more ashen than before.

"That must've been one hell of a test you had," she said. "Or do you have the flu?" Clare didn't *want* to feel sympathy for him, but despite everything, she did. It was impossible not to be affected by someone's pain. Even if that person had ripped apart her life. Even if she'd sworn to harden her heart against him.

"I wasn't at the hospital for tests," he said after a moment. "And I don't have the flu."

Clare glanced in his direction and waited for him to explain, her hand on the ignition key.

"I'm undergoing chemotherapy."

Chemotherapy? Michael?

"You have cancer?" Clare whispered.

"The way I see it, if you want the rainbow, you gotta put up with the rain."

—Dolly Parton

14

CHAPTER

LIZ KENYON

February 8th

I'm worried about Clare and Julia. Our meeting today troubled me.

Clare is my main concern. It didn't take me long to discover why Michael Craig was at the hospital on Monday, and it wasn't for any tests, the way Clare assumed. One look at her ex-husband told me he wasn't a well man. I wonder if Clare knows the seriousness of his condition, but unfortunately that isn't a question I can ask her.

My first reaction was that her son had practically blackmailed her into picking Michael up. I wondered if Alex did this on purpose so Clare would discover the truth on her own. It's a possibility, but not one I mentioned. In fact, as I learned later, she's not sure how much her boys know.

I suspected she was going to need to talk all of this over with someone, and I was right. After work on Monday, I got some Chinese takeout and drove to her house. It took her almost five minutes to answer the door, and she looked pale and shaken and very glad to see me.

We talked for several hours while we ate Szechwan chicken and shrimp egg fu yung, then drank black tea in front of her fireplace. Apparently Michael's still living with Miranda. It couldn't have been easy for Clare to drive him to the house he's sharing with another woman. I don't know what they said to each other, she and Michael. Doesn't matter, though. My main purpose is to help a friend.

Clare's a strong woman. She doesn't credit herself nearly enough. She's been through a great deal and unfortunately, there's more to come. However, by the end of the evening, I felt confident that Clare was handling this news as well as could be expected.

Then at the breakfast this morning, she looked like she hadn't slept all night. She seemed especially quiet, too, and Karen's attempts to draw her out were unsuccessful.

Clare isn't the only one experiencing problems. Julia seems completely drained. This pregnancy hasn't been easy on her physically or, of course, emotionally. She, too, was withdrawn and uncommunicative.

That left Karen and me. Karen, forever the actress, seemed grateful for an audience and did most of the talking. While I enjoy her, I'd hoped Clare and Julia would be more forthcoming, but neither of them really entered into the conversation. Without them contributing, the group simply doesn't work.

I'm making the effort to see more of Clare and Julia. After all, I'm the one with the free time to invest in our friendships. I can certainly give them the benefit of my affection and sympathy—if not my wisdom!

With that thought in mind, I've decided I want to learn how to knit, and Julia's agreed to teach me. She doesn't hold regular classes; she found it was too difficult to run the store and teach at the same time. (She can't afford to hire anyone yet, although that's her eventual goal.) Evenings are reserved for her family and after spending all day at the store, she's ready to go home by six.

I've always wanted to knit (and I'll be meeting one of my goals for the year—a new skill!). I'll buy yarn to make a sweater for Annie, and while I'm learning the basics, I'll have an opportunity to visit with Julia. We've arranged our lessons for two lunch hours a week; I'll bring the sandwiches, since she won't accept payment. We'll knit—and we'll talk. About the baby, her feelings, whatever she wants.

Julia's baby must be why Lauren's on my mind so much these days. To carry a child for six months and then lose her, born three months premature, nearly destroyed us. Steve and I were so young and afraid. I've never forgotten her, although I rarely mention her name. Born now, my Lauren might have lived. A doctor like Sean might have given her a chance at life.

He came to my office earlier in the week. I didn't see him, but I knew he'd been there. I was in a meeting with the nursing director, finalizing the details of the new contract. When I returned, a long-stemmed rose had been placed on my desk. It's been almost a month since Sean and I talked. I'm not even sure if he's still seeing the physical therapist.

I wish I could pinpoint what it is about this man that I find so attractive. And dammit, I have to admit that I do. I know he's younger and he's arrogant and he's impatient and demanding—and he's got an inflated opinion of his own charms. And yet...and yet I can't stop thinking about him.

He's as different from Steve as any man could be. Perhaps what attracts me is the challenge. But really, do I need that at this point in my life? I don't think so. Then why do I care?

I can't figure it out.

I have plenty of challenges to occupy me. My job, of course. And my volunteer work. Now that I'm reading to the kids at the detention center, I'm finding the experience immensely satisfying.

Anyway, I put Sean's rose in a vase and left it on my desk (right next to my copy of the second Harry Potter book). All week that rose has been there to remind me of him. It's the first thing I notice when I walk into the office each morning and the last thing I see at the end of the day. I should have tossed it immediately, and didn't.

I generally trust my own judgment about people and relationships. This time I have the distinct feeling I'm setting myself up for a major letdown.

It's not a comfortable sensation. Sean obviously feels the same way or he would have asked me out again and he hasn't.

I can't decide if I'm relieved or disappointed.

> "It goes without saying that you should never have more children than you have car windows."
>
> —Erma Bombeck

CHAPTER

JULIA MURCHISON

February 12th

List of Blessings
1. Hot baths and lavender soap and a matching cream that feels like silk on my skin. An early Valentine gift to myself.
2. A full night's rest—something I really appreciate now that I have difficulty sleeping.
3. Attics.
4. Heartburn medication.
5.

I was in for my monthly visit with Dr. Fisk, the OB-GYN who delivered both Adam and Zoe. We talked for almost fifteen minutes and probably would have spent more time discussing the pregnancy if she didn't have such a tight appointment schedule.

My attitude isn't good. I'm making an effort, but so far it hasn't really worked. My due date is September seventh. The ultrasound showed a healthy pregnancy; the fetus is developing normally. But I don't remember the nausea or the heartburn being this bad with either Adam or Zoe.

I might as well accept the fact that Peter and I are about to add another child to our family. I might as well assume that things will work out. I'm sick of worrying about how we're going to manage, sick of thinking about the complications a baby is adding to our lives. Babies are expensive, and our finances are already strained.

Peter has taken this pregnancy in stride—easy to do since he isn't the one who's pregnant. When the baby arrives, I'll let my good-natured husband worry about finding day care. I'll suggest he get up in the middle of the night to deal with the feeding and the constant needs of a newborn. Peter's conveniently forgotten how demanding an infant can be, but he'll remember soon enough.

The kids know something is up. We can't delay telling them much longer. Once again my husband has this rosy, unrealistic picture of how they're going to react. I hate to disillusion him, but I know exactly what Adam and Zoe will say, and it doesn't bear any resemblance to what he expects.

Saturday, while Peter had Adam and Zoe with him, gallivanting from one sporting event to the next, I went to the attic. I can't remember the last time I did that. What a mess. Obviously the kids have been up there.

I sought out anything we could use for this baby. As I recall, we gave the crib, high chair and other furniture to my sister, but Peter was sure we kept the bassinet. If so, I didn't find it. I looked everywhere, to no avail. There are no baby clothes to be found. Nothing. Zilch. Nada.

We'll have to start completely over. I simply don't know how we're going to afford all this. My shop's income has dropped—it's no wonder since I've had to close once or twice a week for doctor's appointments and all these tests Dr. Fisk considers necessary. Thank God Peter has excellent health benefits.

* * *

Nervous about confronting the children with news of her pregnancy, Julia took the chicken casserole from the oven and carried it to the table. She'd gone to extra trouble this evening, preparing a family favorite, accompanied by fresh green beans and hot rolls and followed by dessert.

Julia insisted on family meals, although Adam and Zoe were involved in a number of school activities that often ran late. Getting everyone to the dinner table at the same time was becoming more and more of a challenge.

"Dinner's ready," she called out when she'd finished. She stepped away from the table and waited for her husband and children to join her.

Peter was the first one in the kitchen. His eyes met hers, and Julia read the question in his gaze.

"Tonight?" he asked.

Julia nodded.

"How'd the doctor's appointment go?"

She shrugged. The appointment had been to discuss the ultrasound, and it had taken longer than she'd hoped. She was more than an hour late in opening the shop, which left her wondering how much business she'd lost. Or worse, how many people she'd irritated by not being there at the time posted. Between today and the two hours she was closed while she had the ultrasound on Monday, that was twice just this week.

"You're sure everything's all right?"

"Yeah." He knew the ultrasound revealed no problems; she'd mentioned it earlier. Peter had been relieved and so, of course, was she. This whole situation was hard enough without worrying about Down's Syndrome or spina bifida. Not that they'd know about *that* until she'd had the amniocentesis.

"Adam. Zoe," Peter yelled. "Dinner!"

As though he was doing his parents a favor, Adam slouched into the kitchen. He'd shaved his head recently, and after a growth spurt the past summer, was an inch under six feet. He was lanky and awkward and painfully conscious of his new height.

He pulled out his chair and fell into it. "I was on the computer," he said, as if that explained the delay.

"Where's your sister?" Julia set the milk carton on the table next to the salad and the green beans.

Adam raised his thin shoulders. "Her bedroom, last time I looked."

Peter walked to the hallway and shouted for Zoe again.

The thirteen-year-old arrived a minute later, full of high spirits. "Sorry," Zoe said, as she flew into the room. "I was on the phone with Ashley."

Ashley and Zoe were in constant communication. Julia's own best friend when she was thirteen had been Kathleen O'Hara, who now lived in Seattle and worked as a journalist. Theirs had become merely a Christmas-card friendship, and she'd forgotten the intensity of relationships at that age. The two girls found it impossible to be separated for more than a few hours. All this would change, Julia realized, when boyfriends entered the picture; she hoped that wouldn't be for a few more years. As it stood now, Ashley and Zoe were at school together every day, then talked on the phone half the night, with e-mail to fill in any gaps. Weekends were spent at each other's houses.

"Shall we eat?" Peter suggested, sliding into his chair.

Julia sat down at the opposite end of the table.

Once they were all seated, they bowed their heads for a brief prayer. As soon as they'd finished, Peter reached for the spoon to serve himself some casserole. "Your mother and I would like to talk to you both after dinner," he said casually.

"Talk to us?" Zoe asked.

"About what?" Adam pressed.

"We'll wait until we've finished with dinner," Julia inserted, unwilling to disrupt this congenial time.

"Is it about me driving?" Adam was due to get his driver's license soon. Already he was pressuring Peter and Julia about purchasing an extra vehicle for him. Naturally, he assured them, he'd get a job to pay for the insurance, gas and maintenance.

Julia stabbed a green bean. She didn't have the heart to tell Adam that with the extra financial burden of a third child, there wouldn't be money for a car. They'd discussed buying a reliable used one, but that was completely out of the question now.

"I know what it is," Zoe burst out excitedly. She tossed her brother a superior look.

Adam scowled in her direction.

"We're taking a family vacation this year, aren't we?" Zoe said.

Julia and Peter exchanged glances.

Zoe's eyes brightened. "We're going to the Grand Canyon, right?"

"I'll drive," Adam offered.

"Do you mind if we put this discussion off until after dinner?" Julia said, wishing Peter hadn't announced their intention beforehand.

"I need forty dollars for gym class tomorrow," Adam announced, grabbing a second roll from the basket and slathering butter on it.

"Forty bucks?" Peter repeated, looking aghast.

"Children are expensive," Julia said pointedly. Peter didn't appear to recognize the sacrifice this new child was going to require, and she wasn't even thinking of the emotional implications, of which there were plenty.

"Speaking of money, I need new reeds for my clarinet," Zoe added.

School. Music lessons. Sports. Scouts. Church. All required commitments of money and time. Both Adam and Zoe were active teenagers, and a new baby wasn't going to change that. Last week alone, there'd been some meeting or other involving one of the kids every night for five evenings straight.

Julia couldn't imagine what they'd do next year when they had an infant at home. An infant who was on a feeding, eating and sleeping schedule. It wasn't as though she could drag a baby to these functions and expect anything to get done. Peter wouldn't always be available to baby-sit either. He had work obligations of his own—PTA meetings, parent conferences and the like—that often took place in the evenings.

"*Are* we taking a vacation this year?" Adam asked.

"No." Julia corrected him before this line of questioning got out of hand and led to yet another disappointment.

Both children stared at her.

"Just tell us what it is then," Zoe pleaded.

"Yeah," Adam agreed. "Why don't you tell us?" He heaped another helping of the casserole onto his plate. During the last six months, their son's appetite had increased tenfold. Peter had joked recently that he was going to have to take on a second job just to afford groceries. A joke Julia now recalled with some bitterness.

"Maybe we should just tell them and be done with it," Peter said, looking at Julia.

"It's not fair to make us guess," Zoe said, her eagerness to hear this news spilling over.

"Gotta get back to the computer. I have a ton of English homework," Adam said, implying that he'd be working on it the instant dinner was finished. He'd be at the computer, all right, but it was doubtful he'd be tackling his English project. Julia was well aware that her son was hooked on "Age of Empires."

"I don't object, if your mother doesn't," Peter said.

Both children turned to Julia. "Tell us, Mom." "Come on, Mom."

Actually, she'd hoped Peter would be the one to make the announcement. Realizing she couldn't postpone it any longer, she set her fork down and placed her hands in her lap. She put on a brave smile. "Your father and I have some good news." She was determined to put a positive slant on this despite her own less-than-enthusiastic attitude.

"I *told* you it was good news," Adam shouted, exchanging a high-five with his sister.

"We're headed for the Grand Canyon," Zoe said. "Mom just said no 'cause she wanted it to be a surprise."

"I'm not sure a baby is what either of you have in mind." Peter threw out the words a bit desperately.

"Yellowstone Park." Adam's eyes flashed with enthusiasm. "I could help with the driving. We could be there in eighteen hours. We'd stay at the National Park, wouldn't we?"

"*Baby?*" The excitement vanished from Zoe's face as she took in her father's words. "What's this about a *baby?*"

Julia wished her husband had led into the subject with a little more finesse. Doing her best to appear pleased, she leaned forward and looked both her children in the eye. "You heard that right."

"A baby?" Adam shared a puzzled frown with his sister.

"Your mother's pregnant," Peter said. Julia preferred him to do the talking, since he was so damn thrilled about this baby. From Adam and Zoe's horrified expressions, he seemed to be the only one in the family who was. "Your baby brother or sister is due in September."

Both children turned their heads and stared at Julia as though they found this impossible to believe.

"I didn't know women as old as Mom could have babies," Adam said.

"This may come as a shock, but your mother isn't old," Peter told him, doing nothing to hide his amusement.

"I'll be forty this year," she murmured, in case Peter had forgotten the significance of that.

"You're honestly having a baby?" Zoe asked, her head cocked to one side. "You mean, we aren't going on a family vacation?"

"Not this year," Julia said. *And probably not for the next five. Or more.*

"Where will a baby sleep?" Adam asked, as if that thought had just occurred to him.

Julia understood her son's reasoning. Adam was concerned about being forced to share his room.

"We won't know that until the baby's born," Peter answered. "If it's a boy, then eventually he'll be with you. A girl will move in with Zoe at some point."

The ultrasound hadn't revealed the sex; at the moment Julia didn't care. She was merely grateful that the baby was okay—and that there was only one. She'd read that twins were more frequent with older mothers.

"Wouldn't it be better to move into a bigger house?" Zoe asked, looking from one parent to the other.

"We can't afford to do that," Julia said, pushing her dinner around the plate with her fork. Her appetite hadn't been good for several weeks, and this discussion wasn't helping.

"You mean if the baby's a girl, she'll be in the same bedroom as me?" Zoe's outrage echoed in each word. "I have the smallest bedroom already! Make Adam change rooms with me, then."

"Adam. Zoe." Peter entered the fray, his voice full of authority. "There's no need to argue about this now. After the baby's born, he or she will be with your mother and me for the first few months."

"Why can't you keep him with you all the time?"

"Don't you think you're both being a little selfish here?" Peter asked mildly.

Julia could tell he was disappointed by their children's reaction. Well, she'd done her best to warn him.

"No one my age has a baby brother or sister," Zoe said next, glancing at her brother for support. "This is...embarrassing."

"You might say we're a bit surprised ourselves," Peter countered. "It wasn't like your mother and I planned this."

"A baby now will change all our lives," Adam said and his insinuation was that any change couldn't possibly be for the better.

Which had been Julia's main concern from the first. "You're right. This pregnancy is going to alter the makeup of our family."

"Is that why Grandma's been phoning you so much?" Zoe suddenly asked.

Invariably, Zoe was on the line whenever Julia's mother called. Zoe made it abundantly plain each and every time that she resented having to end her conversations for something that wasn't related to her own small world.

Julia nodded. "My mother and sister both know."

"You told Grandma and Aunt Janice, but not us?" Adam scowled again.

"What am I going to tell my friends?" Zoe sounded near tears. "I can't *believe* you'd let something like this happen."

"Tell your friends you're about to become a big sister," Peter suggested.

"Oh, Daddy, how juvenile. This is so stupid."

Adam didn't say anything for a couple of minutes. Then he muttered, "This means you won't be able to afford a car for me, doesn't it?"

"We don't know that yet." Julia hurried to answer before Peter could say something too blunt and destroy their son's dream. "Maybe next year..."

"Are you closing the yarn shop?" Zoe asked.

"No." Of that Julia was certain. She'd come too far, sacrificed too much, to abandon everything now.

"Did you *want* more kids?" Adam asked her.

"No," Julia admitted.

Zoe stood and glared across the table at her and Peter. "Why'd you have to go and do this?" she wailed. "I don't want to share my room and furthermore, I refuse to baby-sit every afternoon after school. I know that's what you're thinking."

"Zoe, we haven't gotten that far. Your father and I are still dealing with this news ourselves. Don't worry, we won't ask you to baby-sit unless it's an emergency."

"What am I supposed to tell my friends?" she cried, tears glistening in her eyes.

"Tell them your parents are having a baby."

"At *your* age?"

"I'm not telling anyone," Adam announced. "They'll think it's a big joke."

"I hate you for doing this to us!" Zoe raced out of the kitchen. A few seconds later, her bedroom door slammed, the sound echoing throughout the house.

Wordlessly, Adam shoved his plate away. He left the table and marched down the hallway leading to his room. Seconds later, his door banged shut, too.

The kitchen was suddenly silent. Julia thought she was going to throw up. This had gone even more badly than she'd feared. She'd known the children would be surprised, and perhaps embarrassed, but she hadn't expected them to react this vehemently.

"Well," Peter said, leaning back in his chair. "What do you think?"

"Think?" Julia echoed as the knot in her gut tightened.

"It didn't go well, did it?"

"No, Peter," she said. "It didn't go well."

"Let me listen to me and not to them."

—Gertrude Stein

16

CHAPTER

LIZ KENYON

"He's here," Donna DeGooyer, the hospital social services director, said, peeking inside Liz's office on Thursday afternoon.

"Who?" Liz asked, playing dumb.

"You *know* who. I just saw Dr. Jamison down the hall and he's headed in this direction."

"Really?" Liz's pulse reacted immediately. For some unknown reason, she'd expected to hear from him yesterday—Valentine's Day. It was ridiculous to entertain any such notion. Men were not romantic beings. Steve's love for her was never in question, but he'd struggled with gift-giving and creating romantic interludes. Dr. Jamison had proven more than once that, except for his patients, he didn't spare a thought for anyone other than himself. Or as Karen succinctly put it, "The ego has landed." Even thinking he'd remember her on Valentine's Day was foolish. Embarrassing. And indeed he hadn't. Yet he was on his way to her office that very minute.

"He's probably going to ask you out."

"Probably," Liz agreed, although she didn't think it was probable at all. She'd spoken her mind to the good doctor and hadn't heard from him since, with the exception of the rose on her desk. He'd kept his distance and was, in fact, dating someone else.

"How are you going to answer him?" Donna asked.

Liz shrugged, trying to look cool and indifferent despite her spinning head and sweating palms.

Donna glanced over her shoulder. "See ya," she said, and with a naughty grin, she strolled calmly away.

No sooner had Donna left than Sean appeared, looking better than any man had a right to. "Good—you're still here," he murmured. "I thought you might be."

Liz glanced at the clock on her desk, surprised to see that it was after six-thirty. "I was just finishing up some paperwork," she said.

"You sure you weren't waiting for me?" Only his light, teasing tone kept his remark from sounding arrogant. She bit back the reply that sprang to her lips. Sean would believe what he wanted to believe—which was, apparently, that she spent her days longing to hear from him. Since it wasn't far from the truth, she let it go. "Thank you for the rose," she said instead.

"What rose?" He leaned against the door frame and crossed his arms.

"The one you left on my desk last week." He knew damn well what she was talking about.

"Oh, the *rose.*" He grinned that sexy, charming grin of his, and her heart began to race.

"You have plans for tonight?" he asked.

She hesitated—but not for long. "Um, no."

"How about a drink?"

"I thought you were dating...what's her name? The physical therapist."

He shrugged. "Not anymore. She's too manipulative."

It took her a moment to catch the pun, bad as it was. Then, despite herself, she smiled. A drink wouldn't hurt.

"Where?" she asked.

"The Seaside," he suggested.

"Sure." Liz was a little apprehensive, especially since it felt as though she'd just done something irrevocable and maybe dangerous: by agreeing, she'd acknowledged her attraction to him. And yet she couldn't have said no. For one thing, she was profoundly curious about *why* she found this man so attractive when he infuriated and annoyed her so much of the time.

Sean glanced at his watch. "Shall we meet there in fifteen minutes?"

"Fine."

He flashed her another easy smile, then turned and walked away.

Twelve minutes later, Liz was fortunate enough to find a spot in the parking lot outside the popular restaurant. She used another minute to refresh her makeup and dig around the bottom of her purse until she unearthed a miniature spray bottle of her favorite cologne.

"Here goes nothing," she said as she slid out of her car and locked it. At the very least, she'd have something to tell the breakfast group next Thursday.

They'd met that morning, and Clare had revealed that Michael was undergoing cancer treatment. Clare vacillated between pity and wanting to remain indifferent. With one breath she'd say it was Miranda's problem; with the next, she'd worry frantically about his prognosis and the chemo's side effects. Julia had finally told her children she was pregnant, with predictable results, and Karen was still upset about being disliked by the cocker spaniel, as if her entire career hung in the balance. Liz had listened to them all, but she'd left with the feeling that her own life lacked meaning, and nothing to report.

The Seaside's bar was smoky and crowded. Valentine decorations—hearts and cupids—were still suspended from the ceiling, and the usual classic jazz had been replaced by schmaltzy love songs. Sean had yet to arrive, and she wished now that she'd waited for him outside. If he stood her up, she swore he'd never hear the end of it. A table became vacant when the hostess led its occupants into the dining room. Moving quickly, Liz claimed the space.

A couple of minutes later, a harried waitress approached; Liz ordered a glass of Merlot and instantly attacked the small bowl of peanuts, feeling she needed something in her stomach.

Sean arrived before her wine did. He paid for her drink and ordered an old-fashioned for himself. Neither seemed to have anything to say, and Liz started to feel a bit desperate.

"I wish..."

"Well, what do you..."

Naturally, when she went to speak, he did, too. Sean grinned and motioned for her to talk first. She nodded, figuring they could make polite conversation, get involved in hospital gossip or discuss books, politics, films, but what interested her most was Sean himself.

"Tell me about you."

He chuckled and reached for a handful of peanuts. "My favorite subject. What would you like to know?"

She imagined that he often spoke of his career, his success, but she was already aware of all that. "What would you like me to know?"

"All right." He took his time, munching on the peanuts, sipping his drink. "First, I don't usually work this hard to get a woman to go out with me."

She rolled her eyes. "Wrong path, take another."

He grinned. "All right. I've been divorced for ten years."

That was what he wanted her to know? It made her wonder if this was his way of saying there was no chance of a long-term relationship.

"Any children?" she asked while she sorted through her various unspoken questions.

"One. A daughter, Eileen. She lives in Seattle with her husband, who's a scientist for Boeing. They've got a three-year-old daughter named Emily."

"So you're a grandfather."

He looked away and nodded.

"Do you have pictures?"

He shook his head. "My daughter and I aren't particularly close."

"My daughter has two children," she told him to cover the awkwardness of his confession. He clearly had regrets, but this wasn't the time to ask him what had gone wrong, why he and Eileen were no longer in touch.

"How'd you get into hospital work?" he asked, obviously wanting to turn the subject away from himself.

Emboldened by the wine, Liz wagged her finger. "We were talking about you, remember?"

"All right." He seemed deep in thought for a few moments, then shrugged almost comically. "Not much else to say."

Liz didn't mean to laugh, but she did. "I can't believe that."

He laughed, too. "Well, not much more about my personal life," he said with uncharacteristic modesty. "And my professional qualifications you already know."

Liz nodded. She recognized that through this small crack in his ego she'd caught a glimpse of the real Sean Jamison. She had a feeling she'd like him.

But before she could learn more, he sidetracked the conversation, and Liz found she was talking about herself. He was curious about her volunteering at the detention center, which led them into a heated debate about the prison system, capital punishment and youth crime. Predictably, they disagreed vehemently on each topic.

"You are so closed-minded," she muttered.

"And you're just another bleeding heart."

"At least I *have* a heart," she countered.

Grinning, he checked his watch. "Do you have a stomach to go along with that generous heart of yours?"

"Yes..."

"How about dinner?"

By that time they'd had two drinks each and nothing to eat other than a small bowlful of salty peanuts.

"You're willing to continue this conversation?" she asked, certain he'd decided, as she had, that they shared little in common. Much as she respected his medical skills and was beginning to like him—his passion for debate, his intellect, even his humor—they were directly opposed on practically every subject.

"Sure. I'm always willing to argue. Aren't you?"

"If you feed me, I'm game." She needed to eat anyway, she told herself.

He leaned over and kissed her cheek, then stood. "I'll see about getting us a table."

The conversation over dinner didn't lack for stimulation. They argued every point, joked, teased and laughed. When they'd finished, Liz saw that the restaurant was closing for the night.

Sean looked at his watch. "It's 11:30—way past my bedtime. What about you?"

Liz groaned. "Mine, too. I need to be at the hospital early in the morning."

The bill had already been paid, so they got up to leave. Sean helped her on with her jacket and walked her to her car. "Just to be on the safe side, I'll follow you home."

"There's no need to do that."

"Don't argue with me, Elizabeth."

"I've spent the entire evening arguing with you," she reminded him sweetly, but actually she was touched by his protectiveness.

"You'll learn soon enough that I win most arguments."

"Yes, sir," she muttered sarcastically. "Although I'd say it was a draw."

He grinned at that but didn't respond.

Sean followed her home, as he'd promised, and when she pulled into the garage, he eased his vehicle behind hers, turning off the ignition.

Frowning, Liz climbed out of her car and met him. "Thanks again. I had ...an enjoyable evening."

"So did I."

She was gratified to hear him say it.

He reached for her and after the briefest of hesitations, she leaned into him and accepted his kiss. His mouth was warm and moist and firm, and she felt sensations she hadn't experienced in more than six years. She wound her arms around his neck and he held her tightly, his hands finding the small of her back and pressing their bodies close. He wanted her, and she was keenly aware of it.

"Invite me in," he whispered. Before she could respond, he kissed her a second time, then again—short, eager kisses that weakened her resolve. To put distance between them, she dropped her arms and stepped back.

"I'll turn an enjoyable evening into a pleasurable one for us both," he promised, his voice husky with desire.

Liz would be lying to herself if she didn't admit how tempted she was. She rested her forehead against his shoulder and waited for reason and sanity to return.

"Don't think," he pleaded. "Just feel." His lips, nibbling at her neck and earlobe, made for a persuasive argument.

"Sean," she said quickly before she had a change of heart. She lifted her head and placed her hands on either side of his jaw. "Your offer is tempting."

His eyes, clouded with passion, cleared and sharpened. "But?"

"If I was in my twenties, I'd probably do it."

"What has age got to do with anything?" he asked.

"Not so much age as common sense. I'm fifty-seven—" she made a point of reminding him that he was younger than she "—and I've acquired a bit more discretion. I find you stimulating and attractive and you're saying you feel the same way about me."

"Yes, God, yes." He kissed her suddenly in a deep, probing way that made her knees wobble.

When he released her, Liz closed her eyes in a determined effort to clear her head. "Now listen, because what I have to say is important."

He raised his head and their eyes met and held. "All right."

"It would be the easiest thing in the world to fall into bed with you. I'm part of the generation that said if it feels right, do it, and I—"

"Is this a lecture?" he asked, sounding bored.

"No, an explanation," she rushed to assure him. "I was married for thirty-one years, and in that time I learned that sex is more than pleasure. It's commitment and communication, shared dreams and lives. It's wonderful, but for me it has to mean something more than a...than a nightcap. I enjoyed myself tonight. I enjoyed being with you."

"In other words, thanks but no thanks. Some other time?"

She hesitated; it was more complicated than that, but she doubted he understood. "Sort of."

"I enjoyed your company, too, Liz, but I'm not interested in this touchy-feely philosophy you're pushing here. You don't want to go to bed with me? I can accept that. I don't like it, but the decision is yours."

She kissed his jaw to tell him she appreciated his listening.

"Tell you what I'll do," he said, heaving a ragged sigh. "I'll wait until you're ready and then you can give me a call."

"What?" He'd confused her.

"I don't ask a woman twice, Liz."

She glared at him, furious he'd turn this into a battle of wills. He hadn't heard a word she'd said. "You'll have a very long wait, Sean."

He chuckled, evidently amused. "I doubt that," he said with maddening confidence. "You'll come around soon enough and when you do, I'll be ready, willing and able."

> "Expecting life to treat you well because you are a good
> person is like expecting an angry bull not to charge because
> you are a vegetarian."
>
> —Shari R. Barr

CHAPTER 17

KAREN CURTIS

February 23rd

Glen Trnavski, the high-school chemistry teacher I met in the parking lot a few weeks ago, called me after school yesterday. I guess he knew I needed some emotional support after eight-plus hours with fifth-graders. Despite what my mother thinks, I was never cut out to be a teacher. However, one bonus has been working with Peter Murchison, Julia's husband. I really like him and he's wonderful with the children.

Glen is actually kind of like Peter. Quiet, calm, a good sense of humor. He's different from the guys I know through drama—like Jeff. But quiet as he is, he's one of the most comfortable men I've ever met and when I analyzed why, I discovered it's because he *listens.* Not only does he listen, he seems to appreciate what I have to say. One thing I particularly like about him is his laugh—it comes from deep in his chest. He's *NOT* my type, though. Too even-tempered. Not bland, I don't mean that, but predictable. There's no fire in his belly, no all-consuming zeal.... Maybe I have enough for both of us?

I like his company and he understands that we're only friends, although he seems to want more. With all the rejection I've had lately, I need a man who's obviously falling in love with me—even if I can't return his feelings. I crave the attention. I'm not proud to admit it, but unfortunately it's true.

Speaking of rejection... I tried out for another commercial on Monday. This one was for hair spray and I should hear soon. I think I did well. I might not fit the role of meticulous housewife, but I can play an airhead to a tee. I've got real hopes this time. My agent said I should know what's up by the end of next week at the latest.

I haven't heard from my mother. That doesn't bother me, and I consider it a gift that she's decided to stay out of my life. Who needs the constant criticism? I'm always falling short of her expectations. Why can't she just accept me for who I am? Isn't that what every child needs? Love and acceptance. Mother wants me to do what *she* considers acceptable, so she can brag about me to her friends—and *then* she'll love me. That's completely backward! And it isn't fair and... Obviously this is still a big issue with me, otherwise I wouldn't continue to write about it. And I wouldn't have chosen "acceptance" as my word for the year. (Well, also I'd like to be accepted for an acting job! Positive thinking or what?)

Getting back to Glen. We're going to a movie tomorrow night. I probably shouldn't have agreed. I hate to string him along, but he did ask and it isn't like I've got hordes of men clamoring at my door. More's the pity. I love movies, and I don't mean to complain, but I find Glen...unexciting. Comfortable but unexciting.

I see as I review this journal entry that I've stayed away from the subject of my sister. She's been creeping into my Thursday morning conversations lately. Liz noticed. Nothing escapes her. Julia said she did, too.

When I asked them what they were talking about, Liz said I've spent my entire life competing with Victoria for my mother's attention. Well, duh! I knew that. Although Liz did say something that made me think. It annoyed me, too. She suggested I dress outrageously, (according to whom?) in order to provoke my mother. To get negative attention, in other words. I disagree. I don't do *anything* to get a reaction out of my mother.

I dress the way I dress, which is stylish and unique (in my humble opinion, anyway). Because that's who I am. I'm me and nobody else.

Now that was profound!

Anyway, I hate to tell my friends they're wrong. My relationship with my mother has practically nothing to do with my older sister. Yes, I'm competitive with Victoria, but *she's* the one responsible for that.

She didn't have to be so perfect. She's always done everything according to form. The classic good girl. It was like she set me up to fail because there was no way I was going to be prettier or smarter or more successful than she is. Enough said. The subject is closed and I'm going to bed.

* * *

By the time six o'clock arrived on Saturday night, Karen had serious doubts about her seven o'clock date with Glen Trnavski. She worried that she was using him to flatter her sagging ego, and worse, that he might read more into their date than he should. Friday night, she hadn't felt too concerned about this prospect, but in the light of day, her behaviour didn't seem fair. She'd stressed the "just friends" stipulation, but still...

She'd halfway decided to phone and beg off when she got a call. If luck was with her, it would be Glen and he'd be the one canceling. That way, the problem would be solved without any action on her part.

"Hello," she said cheerfully.

No response.

"Hello," she said again, more loudly this time. "Is that you, Jeff?" she snapped. She hadn't heard from him since their spat and couldn't help wondering—and hoping....

Silence.

"You're really sick, you know that? If this is Jeff, then you already know what I think. If this is someone else, all I can say is *get a life.*" With that, she banged down the receiver emphatically enough to make the person on the other end regret phoning.

Glen Trnavski arrived five minutes early with a bouquet of pink carnations.

Karen instantly felt guilty for wanting to cancel.

"How thoughtful," she said, holding the flowers to her nose. Pink carnations might not be original, but it'd been a long time since any man had done anything so sweet and, yes, traditional. Karen was touched, although she reminded herself that this first date was supposed to be a non-date, more of an outing between two friends.

"Have you decided on a movie?" he asked, following her inside the studio apartment.

"You're letting me choose?" Other guys she dated generally decided in advance what movie they'd see. Or it was a decision they made together. "There's a new Julia Roberts film I wouldn't mind going to," she suggested. A "chick flick." Most guys were more interested in high adventure, blood and guts, gasoline explosions.

"Fine with me." He was so agreeable; she liked that and she didn't. This was not a man who was likely to argue anything to the wall. Or generate any fireworks.

After setting the carnations inside an empty mayonnaise bottle, one she'd saved for just such an occasion, Karen reached for her jacket and purse. Just as they were about to leave, the phone rang again.

"I'd better get that," she said hurrying across the room to pick up the receiver. She wasn't expecting to hear from her agent on a Saturday night, but she didn't want to miss anything important, either. Her cheap answering machine wasn't always reliable.

"Hello?"

Nothing.

Impatient, she slammed the receiver down and complained, "That happened earlier. I answer the phone and there's no one there. Well, there is, but they aren't speaking."

"Do you have any idea who it might be?"

"Not a clue." She certainly wasn't going to mention Jeff.

"What about caller ID?" Glen asked.

"Don't have it." She hated to admit she pinched her pennies to the point that she'd never enjoyed the luxury of caller ID. It was difficult enough paying her phone bill without all the extras. Her one extravagance was call waiting. Heaven forbid she miss a call from her agent because she was chatting with a friend. Of course, she could always punch star 69. She decided to try that now. Naturally, the number was unlisted and she groaned in frustration.

"If they call again, you simply won't be here," Glen said with such perfect logic she had no comeback. "They can leave a message—or not."

He was right, of course; there was no reason to worry about it. She turned on the machine, and with a lighter heart, grabbed a woolen cape she sometimes liked to wear. Glen took it from her and placed it around her shoulders. He was being traditional again, and she decided she rather liked it. This wasn't a gesture she was personally familiar with—except in old movies and period plays.

The movie was delightful, and they both laughed their way through it. Afterward they shared a gourmet veggie pizza and glasses of red wine at a popular Italian restaurant in the area. Despite her reservations about the wisdom of seeing Glen, Karen enjoyed herself and their time together. Her one disappointment was that she was home by eleven. When she invited him in for coffee, Glen politely declined.

As she entered her apartment, she couldn't help wondering if *she'd* passed muster. The first thing she noticed was the flashing light of her answering machine. In replaying the tape, she discovered there were no less than six hang-ups. *One* she could understand, even two, but six?

Whoever had called earlier and said nothing had obviously continued phoning. Karen was tempted to unplug the phone and be done with it.

She turned on the television for company, then stripped out of her jeans and vest. She'd just pulled on her pajamas when the phone rang again. Karen stared at it, certain that her caller was the jokester. The best thing to do was let the answering machine pick up, she told herself. However, seconds before the machine kicked in, Karen impulsively grabbed the receiver. She wasn't sure why, hadn't even known she was going to do it. One second she was staring at the phone, willing it to stop ringing, and the next she had the receiver in her hand.

"Hello," she yelled, furious with herself as much as the anonymous fruitcake on the other end.

Silence.

Karen was about to slam down the receiver and unplug her phone when she heard a soft, unrecognizable female voice say her name.

"Hello," Karen tried again. "Who is this?

"It's me."

Karen strained to make out the voice, but couldn't. "Who?" she demanded.

"It's Victoria."

"What's the matter with you?" Karen asked aggressively. "Are you the one who's been calling and hanging up? Why? You scared me, dammit!"

"I...I can't talk any louder, Roger might hear me."

Roger the twit, her brother-in-law. "You don't want him to know you're on the phone?"

"No..."

Karen thought she heard a soft intake of breath that might have been a sob. "What's wrong?" she asked more gently.

No response.

"Victoria? Are you still there?" The line hadn't been disconnected, but there was no further sound.

"I'm here," Victoria finally whispered.

Karen guessed her sister was in some kind of trouble, otherwise she wouldn't be phoning her, especially this late. And all those hangups... A sense of urgency filled Karen. The kind that required action. Something was terribly wrong. "I'm coming for you and Bryce."

"No." Her sister's response was sharp and immediate.

"Tell me what happened."

Victoria hesitated, sobbed once, then spoke again, her voice so low Karen had to concentrate in order to make out the words. "Roger and I had an argument."

Karen couldn't understand why her sister was calling her. What did Victoria need her to do? Sympathize? Give advice? That seemed unlikely, but just as she was about to ask, Victoria explained. "You were always so brave..." she said in a quavering voice. "You never let people get away with anything. I—I've always admired that. I...wanted to talk to you, tell you..." The words trailed off.

"Is everything all right between you and Roger now?" Karen asked. Again the hesitation. "No."

"Are you sure you don't want me to come and get you?"

"I'm sure."

"Is there anything I can do to help you?" Karen asked, sitting down on the sofa and folding her legs beneath her. "Do you want to get away, talk, whatever?" She couldn't remember the last time she'd talked to her sister—*really* talked. Years ago, she guessed. Long before Karen had graduated from high school. Victoria was two years older, and Karen had looked up to her sister. Their real troubles had started when Victoria was away at college and Karen had gotten involved in the school acting ensemble.

"I don't think there's anything anyone can do," Victoria whispered.

Her sister was sobbing quietly and trying not to let Karen know. Karen's heart went out to her. "Did I ever tell you I think Roger's a total twit?"

Victoria responded with a hiccuping sound that was half laugh and half sob. "No, but I guessed. And...he knows."

"Good." Karen was glad to hear it.

"Oh, Sis, sometimes I think..." She didn't finish.

"Think what?" Karen probed.

"Nothing," Victoria said after a moment.

"Do you want to tell me about the argument?"

"It...it isn't important. The reasons never are."

"Victoria, listen. People don't always agree. We fought enough as kids, didn't we? It doesn't mean we don't love each other. We all say and do things we regret." Karen wasn't taking sides, nor did she want to put herself in the middle of a disagreement between her sister and brother-in-law. What she wanted to do was present a mature option, and give them both some breathing room. "Why don't you hop in the car and come on over here with Bryce? We can sit up all night and have a gabfest the way we did when we were kids."

"I can't."

"Sure you can. If you prefer, I could drive over to your place."

"No...no, that wouldn't work."

Karen's hand tightened around the receiver as a horrifying thought occurred to her. "Is there a reason you don't want me to see you?"

A soft sob, then, "Yes."

A chill ran down her spine. "The son of a bitch hit you, didn't he?"

"We're all in this alone."

—Lily Tomlin

18

CHAPTER

CLARE CRAIG

March 9th

Most of my day was spent with Michael. Not *with* him as in the same room or even the same vicinity. But I thought about him constantly. He was back in the hospital for his second bout of chemotherapy and Alex was scheduled to pick him up at the same time as before.

Apparently Miranda can't be bothered. Her excuse is that she's building her customer base and can't be dragged away from the nail clinic without missing appointments. I can't stand the way Michael defends her!

Alex knows better than to discuss the little darling with me, although I doubt he would, anyway. He finds the subject of Michael's live-in lover as distasteful as I do.

I know it's hard for Alex to see his father this ill. It is for me, too. I can sympathize with my son; Michael's his father, after all. My own reaction is harder to understand. Why should I care so much? But I do, especially since Michael's condition appears to be fairly serious. He's avoided my questions so far, but from what I've been able to learn, it's some form of liver cancer. Alex doesn't know any more details than I do, but this can't be good.

While we were going through the divorce, I thought I'd enjoy seeing Michael suffer, but surprisingly I don't. Twenty-three years of marriage, most of them good, two children plus a successful business we built to-gether—we shared all that. I think this is why I can't remain unaffected by his illness. If ever I needed proof of the thin line between love and hate, here it is. The line's so thin, in fact, that sometimes it's transparent.

Michael's chemotherapy, and apparently he's being given one of the more aggressive drug combinations, takes nearly all day. He's at the hospital for almost eight hours and so weak he can barely walk when he's finished. For four consecutive days he receives the drug cocktail, then he doesn't get it again for three weeks. I don't know how many treatments he'll require, but Alex mentioned four sessions. Four months of this seems like a very long time.

Twice now, because of Alex's schedule at school and my part-time hours, I've been the one to chauffeur Michael home from the hospital. My friends in the Thursday morning group fear I shouldn't be doing this. As they pointed out, Michael does have other options that don't need to in-volve me. I understand their concerns and yet I still find myself volunteering.

I'm confused about my feelings for Michael right now. Love, hate. Compassion, anger. It's all there.

And apparently I'm not the only one who's confused. Michael doesn't know what to think about me, either. We talk more, but never about *her* or the divorce. The ride between the hospital and his place takes about thirty minutes, depending on traffic. So I guess it's only natural that we talk. After all, we spent more than two decades talking to each other.

The first time, our conversation was stilted and uncomfortable. More recently Michael described the side effects of chemotherapy. The weakness and nausea, the continuing weight loss, the depression. He's losing his hair but that seems too insignificant to mention. (Although it probably bothers his girlfriend.)

I was forced to stop the second time I drove him, too. I pulled off to the side of the road and just as before, Michael stumbled out of the car and immediately vomited. Then he did the oddest thing. He reached down and touched his vomit. *Touched* it. I had to know why. Michael would never do anything like that under normal circumstances.

After he'd rinsed his mouth, he explained. It's the fire, he said. It feels as though his entire body is burning from the inside out. The reason he touched the vomit was to see if it was boiling. That's the way it felt coming up from his stomach and through his throat. Like molten lava.

I gave him a few minutes to regroup and breathe in the fresh air. He leaned against the bumper, too weak to stand upright.

I had to help him back into the car and I know he found it embarrassing. Once he was settled and we were on our way again, he casually asked about Mick. Apparently our oldest son remains unwilling to speak to his father. He knows about the cancer; I told him myself. But Mick is as stubborn and unforgiving as I am. It gives me no pleasure to write this.

Michael isn't the only one Mick isn't speaking to these days. I wonder if he knows that his sons are estranged from each other because of him. Alex and Mick haven't talked in weeks. It hurts me to see it, knowing how close they once were. The boys and I clung to one another all through the divorce, and now Mick can't forgive his brother for reconciling with their father. He was upset with me too when he learned I'd driven Michael home from the hospital. I guess I should count my blessings that he's still speaking to me. It's probably just as well that Mick's at college and not living at home right now, much as I hate to say that.

When we reached the place Michael's renting, he told me how much he regrets what's happening between him and his sons. Even though he sees Alex every week, Michael realizes their relationship will never be what it was. And Mick, of course, won't have anything to do with him.

Michael wanted me to know how much he loves them and how sorry he is, how he'd do anything to repair the damage. He looked sad and broken as he climbed out of the car and headed toward the small, dumpy rental house.

Not until he disappeared inside did I realize something important. When he talked about his remorse over everything that's happened, my name was missing.

> "See into life—don't just look at it."
>
> —Anne Baxter

19
CHAPTER

LIZ KENYON

March 13th

Annie wrote me, and her sweet, precious letter was waiting when I arrived home from work. It thrilled me to hear from my granddaughter, but I felt restless and sad for the rest of the evening. Just a few months ago she lived here in Willow Grove and we had all the time in the world to be together. I miss our tea parties and baking muffins and snuggling up together in bed.

I read the letter twice, then wandered into the bedroom. The big fancy hats and white gloves we used for our tea parties are on the top shelf of my closet, gathering dust. What fun Annie and I had as we sipped tea—hers cooled with milk—from delicate china cups, the ones I inherited from Steve's mother. We'd nibble on cookies, having silly conversations with lots of laughter. It's a memory that brings tears to my eyes.

Amy and the kids and I chat every week, but it's not the same. I miss Annie and Andrew so much. They're my only grandchildren, an extension of my children, an extension of Steve and me and the wonderful years we shared.

My appetite was nil tonight, but I forced myself to eat dinner, although I didn't put any effort into cooking nor did I experience any pleasure when I sat down at the kitchen table to eat. When Steve was alive, our dinners were an occasion, always served in the dining room with good linen and china, usually accompanied by a glass of wine. I took pride in cooking. Now dinner is simply a necessity, a chore.

As soon as I finished eating and feeling sorry for myself, I wrote Annie, holding Tinkerbell in my lap, making a rash promise. I told her I'd visit her this summer. The thought lightened my mood and then on a wild impulse, I made the decision to drive from California to Oklahoma. I hate flying. I detest being cramped in a narrow seat, breathing recycled air. Invariably I'm stuck with an inconsiderate jerk who rams the back of his seat into my nose. Why should I fly when I have the time and the desire to drive?

I can already hear Amy and Brian's objections. My children are going to remind me that it's not safe for a woman to drive a distance of that length alone. They'll want to know why I'd take the risk when air travel is so convenient. And I can almost guarantee they won't like my answer.

Over the years, Steve and I took a number of driving trips, with the kids and without them. We always enjoyed our time on the road. Like so much else in my marriage, I've missed that. Spending all those days in the car is far from a hardship when you're with a person you love, a person you know so well. It's a distinct pleasure and definitely my favorite way to travel. However, it's just not a possibility now; there's no one like that in my life. But I can still enjoy my vacation. With three weeks due me, I can drive leisurely, stop when I feel like it, tour where I want to and still spend plenty of time with Amy and the kids.

I don't intend to be stupid about it, but if something dreadful happens, an accident of some kind, then so be it. I refuse to live the rest of my life in fear. I enjoy driving, I miss my grandchildren and I'm heading for Tulsa.

Only I won't mention my plans to the family. Not yet. No need to stir up their concerns this early. Besides, it won't matter; I've made up my mind. First thing tomorrow morning, I'll book the time off. I feel better already, just knowing I'll be with Annie and Andrew this summer.

Karen phoned just before I got ready for bed. She asked several questions about reporting spousal abuse. It didn't take me long to figure out who she was talking about, although she didn't actually mention her sister by name.

Karen is outraged and rightly so. She wants *the son-of-a-bitch* arrested. Although I don't know why she phoned *me* to ask these questions. I guess it's because I'm older and supposed to be wiser. And maybe she figures that I know about domestic crime because I work in a hospital. I told her that, to the best of my knowledge, a third party can't file charges. I explained that whoever was abused had to be the one to do it.

It was fairly easy to decipher what went on, although she was careful not to break any confidences. Karen has rarely mentioned her brother-in-law and never by name. She calls him "the twit," which appears to be a fairly accurate characterization. Reading between the lines, I listened as she explained that this *son-of-a-bitch* took a heavy hand to his wife. Just when it looked as if Karen had convinced *the wife* to file a report with the police, the twit sobered up and apologized. *The wife* has apparently forgiven him.

Karen is furious, not only with "the twit," but with her sister. She's having a difficult time accepting Victoria's decision. Again and again she talked about the danger she felt *the wife* and her child were in and how the *son-of-a-bitch* couldn't be trusted. I told her there was nothing more she could do without the wife's cooperation.

She didn't like hearing that any more than I liked telling her.

I will say one thing. For months now I've heard Karen complain about her sad relationship with her family. Even her word for the year has more to do with her family than with Karen herself—or so it seems to me.

At one breakfast meeting, she spoke of severing her relationship with her mother entirely. Each of us advised her not to do anything so rash, told her she'd regret it later. We all said family's too important to throw away like that. Karen took our words to heart, and I think she's glad she did. If ever her sister needed her love and support, it's now. From what Karen's said, *the wife* can't go to her parents. Karen might well be the only person Victoria can turn to.

* * *

It was nearly two and Liz still hadn't taken a lunch break. The way things were going, thirty minutes away from her office just wasn't feasible. Her one solution was to run down to the cafeteria and grab a sandwich to eat at her desk.

"You leaving?" Donna DeGooyer, the hospital social worker, looked stricken as she raced into Liz's office.

"What do you need?"

"Help and lots of it. I've got an adoptive couple coming to pick up a baby and an attorney who hasn't got the paperwork finalized and a young mother who's having second thoughts. The attorney and the birth mother are on their way to my office right now."

"I was just going to get a sandwich. Do you want to come with me?"

Donna did a double-take as she looked at her watch. "It's after two. Already? Go have lunch and I'll catch you later." Then she was gone as quickly as she'd arrived.

Taking her wallet with her, Liz headed for the basement where the hospital cafeteria was located. The food was cheap, and for institutional fare, she found it surprisingly good. The lunch crowd had thinned considerably and the room was nearly empty. She reached for a tray, sliding it along the steel rails as she studied the remaining choices.

This late in the afternoon the selections were narrowed down to only a few. As she picked up an egg salad sandwich and a small pastry, Sean Jamison stepped next to her and slid his tray alongside hers.

"Egg salad?" He sounded skeptical. "Hmm. And a danish. High fat, empty calories. I don't recommend it."

Ignoring him, Liz placed both items on her tray.

"You're a stubborn woman, aren't you?"

She didn't so much as glance in his direction. "If you haven't figured that out by now, you're a slow learner."

It'd been nearly a month since she'd last seen him. They'd parted on pleasant terms—sort of. He had said he'd wait for her to call him, and that wasn't going to happen. She liked Sean, enjoyed his company, but she wasn't interested in a casual affair, which was all he seemed to be seeking.

He helped himself to a sandwich—*and* a danish, Liz noted. What a hypocrite! She poured a cup of coffee and he did likewise.

"You eating here?" he asked as they moved toward the cashier.

Liz's original intention was to take lunch back to her office, but now she hesitated. "I was thinking of it."

"I was, too."

She paid for her meal, then chose a seat close to the window.

Sean paid for his lunch and positioned himself at the table directly across from hers. Liz glared at him. "Aren't you being a bit ridiculous?" she asked.

"Is that an invitation to join you?"

She sighed. "Don't be silly. You can sit here if you want."

He was out of his chair and at her table within seconds. She could tell by his cocky grin that he was pleased, as though her invitation—such as it was—had been a concession.

"It's good to see you," he said as he unwrapped the cellophane from his sandwich. "I'd hoped we'd get together before now. I don't mind telling you, it's been a long month. You're trying my patience, Liz. We both know what we want, so let's be mature about it."

Liz reached for the salt and pepper shakers and peeled back the bread to dump liberal doses on the egg salad. "Don't you ever give up?" she asked, not in the mood for verbal sparring.

"What?"

"You're wasting your time. I'm not calling you."

"Ah," he said with a beleaguered sigh, "so this is all a matter of pride."

"Come on," she scoffed, "you know better than that. I came away from our dinner date feeling good—until you wanted to turn me into one of your sexual conquests."

"Wrong. I happen to think you're an attractive woman and I believe we could enjoy each other in a mutually satisfying arrangement. What's so terrible about that?"

She was about to explain once again exactly what she objected to, but he cut her off.

"You're sexually repressed, aren't you?" he said. He seemed to be serious.

Laughing probably wasn't the most tactful response to his assessment, but Liz couldn't help herself. "You know what I've decided?"

she asked, and then didn't give him a chance to answer. "I like you. I'm not sure why, because when it comes to male-female relationships, you're about as shallow as a man can get."

"Insults now?"

"No, the truth, and apparently there aren't enough people in this world brave enough to give it to you."

"Should I be grateful you're so willing to enlighten me?" He looked more entertained than insulted.

"Yes, but I doubt you will be. Frankly, I don't know who you've been dating for the last ten years, but the Hugh Hefner image lost its appeal a long time ago."

"Hugh Hefner?" he repeated as though that amused him. "Are you kidding?"

"I'm disappointed in you, Sean." This, too, was the truth. Her sincerity must have reached him because his grin slowly faded. "You see me as nothing more than a challenge," she said in a matter-of-fact tone.

He pushed his unfinished sandwich aside. "Hey, it's something we share because that's exactly how you see me. The only thing you're interested in is a ring on your finger. I went the marriage route once, remember, and all that got me was a whole lot of pain."

"I'm not asking you to marry me. I'm simply stating that I won't fall into bed with you without a committed relationship on both our parts."

"Sex isn't a four-letter word," he sputtered.

"But it is," she countered. "L-O-V-E."

"Been there, done that, not interested in doing it again."

Liz stared at him. She recalled that the only personal thing he'd told her was that he'd been married at one time. She hadn't realized the significance of that earlier.

"Was the marriage that bad?" she asked.

His face hardened. "Leave my ex out of this."

"All right." Apparently he'd carried the burden of his failed marriage for the last ten years. Everything he said proved he'd never moved beyond the regrets and the pain.

"I don't need any more lectures from you or anyone else." He stood and emptied his tray, pastry, coffee and all, in the wastebasket on his way out of the room.

Liz knew it was unlikely she'd see him or hear from him again, unless it was work-related and unavoidable. Actually, that was for the best all around. They had nothing substantial in common, she decided, and a sadness settled over her.

She knew she had to relinquish the hopes she'd centered on Sean Jamison. Her natural tendency was to hang on, to keep hoping, but if she'd learned anything in the last six years, it was the danger that posed to her sanity and her heart. Sometimes you had to let people go—let your *feelings* for them go—in order to protect yourself.

She was back in her office when Donna returned, and from the relieved look on her face, Liz assumed that the adoption crisis had been resolved. Donna paused halfway inside the room. "You okay?"

"Of course I'm okay." Liz was surprised her friend could read her this readily.

"I just saw Dr. Jamison, and he's on another of his rampages. You two didn't happen to cross paths, did you?"

Liz nodded. "You could say so," she muttered. "We don't see eye to eye on certain subjects."

Donna sank down on the chair and crossed her legs. "I don't get it. As a physician he's brilliant and wonderful, and as a man he's a major jerk. The way he treats women is deplorable."

"I agree." And she did.

"The entry of a child into any situation changes the whole situation."

—Iris Murdoch

20

CHAPTER

JULIA MURCHISON

The Wool Station had been quiet all morning. Not an encouraging sign, Julia mused as she sat in her rocking chair and knitted a swatch to display the latest double-knit cotton yarn. She wanted this to sell, *needed* it to sell, seeing that she'd ordered it in fifteen different colors. The steel needles made a soft clicking that disrupted the silence. Her stomach had been queasy all morning, but she'd done her best to ignore it. Nor did she allow her mind to dwell on the battery of tests she'd recently undergone. The final results weren't in yet, and Julia wasn't sure she wanted to know. She'd had all the reality she could handle at the moment. If the baby did have Down's Syndrome or spina bifida or whatever, she'd deal with it when necessary and not before.

Some days the denial tactic helped, and she could pretend everything was okay. On other days, that was impossible. Her stomach rebelled. The morning sickness wasn't as bad as it had been when she first discovered she was pregnant. But it was bad enough.

A Mercedes pulled into the parking space in front of the store and Julia recognized Irene Waldmann. Great. Mrs. Waldmann wasn't Julia's favorite customer and she took every opportunity to remind Julia of her one small mathematical error. In fact, the older woman was often difficult, changing her mind frequently and making unreasonable demands—like expecting Julia to keep a particular wool in stock when it had been discontinued by the manufacturer. The root of the problem, in Julia's opinion, was that Mrs. Waldmann didn't really know what she wanted herself. Clearly wealthy, if her clothes and vehicle were any indication, she drifted from one project to another.

"Hello." Julia greeted her with a smile.

Mrs Waldmann ignored the greeting and headed for the rack where Julia kept the pattern books.

"Is there anything I can help you find?" she asked.

"Not just yet."

Finishing her row, Julia stood—and the room started to spin. She gripped the chair in an effort to steady herself. A moment later, her head cleared and then almost immediately her stomach heaved. The sensation was unmistakable.

"You'll have to excuse me for a moment," Julia said, rushing to the back of the store. She made it to the small rest room just in time. The little breakfast she'd managed to eat was soon gone.

Mrs. Waldmann's eyes were wide when Julia reappeared. Until recently she'd kept the news of her pregnancy from her customers. But instances such as this needed explaining.

"You'll have to forgive me," she said, faltering slightly. "I'm—I'm pregnant."

Mrs. Waldmann stared back at her in open curiosity. "Pregnant? At your age?"

"It looks that way." How comforting to be reminded that she was past her prime. Her instinct had been to explain that this pregnancy wasn't intentional, that she and her husband were as surprised as everyone else. But she held her ground, refusing to defend herself or her situation. It was private—no one's business but theirs.

"Well," the other woman said, spinning the pattern rack. "That settles that."

"I beg your pardon?"

"I was just wondering what I should knit next." She twirled the rack until she found the infant section and reached for a pattern.

Julia was confused. "I'm sorry, did I miss something?"

"Apparently so," the older woman said dryly. "I've decided to knit a baby blanket for this new child of yours."

"For me?"

"Do you have a hearing problem?"

"N-no, I mean, b-but why..." Julia knew she was stuttering; she couldn't help it.

"I imagine this is a case of the cobbler's children without any shoes. I take it this pregnancy is unexpected?"

"Well, yes but—"

"Have you knit anything for your baby?"

"No, not yet, but—" She had every intention of doing so. The problem was finding the time between her family and her commitment to The Wool Station's customers.

"Just as I thought," Mrs. Waldmann said, with—could it be?—a hint of humor. "You can use a blanket, can't you?"

"You'd do that for me?" Julia asked, taken aback by the generosity of the offer. Especially from a customer she'd often considered a burden.

"Boy or girl?" Mrs. Waldmann asked gruffly.

"We chose not to know," Julia answered.

Mrs. Waldmann nodded approvingly. "Good for you. There are too few surprises left in this life."

At the moment, Julia would happily live with fewer. The last four months hadn't been easy. Adam and Zoe's attitudes toward her pregnancy hadn't improved. The only people who seemed happy about it were her husband and her mother. All right, her sister and Georgia, too. George seemed to think the baby was destined to be "special."

"What do you think of this?" Mrs. Waldmann handed her a complicated pattern.

"This is an heirloom piece," Julia commented, wondering if the other woman realized the work involved in such a blanket.

"My thought exactly."

"But—"

"Shall I do it in ecru or would you prefer a soft yellow?"

"Ah..."

"Don't suggest that sickening lime color. I never could stand that."

"The yellow sounds very nice." Julia couldn't quite hide her astonishment. Mrs. Waldmann—of all people—knitting her a baby blanket!

"Good, that's what I would have chosen myself. There's something so...warm about yellow, don't you think? So uplifting."

"Yes," Julia agreed. Turning over the pattern, she read the amount of yarn required, then counted out the skeins, selecting the lemony yellow fingering weight.

Mrs. Waldmann concentrated on the pattern, her brow furrowed. Never having seen anything the other woman had completed, Julia worried that his project might be beyond her capabilities, but she dared not suggest it.

"You don't need to do this," she felt obliged to tell Mrs. Waldmann a second time.

"Didn't anyone ever warn you not to look a gift horse in the mouth?" Mrs. Waldmann asked her briskly.

"Yes, but really this is too much."

"Don't you tell me what is and isn't too much. I want to do this and I will."

"It's so nice of you."

"Oh, hardly. I know I'm not the easiest woman in the world to deal with. But you've always been patient with me and I appreciate it."

"I appreciate the business," Julia told her in turn, and it was true, especially on days like this. She needed to take in two hundred dollars a day just to meet her rent and utilities. The morning was half-gone and this was her first sale. Some days were like that.

Mrs. Waldmann wrote the check, tore it out and gave it to Julia. She hesitated as though she was about to say something, then evidently changed her mind. Julia handed her the bag.

"Thank you again," she said.

Mrs. Waldmann nodded. "I'll see you in a few weeks."

"I'll look forward to it."

At dinner that evening, Julia mentioned Mrs. Waldmann and what she'd done. It was a way of bringing the baby into the conversation in a casual manner; she thought this kind of comment might help the children adjust.

"Why would she do something like that?" Adam asked, sounding more annoyed than pleased.

"Some people like babies," Zoe answered, in a tone that suggested she wasn't one of them.

"What did you say her name was again?" Peter asked, frowning as he propped his elbows on the table, dangling his fork above his dinner plate.

"Irene Waldmann."

"Waldmann, Waldmann," he repeated thoughtfully. "The name rings a bell."

Julia noticed that as soon as she mentioned the baby both Adam and Zoe had grown sullen and unpleasant. She'd hoped that in time they'd be more accepting, more generous of heart.

She glanced at her family. She hated to bring discord to the table, but she couldn't ignore their attitude.

"I understand that this isn't easy," she said to her children. No further explanation was needed; both Adam and Zoe knew she was talking about the baby.

"How could you do this?" Zoe demanded, once again. "Nothing will ever be the same."

"We can't afford a car now." Adam glared at her, resentment in every word.

"Or a vacation," Zoe chimed in, close to tears.

"Stop it!" Peter banged his fist on the table. "Just listen to you," he said. "Just listen! You're only thinking about yourselves."

Rarely had Julia seen her amiable, easy-going husband display such anger and disgust.

"No one said it was our duty to provide you with a vehicle just because you're turning sixteen. Nor is there anything written about a parent's obligation to take children on expensive vacations. Your mother and I know you're disappointed about missing out on those things, but guess what, life is filled with disappointment. I'm ashamed of your selfishness. You think a little embarrassment in front of your friends, or having to share your bedroom with a younger brother or sister, is some major tragedy. Get a little perspective!"

Both children stared openmouthed at their father.

"Your mother and I have tried to be patient, to give you time to accept our news. But you know something? This baby is entitled to as much love and welcome as you received when you came into our family."

Silence followed. Then Zoe sniffled and bowed her head. "Can I be excused?"

"You're finished with your dinner?" Most of her meal remained untouched.

Zoe nodded.

"All right."

"Me, too," Adam muttered.

Frowning, Peter waved him off and the children hastily left the table.

Julia could tell by the belligerent way they stalked out of the room that nothing had changed.

Her husband shook his head. "I don't think I've ever been more disappointed in my children."

"Give them a chance," Julia urged, feeling guilty about her own ambivalence and resentment. Peter was right. This child deserved the same love as Adam and Zoe. Unfortunately the kids weren't the only ones who needed to hear it. Julia had to remind herself, as well.

* * *

List of Blessings
1. Irene Waldmann
2. Salt and how desperately I miss it
3. Comfortable shoes
4.
5.

March 21st

Adam and Zoe are barely speaking to Peter and me. The last few days have been a real strain. Peter suggested we just let them have their little temper tantrum and not react to it. Eventually they'll come around. I only hope he's right. I knew they were upset with us; I hadn't realized it was to this extent.

Peter came to the shop after school this afternoon. He had a copy of a newspaper article from the early 1990s. It was about a Manchester high-school graduate by the name of William Waldmann who'd been killed in Desert Storm. He was the only child of Irene and Brad Waldmann.

The other night at dinner, when I mentioned Irene's name, Peter had said it sounded familiar. So he looked it up on the school Internet and found the article.

My heart aches for Mrs. Waldmann. Her only son. I can't imagine what it would be like to lose a child. The grief would be unbearable. Knowing this helps me understand why she was so willing to knit a baby blanket for me. There are no grandchildren in her future.

Georgia stopped by the store this morning on her way home from work. Her job at the gallery has the craziest hours; they spent all night setting up for a major exhibit that's opening today. She filled in for me while I ran to Dr. Fisk's for my appointment. Thankfully I was in and out in forty minutes, which is something of a record. I hate leaving the shop, but there's no help for it. Nor was I comfortable closing for even an hour; I've done that too many times already. If there's one thing customers demand, it's consistency. If I say my store's open from 10 to 5, then I'd better be open during those hours.

Georgia brought me a new maternity top. I looked at it and wanted to weep. She was only trying to be kind, but I hate the thought of growing into *that*.

Liz came for her knitting lesson at lunchtime.

She says the tension at the hospital is getting to her, and she finds that knitting helps relax her at night. We've done some squares, just to practice different stitches, and today she bought yarn to make a sweater for her granddaughter. We cast on and began, following a simple pattern I selected for her.

I wasn't fooled. She comes more to check up on me than because of any real desire start knitting. I know she and the others are worried about me. The last few weeks I haven't said much at breakfast. I won't for a while yet. I told Liz that, and the reasons for it, and she understood. I'm trying my hardest to make the best of this situation. I'm disappointed in my children, but no more than I am in myself.

"Only friends will tell you the truths you need to hear to make...your life bearable."

—Francine du Plessix Gray

21

CHAPTER

THURSDAY MORNING BREAKFAST CLUB

Karen arrived at Mocha Moments early, and ordered her current favorite latte, a caramel and mocha combination that tasted like a liquid candy bar with twice as many calories. Luckily, Karen didn't need to worry about her weight. A lot of her friends were fanatical about every morsel they put in their mouths. Not Karen; she ate what she wanted and when she wanted. A good metabolism was just the luck of the draw, she supposed.

She carried her drink to the table and slid into a chair, planning to talk to her friends about Victoria. She had great news, too, about getting the hair spray commercial, and she was eager to let everyone know. Still, it was her sister's dilemma that preoccupied her most. She was grateful Victoria had reached out to *her*, even if she'd now begun to back off. Karen wanted to help her older sister, but deciding how to do that was giving her a major headache.

Liz entered the coffee shop and walked up to the counter to order her breakfast. Liz was almost always the first to arrive, but today Karen had come early.

The majority of people were creatures of habit, she mused, and the four of them were no exception. They sat at the same table whenever they could, even choosing the same chairs. Every week Liz ordered the same thing. Plain ol' coffee and a croissant. Clare had an espresso and a scone with blackberry jelly, and Julia always ordered tea, herbal tea now that she was pregnant, and a muffin. Only Karen varied her orders; there might be comfort in predictability, but she found more reassurance in being different.

She wished again that her mother was more like Liz. Karen got on far better with her father, but her mother had dominated him for years. She used to wonder if there'd been a mix-up at the hospital and she was actually someone else's daughter. Or if she'd been adopted— a favorite childhood fantasy of hers.

"Good morning," Liz said, sitting down gracefully. "You're bright and early this morning." She wore a dark red suit with a double-breasted jacket and straight skirt. The matching high heels were fabulous. So few women wore heels anymore, and Liz, already tall, didn't need the height. They made her look more powerful, yet strikingly feminine.

"Morning," Karen returned with a smile.

Clare and Julia were only minutes behind Liz. Soon all four were at the table, each with her signature breakfast.

"Karen was here when I arrived," Liz said, and the other two women turned to her. This was obviously Liz's way of letting them know there was something on Karen's mind.

"Is it your sister?" Clare asked. At their previous week's breakfast, Karen had finally told them about Victoria's situation.

"Yeah," she said. "Guys, I want to throttle her. Her husband punches her in the face. First she won't let me call the police, and now...now she's acting like it was all a big mistake."

"She wants to put the whole thing behind her, right?" Liz asked, frowning thoughtfully.

"Yes, but it's more than that. She's embarrassed she even phoned me."

"This isn't the first time Roger's hit her, is it?" The question came from Clare.

Karen couldn't be sure, but she guessed this was a pattern between Victoria and her husband. Abuse, followed by apologies and promises. Roger was a bully who took out his frustrations on his wife. Six years earlier, when Victoria had started dating Roger, there'd been an incident that Karen had never forgotten. It'd happened at a family function—Thanksgiving dinner, if she remembered correctly. A command performance.

Victoria had brought Roger to meet the family, and all through dinner her mother had fussed over him, ingratiating herself in a way that made Karen cringe. The entire meal had been a disaster. Her mother had set out her best china and silver in an effort to impress Victoria's wealthy beau. She'd chatted endlessly, casually dropping names as if their family was part of the social circle that frequented the elite clubs and shops of Beverly Hills.

As the miserable meal progressed, Karen had watched Roger drink glass after glass of wine. She noticed that at every opportunity he criticized Victoria until her sister had dissolved into tears and run from the table.

Karen's first inclination was to go after her and advise her to dump the creep. He might come from a wealthy family and work at an established law firm, but that didn't excuse bad manners or classless behavior. Before she could move, their mother had apologized for Victoria's rudeness.

Karen had been furious. To her parents' dismay, she'd stalked out of the room. The ensuing argument with her mother had resulted in Karen's leaving in a huff. She'd threatened never to return, although of course she did. But her already difficult relationship with her mother grew even more strained.

Within a week of that infamous Thanksgiving, Victoria and Roger were engaged. Their wedding had been a gala event, with her mother using the opportunity to do some major sucking up. From the moment Victoria married Roger, Catherine Curtis had placed her eldest daughter on a pedestal. Karen thought wryly that her mother never complained about *Victoria* not using her college degree; in fact, she'd encouraged her to stay home and be the kind of wife "a man of Roger's standing" required.

"I think Roger might have hit her before," Karen said, although she had no actual evidence. "I do know he's been abusing her emotionally for years."

"You weren't able to convince her to file a police report?" Julia asked, shaking her head as though she found it difficult to comprehend how any woman would endure such treatment from her husband.

"Not for lack of trying," Karen informed her friends. She'd done everything but make the call herself. Victoria had seemed so small and broken when they'd first talked. Karen was forced to wait until Monday morning, after Roger had left for the office, before Victoria would let her visit.

The bruises on her cheek and upper arms were dark and ugly. Karen was enraged, but didn't dare show it. She talked to her sister about contacting the authorities, calling her doctor, visiting a women's crisis center—taking some kind of action—but Victoria wavered and then later refused to discuss it.

"It was all her fault, right?" Clare said. "That's what she told you, isn't it?"

Karen nodded. "That's exactly what Victoria said. If she'd had Bryce in bed when Roger returned from his client dinner, everything would've been okay. Can you *believe* it?"

"I'm afraid that sort of confused thinking is typical of abused women."

"I just can't understand why this is happening to my sister," Karen said.

"It's not uncommon," Liz told her. "And the women's reactions are more complex than many people understand. It's easy for us to say she should leave him, but she may be feeling shame, fear, desperation, even a sense of aloneness."

"In a way, things are even worse now," Karen murmured.

"Worse?" Julia repeated. "Has he hit her again?"

"I almost wish he had. It might help Victoria see the light."

Liz pulled the corner off her croissant and slowly shook her head. "My guess is the bastard's turned into a regular Prince Charming."

Karen stared at the older woman. "How'd you know?"

Liz answered with a sad smile. "I've seen it far too often. And I've heard of quite a few similar cases."

"He's so sorry," Karen said in a syrupy sweet voice, imitating her sister. According to Victoria, Roger was sick with remorse the minute he saw her bruises. He'd begged her forgiveness, apparently close to tears, and seeing how sorry he was, Victoria agreed. "It'll never happen again," Karen reported, "or so Victoria claims."

"Until next time," Clare added, her deep voice weighted with sarcasm.

"What can I do?" The frustration and anger were consuming her. Any excitement she felt over getting a role in a commercial paled against what she'd learned about her sister. Victoria was all she could think about. This was her *sister,* and although they had their differences, Karen couldn't tolerate the thought of anyone mistreating her.

"You can't talk to your parents?" Julia asked.

"No. I wish I could, but...I can't." Karen had considered that herself, and after careful thought, recognized that it would only cause more problems within the family. In Victoria's current state of mind, she might deny the entire incident and then hate Karen for breaking her confidence. The same went for contacting social services. Roger would be furious and Karen was convinced he'd take it out on Victoria.

"You could suggest Victoria get some counseling," Liz advised.

"I've already tried that—she said no. Besides, it wouldn't do any good. Roger's the one who needs therapy."

"Your sister could use some help herself," Clare said, not mincing words. "She's letting her husband beat her and then making excuses for him."

"True." But Karen hated to admit it.

"Talking out my feelings with a counselor after Michael left helped me tremendously," Clare told her.

"Speaking of Michael, how is he?" Karen asked, anxious now to change the subject.

"He's finished with the second round of chemotherapy," Clare said. She pulled her scone apart, turning it into a pile of crumbs. "I haven't seen him in several days, but Alex calls him every afternoon."

"Does that bother you?" Julia asked. "Because it would me."

Clare shook her head, but Karen didn't know if that was an answer to Julia's question or if she simply didn't have one.

"I always thought I wanted to see him suffer...." she finally said.

"And now that he is, you're finding it difficult to watch," Liz murmured.

Clare nodded.

"Is the...girlfriend around?" Karen wondered whether Michael was getting any support, emotional or otherwise, from Miranda Armstrong.

Shrugging, Clare reached for her espresso. "I wouldn't know. She must be, because he's still at the house."

Michael had moved into a rental place with Miranda Armstrong and if he was still living at the same address, presumably it was with her. Karen thought that was a reasonable assumption.

"How's Mick dealing with this?" she asked.

Clare's sigh said it all. "Not well. He isn't speaking to his father. He's angry with Alex and infuriated with me. He said we're the most screwed-up family he's ever known and wants nothing to do with us."

"He doesn't mean it," Karen rushed to assure her friend. "I'm always saying stuff like that to my parents. Oh, I mean it at the time, but I regret it later."

"When was the last time you talked to Mick?" Liz asked.

"Sunday afternoon."

"Give him a week," Julia suggested.

"Two weeks," Karen said, "then call him yourself. That's what my father usually does. He has his little speech down pat. I can almost recite it along with him, but by the time he phones I'm always glad he does, so I listen and pretend to take his advice." It was all part of her family's particular routine; every family had its own version. Actually, she was grateful her father stepped in when he did, breaking the stalemate between her and her mother.

"Little speech?" Clare was smiling, which pleased Karen.

"Yeah. First Dad says he can't understand why my mother and I can't get along. Then he goes on to remind me of the importance of family. He finishes up by telling me how much he loves his girls. When we're done, I feel better and apparently so does my mother."

Karen didn't mention that she never spoke to her mother during these conversations. Vernon Curtis was the peacemaker in the family.

"How's life treating you?" Julia asked, looking at Liz.

"No complaints," she responded.

"Have you run into Dr. Jamison lately?" Clare wanted to know.

For all her bitterness over her failed marriage, Clare was something of a romantic, Karen thought.

"No," Liz said abruptly.

"He's been at the hospital, though, hasn't he?"

"I wouldn't know." She focused her gaze across the room, refusing to meet their eyes. "Sean and I have agreed to disagree."

"Is that regret I'm seeing in you?" Julia asked softly.

Liz considered her question for a long moment. "Perhaps. But it's been six years since Steve was killed. In that time, I've learned I don't need a man in my life. If and when I decide to become involved, it'll be with a man who appreciates and respects me."

"You might not *need* a man," Karen said, leaning closer, "but that's not the same as wanting one."

"Besides, you had your kids around for most of those six years," Clare added, "and now you're alone."

"She's right," Julia said emphatically. "With your son and daughter moving out of the area, this is the first time you've had to deal with certain issues—like being alone and what you want to do with your future. There are no distractions around you now, and it makes a difference."

Liz would make a great poker player, Karen decided. Her face was unreadable. "Maybe I'll get serious about dating," she said, but Karen couldn't tell if she meant it or not.

"*You* need to start dating, too," Julia said, staring at Clare.

At the shocked look that descended on Clare's face, they all burst into laughter.

"You're joking, right?" Clare shook her head as though the idea was ludicrous.

"No, I'm not," Julia insisted. "In fact, I have an uncle I want you to meet."

Clare's mouth opened and then closed, but no sound came out. Finally, she asked, "Who?"

"My uncle Leslie. He's gorgeous and fun and visiting the family. We're having him to dinner Saturday night, and I want you to join us."

"Me?" Clare pressed her palm to her chest. "What about Liz—she doesn't have all the baggage I do. Anyway, I'm not ready. I—"

"This is totally nonthreatening," Julia broke in. "My uncle's only going to be in town for a couple of weeks. He's divorced, too. He understands."

"I don't know..."

"You're going," Liz stated in no uncertain terms.

"Why me?" Clare challenged. "*You* should be the one."

Karen caught the glance Liz and Julia exchanged. It told her what she'd already suspected. Julia had originally gone to Liz, but she'd refused and suggested Clare instead.

"You'll come, won't you?" Julia pleaded.

"I..." Clare looked uncertain and then seemed to arrive at a decision. "Yes, I think I will."

Liz positively beamed.

"Are you sure you're up to this?" Clare asked Julia. "Entertaining and all?"

"Of course I am."

"The pregnancy's going okay?"

She nodded, but Karen noted a small hesitation. "I haven't been sick all week."

"Has the baby moved yet?" Clare asked.

"She's moving all the time."

"She?"

"I don't know, but I like to think I'm having a girl."

"I have a name for her," Karen said. "You should call her Thursday."

"Thursday?"

"Sure, why not? You could name her after us."

"Sorry," Julia said, instantly nixing the idea. "I'm far too traditional for something like that. Besides 'Thursday's child is full of woe'— don't you remember the old rhyme?"

"Before we get sidetracked," Liz said, "I believe Karen has something else she wants to tell us."

All eyes turned to Karen.

Karen blinked and stared back at her friend.

"Don't you have some good news about a recent audition?"

Karen shrugged, pretending to make light of her success, then joyfully threw her arms in the air. "I got the role!"

> "It is not easy to find happiness in ourselves, and it is not possible to find it elsewhere."
>
> —Agnes Repplier

22

CHAPTER

CLARE CRAIG

April 7th

I can't believe I actually agreed to this dinner party. It's insane! The last time I went out with a man other than Michael was nearly twenty-six years ago. The minute Julia suggested the idea I should have refused. I have no idea what made me agree. How could I have done such a thing without thinking it through more carefully?

I'm not ready to date again. But if I phone now, just hours before I'm supposed to show up, I'd be putting Julia on the spot. To be honest, I'm not as worried about that as I am about what she'd tell the others in our group. Then everyone would know what a coward I am.

Okay, the decision is made. I'm going.

No, I'm not. I can't. I wouldn't know what to say. Idle chitchat with a stranger has never been my forte, even if this stranger is the nicest man in the world (according to Julia, anyway, who also says we'll have lots in common). The truth is, I don't know why I'm afraid. As Julia pointed out, this is totally nonthreatening. Having dinner with the uncle of a good friend. Really, what's so scary about that?

I think what terrifies me is the idea of any man in my life other than Michael. I didn't realize how insecure I am.

I refuse to believe that after all these years as a competent businesswoman, I'm letting a dinner date do this to me. I guess it isn't insecurity as much as the fear of making myself vulnerable again. I don't *want* to put myself at risk, especially when I know how crippling the pain of rejection can be.

Liz reminded the group that she doesn't need a man in her life. I agree with her. I don't need a man, either. I'm a smart, attractive woman, dammit! I'll admit my personal life has been a disaster recently. I'm coming back, though, slowly but surely, from the edge of insanity. I'm recovering from the grief of Michael's betrayal. Getting over the anger.

This evening, I'll go to Julia's with a brave smile and zero expectations. I have something to prove to myself. *I am healing.* I'm almost whole again. Oh sure, I take a few steps backward every now and then. For instance, my job with Murphy Motors—in some ways, that was a mistake. The main reason I wanted the job was to get back at Michael. I wanted him to spend his nights worrying about what I was doing, but my ploy lost its effectiveness when I learned he had other, more important things keeping him awake.

* * *

"Clare," Julia said, reaching for her hand when Clare arrived, giving her fingers a brief squeeze. "You look wonderful."

She should, Clare mused, seeing the time and effort that had gone into her appearance. She'd chosen a velvet cocktail suit in deep green, with a silk camisole, after trying on every party outfit she owned. Thankfully, Alex wasn't home and hadn't been around to see her agonizing over this dinner party—or to scoff at her primping. She was afraid he'd disapprove, which was the last thing she needed right now. In any event, he'd taken off that morning and she hadn't seen him all day. That wasn't unusual. She'd left him a note saying she'd gone out for the evening. Hey, she could be just as mysterious as Alex!

"Come and meet my uncle Leslie." Julia led her into the family room, where Peter sat talking to a distinguished-looking older man. Each held a glass of wine and glanced in Clare's direction.

Leslie and Peter stood as she entered.

"Clare, this is my uncle, Leslie Carter."

She stepped forward, her hand outstretched. "I'm delighted to meet you." Then smiling at Peter, she added, "And it's good to see you again, Peter."

"You, too." He headed into the open-plan kitchen, where an empty wineglass was waiting. "Can I pour you some wine?"

"Please." The dining-room table was set for four. Julia had mentioned earlier that the children were out with friends.

They all sat down on the two comfortable sofas in the family room. Julia placed a dish of baked artichoke dip and crackers on the coffee table in front of Clare.

"I understand you're visiting the area," Clare said, helping herself to a cracker and dip. Leslie Carter was a handsome man, just as Julia had promised. He had clear blue eyes, and was beautifully tanned. He'd gone almost completely bald, but it was extremely attractive on him—sexy in a Sean Connery way, Clare thought. In contrast to her, he'd dressed casually in a white polo shirt, crisp slacks and deck shoes. She guessed he was somewhere in his late fifties, perhaps early sixties. Julia hadn't said.

"I retired a few years ago," Leslie explained.

"He's a whiz with finances. In fact, he's been giving Peter and me lots of tax tips and he's got some good financial advice about the store."

Clare smiled.

"He's traveling around the world in his sailboat," Peter said enthusiastically.

"So far I haven't gone any farther than the West Coast of the United States," Leslie corrected.

"But you're going to Hawaii from here, right?"

"That's the plan."

"Alone?" Clare asked, thinking such a venture must surely be unwise.

"No. I have a small crew accompanying me."

"You must love sailing," Clare said.

"I do, but it's a recent passion."

"Uncle Leslie didn't even own a sailboat until three years ago," Julia told her.

"It was something I always thought about doing, but delayed. Then the excuses seemed to run out." Leslie leaned forward and reached for a cracker. "Once I got started, I wondered what took me so long."

"You say you retired a little while ago?"

"Yes, I was a management consultant for a number of companies in the Pacific Northwest."

Julia stood and headed into the kitchen. "Is there anything I can do to help?" Clare asked.

"Not a thing," Julia assured her. "Go ahead and visit while I put the finishing touches on the salad."

"Let me help," Peter said, as if on cue.

All at once Clare and Leslie were alone. She nervously twirled the stem of the wineglass between her hands while her mind raced with possible conversational gambits.

"I understand you were recently divorced," Leslie said.

"Actually, it's been a while. A little more than a year, I believe." She knew exactly how long it'd been, practically down to the hour. "You're divorced, too?"

He nodded. "Five years now. It was an adjustment at first. I was prepared to grow old with Barbara, but she... It seems we grew in different directions. She wanted a new life that didn't include me."

"So did my ex," Clare said with a short, humorless laugh. "Only Michael found a younger woman who made his new life a little more exciting." She gave a small shrug. "Why stick with apple pan dowdy when there's cheesecake available?"

"Barbara's new friend is named Troy. They're living together."

"Children?"

He shook his head. "I suppose I should be grateful for that, but I'm not. My life felt damn empty for a long time following the divorce. How about you?"

"Two sons. Mick's almost twenty and Alex is seventeen. I don't know what I would've done without them."

Leslie nodded. Clare sensed that the failure of his marriage had damaged this man, and that he was still recovering, just as she was.

"The salad's ready," Julia said, entering the room again.

"In case you weren't aware of it, my niece is an excellent cook," Leslie informed her as he got to this feet.

This was Clare's first opportunity to sample Julia's cooking. If the artichoke dip was anything to go by, she was in for a treat. The salad was impressive—a rich mixture of greens topped with slices of fresh pear, crumbled bleu cheese and walnuts, served with a raspberry vinaigrette.

"Julia, you've outdone yourself," Leslie said after the first bite.

Clare agreed. "This is fabulous."

Julia beamed at their praise. "Thanks. If you want I'll bring the recipe to breakfast next week."

"I'd love a copy," Clare assured her, although she didn't know when she'd get a chance to prepare it. Alex and Mick were meat-and-potatoes eaters, the same as their father.

After the salad, Julia brought a baked salmon and a scalloped potato dish to the table. Both were beautifully presented and delicious. Clare had always suspected that her friend possessed finely tuned domestic talents, but she'd never guessed Julia was this accomplished. Dessert was a lemon torte.

Over coffee in the family room, they chatted about Leslie's upcoming trip to Hawaii. Julia got out her knitting and, for the first time that evening, Clare was aware of the bulge outlined by her dress. She wondered whether Julia had mentioned the pregnancy to Leslie, then realized that Peter probably had. Julia's husband and uncle seemed to get on well.

Clare found that Peter and Leslie were good company and entertaining conversationalists. Julia was quieter than usual but seemed content. She concentrated on her knitting and made only the occasional remark.

At nine-thirty, Clare decided it was time to head home.

"I should be leaving, too," Leslie said and stood with her.

"I had a wonderful evening," Clare told Julia and Peter, but the message wasn't for them alone. Despite all her anxiety, she'd actually enjoyed herself.

After another round of farewells and thank-yous, Leslie walked Clare to her car, which was parked behind his at the curb. The night was lovely and warm, the stars were out and the scent of blooming lemon trees filled the air.

"Thank you, Clare," he said as she unlocked her car—the newest Chevy Tahoe.

Clare knew what he meant. "Thank *you*."

He grinned; they understood each other. Not only had the evening been pleasant, it had given them hope for the future—not necessarily a future together, but with *someone*. Romance and male companionship weren't lost possibilities, Clare thought, as long as there were men like Leslie Carter.

"Enjoy your adventures," she said as she slid into the car. "I'd love to see you when you get back."

"Same here." Leslie closed the door for her, then walked to his own vehicle.

Clare drove home, feeling better about life than she had in...well, in years. Two years. She parked in the garage and was climbing out of the car when the door leading to the house was thrust open. Alex stood on the threshold.

"Where were you?" her son demanded.

"I had a dinner engagement," she answered calmly. Judging by his tone, he'd been worried. Maybe he'd be a bit more considerate about letting her know where *he* was from now on.

"You had a date?" Alex asked, his tone bordering on the belligerent.

"Hey, be reasonable! I didn't shrivel up and die after the divorce, you know."

Alex followed her into the house. "Who'd you go out with?"

"Who?" she repeated, frowning. "Why do you need to know that?" When he continued to glare at her, she asked, "Is my going out really so remarkable?"

"Yes."

Taken aback, she just looked at him.

"Where were you?" he asked again.

"Julia and Peter Murchison's house, if you must know."

"She's in your breakfast club, right?"

"Right." Clare went into her bedroom, kicked off her shoes and removed her earrings. Alex trailed behind her, then slumped onto the end of the bed.

"Did you have a good time?" he asked, obviously making an effort.

"Wonderful. Julia's uncle Leslie was in town and I met him." She went on to mention Leslie's sailing trip to Hawaii.

"That's cool." But Alex didn't sound overly impressed.

"Did anything happen while I was gone?" Something was troubling her son. Alex didn't generally follow her from room to room, nor did he grill her about where she'd been.

"Dad called," Alex said, his voice deceptively casual.

"And?" She didn't know what was coming but she tensed, anticipating bad news. With Michael she no longer knew what to expect.

"He wanted to talk to you."

"Me?" Now, that was a first.

"He...he—" Alex's voice faltered and he bit his lower lip.

Clare turned around to face her son. "What's wrong?"

"Dad didn't want to ask me. Dammit, Mom, you should have been here! Dad needed you and you weren't here." Alex stood, his hands clenched at his sides.

"Why did your father need me?" she asked, ignoring the accusation in his voice.

"He needed someone to take him to the hospital—he didn't want to ask me."

"Did you drive him?"

"No... When I got there, he was so sick Mom, I didn't know what to do so I called 911. I thought he was going to die." Alex's voice broke. "You should have been there, Mom, you should have been there to help Dad. He needed you."

"It is never too late to be what you might have been."
—George Eliot

23

CHAPTER

LIZ KENYON

"Sharon Kelso is here," Liz's secretary announced over the intercom. "She's asked to speak to you and says it's important."

Liz sighed. Her afternoon was booked solid but her secretary certainly knew that. If the head of the nurses' union sought an impromptu meeting, then it went without saying something was up. In all likelihood, it meant trouble.

"Show her in," Liz said. She felt slightly sick to her stomach. Although a strike had been averted, relations between the hospital and the nursing staff remained tense.

Sharon Kelso was a large woman who presented herself as a no-nonsense professional. Liz liked and respected her. She considered her fair-minded but a tough negotiator.

Liz stood as Sharon marched purposefully into her office.

"Liz." The other woman inclined her head in greeting.

"Hello, Sharon, what can I do for you?" No need to delay this with idle conversation; they were both busy women.

"I'll need about ten minutes of your time."

"You have it," Liz told her and motioned to the chair. She waited until Sharon was seated before sitting down herself.

The head of the nurses' union paused to collect her thoughts before speaking. "I don't mean to be telling tales out of school," she began. Her pinched lips made it clear that she was upset. "One of our nurses is experiencing a problem with a certain visiting specialist."

There were procedures to be followed in cases like this and Sharon knew them as well as Liz did.

"Do you want to file a complaint?" Liz asked.

"That's an option we've considered," Sharon said.

"Can you tell me what this is about?"

"It involves recent corrective actions taken by Dr. Sean Jamison."

Liz should have known it had to do with Sean. She could barely keep from groaning aloud.

"At this point, the staff member involved and I prefer to handle the situation without the formality of filing a complaint," Sharon said. She appeared to be selecting her words carefully. "Once you hear what happened, you'll understand our hesitation. We don't feel it would serve a useful purpose to make an issue of this. There are extenuating circumstances."

There almost always were, but Liz didn't say so.

"Before I go any further, I want you to know my staff member accepts full responsibility for her part in this. However, I find Dr. Jamison's behavior offensive and unacceptable."

"Tell me what happened," Liz suggested.

The story that followed was short and to the point. "One of my staff made a small clerical error on one of the charts."

Liz knew there was no such thing as a small error, but didn't point that out.

"It was caught almost immediately, but when Dr Jamison learned about it, he blew a gasket. He insisted that the nurse in question not be assigned to any of his patients. Now, Liz, you and I both know that's an impossible request."

She nodded.

"He was rude, belligerent and unnecessarily harsh. We're not perfect. We can only do our best. No one deserves the kind of tongue-lashing Dr. Jamison gave her. It was humiliating and downright scathing, and furthermore he yelled at her in front of other people. I simply can't allow such unprofessional behavior to go unreported."

"I agree." Liz understood Sharon's dilemma. Knowing Sean, she could well imagine the scene. She was surprised she hadn't heard about it before now. Liz didn't blame him for his anger but took issue with the manner in which he'd expressed it. Under normal circumstances, Sharon wouldn't hesitate to file a formal complaint. The reason she didn't was understood; the nurse had been in the wrong and she didn't want documentation acknowledging her error.

"You'll talk to Dr. Jamison?" Sharon asked—less a question than a demand.

"I will," Liz promised, although it was the last thing she wanted. To this point, they'd managed to avoid each other. It wasn't difficult. Other than instances such as this, there was no reason for any contact.

"Thank you," Sharon said, rising. "We're pleased with our new contract, and don't want anything to stand in the way of a long and healthy working relationship."

"I couldn't agree with you more," Liz returned, the knot in her stomach tightening.

Sharon left then, but Liz remained standing, considering how best to handle this situation. Sean might assume that her asking to speak to him was a convenient excuse to see him again. She shook her head in frustration; getting involved with him, however briefly, was a mistake.

She walked over to her desk and pushed the intercom button. "Cherie," she said, "leave a message for Dr. Jamison to stop by my office at his earliest convenience, would you?"

"Of course," Cherie returned, sounding delighted at the prospect. "I'll do it right away."

Sean didn't keep her waiting long. That very evening, just as Liz was shutting down her computer for the night, Sean appeared at her door. Cherie had long since gone home and Liz was there by herself. Sean often seemed to plan it that way.

"You wanted to talk to me?" He wore his usual cocky grin as he strolled casually into her office.

"This is a professional matter," Liz told him immediately. "Please sit down."

His face was carefully neutral as he claimed the chair across from her. "This has to do with the Tucker baby, doesn't it?"

"I wasn't given the full details."

"Was a formal complaint made? If so, I'm here to tell you the woman deserved everything I said. There's one thing I won't tolerate and that's—"

Liz held up her hand, stopping him. "A complaint wasn't filed."

He indicated no relief. "The woman deserved to have her wrist slapped. Her carelessness could have cost the Tucker baby his life. There are a lot of things I'm willing to put up with at this hospital, but sloppy record-keeping isn't one of them."

"No one's saying you were wrong about the nature of your criticism."

"Naturally, because I was right. Believe me, if I hadn't been, Sharon Kelso would have filed a complaint so fast, it'd make your head swim."

All of that was true, but Liz chose not to respond.

"What does she want?" Sean demanded. "An apology? Because I don't owe *anyone* an apology."

"Actually, no. The nurse in question is willing to accept responsibility for this error."

"Good, because that's what she needs to do."

"I believe," Liz said, "that Sharon came to me as a gesture of good faith. She wants to keep things low-key and nonconfrontational. She—"

"Like hell! She wants me reported as an unreasonable jerk." He shrugged. "I already know that, and so do you. When it comes to my patients I'm like a wounded bear."

"No one's faulting your skills or your commitment."

"Just my bedside manner?"

"No, I'd say it's your nurses' station tactics that are causing the problems."

His frown relaxed. "I'll admit I got damned angry." A grin began to emerge.

That was an understatement, Liz was sure.

He rubbed the back of his neck and expelled a slow sigh. "I probably did come down on her a little too hard," he was willing to admit, but with reluctance as if he, too, was making a concession to keep the peace. "I was afraid I was going to lose the Tucker boy. I hadn't slept in over thirty hours. I'll say something to her in the morning. That'll smooth things over."

"You were up for thirty hours? That's not good for you or your patients." Although she chastised him, she remembered doing the same thing herself once, years earlier, when her baby's life hung in the balance. Liz had been afraid to leave Lauren, afraid to fall asleep, afraid to even take her eyes off the baby. The staff had been gentle with her and Steve, but there'd been no physician by their side. No one to comfort her when her baby girl died.

How grateful the Tucker family must be to Sean. Liz found it difficult to think ill of a physician as dedicated to the well-being of his patients.

Sean glared at her. "Don't tell me how to do my job and I won't tell you how to do yours."

She remained calm. "You should learn how to deal with pressure—some method other than terrorizing staff. You need to find some kind of release."

"I know, but you won't cooperate. A week in bed with you would cure everything that ails me, and it'd probably do you good as well."

Liz gasped; she couldn't help it. She wasn't sure if she should be furious or just plain insulted. "I don't appreciate your making comments like that," she said in a stiff voice.

"Of course you don't. Why else would I make them?"

She stared at him and saw that he was smiling. Ten minutes with Sean Jamison and *she* was the one struggling to hold onto her temper.

"How do *you* relieve the stress of the job?" he asked, sounding genuinely interested.

"I...I do a number of things." Liz wasn't ready for his rapid switch from provocative to serious.

"Such as?"

"Most recently I took up knitting," she said, although she'd had to cancel her sessions with Julia this week.

"Knitting." His gaze was skeptical.

"One of the women in my breakfast group owns a yarn shop."

He grinned. "Ah, yes, this breakfast group of yours. Tell me, are the meetings just an excuse for men-bashing?"

Leave it to Sean to suggest such a thing. "Oh, hardly. The problem with you men is that you're so threatened by women getting together, you naturally assume it's all about you."

"Well, isn't it?"

"No," she said emphatically.

"All right," he said, sincere once again. "I agree with you, I need a way to release work pressure, but I don't know that knitting's my thing."

"Don't knock it until you've tried it," she joked.

He considered her words, then slowly nodded. "All right, I'll try it. Are you willing to teach me?"

This was more than a casual question, and Liz knew it. The last time they'd talked, Sean had made it clear that she'd have to come to him if their relationship was to advance. He'd riled her so much with his attitude and his arrogant tactics she'd vowed never to see him again. That hadn't stopped her from thinking about him, though. For weeks she'd pushed any thought of Sean Jamison to the farthest reaches of her mind. What irritated her was how often she'd been required to do so.

"It's a simple question," he teased, obviously well aware that it wasn't.

"Just you and me and a ball of yarn?" she asked, delaying a response while she weighed the risks.

"Sounds kinky, but I'm game if you are."

Liz groaned.

He knew she hated the sexual innuendoes and with a sheepish grin, raised both hands. "Just kidding."

She folded her arms across her chest. "You're serious about knitting?"

The teasing light left his eyes. "I promise to make an honest effort."

They both understood that he wasn't talking about knitting.

"What do you say, Liz?" His eyes continued to hold hers.

Her first inclination was to tell him to forget it; she didn't need the grief. Instead she found herself tempted. They'd gotten off to a bad start. He'd wanted one thing and she another. Finding a middle ground might not be possible, but if he was willing to try again, then she could do no less.

"All right," she agreed. "Don't make me sorry," she muttered as an afterthought.

He laughed, and the robust sound made her smile, too.

"Would I do that?" he asked.

> "You don't have to know how to sing. It's feeling as though
> you want to that makes the day worthwhile."
>
> —Coleman Cox

24

CHAPTER

KAREN CURTIS

April 19th

The breakfast group met this morning, and as usual we were all full of chatter and news. Julia and her husband bought a crib for the baby and set it up in their bedroom. Clare got a humorous card from Julia's uncle Leslie and showed it to everyone. She was a little giddy about it, and I found that rather endearing. Here she was, married all those years, and then she gets flustered over a silly card. Apparently the dinner party went well, although neither Julia nor Clare said much about it. We get sidetracked so easily.

The one who surprised us all is Liz who, just before we broke up, casually mentioned that she's seeing Dr. Jamison again. You could have heard an egg crack when she dropped *that* news. Everyone went quiet. No one likes him, (well, not that we've actually met him, but we have a pretty clear picture). We're all wondering what a savvy, sophisticated businesswoman sees in a man who treats women like objects. On second thought, there must be more to the man. I sure hope so. I'd hate to think Liz is another Victoria.

Speaking of my sister, I heard from her. She mailed me one of those sappy, sentimental cards about how great it is to have a sister. If she truly felt that way, she'd listen to me. Hey, I understand about her staying with the twit, but the abuse isn't going to stop unless some changes are made. Victoria claims Roger loves her and is genuinely sorry. I'm sure he is and will continue to be—until the next time he slaps her around. Thinking about my sister and her marriage depresses me. So does the state of my own love life.

I haven't been out on a date for so long that I'm beginning to lose hope. I've been busy, but it isn't like there's someone in the wings just dying to ask me out, either. Glen Trnavski, maybe, although I haven't heard from him in a while. I've been substitute teaching at different schools lately, so I haven't had a chance to run into him. It's sort of pathetic that I'm even thinking about him, since we only went out once. He's a nerd, the kind of guy who dangles a slide rule from his belt loop, but a nice one and really very sweet. Doesn't matter—he hasn't called and neither has Jeff. Jeff and I will only argue, so it's just as well we're not in touch. Especially after our last conversation... Glen might be a little on the dull side, but at least he's focused. (Not on me, though. Ha! Ha!)

On a more positive note, the hair spray commercial airs for the first time next week. The filming took forever. I liked the director, but this ten-second spot isn't exactly *Gone With the Wind*. Unfortunately, the only part of me that shows is the back of my head. The camera shows me tossing my head as my perfectly shaped hair bounces about with every curl perfectly in place, thanks to "Beauty Hold." It's supposed to look like I'm playing tennis, but in reality I was hopping up and down on a trampoline. Needless to say, Mother's relieved no one will know it's me.

My rent is paid and I just got a check from the school district. I feel flush! It's only fitting that I celebrate my first national commercial. I haven't been to a movie in forever, but it's getting harder and harder to find someone who isn't one half of a couple to do things with. I never thought I'd have this kind of problem, but nearly everyone I know, male or female, is either married or has a significant other.

I could always ask Liz, but she works such long hours and besides, the little time she does have available is about to be taken up by the good doctor. Clare might be interested. She's fun, and I find myself liking her more and more.

* * *

"Do you want me to pick you up?" Karen asked. She'd followed her impulse and phoned Clare Craig, and to her delight Clare had immediately agreed. She seemed surprised that Karen had a Friday night free.

They took a few minutes to choose a film and decided on a comedy.

"Sure, pick me up," Clare said, "that way you can meet my son."

"Alex will be home?"

"He makes pit stops every weekend." Clare laughed. "I told him I should install a drive-through window so all I have to do is lean out and hand him money and food."

Karen laughed, too, and wished her mother had half the sense of humor the women in her Thursday morning breakfast group did. She and Catherine might have gotten along better if they'd found a reason to laugh together.

She finalized her arrangements with Clare and they ended the conversation.

Predictably, on Friday morning Karen got called in to substitute teach at Manchester High School. In the English department this time. She hesitated before taking the assignment, but not for long. The money was too good to ignore and besides, Manchester High was where the elusive Glen taught chemistry.

High school was Karen's favorite age group. Somehow—maybe because of her own age—she found it easier to relate to the kids. She had three periods, then an hour's break before her two afternoon classes. The eleventh-graders were studying *Macbeth,* a play she knew fairly well, since she'd been in a college production, playing one of the witches. She gave the ninth-graders a creative-writing project. During her lunch break she ate in the teachers' lounge, thinking she might accidentally-on-purpose run into Glen.

She didn't, but when she asked about him, several of the other teachers sang his praises. Apparently he was popular with the staff. He might be popular with her, too, if he made more of an effort to seek her out. After school, Karen decided it would be all right to casually wander the halls until she located him. She found him in the chemistry lab with a handful of students clustered around him like groupies around a rock star.

Standing in the doorway, Karen was uncertain if she should interrupt. She cleared her throat. "Mr. Trnavski?" she said.

Glen glanced up and did a double-take. He was pleased to see her and made it obvious. "Karen, hi!"

"Hi," she said. "Um, I was subbing here and thought I'd stop by and say hello." She held up her right hand. "Hello."

"I was just finishing," he said, closing the text with a snap.

The students exchanged shocked glances, as though stunned that their teacher had a life outside of chemistry. "But..." one of them began.

"We'll go over this again on Monday," he said, dismissing them.

"But the test..."

"Has been postponed until Tuesday."

From the way they reacted, Karen knew the extra day to study had been an unexpected gift. The six students left, chattering away and patting each other on the back as if they'd just been granted parole.

He waited until they'd disappeared down the hall before he spoke. He might not have the sleek good looks that would attract Hollywood, she thought, watching him, but he wasn't bad on the eyes, either.

"You're looking fine," he said as the last student vacated the room.

His admiration was just what Karen's sagging ego needed. But if he was as interested in her as he seemed to be, she couldn't understand why he hadn't contacted her. "I haven't heard from you in a while."

Glen turned away and erased the blackboard. "As I recall, you said you wanted to be friends. Nothing more and nothing else."

"I said that?"

"Maybe not in so many words. But I got the message and decided not to waste either your time or mine." He brushed chalk dust from his palms.

"Oh." She did remember making some remark to that effect, but only because she hadn't really known what she wanted. Anyway, she'd said it months ago. Couldn't a girl change her mind? Glen was smart and funny, and the more she was around him, the more she liked him. "I've been known to make statements I later regret."

"Really?"

Karen nodded, hoping he'd take the hint and ask her out again.

He didn't.

Glancing at her watch, she decided to make a quick exit. No need to hang around, possibly waiting to be humiliated. The sole purpose for seeking him out was to let him know she was available, which she'd now done. She briefly considered asking him out, but figured he was too traditional to be comfortable with that. "Okay...see you later," she said breezily, then turned to leave.

"Can I phone you?" he called after her.

She turned back. "I'd be disappointed if you didn't."

"Do you have a date tonight?" he asked, following her into the hallway. He struck a casual pose, leaning against the doorjamb and crossing his arms. "Or would you like to go out?"

"Sorry," she said, "I already have plans."

"Another time, then?"

"I'd like that," she said, walking backward until she collided with the janitor, which totally ruined her exit.

Two hours later, Karen drove to the address Clare had given her and parked in front of the large, professionally landscaped house. It was the first time she'd been to any of the other women's homes, and she was impressed.

Alex answered the doorbell and stared at her.

"Hi, I'm Karen Curtis," she said, introducing herself. "Your mother's friend."

Alex was a tall seventeen-year-old, and although they'd never met, he seemed vaguely familiar.

"You came looking for Mr. Trnavski this afternoon, didn't you?" he asked as he held open the screen door.

"Is that Karen?" Clare's voice came from down a hallway.

"Yeah," Alex shouted over his shoulder.

If the outside of Clare's home was impressive, it paled in comparison to the inside. Every aspect of the house spoke of quality and craftsmanship. Karen thought about her parents' place, where her father's desire for comfort—comfortable armchairs, big TV—warred with her mother's often pretentious decorating ideas.

"Are you dating Mr. Trnavski?"

"We're friends."

"Man, I've never seen him get so flustered before."

Karen was thrilled to hear it.

"I see you've met my son," Clare said, entering the living room. She was trying to fasten an earring in place. She leaned her head to one side as she fiddled with the gold loop.

"Mom, this is Ms. Curtis from school."

"Yes, sweetheart, I know. Karen's in my breakfast group."

"Your breakfast group? I thought that was a bunch of old women like you."

Despite herself, Karen laughed. "I don't think you're earning points with your mother," she said.

Alex looked embarrassed. "You know what I mean."

His mother closed her eyes for a moment, as if to avoid the subject entirely. Then she resumed her struggle with the earring, finally succeeding.

"You're divorced, too?" Alex sat down on the sofa arm and gazed up at Karen.

"No. I've never been married."

"Not everyone in the group is divorced," Clare informed her son.

She didn't mention that she was, in fact, the only one of the four who was. Karen wondered why.

"Aren't you going to—" He stopped and frowned. "Isn't this Friday night?"

"Yes." Karen frowned, too. "Is that a problem?"

"Your divorce support group is tonight, isn't it, Mom?"

"Oh," Clare said. "That's what you mean. Well, it's an ongoing session and the people change."

"You're not going?"

"Not tonight. Karen and I are taking in a movie."

"Oh."

"I'll be just a moment longer," Clare told her, hurrying down the hallway.

Alex continued to stare at Karen.

"What's the matter?" she asked. "Didn't you realize teachers had a life outside the classroom?"

"It's not that," he said. "It's my mom."

Karen waited for him to finish.

"You don't understand. She's never missed a meeting of that group. She *needs* her group."

"Maybe she doesn't need it as much as you think."

Alex shook his head. "She needs it," he insisted.

"Then ask her."

"I will," Alex said, standing as his mother came back into the room. "What about the divorce support group? Don't you think you should go?"

Clare reached for her purse. "I decided not to."

"Well, I can see *that*. Why not?"

"Because, my dear son," Clare said and pressed her hand to the side of his face, "it's time to move on. I'm ready," she said, glancing at Karen. "How about you?"

"Ready," she echoed and smiled to herself.

"You don't get to choose how you're going to die. Or when.
You can only decide how you're going to live. Now."

—Joan Baez

CHAPTER

CLARE CRAIG

Clare turned off the vacuum and heard the phone in the background as the Hoover moaned to a stop. Lunging for the cordless she had no idea if this was the first ring or the fifth.

"Hello," she said, slightly breathless. Although she could well afford a cleaning service, she preferred to do her own housework. She joked that it helped her work out her aggressions, which was true; she also felt that she could better maintain the kind of control she wanted over her environment.

Her greeting was met by a short hesitation. "Clare, it's Michael."

She knew he'd been released from the hospital a few days earlier; after Alex's 911 call, he'd been admitted a second time—and now he was home, in the tender, well-manicured hands of Miranda.

"Alex is at school," she reminded him in case he'd forgotten.

"Actually, I wanted to talk to you."

In the beginning she'd dreamed about the day Michael would need her, reach out to her, want her back in his life. During the two years since he'd moved out, it hadn't happened. But Clare had learned valuable lessons about herself. Each day she grew stronger, more confident and self-assured. They'd always been a team, the two of them, but she'd learned to fly solo.

"I'd like to invite you to lunch," Michael shocked her by asking.

"Lunch?" She nearly choked on the word.

"It's my way of thanking you for your kindness while I underwent chemo."

Clare sank onto the edge of the coffee table. He was telling her this was simply to let her know that he appreciated her help; she shouldn't put any stock in the invitation. He didn't want her back any more than she wanted *him* back, she told herself fiercely.

"No thanks are necessary." And they weren't. Her reasons were too complex to analyze. Suffice it to say she'd done it for him *and* for her. Because of their shared past and because of their children.

"I insist. I'd like to take you to Mama Lena's."

Her favorite Italian restaurant, no less. When they were first married and lived paycheck to paycheck, it was a special indulgence to dine at Mama Lena's. Every birthday and anniversary found them enjoying ravioli and eggplant Parmesan. The breadsticks and cheese, the antipasto, a glass of red wine—followed by espresso and tiramisu for dessert. The memories scrolled through her mind like silent movies.

"I...don't think that's a good idea," she said, fighting the urge to agree.

Michael paused. "Another restaurant then. You name it, any place you want."

"I know you appreciated my help, Michael, but I don't believe our having lunch is the right thing to do. Not at this point in our lives."

"I need to talk to you," he said after another long pause.

"Talk to me now."

"I can't," he told her with what sounded like regret. "All I'm asking is that you meet me. Any place you want, any time."

"All right," she said, curiosity getting the better of her. "Meet me at Mocha Moments at three o'clock tomorrow afternoon."

She felt comfortable there, safe. Michael wouldn't tell her what this was about over the phone, but she wasn't meeting him at Mama Lena's, where he could evoke memories of happier times, when life was sweet and all her illusions had yet to be shattered.

Clare didn't mention the phone call, not to Alex and not to Karen who called that evening to tell her excitedly about Alex's chemistry teacher asking her out to dinner. If Clare was tempted to discuss Michael's call with anyone, it would have been Liz. Instead, she kept the information to herself, wondering what it meant, and what the hell was so important that Michael had sought her out.

Perhaps she was reading more into this than she should. Since their relationship was fairly amicable now, Michael might simply want to discuss their sons. Maybe he wanted her advice about reconciling with Mick....

Then again, this might have to do with Alex's upcoming high-school graduation. Should they both attend and pretend to be a happy family for the sake of their sons? No. She couldn't see that happening, and there was Mick to consider. Naturally Michael was free to attend, but Mick wouldn't want his father sitting anywhere near him.

Another thought occurred to her as she sat with a cup of strong coffee the following day, waiting for her ex-husband to show up. Perhaps this was connected to his cancer treatment.

Precisely at three, Michael walked into Mocha Moments. He was even thinner than the last time she'd seen him but not so horribly pale. Some of the color had returned to his cheeks. He paused just inside the door and smiled when he saw her.

"Hello, Clare," he said, making his way to the table.

"Hello, Michael." She inclined her head toward him, choosing not to study him too closely for fear he might misinterpret her interest. He glanced over his shoulder at the counter and the printed menu above the cash register. "I take it they don't have a waitress here."

"Everyone sees to his or her own."

"You want a refill?" he asked, and shoved his hand in his pocket, removing his money clip.

When she shook her head, he stepped toward the counter, returning a few minutes later with a latte. Pulling out a chair, he sat down across from her.

"How are you?" she asked. Now that he was close, she realized he didn't look as good as she'd first assumed. The whites of his eyes had a yellowish tinge and while there was color in his face, his cheeks were still gaunt.

"I'm better now, thanks," he answered and sipped from his latte.

"The cancer?"

He didn't respond right away. "I didn't come here to exchange news."

"Fine, then get to the point and be done with it," she snapped, feeling a little hurt, a little insulted.

"Actually, I have a favor to ask of you."

He had a funny way of leading up to it, she thought, considering he'd just antagonized her. *She* wasn't the one who'd asked for this meeting; her being here was a favor to him.

"I don't have any right to ask this," Michael went on, his voice lower now. He stared down at his latte as if he'd find the solution to his troubles in the frothy milk.

"Ask me what?" she demanded, trying to temper the defensiveness she heard in her own voice.

"I wouldn't, if it wasn't for our sons."

"What is it?" she asked. Enough with this preamble!

"I want you to come back and work at the dealership," he said, his eyes boring holes in her.

"No—no way." She didn't need to think it over, didn't need to hear the reasons. Her answer was instantaneous.

Michael raised his hand. "Let me explain."

"I've already got a job." She'd set out to be an irritant to him by taking the part-time job at Murphy Motors. She regretted it; apparently Michael had lost business and now he was afraid.

"Give Murphy two weeks' notice."

"Michael, I can't... Listen, I made a mistake. I should never have taken that job, and—"

"Hear me out," Michael interrupted.

She laughed, and shook her head. It was as though they were still married. He hadn't bothered to listen to her then, either.

"This doesn't have anything to do with Murphy Motors," he said impatiently. "The entire future of Craig Chevrolet hangs on your answer."

"Michael, please..." He was overreacting. Naturally, he didn't want her working for his biggest competitor and now he was trying to lure her back. What he didn't understand, hadn't bothered to hear, was that she regretted the whole stupid idea.

"I swear to you, this isn't personal. I need you to assume my role."

"And just where will you be?" If he told her he needed time to take Miranda on some exotic vacation, she'd tell him exactly what he could do with his job offer.

He wouldn't look at her.

"What exactly will you be doing while I'm taking over as general manager?" she repeated. Although her voice remained calm, she refused to answer his question until he answered hers.

"It's not what you think," he hastened to add.

"How do you know what I'm thinking?"

"Oh, Clare, you've forgotten I was married to you for twenty-three years." Although he was smiling, there was little humor in his words. "Fine, I'll tell you." He dragged a shaky breath through his lungs. "I've been selected for an experimental drug treatment. It means I won't be able to continue my duties at the dealership."

"This has to do with the cancer?"

Again he wouldn't meet her gaze.

"You know the car business better than anyone. Despite our differences over the past few years, I trust you."

She didn't know what to say. Earlier, he'd avoided the question of his health, sidestepping it with the pretense of getting on with their discussion.

"The dealership is heavily mortgaged now, and unless this transition is smooth, I could lose everything."

He was afraid of losses? Clare was stunned by his insensitivity. She'd had her life ripped apart, her security shredded, her heart broken. Now he was afraid that if he spent a few weeks away from the business, it might falter—so he'd come to her. Yes, any erosion of the dealership's finances would have an impact on her and the boys, but to ask her to step in like this! As though they were still a married couple, still a team... Well, they weren't and that was entirely his doing.

She wanted to tell him what she thought, but the words lodged in her throat, making it impossible to speak. Then Michael astonished her even more, by laughing.

"You find this *humorous?*"

"No." He shook his head. "Not at all. I'm just amused by your predictability. You're so mad right now, you can barely think."

"You've got it. Hire Miranda, Michael, because I'm not interested." She stood to leave, but his hand on her arm stopped her.

"Miranda left me." The pain behind those words was barely concealed.

Clare felt her knees buckle. For two years she'd wanted him to experience just a fraction of the emotional agony she'd endured when he walked out on her.

"Aren't you going to remind me that what goes around comes around?" he asked hoarsely.

"No," she whispered. Not when he'd so plainly learned that lesson on his own. What surprised her was his willingness to admit it, especially to her.

"Clare," he said, pleading with her now. "Sit down, please."

She reclaimed her seat, not that she had any choice, since her legs were about to go out from under her. "When did she leave?" Clare asked, wondering how long Michael had been on his own.

"A while ago now."

She nodded.

"Actually, she moved in with a friend soon after I learned about the cancer. She has...trouble dealing with sickness."

Clare found it interesting and rather sad that he'd continue to make excuses for Miranda.

"I should have told you sooner." His voice had grown soft, and he slouched forward, looking suddenly old.

"It isn't any of my business." She glanced away, finding it difficult to look at the pain in his eyes. Michael was alone and knew what it was like to come home to a cold, empty house. She studied him for any signs of regret and saw none. Even now, sick and abandoned by the woman he'd given up so much for, he revealed no contrition, despite what he'd done to Clare and their family. That hurt, and she silently chastised herself for seeking more than he could give.

"Aren't you going to gloat?" he asked, some of the old fire returning to his eyes.

"No," she whispered.

"Will you do it?" he asked again. "Will you take over for me when I go into the hospital?"

Clare couldn't meet his eyes. "Let me think about it."

"I'll make it worth your while," he promised. "The dealership belongs to the boys. I don't want to lose it. And, of course, there are your support payments...."

She nodded. She wasn't likely to forget those.

"How long will it take you to have an answer?" he asked.

Rushing her into a decision wasn't going to help. "I don't know," she said, hardly able to take it all in. "I—I need to think through my options."

"A day."

"Longer."

"A week then?"

Why was he rushing her like this? "I don't know," she said a second time, resenting the pressure. "If you're going to force me to answer right away, then the answer is no. I've made a new life without you, Michael, and I can't see the point of getting our personal and financial affairs all tangled up again."

"Think it over, Clare. This is important."

"To you, you mean."

"It's important to our children," he reminded her.

"I need time," she repeated.

"Dammit, Clare, I don't have time. Can't you see? Do I have to spell it out for you? I'm dying."

"Dying?" The word barely made it past the constriction in her throat.

"According to the specialists, I'll be lucky if this treatment buys me six more months. The cancer is spreading.... Look at me, Clare. Look at me," he insisted. "I don't have much longer. Now, are you going to help me or not?"

* * *

April 25th
2:34 a.m.

I can't sleep. Every time I close my eyes I see Michael sitting at the table at Mocha Moments, telling me he's dying.

Dying!

He seemed to accept it, as if it were a foregone conclusion. After the initial shock, I had a thousand questions. He answered the first few, but didn't want to go into detail. The cancer started out in his liver and has spread throughout his body. There's nothing to be done. No miracle drug, no clinic that can save him and no cure in sight. He doesn't want the boys to know and begged me to keep his secret.

Everything about this afternoon is so vivid in my mind. I keep going over it and over it, almost obsessively. Miranda left him—I never did learn exactly when she moved out. I'm sure Michael didn't want me to know.

That made me wonder if he delayed seeing the doctor because of her. And I wondered—if we'd still been together, if there'd never been an affair or the subsequent divorce—whether I would've detected something wrong before it was too late. If Michael had gotten medical treatment sooner, would that have made a difference?

I'll never know.

I've been walking around in a haze ever since. Michael asked me to assume the management of the dealership, but he made it clear that once he leaves, he won't be back. Mick's major is business, and Michael's hope is that our eldest son will eventually step into the role of manager and shared ownership with his younger brother. Until that happens, Michael needs me to run the business.

I remember, soon after I filed for divorce, pleading with God to let Michael suffer. My sense of outrage demanded it. I wanted him to know that betrayal can destroy you, wanted him to feel the bitterness corroding everything he once considered decent and fair. But even in my most desperate moments, I wouldn't have wished this on him.

Alex, the son of my heart, knew the minute he walked in tonight that something was drastically wrong. I kept my promise to Michael, but I don't know how long I'll be able to hold back the truth.

I'll do what Michael asked, give my notice at Murphy Motors and return to the dealership. With the two of us working together, the transition should be seamless.

Michael is dying and he's come to me for help. I'm willing to step in and do what I can, for my children's sake...and for his. I don't *want* to care, don't want to become emotionally involved. But I am, and even though we're divorced, that's not going to change.

> "The greater part of our happiness or misery depends on our dispositions and not on our circumstances."
>
> —Martha Washington

CHAPTER

JULIA MURCHISON

List of Blessings
1. My mother
2. Comfortable shoes
3. Consignment maternity clothes
4.
5.

May 13th—Mother's Day

The house is quiet and everyone's still asleep. I woke early, although this is the one day of the year I can sleep in without feeling guilty. The peacefulness was just too wonderful to ignore, so I'm sitting here in the family room, thinking over the events planned for today.

My mother's coming for brunch after church, and then she's going to my sister's for dinner. Janice wanted all of us to celebrate Mother's Day together, but I couldn't.

I wanted this day with my own husband and children—although that's not working out exactly as I'd hoped. Peter's mother is joining us. Two visits within a year. Now, that's got to be a record! Naturally she's in the area for some meeting. We just happen to be unlucky enough to be here, too. How ungracious of me, but that's the way I feel.

I've never had much enthusiasm for my mother-in-law. She's so unlike my husband that it's difficult to see them as mother and son. She flew in from Seattle for a business meeting and insisted on staying in the hotel room her company arranged. I got the distinct impression that visiting us is a burden. It's as though she'd like to forget she has a son and grandchildren. I sometimes find it difficult to hold my tongue with her. I have a wonderful, loving husband, but Peter owes his upbringing to a hodgepodge of daycare workers and nannies who provided him with the love and emotional support his mother was unable or unwilling to give her only child.

We invited Peter's mother to join us for church and then brunch afterward, but she declined, which didn't surprise me. Her excuse was that she didn't want to "intrude" on our time with my mother.

Peter is kind of defensive about his mother, so I said nothing, but I'm not looking forward to this afternoon. I only hope the children will behave themselves. This is probably wishful thinking on my part. Our kids are typical teenagers; the only people they care about are themselves.

* * *

"I am *not* playing the clarinet for Grandma," Zoe insisted as Julia added slices of cucumber to the salad, then placed it inside the refrigerator.

"Your father asked you to," Julia reminded her rebellious daughter.

"I hate it when he does that."

Julia understood her daughter's reluctance, but at the same time, she sided with Peter. He was proud of Zoe and wanted to impress his mother with her musical ability.

"When's Dad gonna get back?" Adam asked, slouching on the sofa, thumbing through the latest issue of *Car and Driver* magazine.

Julia read the digital readout on the microwave. "It's three-twenty. Give him another ten minutes."

"How come Grandma Murchison didn't want to sleep here?" Zoe asked, following Julia around the kitchen.

"Would you?" Adam demanded, his face hidden behind the magazine.

Zoe seemed to consider her brother's question. "Yeah, I would. If I only had a few hours to spend with my grandchildren, I'd make the most of every single one." She gave a slight shrug. "I mean, she doesn't get to see us very often."

"Grandma Murchison didn't come to see us this time, either," Adam told his sister.

"Yes, she did!"

Adam lowered the magazine. "Tell her, Mom."

"Tell me *what?*"

"I believe your grandmother flew in on a business-related matter," Julia confirmed, choosing her words carefully.

Zoe frowned. "What?"

"She's here for a finance meeting with some corporate bigwig," Adam said.

Peter's mother had seen her grandchildren maybe a dozen times in their entire lives. Adam was right; the only reason she was with them now was because her company had sent her.

"Apparently Grandma's real important," Adam continued, clearly in the know.

"That's what I hear," Julia muttered.

Zoe ran to the living-room window at the sound of the minivan pulling into the driveway. "Dad's back," she cried excitedly. Shoving her feet into an old pair of sandals, she raced out the front door.

Adam slowly set aside his magazine and stood, his shoulders hunched.

Julia removed the apron and brushed her hand down her blouse to remove any crumbs. She sighed deeply; other than a half-hour's respite when she first woke, all she'd done today was cook and clean.

Peter, ever thoughtful, had brought her a plant yesterday, but she'd been the one who'd organized two family meals to honor first her mother and now his. Everyone took for granted the effort and planning that went into each event. For brunch, she'd served a smoked salmon and asparagus frittata—admittedly wasted on her children—plus homemade rolls, muffins and fruit salad. Not to mention fresh-squeezed orange juice. Dinner was going to be a barbecue. At least Peter would do that part, Julia thought grudgingly, although she'd marinated the chicken, made the salads and prepared dessert. She sighed again, feeling tired and out-of-sorts.

"We're back," Peter announced as he escorted his mother into the house.

"Brenda, welcome," Julia said, moving toward her. "It's so good to see you."

"Hello, Julia." The other woman leaned forward and pecked Julia's cheek. But her eyes didn't leave the small mound that identified the pregnancy.

"When is the baby due again?" she asked, eyebrows raised.

"September seventh," Adam said in a loud, clear voice. He sounded as though the date had been burned in his mind like a historical day.

"Adam's shot up about a foot since you last saw him," Julia said, sliding an arm around her son's shoulders.

"Hi, Grandma," he said with little warmth.

"Zoe, say hello to your grandmother," Peter instructed.

"Hi," Zoe mumbled, clasping her hands behind her back as if to say she had no intention of playing the clarinet on command.

"Please, come in," Julia said. This was all rather awkward, with the five of them standing in the entryway.

Brenda walked into the living room and sat down, choosing the most comfortable chair for herself.

"Iced tea, Mother?" Peter asked, evidently eager to please her.

"That would be nice." She patted her brow with a lacy cotton handkerchief. "The weather in southern California is considerably warmer than it is in Seattle this time of year," she murmured.

Peter hurried toward the kitchen. As soon as he'd left the room, Brenda turned to Julia.

"So, the new baby is due in September?"

Julia nodded and sat down, too. It was the first time since early morning that she'd had an opportunity to relax.

"Do you think a third child is wise at this stage of your life?" Brenda asked, her question as blunt as it was unwelcome.

"I beg your pardon?" What she *wanted* to do was scream"That's none of your business!" Brenda had no right whatsoever to comment on their personal lives and decisions. This was a woman who barely knew her grandkids' names, Julia thought angrily.

"The baby is a surprise," she managed to say calmly.

"This is a three-bedroom house, isn't it?" Brenda asked, looking around critically.

"Mom and Dad want us to share our rooms with the baby," Adam informed her. He ignored the furious glance Julia threw him.

"You can't do that to Adam and Zoe," Brenda said.

"For the first few months, the baby will be in our room," Julia told her.

"It'll ruin your marriage."

"Peter, I'd like a glass of tea, too," Julia said, in an effort to turn the conversation from the volatile subject of her pregnancy.

"Coming right up," he called back.

Julia wanted to wring her hands in despair when she realized that all her request had done was delay Peter's return.

"Zoe," Julia said, smiling grimly at her daughter. "Go get your clarinet."

The girl's eyes widened. "Mother, I *told* you I didn't want to play for Grandma."

"Please, Zoe," she whispered, desperately needing an ally.

The thirteen-year-old stamped out of the room, muttering as she went. Julia's feelings vacillated from embarrassment at her daughter's bad manners to relief at the coming distraction.

"Here we are," Peter said, returning with a tray of iced tea, clearly oblivious to the tension in the room. He served his mother first, then Julia, and took the third glass himself. The three of them sat in a small circle, with Adam standing next to his father.

"I thought we'd barbecue later, when it cools down a little," Julia said in an effort to fill the silence.

No one had anything to add to that.

"Do you like my purse?" his mother asked, holding up the brief-case-style leather bag. "I bought it specially for this trip."

"It's lovely," Julia said. *And obviously expensive...*

"It's my Mother's Day gift to myself." She turned to Peter. "Thank you, dear, for the flowers in my room."

Julia decided she should learn from her mother-in-law. Brenda wasn't waiting for her son or anyone else to go out and buy her what she truly wanted. Instead, she'd purchased it herself.

Julia had received a potted azalea from her husband. The kids had given her cards and gone in on a small basket of scented soap. She loved the significance of those gifts—but what she really longed for was a silk nightgown in a pale shade of ecru with a matching robe. The gown was on display at the local Nordstrom's, and Julia had been back to look at it three times. She wanted something beautiful, something to remind her that she was attractive and desirable even at five months pregnant. Unfortunately, the price tag was more than her shop pulled in during an entire day.

"Do I *have* to play?" Zoe bemoaned her sorry fate as she clumped back into the room, clarinet in hand.

"I'm sure Grandma would be happy to hear you perform," Peter told his daughter with a look that defied her to suggest otherwise.

"Do you know anything by Bob Dylan?" Brenda asked. "Maybe one of the early protest songs?"

Zoe glanced at her mother for the answer. Julia shook her head.

"Sorry, no."

"You choose then," Brenda said, with a resigned expression as if she had about as much interest in listening as Zoe did in playing.

The next ten minutes were taken up with Zoe's all-too-short performance.

"I'll have my driver's license this summer," Adam said as soon as his sister had finished playing and hurried back to her room.

Julia wished there was somewhere she could hide.

"Driving?" Brenda seemed astonished.

"I'll be sixteen next month," Adam boasted.

"And you're pregnant," Brenda said, turning to Julia.

Julia looked away.

"I certainly hope you can afford this child."

"Mother..." Peter murmured.

"Think about it," her mother-in-law pressed. "You're just making ends meet as it is. Julia's business is barely off the ground. What are you going to do with the baby while you're at work? Have either of you given that any thought?"

"My mother's retiring this year," Julia began.

"You expect your mother to step in and provide day care?" Brenda asked sharply. "That's completely unfair of you."

"My mom—"

"Mother," Peter said, more loudly this time.

"Far be it from *you* to offer any help," Julia cried, feeling trapped.

"Do you expect *me* to pay for your mistakes?"

Zoe came back to the living room, obviously drawn by the shouting. She and Adam stared wide-eyed, listening to the heated exchange between their mother and grandmother. Peter was trying to calm them down, without success.

Julia stood abruptly and glared at her mother-in-law, husband and children. "This might come as a shock to you all, but my baby is not a mistake."

"You mean to say you got pregnant on purpose?" Brenda demanded.

Julia stiffened. "No...no more than you did." She was instantly ashamed of her outburst. Brenda had chosen never to marry and had raised Peter entirely on her own. "My child is a surprise, but he or she is no mistake." Then, because the entire episode had distressed her so much, she left the room.

Peter followed her into the bedroom a moment later. "Honey..."

"All I want is a few minutes alone. I'm sorry if I upset your mother."

"No. I'm sorry *you're* upset." He sighed, and slowly exhaled. "Things got out of hand before I realized what was happening. I'm sorry, sweetheart." He sat on the edge of the bed. "What would you like me to do now?"

"I...don't know. Give me a while to rest and let our tempers cool, and I'll come back and apologize."

Peter rubbed the length of her arm. "Take as long as you need. And Julia?"

She glanced up at him, raising her head from the pillow.

"Don't apologize."

Exhausted and emotionally drained, Julia decided to rest her eyes and immediately fell asleep, waking two hours later. When she rejoined the others, it was as if nothing had happened. She found her mother-in-law with Adam and Zoe, arranging dinner dishes on the patio table. Brenda had rolled up her sleeves and donned one of Julia's favorite aprons.

"We were about to wake you," she said, setting a couple of salad bowls in the center of the table. "The potatoes are roasting in the oven. I hope that's okay."

"Thank you," Julia said faintly.

"You're up," Peter said, carrying a platter of barbecued chicken toward them.

"Just in time, too." She kissed his cheek, letting him know she felt much better. Because she'd been so exhausted, she'd allowed his mother's attitude to get the best of her, something she genuinely regretted.

"We wouldn't have eaten without you, Mom," Zoe assured her, slipping an arm around Julia's thickening waist. It was the first time in weeks that her daughter had made such a loving gesture. Julia felt tears gathering behind her eyelids; she blinked rapidly, determined not to let them fall. With pregnancy she'd become so emotional.

While Peter turned off the barbecue, the kids went to the kitchen to bring out the potatoes and collect drinks.

Julia approached her mother-in-law. "I'm sorry," she said in a low voice.

Brenda hesitated, then nodded and without looking at Julia, whispered, "Me, too. I have a bad habit of saying things I shouldn't—poking my nose in. You and Peter are wonderful parents. Everything I never was." Her mother-in-law busily rearranged serving dishes for a moment. "I realize this pregnancy is unplanned, but you're right, the baby's no mistake." She glanced toward Peter and her eyes softened. "I was never meant to be a mother, and when I discovered I was pregnant with Peter, I had doubts about my ability to raise a child. Over the years, I made my fair share of mistakes, but I've always loved my son and wouldn't exchange the experience of motherhood for anything in the world. You and Peter will be just fine." Having said that, Brenda did something completely and totally out of character.

She hugged Julia.

> "Make no judgments where you have no compassion."
> —Anne McCaffrey

27

CHAPTER

LIZ KENYON

May 17th

Amy's belated Mother's Day gift arrived in the mail this afternoon. It was an eight-by-ten portrait of Andrew and Annie. My goodness, how my grandbabies have grown. I had to work hard not to break down and weep. I miss them all so desperately.

The gift certificate Brian sent me is on the kitchen counter. I haven't gotten down to Barnes and Noble to use it yet. At first I was disappointed that he'd mail me a generic present instead of coming up to spend the day with me. On second thought, it seemed a perfectly wonderful gift. Thoughtful, too. It's my son's way of saying he approves of me volunteering at the juvenile detention center. I think I may start reading the C. S. Lewis books next—once the last Harry Potter is finished. I'll have to see if that's okay with Ruth, although I'm sure it will be. I'll get a copy with the gift certificate—which is fitting because the Lewis stories were

Brian's absolute favorite childhood reading. Okay, that settles it. I'll use my gift certificate to buy *The Lion, the Witch and the Wardrobe,* plus a book on knitting and, if there's any money left, the new Barbara Kingsolver. A satisfactory decision, if I do say so.

The kids called me Sunday morning, but if not for Sean, I would've spent Mother's Day alone. I've discovered something about him. All his provocative remarks about women are intended to get a rise out of me. It used to work, but lately I've been letting the ridiculous things he says just pass me by and that flusters him so much he doesn't know how to react.

Well, I'm on to his game. From now on I'll just pretend not to hear him. Maybe I should occasionally mutter a disparaging remark about men in the medical profession, just to rattle his cage, and see how he likes it.

He still makes cursory efforts to talk me into bed, but I'm not easily persuaded. He'd enjoy a weekend fling, or so he's let me know. The problem is, I'm confused. He can have his pick of women and he seems to want me.

We've gone out to dinner twice in the last week, and I cooked him a meal Sunday night. Afterward, I broke out the yarn and knitting needles and attempted to teach him to knit, which was hilarious because Tinkerbell thought the yarn was for her. I can't remember a time I've laughed more. I know why he chose not to be a surgeon! All his talk about agile fingers was simply that—talk. Sean was all thumbs. Somehow in the process of casting on stitches, he got the yarn completely twisted around his fingers. After fifteen minutes he gave up entirely and suggested we take in a movie. We saw the latest Mel Gibson film and shared a bag of popcorn. After the popcorn was gone, we held hands for the rest of the show.

He asked me not to tell anyone that all we've done is hold hands (and kissed once or twice—let's not forget that). But if word got out that we've spent all this time together and none of it in bed, it'd destroy his reputation. I had to roll my eyes but agreed to keep quiet.

I'm actually beginning to wonder if there's any truth to the rumors about him and all these women he supposedly dates.

* * *

The doorbell chimed and Liz set aside her journal. A check of the peephole revealed Sean standing on the other side. Liz was dismayed by the way her heart reacted at the sight of him. He'd come to mean so much to her, and that kind of feeling left you vulnerable. In a split second, she shook off her sense of fear. *Seize the moment*, she told herself.

"Surprised to see me?" he asked as she opened the door. When she merely smiled, he stepped into the house and leaned forward, kissing her briefly on the mouth, as though this was an accepted practice between them.

He had kissed her before, and both times the kisses had been full and passionate. This casual approach was welcome. But when he started to pull away, Liz stopped him, splayed her fingers through his hair and stepped closer to kiss him herself.

When she lifted her head, she found him staring down at her with an oddly puzzled look. Obviously he didn't know what to make of this sudden change in attitude.

"You must be really glad to see me," he whispered.

"I am," she assured him. He followed her into the kitchen. "Have you eaten?"

"I had something at the hospital earlier. Have you?"

"A while ago." It was after eight.

"Am I interrupting anything?"

"Nothing that can't be put off until later. What can I do for you?"

"Now that was a leading question if I ever heard one."

"Okay, bad choice of words."

"Have you got an hour or two?" he asked with a grin.

"Of course."

"Grab a sweater then."

Curious, she did as he asked, returning from her bedroom with a light sweater and her purse. He held out his hand and she took it.

"Tell me where we're going," she said as he led her outside to his Lexus and opened the passenger door.

"You'll find out in a few minutes."

A few minutes turned into twenty. He headed toward the freeway on-ramp, drove for several miles, then exited, ending up in a residential neighborhood that was unfamiliar to Liz.

She noticed that the houses were middle-class, with well-maintained yards. Sean eased to a stop in front of a corner house. Nothing distinguished it from any of the others.

"You're taking me to meet friends?" she asked. Then why didn't he say so?

"My very best friends," he said, climbing out of the car.

Liz looked around. "Do you mind telling me where we are?"

"Thirty-fifth and Jackson," he returned without a pause.

"All right, *why* are we here?"

"Ah," he said grinning broadly. "Now you're asking the right questions. My dear Liz, I'm about to show you what I do to release the tension in my life." He gestured to the house. "My alternative to knitting."

"You didn't mention anything about this earlier."

He grinned again. "I had my reasons."

"Does your tension relief have anything to do with Rolfing?" she asked, wondering if this place belonged to some kind of massage therapist.

"Rolfing," he echoed and laughed.

"Never mind."

He led her up the sidewalk and gently tapped on the door.

Liz was certain no one could possibly hear his knock. Just when she was prepared to suggest there was no one home, the door opened. A large African-American woman stood there, wearing a stern look. As soon as she saw Sean, she broke into a wide smile, her face brightening with pleasure.

"Dr. Sean, aren't you a sight for sore eyes! Come in, come in."

Sean pressed his hand to the small of Liz's back and directed her into the large foyer. And Liz saw the babies. What would have been the living room was set up with six cribs and an equal number of rocking chairs. Each of the cribs held an infant, and most of them were crying.

"Who'd you bring with you?" the woman asked, eyeing Liz curiously.

"Clarissa, this is my friend Liz Kenyon. Liz, Clarissa Howard."

"Hey." The woman planted her fists on her ample hips. "I thought you said I was the only woman for you."

"Looks like you're going to have to share me," Sean joked.

Clarissa laughed boisterously, then faced Liz, her smile benevolent. "Any friend of Dr. Sean's is a friend of mine. Welcome to Little Lambs."

"These are all crack or heroin babies," he said. "Clarissa and her staff are here to love them through the worst of the withdrawals."

"Dr. Sean is our favorite physician," Clarissa told Liz, her gaze adoring. "The babies love him, too, isn't that right?"

Sean didn't answer. Instead he walked over to the farthest crib. "How's little Donovan doing tonight?"

"Not well, not well at all."

"Rough day?"

Clarissa nodded.

With a tenderness Liz had rarely seen in a man, Sean reached into the crib and lifted the emaciated infant and held him gently. "Only three weeks old," Sean whispered as he settled into the closest rocking chair. "Poor little tyke came into this world facing one hell of an uphill climb."

"Little Faye could do with being rocked," Clarissa said boldly, staring at Liz. "She's over there."

Liz knew an order when she heard one. Smiling, she found the crib marked with Faye's name. She gathered the baby in her arms and sat in a rocker. The baby gazed up at her, eyes wet with tears, lower lip quivering.

"Poor sweetheart," Liz whispered, gently brushing the curls from the baby's brow.

"Like Donovan, our Faye has a struggle ahead of her," Sean said.

Liz had seen a number of reports on crack and drug babies over the years. Women addicted to any illegal substance tended to neglect everything else in their lives. Their health in general was poor. Statistics showed that they ate junk food and skipped meals and had poor sleeping habits. They abused themselves in a multitude of ways. Studies had indicated that a large percentage of pregnant drug-users also smoked cigarettes and drank alcohol throughout the pregnancy. Consequently, the babies were born with low birth weights and often prematurely. Some had Fetal Alcohol Syndrome. Some, as Sean had said, suffered because they'd been born to drug-addicted mothers.

Liz had heard about Little Lambs when it was in the setup stages, but Willow Grove Memorial hadn't been part of the project. She'd never heard anything about Sean's involvement.

Clarissa took a third child and settled herself between Sean and Liz, humming quietly as she rocked, the baby cuddled in her loving arms.

Thirty minutes later, the room was quiet. Liz glanced over and realized that Sean's eyes were closed.

Clarissa's gaze followed hers. "He falls asleep nearly every time."

"Does he come often?" Liz asked.

"Quite a bit, but it's been a week or so since his last visit."

The man was full of surprises.

"Dr. Sean's crazy about babies," Clarissa added. "I don't understand why he didn't have a houseful of his own."

Other than that one mention of his ex-wife and daughter, Liz knew almost nothing about Sean's life outside of medicine. Although he hadn't said so, Liz was under the impression that he hadn't told many people about his family.

"Do you love him?" Clarissa shocked her by asking next.

The question caught Liz unawares, and she wasn't sure how to answer. "I don't know."

"Someone should. He needs a woman, and you're the first one he's ever brought here."

That lifted Liz's spirits. "Have you known him long?"

Clarissa nodded. "He helped create Little Lambs and recommended me for the job. Far as I'm concerned, there's no better man than Dr. Sean. If he wanted me to walk over red-hot coals, I'd do it for him, without asking why."

If Sean was aware of this conversation, he'd be gloating, Liz thought. He must love hearing Clarissa sing his praises. She leaned forward, wondering if she could detect a sassy grin on his face.

"He's out," Clarissa assured her. "It's amazing how rocking the babies calms *him* down."

Liz had to agree that was quite a switch. "He told me this is what he does to unwind."

Clarissa's chair made creaking sounds as she continued rocking, still humming softly.

"I tried to teach him to knit." Which, Liz had to admit, seemed a bit ridiculous now.

"Dr. Sean?" The other woman pinched her lips. "He doesn't need that; you don't either. Both of you just come see me and my babies."

"All right," Liz agreed.

A full hour passed before Sean woke. He yawned, looked in Liz's direction and asked, "You ready to go?"

"Whenever you are."

He replaced a sleeping Donovan in the crib, and within a few minutes they were preparing to leave.

Clarissa walked them to the door.

"It was a pleasure meeting you and your babies," Liz said.

The other woman nodded, then gripped Liz's elbow. "You find out."

"Find out?" Liz repeated.

"What we talked about earlier."

"Oh." Liz was sure her red face gave her away. She didn't dare look at Sean, certain he'd know they'd been discussing him. *Do you love him?* Clarissa had asked, and Liz figured she expected the answer to be *yes.* Clarissa was openly encouraging Liz to delve deeper into her feelings for Sean.

"What was that all about?" Sean asked as they strolled toward his car.

"Nothing important," she said dismissively.

Not until they were on the street, driving back to her house, did she chance a look in his direction. From what Clarissa had said, she was the first woman he'd ever brought to Little Lambs.

What she didn't understand was why. What did she actually mean to him? What did he *really* want from her?

"You're frowning," he said. They'd stopped at a traffic light before heading onto the ramp that led to the freeway. He reached over and squeezed her hand, his fingers lingering in hers.

"Just thinking." Liz smiled so he'd know she wasn't upset, only perplexed by the complicated man she was beginning to know.

"Any thoughts you want to share with me?"

"One," she said, realizing even as she spoke that she was taking a risk. "I think there might be some hope for this relationship, after all."

Sean gave no outward response for a moment. Then he said, "That's what I've been trying to tell you. I don't know why you women don't listen to men more often."

Liz groaned and shook her head, but not before she saw him trying to suppress a laugh. She was smiling, too.

> "Life is the first gift, love is the second, and understanding the third."
>
> —Marge Piercy

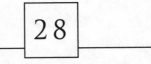

CHAPTER

KAREN CURTIS

"Your father and I would like you to join us for lunch next Saturday," Catherine Curtis informed Karen in her most prim voice. She used the tone guaranteed to set Karen's teeth on edge every time.

Pressing the telephone receiver hard against her ear, Karen felt as if she'd received a summons to appear in court instead of an invitation from her mother. Whatever Catherine wanted was important enough to add the influence of her father's name.

Karen knew it wasn't her company they sought—or at least her mother didn't. Something was up, and she suspected she wasn't going to like it.

"You'll come?" her mother said.

"Don't go to any trouble, though," Karen warned. Lunch for her generally consisted of a sandwich on the run or something she could pick up at a drive-through window.

For Catherine Curtis, on the other hand, every meal was an occasion. Karen didn't know anyone outside her parents' circle of friends who went to such effort for lunch. It was just *lunch,* for heaven's sake. Her mother had built her entire social life around a bridge club that met every Friday at one. The women were constantly in competition, trying to outdo each other with elaborate luncheon menus and fancy centerpieces.

"I'll see you on Saturday then."

"Any reason you and Dad want to talk to me?" Karen asked. Better to get a heads-up now than be blindsided later.

"Can't your father and I invite you to the house without a reason?" her mother asked with a light, tinkling laugh—a laugh that was so forced, Karen had to cringe.

"You always have a reason, Mother," she said grimly.

Catherine gave a beleaguered sigh but no other response.

"I was just there for Mother's Day." Being in close proximity to her mother twice within the same month was above and beyond the call of duty.

"You've already agreed to come," Catherine reminded her.

"Yes, and I will, but I want to know why."

"Because I asked it of you. Let's not get into this now. I'll look forward to seeing you at noon on Saturday."

"Yes, Mother," Karen muttered, banging down the telephone receiver. She'd allowed herself to be manipulated again. Would she never learn?

Saturday arrived far too soon, long before Karen was ready. She chose a dress her mother had bought her when Karen was still in high school. Sensible, demure—and a style completely wrong for her. Karen didn't know why she still held on to it.

By the time she arrived, her stomach was swarming with nerves. She knew from experience that her mother was likely to serve a five-course meal, and Karen didn't have the appetite to enjoy even one bite.

The first thing she noticed when she pulled into the circular driveway in front of her parents' home was that Victoria's car wasn't there. Always before, her sister had been included in these lunches. Not today, which led to immediate speculation that this conversation had something to do with her sister.

Before she could change her mind, Karen parked her ten-year-old Ford Tempo.

The front door opened and her mother stood in the entrance. Karen's engine was still hacking and coughing, although the ignition had been turned off. She was sorry her mother was there to hear it. Catherine had never approved of Karen's car, but to Karen it represented independence and integrity, since she'd purchased and paid for it herself.

She walked toward the door as the old Ford coughed one last time, as if to remind her how badly it needed servicing.

"Could you park your...vehicle over by the garage?" her mother called.

And out of the neighbors' sight, Karen added mentally. "Sorry, Mom, but I'm having trouble with the transmission. It'd be better if I left it someplace where I won't need to reverse."

Her mother started to speak, then seemed to change her mind, and turned away.

Karen followed her into the house. This wasn't the home she'd grown up in and she'd never felt as though she belonged here. Her father's chain of produce warehouses had prospered dramatically over the past ten years, and her parents were living off the fruit of his labors. She smiled at the pun.

Status had always been important to her mother, and the big home, fancy cars and children she could brag about to her friends were included in her requirements.

They were apparently having lunch in the kitchen. The kitchen, though, was the size of Karen's entire apartment. It was newly renovated with oak cabinets, a slate floor and lovely multi-paned windows—a nice traditional look, except that Catherine had added a few too many bits of "country" kitsch. The round oak table held a huge sunflower centerpiece, with sunflower-patterned place mats. Clearly a theme—no doubt based on a magazine article about decorating for summer. Karen glanced around expecting to find her father hiding behind the sunflower display. "Where's Dad?"

"He sends his apologies, but he was called into the office."

"On a Saturday?"

Her mother's sigh said it all. "I wasn't pleased," she said sternly. "You asked that I not go to any trouble, so I thought we'd have lunch in here."

"This is perfect." Karen clasped her hands to conceal any sign of nervousness. She'd hoped her father would be here. If Victoria wasn't around, her father could have served as a buffer.

Catherine opened the refrigerator and removed a sesame chicken and pasta salad. Bread, steaming from the oven, was already out and cooling.

"This is your favorite salad, isn't it?" Catherine asked.

Actually it was Victoria's, but now didn't seem the time to point that out.

"My all-time favorite," she lied. "How thoughtful of you to make it for me."

"Well, to be honest, I had Doris put it together."

Doris was the housekeeper who'd been with the family for a number of years.

"Oh." So much for thoughtfulness.

"You know I play bridge with the girls on Friday." Her mother's tone was defensive. "This salad needs to be made twenty-four hours in advance."

"I wasn't upset," Karen said, wishing they could have a normal conversation, one in which they weren't constantly offending each other.

"Shall we sit down?" Catherine said.

"Sure." Karen slid into her chair and unfolded her linen napkin. Catherine handed her the chicken salad; the warm bread followed.

Karen took her first bite, but it seemed to get stuck in the back of her throat. She knew it would be impossible to down another forkful until she learned what this was all about. "Where's Victoria?" she asked outright. She hadn't talked to her sister in some time and feared there'd been a repeat of the last incident. Karen felt her anger rise at the mere thought of that twit hitting her sister. Maybe she should change *twit* to *brute,* she mused darkly.

"Victoria?" her mother echoed. "Uh, what do you mean?"

"She's always here when we have our lunches."

Her mother paused for a moment. "I believe she's shopping—buying summer clothes for Bryce this afternoon."

"Oh." Karen never had a problem being articulate except when she was with her mother.

Catherine stabbed a shredded piece of chicken with her fork, eyes downcast.

Finally Karen couldn't stand it any longer. "Just tell me!"

Her mother's eyes widened. "Tell you what, dear?"

"Why you invited me here."

Her mother sighed. To Karen's surprise, she capitulated without any more of that conversational thrust and parry. "I'm concerned about Victoria," she said in a flat voice.

She knew. Thank God! Somehow, her mother had learned that Roger was beating Victoria. Relief swept through Karen. Surely her mother would step in now and help in ways that Karen couldn't.

"I'm worried about her, too," Karen blurted out, nearly weak with gratitude. "We need to do something, Mom."

"Yes, well..."

"Has she opened up to you? She called me a few months ago, absolutely desperate. I was deathly afraid of what Roger might do."

Her mother frowned. "Victoria phoned you?"

"I'm sure she would've called you and Dad, but she didn't want to alarm you."

"Oh, dear."

"How'd you find out? Did you see the bruises? She's gotten so good at hiding them, but it's more than the physical abuse, it's the horrible things Roger says to her. The worst part is that she believes them."

Her mother went pale and her hand crept to her throat.

Karen hesitated. "Are you all right?"

"I..."

A sick feeling came over her, and she realized she'd made a serious mistake in assuming that Victoria had confided in her parents. "You didn't know, did you?"

Ever proper, Catherine Curtis squared her shoulders. "I...don't know what to think. I have a hard time believing Roger is the kind of man who'd do the things you're suggesting."

Horrified, Karen vaulted to her feet. Tears of anger and outrage stung her eyes. "You don't believe me? You think I'd make something like this up?"

"Sit down," her mother ordered, voice shaking.

"Do you think I'd fabricate this story out of some perverse jealousy?"

Her mother's hand trembled and when she spoke it was as if she'd forgotten Karen was in the room. "I've known for some weeks that things weren't...right between Victoria and Roger, but I didn't want to interfere." She shook her head. "I thought Victoria seemed depressed—that's what worried me. That's what I'd hoped to discuss with you."

Karen sank into her chair. "I saw what he did the last time. Well, the time she called me... Who knows what's happened since?"

"Roger hit her?"

Karen nodded.

"You say Victoria told you," her mother said, giving up all pretense of eating. Her hand continued to shake as she reached for her iced tea.

"Yes..."

"Did she tell you why she wasn't comfortable talking to me?"

"No," Karen answered. "I'm sure she just didn't want to upset you," she said again.

"Instead, she left that task to you."

"No...no, Mom, Victoria would never do that. I upset you all on my own. I mean, oh hell—you know what I mean!"

"Do I?"

The harder Karen tried, the worse it became. "Mom, listen to me, please. This is too important. We can't get all twisted up in our own egos. We have to help Victoria."

Catherine closed her eyes. "I agree. Tell me what you know."

Karen wasn't sure where to start. She felt tempted to mention that dreadful Thanksgiving dinner years earlier when Victoria had bolted from the table, but she didn't.

"Roger's a twit," she said instead. "And a brute."

"Is he...abusing Bryce?"

"No...not to my knowledge."

"You're absolutely certain about Victoria? Oh, of course you are. It's just that this is far worse than I imagined. Dear God, why couldn't she tell me?"

"I'm sure Victoria wanted to, but she doesn't know how."

Catherine's expression was stricken. "It's such a shock."

"I know it's hard to believe, Mom—it was for me, too. But I swear to you, it's the truth. I've seen the evidence."

Her mother looked away, as though just hearing the words brought her pain. "Why doesn't Victoria come to your father and me—surely she knows we'd do anything to help..." She let the rest fade.

"You said you were worried about her? That she seemed depressed?"

Caught up in her thoughts, her mother didn't immediately answer. "She's been so distant lately," Catherine finally said. "We were always close, Victoria and I, but lately she's made excuses to stay away. I felt something was wrong. I'd hoped you might know what was going on, and as it turns out you do."

Karen had no idea what to say next, what to suggest. She sipped at her iced tea while she waited for inspiration.

"I don't understand why Victoria didn't come to me," her mother wailed. "I really don't." Karen had never seen her lose control to this extent. She realized Catherine was deeply hurt by Victoria's silence and probably felt a large measure of inadequacy.

"Listen, Mom, she's embarrassed and ashamed. Everyone assumes Victoria has the perfect marriage and she didn't want to disillusion any of us."

"But why would she allow this kind of treatment to continue?"

"Mom, the whys don't matter. We can sort all that out later. Right now, we both need to concentrate on how to help Victoria. She's at the point where she can't do it for herself."

Her mother stared down at her lunch plate. "She should have told me," she mumbled again. "She—"

"Yes Mom," Karen said impatiently. "But she couldn't."

"What are we going to do?"

"I don't know. Support and love her, first of all."

"Of course, that's understood."

"I wanted her to leave the jerk, but Victoria wouldn't hear of it. Nor will she involve the police. I talked until I was blue in the face and it didn't do one bit of good. She's afraid of hurting his career."

"If the law firm finds out about it, Roger could very likely lose his position," her mother said.

"That isn't Victoria's fault. He's the one hitting her."

"Oh, I agree. All I'm saying is that I can understand Victoria's hesitation. If Roger loses his job, the entire family will suffer. Plus, there's the humiliation of family and friends discovering she's married to a wife-beater."

"Of course," Karen muttered. "That's why she's kept it to herself."

"We must consider our options very carefully," her mother said. "Karen, let's give this some thought." She'd become the formidable matron once again, the woman whose strength of will wasn't easily defeated. Despite her flaws and pretensions, Catherine Curtis loved her daughters—*both* of them. Karen knew the truth of that, had in a sense always known it, but now she was overwhelmed by the insight. She suddenly understood that she was her mother's equal, in strength and determination, far more than Victoria.

She relaxed in her chair for the first time since she'd arrived. The burden of Victoria's life was lifted from her shoulders; she and her mother were allies, united in the quest to help her sister. She felt a hundred times better.

She shoved her plate and the sunflower centerpiece aside and leaned her elbows on the table. "Okay, Mom, let's get to work."

"Learn the wisdom of compromise, for it is better to bend a little than to break."

—Jane Wells

CHAPTER | 29 |

CLARE CRAIG

The house was in chaos and that wasn't going to change any time soon. Mick was home for the summer. He'd arrived late the night before, his car loaded down with a year's accumulation of dorm room necessities.

Yawning, Clare ambled down the hallway to the kitchen, maneuvering around his half-size refrigerator with a microwave balanced on top. She paused to look inside the laundry room and gasped.

Rather than deal with what appeared to be an entire semester's worth of wash, she closed the door and continued into the kitchen. To her surprise the coffee was already made.

"Morning," Mick greeted her from the family room. All that was visible was his arm, which lay across the back of the sofa, and his head. His hair went in all directions and he was badly in need of a shave.

"How long have you been up?" she asked, reaching for a mug. Mick merely shrugged.

"You haven't been to bed yet, have you?" Her son, like his father, was a night owl.

"I was too keyed up from the drive," Mick confessed. "I sat down in front of the television and then it was too much effort to move."

"Did you sleep at all?"

"Some," he muttered, but from the look of him, Clare doubted it.

She'd never understood why Mick always insisted on unloading the car the minute he arrived home. The boys were still hauling in one load after another when she'd gone to bed. She was relieved that Mick and Alex were back on speaking terms.

Her own relationship with Mick had also been strained, and Clare hoped that everything would resolve itself now that he was home. She hoped he'd make his peace with his father too. Her oldest son's anger toward Michael hadn't wavered. He refused to have anything to do with him, even though Alex and Clare saw Michael regularly.

"Do you feel like talking?" Clare carried her coffee into the other room and sat in the recliner across from Mick.

He stiffened. "Not if it's about Dad."

"All right." Her son was more intuitive than she'd realized.

"I'm glad school's out," he said. Mick was obviously searching for a topic of conversation.

"I'm not going to be around as much this summer," Clare told him. To her relief, her taking over at the dealership had gone relatively well. Because she already knew the staff, the transition had been quick and smooth. Nevertheless, she worked far more than the normal forty hours a week.

"Alex told me you don't get home until eight o'clock," Mick said, frowning.

"Just some nights."

"I don't understand it. Why are you helping Dad? How *can* you, after what he did to you?"

"What he did to *us*," she corrected. That was what Mick was really saying. The pain their sons had endured was as great as her own.

"I can't forgive him."

"I'm not sure I've completely forgiven him, either," she said. Even now, Clare found it difficult to look past the agony Michael had brought into their lives.

"But you're helping him."

"I know."

"Why?" Mick cried. "Is it because of the cancer?"

It deeply pained her that neither boy was aware of the full truth regarding Michael's illness. She'd promised not to tell them Michael was dying, and, in fact, had only a few months to live; it was a promise she regretted now.

"What else could I do?" she asked, her voice low. "Michael came to me. The dealership was floundering, and someone needed to step in. Otherwise the business might fold entirely."

"Are you hoping Dad will come back?" Mick asked angrily.

Clare had given some thought to that question herself. A part of her *wanted* him to want her back, to plead with her to forgive him. The scenario had played in her mind a thousand times before and after the divorce, and in each version she'd rejected him. She didn't know what she would've done if Michael had actually attempted to reconcile.

"Are you, Mom?" Mick pressed.

She shook her head. "He doesn't want me anymore." That was the truth, painful though it was to admit.

Mick's face hardened. "Or Alex and me."

"That's not true," she insisted. "Your father loves you both."

Mick snorted. "Sure he does."

Clare wanted to argue, but stopped herself, hardly able to believe she'd turned into Michael's champion. As far as his father was concerned, Mick had already made up his mind.

"I'm glad Miranda left him," he added.

Clare hated the edge she heard in his voice and realized it was an echo of the anger she'd carried herself for all those months.

"I saw her, you know."

Clare glanced at him. "When?"

"Last Christmas, while I was home. She was with some guy."

"Someone her own age?"

Mick nodded. "She had her arm around his and was looking up at him with these big adoring eyes. I thought, you know, this was what Dad deserved. He cheated on you and now everything had come full circle and she was cheating on him."

"Poor Miranda."

"Poor Miranda?" Mick sounded incredulous. "You've got to be joking."

Clare avoided meeting his gaze. "It's taken a long time, but I finally understand what happened. Miranda lost her father without a minute's warning. One day he was alive, and the next day he was dead. That shook her whole world."

"And there was Dad, so helpful, taking care of everything," Mick said sarcastically.

Clare nodded, her throat tightening. "The poor girl got confused. In her pain and grief, she turned to Michael, somehow transferring the love she had for her dad to him. She was looking for another father figure more than she was a lover. In a way, I can understand that."

"Well, I can't." Mick's voice was stubborn, uncompromising.

"Michael offered her strength and comfort." Clare didn't condone the grief their actions had caused, but she wanted Mick to be a little more compassionate.

"That might excuse Miranda, but what about Dad?"

"I...I don't know. Perhaps there was something lacking in me." She'd gone over her own role in this fiasco again and again. "Miranda needed him and I...I didn't."

"All that tells me is you're strong and Dad's weak." Mick bolted off the sofa and stood in the middle of the family room, fists clenched at his sides. "We weren't going to talk about Dad, remember?"

"Right," she said, forcing a smile. She knew what her son was saying. It had been this way for more than two years now. Everything—every conversation, every argument, every thought—always went back to Michael.

"When I was in high school," Mick said, "Dad was around all the time and it was no big deal."

Even when he'd declared he *didn't* want to discuss Michael, Mick was the one bringing him into the conversation.

"Now Dad's gone, and I feel his absence far more than I ever did his presence."

How articulate Mick was. She stared at him with a renewed sense of love and appreciation.

"I hope you'll go see him," she said.

Mick's response was immediate. "No way!"

"Oh, Mick, don't turn your back on him out of any sense of loyalty to me. Your father needs you."

Her son shook his head vehemently, his face unyielding. "What about all those times I needed him and he was playing daddy with Miranda? Don't push the issue, Mom."

The pain vibrated from him, and Clare could see that Michael had a lot of work ahead of him if he hoped to heal the broken relationship with his oldest son.

"What's everyone doing up?" Alex asked, wandering into the family room in his swimming shorts. He yawned and scratched his head.

"Mick never went to bed," Clare told him.

"Hey, why not?"

"I was watching reruns of *The Brady Bunch.*"

"The Brady Bunch?" Alex repeated. "Why would you do that when there's all those stations? What about VH-1?"

Mick shrugged. "I don't know. I was in a groove."

Strangely, Clare understood. Her son wasn't interested in the entertainment value of a decades-old situation comedy. What he saw was a happy blended family. With the Bradys, problems all seemed trivial and the parents loved each other and everyone worked out their differences. This was the fantasy family, whose lives were far removed from his own.

* * *

June 10th

Michael phoned the dealership six times from the hospital this afternoon. The chemo's especially rough on him this go-round, and the doctors felt it was best if he stayed there for the week.

I was busy each and every time he phoned. I waited until I had a free minute before I called him back. He asked me to take over for him, but I've discovered that he wants to keep close tabs on everything I do. I know I was being unfair and unreasonable, but I let Michael have it.

I should apologize for that outburst. It must have been very hard for him to step down and let me assume the leadership. We're different people and our work methods don't necessarily agree. Nor do we handle staff in the same way.

I don't think Michael has quite realized what a financial mess the business was in. He'd obviously been putting work off for months, letting orders slide. I'm trying to get things in shape, but he has opinions on everything I do. Even from his hospital bed, Michael can't leave it alone. More than once I've been tempted to tell him exactly what he can do with this job.

I haven't, and I won't. I understand how difficult it was to turn the management over to me. He says he asked me to do this for the boys, and I know that's true. The dealership is their inheritance, but unfortunately they're not interested. Neither of them is willing to work here, even for the summer. Alex's job at Softline keeps him busy and Mick got a job as a lifeguard, which he loves. He's tanned and gorgeous and the girls are flocking to the house. Kellie is still dating Alex, but she's got her eye on Mick. A mother knows these things.

On a brighter note, I had an unexpected but welcome surprise. Leslie Carter phoned me from Hawaii. We chatted for nearly thirty minutes. He talked about the sailing trip and what he learned about himself and his limits. I found it really interesting; he's a perceptive man. I told him about working at the dealership. We only met that one time, but he's stayed in my mind and apparently I've stayed in his.

Both boys were home when Leslie phoned and were full of curiosity. It was all a little embarrassing. Mick had a lot of questions, and for a while there, I felt like I was being interrogated. Really, there's nothing to tell. Leslie is a wonderful man and I'm glad I met him. I don't have any idea if I'll be seeing him again.

I hope I do, though. I really would like to know him better.

"The dedicated life is the life worth living. You must give with your whole heart."

—Annie Dillard

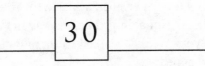

CHAPTER

THURSDAY MORNING BREAKFAST CLUB

Liz, by nature, was prompt and thus the first to arrive at Mocha Moments. She ordered her croissant and coffee, and secured the table by the window so she could watch for her friends.

These few quiet minutes helped her compose her thoughts. She needed to process the conversation she'd had with her son the night before. Brian, spurred on by his sister, was worried about her. Funny, her son had been perfectly content to call her once a month until he'd learned from Amy that their mother was dating again. Now he felt he should visit home and check out the situation.

Liz didn't know if she should be pleased by her children's concern or insulted by their lack of trust in her judgment.

Clare arrived soon afterward, looking harried. The last two Thursdays, she'd only stayed about ten minutes before rushing off to the dealership. Earlier in the week, Liz had left a message with Alex, but Clare hadn't called her back.

"Morning," Clare said, carrying her espresso and scone to the table. She was about to sit down but stopped in midaction. "I never did return your call, did I?"

"No."

"Damn, I'm sorry. It's just that I've been running around like a lunatic for the last couple of weeks." She sank into her seat.

"I noticed," Liz said, without chastisement.

"Hello, everyone." Julia pulled out her usual chair and joined them.

The maternity jumper seemed new and Liz was pleased to see some color in her cheeks. Julia dipped her tea bag in the white ceramic pot.

"How was your week?" she asked them both. Before they could answer, Karen appeared.

"Sorry I'm late." She greeted them with her cheerful smile as she bounced into her seat. The backpack went onto the floor next to her chair; this week's latte was plunked down on the table and some of it sloshed out of the cup.

Liz studied the frothy concoction Karen had bought and wondered what flavor combination she'd selected today.

"How is everyone?" Karen asked.

"I'm feeling great," Liz said and she meant it. She smiled widely; happiness seemed to radiate from her. Everyone at work had noticed. Her secretary, Donna DeGooyer, people in the cafeteria—everyone— and they all knew the reason, too.

"So speaks a woman in love." Julia poured her brewed herbal tea into her mug.

"In love?" Karen raised her voice in excitement. "You're falling for that doctor friend of yours, aren't you?"

All three turned to stare at her.

Liz was uncomfortable with their scrutiny. She was surprised she'd been able to hide her feelings this long. "The operative word here is *friend.* Sean and I are just friends."

Clare eyed her skeptically. "Nothing more..."

"Nothing more," Liz quickly agreed, and she was serious. Sean wanted her in his bed, but he'd accepted her refusal with unexpected grace. As a result, their friendship had flourished, deepening beyond work talk and casual conversation. For the most part, he avoided any mention of his ex-wife and their divorce, but he'd divulged a few of the details. Liz felt certain she was one of the few people privileged with that information.

"Yeah, right," Karen muttered, not bothering to conceal her disbelief. "The way you feel about him is written all over you."

"Don't say that." Liz groaned aloud. "Brian's coming for a visit this weekend."

"To check out Sean?" Clare had two boys of her own and knew exactly what Brian was up to, Liz thought wryly.

"Well, he didn't admit it, but we both know why he's developed a sudden interest in visiting his mother," she replied.

"Amy sent him," Clare said, raising her eyebrows.

"That's my guess, anyway." Liz shook her head. "I never thought my children would react like this."

"React like what?" Julia peeled away the paper lining on her blueberry muffin, then looked at Liz, awaiting a response.

"Like my being attracted to another man is this huge shock." There, she'd come right out and said it. Liz was interested in Sean. Sure, they had their differences, but everything had changed the night he took her to Little Lambs. He'd revealed an unprecedented trust in her and she, in turn, had shed her own prejudices.

"My dad died ten years ago," Julia continued, splaying her hand across her abdomen as the baby kicked. "And if my mom started dating after all this time, I'd wonder, too. It's only natural, don't you think?" She threw the question out to the group.

The other two agreed.

"I'll say one thing," Clare said, "you look happier than I've ever seen you. What was your word for the year again?"

"Time," Liz said. Funny Clare should ask, because she'd given a lot of consideration to her word lately. She'd chosen it because she was afraid life was passing her by and there were so many things she had yet to do, yet to experience. Falling in love wasn't something she'd anticipated. But it made every day, every hour, feel vivid and special—made her conscious of time in a new way.

"I suggest you don't waste any *time* making excuses, either," Karen said, half-humorously. "When Brian comes, just hold your head high."

"She's right," Julia said. "Brian might feel shocked, as I would, but be honest and ask for his support."

"What I can't get over is that my own children doubt my judgment."

"From some of the things you told us about him early on, *I* doubt your judgement," Clare muttered, then refuted her disapproval with a wide smile. "But if you see something redeeming in him, then it must be there."

"There is," Liz said with a soft sigh. She wouldn't be with Sean until the weekend, and already she was counting the days.

"Help me, please," Clare moaned. "My friend is falling in love and she can't think straight."

"Cut it out," Liz returned sternly, but was unable to keep back a smile. She *was* in love, and it felt absolutely wonderful.

"Love can have consequences," Julia said, placing her hands over the small mound that was her baby. "Before you ask, everything's developing nicely. I'm nearly seven months along now. I guess I spent so long trying to deny that I was pregnant, the weeks just slipped away."

"What about Adam and Zoe? Have they had an attitude adjustment yet?" Liz asked.

Julia shook her head. "Most of the time, they're still angry and upset with Peter and me, as though we purposely set out to destroy their self-involved little lives. That's one of the reasons we don't talk much about the baby around them."

"It's fairly obvious you're pregnant," Clare said. "It isn't like they can ignore it."

"Yes, they can," Julia insisted. "And they are. They don't understand that being parents to a newborn means more than having a package of disposable diapers on hand. This baby is going to cause a major lifestyle change, and *everyone's* been ignoring that fact, including me." Julia sounded near-frantic. "To complicate everything, Peter and I still don't know what we're going to do about day care."

"I thought you said Peter could get three months' paid leave after the baby's born, and that he'd bring him or her to you at the store for feedings."

"But that's only three months, and I don't even know how well it's going to work."

"You can't keep the baby at the store?"

"Not if I intend to give good customer service. I think people would be tolerant for a little while, but not on an everyday basis. It is, after all, a retail store."

Liz agreed with her. "It's one thing with an infant," she said. "You might be able to manage. But when he or she begins to crawl..."

Julia nodded.

"I thought your mother was retiring," Karen inserted.

The worry in Julia's eyes diminished slightly, and Liz could see that her friend had pinned her hopes on her mother's help.

"Mom is retiring, but I can't expect her to leave one job and take on another, especially when it's this demanding. If she were to offer, then that'd be great. Peter and I would be thrilled. But she hasn't—and I can't ask her." Julia's voice faded with disappointment.

"What about Georgia?" Karen suggested.

"My cousin? You're joking, right? Georgia hasn't been around babies very much and doesn't know a thing about them. I love my cousin, but she'd hate me if I saddled her with this baby for more than an hour at a time. Besides, she already has a job."

"What about baby clothes and all the other paraphernalia you're going to need?" Liz asked.

Julia looked more distraught than ever. "Clothes are the least of my concerns. Between my sister and the women from church, I'll have more than enough clothes to see this baby through kindergarten."

"Day care is a big problem for a lot of women," Liz said, knowing how heavily the issue weighed on Julia's mind.

"I don't know what I'm going to do," she murmured again, eyes disconsolate. "I might have to close the shop. I'd hate that and it would make me resent my baby—which I don't want. But I don't want to throw away all my hard work, either." She shrugged helplessly. "The baby has to be my first priority."

"There don't seem to be any easy answers, do there?" Clare's voice revealed her sympathy.

"None—and the crazy part is, I'm actually looking forward to having this baby. After all the angst and doubt I had in the beginning, I didn't think that was possible. Now, if only my children would develop some tolerance…"

"Adam and Zoe will come around," Karen said. "Just be patient."

"Six months of substitute teaching, and the girl's an expert on child-rearing," Clare muttered under her breath.

"Hey," Karen countered. "I spend eight to ten hours a day, four days a week, dealing with teenagers. I know how they think."

Liz was surprised. "You must be substituting a lot more hours than you were before." Come to think of it, Karen hadn't mentioned an audition for some time now.

"I've been filling in at Manchester High School," she said.

"Isn't that where the chemistry teacher works?" Liz asked. "The one you hooked up with?"

"Yeah." Karen lowered her gaze.

Liz read the signs like a skilled scout. "You like this guy."

"I do," she admitted. "Glen is wonderful."

She was charmed by the way Karen's eyes brightened when she mentioned his name.

"Glen met my parents this weekend," she said with deceptive casualness.

"You took Glen to meet your *parents?*" Julia asked, unable to disguise her shock.

"Not exactly. Glen and I were rollerblading near the beach and we ran into my parents at the marina."

"Did mom and dad approve?" Clare asked, although the answer to that should be obvious.

"How could they not? Glen is smart and polite and traditional. Plus he's got a respectable occupation." She grinned. "He's everything my parents always wanted for me." After a brief pause, she added casually, "You know, I'm getting along much better with my mother these days."

"That's good news." Liz was sincere. Every week, it seemed, Karen had come with a long list of grievances against her mother. Liz recognized that this was a relationship between two stubborn people, neither of whom was willing to meet the other's expectations.

"How's your sister doing?" Clare asked next.

Karen didn't say anything right away, and it seemed to Liz that she struggled to answer. "Okay, I guess. She isn't speaking to me at the moment."

"Why not?"

If Clare had been able to stay for more than ten minutes the last couple of weeks, she'd know. Karen had told them about the lunch with her mother and how she'd inadvertently blurted out the truth about Victoria's marriage. Her mother had then confronted Victoria, and Karen's older sister had resented the intrusion.

Soon afterward, the two sisters had an angry exchange. In the end, Victoria had slammed the door in Karen's face, but not before she'd screamed that she wanted nothing more to do with her. Karen had felt horrible. She hadn't mentioned the episode since, but Liz knew the strained relationship continued to bother her.

"Here's what I wanted to tell you," Karen said, clearly eager to move on to another topic. "Guess what I've been teaching?"

"English?"

"No. Drumroll, please. Drama classes! And guys, I absolutely love it."

"Drama?" Liz repeated. "Karen, that's great!"

"Yeah, and with the year-round schedule, I can work all summer long, if I want."

Clare rolled her eyes. "I still can't get used to that. I'm just grateful only one of my boys was involved in it. Manchester High School didn't go year-round until after Mick graduated."

"Well, I'm just grateful they did," Karen said. "Otherwise I'd go back to being a starving artist. I've had work and I've had none and—"

"Work is better," Julia finished for her.

"Exactly!" Karen agreed.

"Get back to Glen meeting your parents," Clare insisted. "I want to hear about this. And I mean details, girl."

"Well..." Karen hesitated. She started to laugh. "You know what my mother said to Glen? That he was the first boy I'd dated who didn't have tattoos or a ponytail."

"She didn't!"

Karen nodded. "She did, but I think she was just so happy to meet someone she considered normal, she simply forgot herself."

Although Karen had made it obvious that she didn't want to discuss her sister, Liz was dissatisfied with their unresolved conversation about Victoria. She felt anxious about this woman, felt that her husband was a time bomb, waiting to explode. "Are you sure everything's all right with Victoria?"

"As far as I know," Karen said. "I tried to call her this week, but she hung up on me."

"Could it have been her husband who answered the phone?"

"No, it was Victoria, and as soon as she heard my voice she slammed down the receiver."

"How sad," Liz said sympathetically. "I'm sorry."

"I'm worried about her, naturally, but my fears are for Bryce, too," Karen said. "Every time Roger unleashes his anger on my sister, he's telling his son it's all right to hit someone smaller and weaker." She frowned darkly. "Mother said Victoria denied everything."

Liz had hoped that Karen's mother would be a catalyst in this situation. Realizing she had the love and support of her family might lend Victoria the courage to reach out for help.

"If she doesn't call you or your mother, who can she call?" Clare asked.

Karen lowered her gaze. "I don't know, but I refuse to give up. I'm stopping by her place this afternoon. She won't have any choice but to talk to me then."

"Good!"

"How did Alex's graduation go this weekend?" Liz asked Clare.

A moment's hesitation was followed by, "Good."

From the flat way she spoke, Liz knew something was wrong. So did the others, because everyone stopped to look at Clare.

"What?" Clare demanded.

"You'd better tell us what happened," Liz said. She hadn't noticed earlier that her friend was troubled, but she saw it now. Clare had looked tired and stressed ever since she'd started work at the dealership; today she also seemed distracted.

"Nothing's wrong."

"You might fool some of the people some of the time, but you can't fool us," Karen said, leaning forward, elbows on the tabletop. "Tell us what's going on."

A hint of a smile turned up Clare's mouth.

"We're waiting," Julia said, crossing her arms as though to say she'd sit there all day if necessary.

Clare exhaled noisily. "Michael insisted on attending the graduation."

Liz frowned. "He's been hospitalized all week."

"I know. Alex said he wanted him at the ceremony, if possible, and then Michael said he wasn't going to let his son down."

"How'd he get there?"

"Taxi." Clare drank the last of her espresso, but clung tightly to the small cup. "He wouldn't ask me because we'd had an argument."

"About the graduation?" Julia asked.

"No, the dealership. He's constantly checking up on me and it was driving me nuts. I talk to him nearly every day, but I haven't seen him since we had lunch together at the end of April." She paused and dragged in a deep breath. "Alex didn't say that Michael was going— he couldn't. He was afraid that Mick wouldn't show up if he learned his father planned to be there. He was probably right, too."

"How come you saw each other?" Julia asked.

"Assigned seating. Each family was allowed three tickets, and all three of ours were together."

"Oh, dear," Karen whispered.

"Michael looks dreadful, just dreadful. Mick was shocked... So was

I. At first, he tried to pretend Michael wasn't there. I knew the medical procedure hadn't gone well, but I had no idea how badly he's doing. Later I glanced over and I could tell Mick was having a hard time seeing his father again, especially in this condition."

"How bad is he?" Liz asked, almost afraid of the answer.

"Bad. Really bad. He's down over fifty pounds now and...and his skin is this sickly yellow color." Clare pinched her lips together. "He's dying... He told me he was, but I don't think I actually believed it. I guess I couldn't bring myself to accept it."

"Now there's no denying it, is there?" Julia reached across the table and placed her hand on her friend's.

Liz placed her hand on top of Julia's and Karen set her own hand over all of theirs.

"I don't know how he endured the two-hour ceremony. He was so weak he could barely sit up."

"I wonder if Mick understood how ill his father is?"

Clare's eyes teared. "I think he knew more than I realized. Alex must have said something."

"It's so hard." Liz knew this from experience. Unlike her husband, her father had died a lingering death. "Even when you're prepared for a death, you're not really."

"Did they talk?" Karen asked.

"Not at first." Clare dug in her purse for a tissue. "It was as if they were invisible to each other. Then the graduates entered the auditorium and everyone stood as "Pomp and Circumstance" was played. Mick and I stood and...and Michael tried to."

"He fell?"

"No...Mick caught him and helped him back into his chair. The next thing I knew, they were both weeping and clinging to each other." Tears rolled down Clare's face. She half-sobbed, half-laughed as she said, "It was quite a display for the rest of the audience. Some of them were crying, too."

"Is Michael back in the hospital now?" Liz asked quietly.

Clare didn't answer immediately. "He's with us."

"With you?" Karen repeated.

"He can't go back to the rental house. At this point he's incapable of living on his own. So...he's living with the boys and me." She bit her lip hard, leaving tooth marks. "He's come home to die."

> "Time is a dressmaker specializing in alterations."
>
> —Faith Baldwin

31

CHAPTER

JULIA MURCHISON

July 4th

List of Blessings
1. Sleeping in on a holiday.
2. America the Beautiful.
3. Fireworks.
4. Family barbecues, especially when Peter does the cooking.
5. Georgia, who helps me laugh at myself and at the curve life's thrown me.

I slept in late this morning, and while Peter and the kids are out picking up some last-minute supplies for the barbecue, I'm taking an hour for myself. After a long soak in the tub, I decided to write in my journal.

The last time I did that was a week ago. I can hardly believe seven days have passed. Usually I write every morning, but my body seems to require more sleep lately and when the alarm rings, I just can't drag myself out of bed. Peter feels that if I'm in need of extra sleep, I should take it. I do, but then the morning's one mad rush and my day's completely off-kilter.

This pregnancy is completely different from my previous two. At first I assumed it was because I'm fourteen years older, and my body knows it. I suspect there's more to it, though; the fact that I'm 40 explains some of the differences but not all of them. However, Dr. Fisk keeps telling me that every pregnancy is unique. Maybe this is just going to be a more difficult baby. That's certainly been the case so far!

At least my fears that there's something wrong with the baby have been calmed now that all the test results are in. I thank God we're going to have a healthy child. It was a real worry, although both Peter and I pretended not to be concerned, something we each did for the other's sake. I know how relieved I was with the good news and I could tell he was, too.

Today is going to be fun. Georgia and Maurice are coming over for a barbecue. The kids get a real kick out of my cousin, and she thinks they're fabulous. Georgia can be outrageous but these last few months I've been more grateful than ever for her friendship and emotional support.

Throughout this pregnancy, she's cried with me and laughed with me. When I was down in the dumps about being forty and wearing maternity clothes, she put on a smock and stuffed a pillow in her waistband just so I wouldn't feel foolish. You gotta love a cousin like that!

After the barbecue, we're all heading over to the pier to watch the fireworks. Adam and Zoe will probably meet up with their friends before then, and everyone will rendezvous back at the house at ten-thirty for banana splits, a family Fourth of July tradition.

Today, I refuse to worry. I refuse to give one minute's thought to the lack of day care arrangements for this unborn child. I refuse to feel upset about Adam and Zoe's selfishness. I will not, under any circumstances, weigh myself.

On the other hand, I will laugh and enjoy my family. I will eat whatever I want this afternoon and refuse to feel guilty for doing so. Also, I'm going to find an excuse to let others wait on me. I intend to sit with my feet up and enjoy the sunshine, appreciate my family and salute my country.

That's quite a manifesto for one day, but I plan to do everything within my power to make it happen.

* * *

"Don't *you* look comfortable." Georgia stood, hands on her hips in front of the lounge chair.

Shading her eyes, Julia glanced up. She smiled, revelling in the late-morning sunshine.

"I am in hog heaven." Julia rarely had an opportunity to indulge herself like this—to actually lie in the sun and do nothing. It was an interlude she cherished all the more for its brevity. Everything for the barbecue was in the refrigerator, including three different salads. For the first time in her married life, she was about to serve deli-made potato salad to her family.

Adam was sure to complain about that and he could go right ahead. If he wanted to peel potatoes for an hour, then more power to him!

"Where's Maurice?"

"He's smoking a cigar with Peter."

Julia swung her legs off the cushion. "Not in my house, they aren't."

"Hold up," Georgia said, giggling. "They're out front chatting with one of the neighbors."

"You should've said so earlier."

"And missed seeing you move so fast? That was an impressive feat."

"Especially in my condition." Julia rested her hands against her abdomen and admired Georgia's slim waist. Her cousin wore white slacks and a red, white and blue T-shirt with gold embroidered stars across the yoke. With her huge star-framed sunglasses and California beach tan, the effect was stunning.

"What do you mean, your condition? You've never looked better."

Julia rolled her eyes.

"None of that, either." Georgia wagged her finger at Julia. "It's true."

Every woman wants to believe she's beautiful while pregnant, Julia thought, but if ever there was a delusion, this was it. Her appearance was something Julia had avoided thinking about, along with day care, baby supplies...and just about everything else.

All her life, she'd been the organized one, the list-maker, the planner. This pregnancy had completely thrown her. She had two months to prepare everyone for the impact this baby would have on their lives. So far, all she'd done was buy a crib.

But she'd promised herself she wouldn't think about any of this today. Fortunately, Zoe provided a distraction.

"Mom, should I bring out the cheese dip?" she called from the house.

"Not yet," Julia called back.

"I'm hungry," Adam muttered, coming onto the patio and slumping into the chair next to Julia.

"So what else is new?" She twisted around. "All right, all right, you can bring out the goodies."

Adam rushed into the house to help his sister.

Georgia took the lounge chair he'd abandoned. "This is the life." She lay back with a long sigh and smiled into the sun.

"What's this?" Adam demanded, holding a plastic-coated nut-crusted cheese ball.

"What does it look like?"

"What happened to the one you always make?"

"I didn't make it this year."

"But—"

"Adam" Georgia inserted, "your mother's pregnant and she doesn't need to be standing on her feet all day cooking for the rest of us."

"Everything doesn't have to change because my mother was dumb enough to get pregnant," Adam exploded. "Nothing's the same anymore, and I hate it. She used to be a real person and now all she is...is pregnant." He pitched the cheese ball at the lawn and stormed back into the house.

"What got into him?" Georgia asked, frowning as she removed her sunglasses.

Julia shrugged. "He's sixteen, has his driver's license and doesn't have his own car the way most of his friends do."

"Now, just a minute here," Georgia drew herself to a sitting position. "Who said it was the parents' responsibility to provide their children with their own personal vehicles?" Her words echoed Peter's outburst of a few months ago. Correct though he was, his comments hadn't done a thing to change the kids' attitudes.

"It isn't that," Zoe said, walking onto the patio. "Adam's upset because he would've had a car if it wasn't for..." She angled her head toward Julia's abdomen.

"There was no guarantee of that," Julia argued. She'd heard all this countless times. "Can we talk about something else, please?"

"Like what?" Zoe asked.

"What about names for the baby?" Georgia suggested cheerfully. "Personally, I think babies should always be named after someone, like a favorite cousin," she said. "That would mean George or—"

"The baby's all anyone wants to talk about," Zoe cried. "It's the baby this and the baby that. If Mom's sick of Adam wanting his own car, then I can be sick of this baby." She raced back into the house and slammed the sliding glass door so hard it bounced and slid partway open again.

"My goodness, what's *with* those two?"

"The joys of sharing and family life," Julia said. But she wouldn't let either one of them ruin her stress-free, worry-free holiday. "I'm ignoring them both and suggest you do likewise."

Georgia didn't say anything for a moment. "Are you running a fever?" she finally asked. "Are you unwell?"

"Me? What makes you say that?"

Georgia hesitated. "Being able to ignore this stuff doesn't sound like you."

"Well, it is for today." Julia settled back in the lounger and closed her eyes. That was when she felt a sudden, inexplicable pain. She froze for a moment, then placed her hands on her stomach. It wasn't the onset of labor; that she would have recognized.

"Something's wrong." She choked out the words, holding her abdomen tightly, nearly blinded by pain.

"Julia, what is it?"

Julia heard her cousin but couldn't answer. Suddenly she felt liquid gush from between her legs. At first she assumed her water had broken, then she saw the blood and nearly fainted.

"Blood...oh my God, there's blood everywhere!" Georgia ran toward the house screaming, her voice filled with panic. "Call 911! Someone do something."

Peter was at her side almost immediately, his face pale. "Honey, it's all right. Help's on the way."

"What's happening?" Julia cried, clinging to his arms. "What's wrong?"

"I don't know... We need to get you to the hospital."

"It's the baby...the baby's in trouble." The panic was rising in Julia. She saw it reflected in the face of her cousin who stood next to her sobbing, hand over her mouth. Peter looked wild-eyed as he tried to comfort her. Zoe was off to one side, crying all by herself.

The next few minutes were a blur until Julia heard the sound of the emergency siren. The paramedics, directed by Adam, came through the gate into the backyard. Two young men lifted Julia from the lounger and placed her on a stretcher.

"Mom, Mom..." Zoe, weeping and nearly hysterical, grabbed her hand. "What's wrong? Tell me what's wrong."

"I don't know, honey, I don't know."

"Everything's going to be all right," Peter assured them both, but his words rang false.

The paramedics carried the stretcher toward the waiting ambulance. The blood continued to gush from between her legs. So much blood. Such intense pain and a fear so paralyzing Julia could barely think.

"I'll bring the children to the hospital."

Was that Georgia? Julia could no longer tell. Peter climbed into the ambulance with her. One of the paramedics wrapped a blood pressure cuff around her upper arm and shouted out a series of numbers to the driver. The siren blared.

"Everything will be fine in a few minutes," Peter told her, holding tightly on to her fingers.

She clutched his hand hard, but she could feel herself weakening. "Call Liz," she pleaded, certain she was about to pass out. As the hospital administrator, Liz could ensure that Peter and the children would be kept informed of her condition.

"Liz?"

"Kenyon," Julia whispered, fighting off unconsciousness. "Thursdays at eight."

"The breakfast group friend."

"Yes...yes." Her eyes remained closed. She felt lightheaded, dizzy. Unreal. She had to make a determined effort to hold onto consciousness. Yet she felt almost euphoric and couldn't understand why.

The next time she opened her eyes, she realized she was at the hospital. There was a brilliant light suspended above her. Although it took a tremendous effort, she tried to lever herself up on one elbow to see who was in the room. An IV bottle hampered her progress. The nurse who stood beside her pressed a gentle hand to Julia's shoulder.

"Mrs. Murchison..."

"My husband, I want my husband."

"You'll see him soon, okay?"

Julia couldn't imagine where Peter would be. She needed him. She wanted him with her.

"What's happening to my baby?" she asked a moment later. It was difficult to think clearly with everyone about her moving in slow motion.

A sympathetic nurse clasped her hand. "We're doing everything we can to look after your health and that of your baby."

A man she couldn't see said something Julia didn't understand.

"Who are you?" she demanded. Julia hated it when people didn't identify themselves.

"Dr. Lowell. You're at Willow Grove Memorial Hospital. Your placenta has ripped away from the uterus. We've called in Dr. Fisk and as soon as she arrives we'll be taking the baby by Caesarian section."

"It's too early." She wasn't quite seven months pregnant.

"Don't you worry, we have one of the finest preemie doctors in the state."

"Dr. Jamison?" Julia asked, remembering what Liz had told her about Sean Jamison.

"Yes. He's already on his way."

Relief washed over her, and she relaxed. Liz had repeatedly lauded Sean Jamison's qualifications; she obviously held his medical skills in high regard. "Good."

"I'm going to give you something that'll make you feel sleepy now," the nurse told her.

"All right...but please tell my husband everything's going to be fine. Can you do that for me? He's very worried and I want him to know I'm okay."

"I'll tell him right away." The nurse patted her hand. "Everything *will* be fine."

"Thank you," she whispered, her voice thick and a bit slurred. Julia sincerely hoped the nurse knew what she was talking about.

"The ultimate lesson all of us have to learn is unconditional love, which includes not only others but ourselves as well."

—Elizabeth Kubler-Ross

32

CHAPTER

LIZ KENYON

Sean had found a premium parking spot at the beach. Liz could hardly believe their good fortune. The sky was the purest shade of blue, and the sun, as always, shone bright along the California shoreline. A refreshing breeze blew off the water. A perfect fourth of July.

With his radio playing a Lovin' Spoonful ballad from the sixties, Sean eased his convertible into the empty parking slot. Liz could have driven around for hours and not located a single space within a mile of the beach.

"Hey, it's just clean livin'," Sean said with a chuckle when she said as much.

"Sure it is," she joked back, happier than she could remember being in a long while. They'd spent the morning at Little Lambs. Sean had brought Clarissa a bouquet of red, white and blue carnations as a Fourth of July gift. They visited with each of the babies and Liz was delighted to see that little Faye showed some improvement. As they were about to leave, Clarissa had pulled her to one side.

"I see you have your answer," the other woman whispered.

Liz hadn't immediately made the connection. Then she recalled Clarissa's question during that first visit and understood. *Do you love him?* Liz didn't respond, merely nodded.

"Good for you," Clarissa said, chuckling to herself as she let them out the front door.

From Little Lambs, they drove to the beach. Sean waited until they were strolling along the crowded sidewalk before he broached the subject of her son's recent visit. "Are you going to tell me if I passed inspection or not?"

He tried to sound casual, but Liz knew he was concerned about the meeting with Brian.

"Feeling insecure, are you?"

"You haven't said a damn word," Sean muttered as they walked side by side, holding hands.

"That was intentional."

"Dammit, Liz, I was on my best behavior. I was as good as I can be. If your son found fault with me, then—"

"Brian thought you were fabulous," she interrupted. "He thinks you're the best thing since bottled water." Restraining her smile would have been impossible.

"He's a great kid."

"Of course you'd think so," she teased, "since he likes you."

"Yup." He grinned. "One thing's for sure, Brian's got terrific judgement."

"Would you stop?"

"Hey," Sean countered, "I'm just getting started. Naturally, once he's back, Brian will call Amy and tell her everything's copacetic. Then Amy will be reassured that you're seeing a real prince of a fellow, and all will be well."

Liz smiled at his enthusiasm. She didn't bother to add that neither of them needed a course set for this relationship. Not at this stage of their lives. For now Liz was content to have someone special to share

the small everyday things. A companion, a friend, maybe—in time—
a lover. Someone who loved and appreciated the woman she was.
Someone who made her laugh. Someone who inspired her and encouraged her to take the occasional risk. Liz hoped for the opportunity to play that role in Sean's life as well.

"Will I meet your daughter one day?" she asked.

Liz saw the pleasure leave Sean's face. "Unfortunately that isn't
likely," he said in a stiff voice.

"Why not?"

"First of all, Eileen lives in Seattle."

"She never visits?"

"No. Say, I could go for an ice cream bar. How about you?"

"Quit changing the subject. The only thing I want is more information about you."

Sean sat down on a nearby bench and leaned forward, bracing his
elbows on his knees. "I don't want to talk about Eileen."

"I can see that, but why not?"

"If you must know," he snapped, "the subject of her mother invariably comes up and my ex-wife is off limits, even with you."

Liz sat on the bench beside him. She didn't remark that this wasn't
always true; he'd mentioned Denise any number of times. But every
mention was a glancing one, as though he couldn't bear to linger on
her memory. "You must have loved her very much," Liz said quietly.

Sean turned away. "It's a beautiful day. Let's not spoil it with talk
of a relationship that's been dead for years."

"Why don't you tell me what happened and get it over with?" she
urged softly, her hand on his forearm.

"Happened?" he repeated. "Just what generally happens when a
man's foolish enough to fall in love with a fickle woman. I don't mean
to be rude, Liz, but I'm serious. I don't want to discuss Denise."

"Then we won't." She respected his wishes and wouldn't pressure
him. She believed that eventually, as the trust between them grew, he'd
tell her more. No point in forcing the issue.

Sean reached for her hand just as his beeper went off. Liz knew the
sound all too well. Earlier he'd warned her that he was on call, and the
beeper meant that her Fourth of July was about to be interrupted.

While he read the message on his pager, Liz's cell phone rang inside her purse. So few people had the number that she knew it must be important.

Liz felt around until she found her phone, and flipped it open on the third ring. "Hello."

"Is this Liz Kenyon?"

Peter Murchison introduced himself and explained the circumstances. "I'm leaving now," she told him, then snapped the phone closed and dumped it back in her purse.

Sean waited for her. "I've got to get to—"

"I know. The Murchison baby's mother is a good friend of mine. That was her husband. Julia asked if I'd come to the hospital."

"Let's go."

When they relinquished their parking space, there were a hundred vehicles all eager to claim the same spot. No sooner had Sean backed out than it was filled. Liz didn't spare even a thought for the leisurely day that had just disappeared.

As they headed toward the hospital, Liz reached for her cell phone again. She hit the "on" button and saw Sean giving her a puzzled look.

"Who are you calling?"

"The rest of the Thursday morning breakfast group."

"How likely is it that you'll reach them?"

"About a hundred percent," she assured him with total confidence.

"On a holiday?"

"Sean, I'll reach Karen and Clare because I won't give up until I do."

"Why? You aren't Julia's family."

"No, we're her *friends,* and this baby is important to us. We were there when she found out she was pregnant. We've watched her deal with family, friends, even her customers' reactions, and we're going to stand by her now."

"Must be a woman thing," he muttered. "If I needed emergency surgery, my golfing buddies wouldn't parade over to the hospital and sit there worrying about me."

"I would."

He turned to stare at her and nearly ran a red light.

"Sean!" she screamed as he entered the intersection.

Sean slammed on the brakes and Liz vaulted forward, the seat belt cutting into her shoulder. Her phone flew onto the dash.

"Dammit, Liz, you can't go saying things like that when I'm driving."

"Things like what?" He frowned at her and she couldn't imagine why.

"Never mind."

She shook her head and retrieved her phone to resume her calling.

By the time Liz and Sean arrived at the hospital, Julia had delivered a baby boy, weighing in at two pounds, ten ounces.

Sean went to assess Baby Murchison's situation while Liz made her way to the waiting area. The room was full of people who milled around, most of them pacing restlessly, talking in low, anxious voices. She recognized Julia's cousin Georgia from the journal-writing class and introduced herself to the others.

"I have a brother," Adam said beaming proudly as he repeatedly shook Liz's hand.

Was this really the same boy who'd given his parents nothing but grief from the moment he learned Julia was pregnant? Right now, he seemed pleased and excited. Liz hoped his enthusiasm lasted.

"Dad said we're going to name him Zachary Justin," Zoe said and impulsively hugged Liz. "Mom talks about you all the time," she whispered.

This was Zoe who did nothing but complain how embarrassed she was about the pregnancy?

"I think your mother's wonderful," Liz told her. "She's very proud of you and your brother."

Zoe's eyes filled with tears. "I think my mom's wonderful, too."

Clare arrived ten minutes after Liz, with Karen following a half hour later. The three of them stood in one corner, talking quietly while Peter, the kids, and Julia's family settled in another section of the room. Every now and again they'd exchange comments or questions.

At about four-thirty, Peter was summoned by a nurse, apparently for a conference with Sean. As he left, tension in the room increased perceptibly.

"Two pounds is terribly small," Clare murmured.

Liz didn't want to alarm the others, but the fact remained that poor Zachary faced a life-and-death struggle.

The room went quiet when Peter returned. "According to Dr. Jamison," he began, "Zachary's chances of survival are very good." He paused, then continued in a steady voice. "About ninety percent of infants born weighing less than three pounds survive."

"Ninety percent?" The odds sounded good to Liz, who felt a giddy sense of relief.

"Just a minute." Peter held up his hand and silenced the group. "Before we start celebrating, we need to recognize that there could still be problems."

Liz thought Peter Murchison looked as though he was close to collapsing from the strain.

"What else did the doctor say?" Adam pressed his father. It was the question they all wanted to ask.

"Dr. Jamison said there's no guarantee Zachary won't develop any number of other complications."

"Such as?" a woman asked fearfully. Liz knew her to be Julia's mother.

"Cerebral palsy."

Everyone grew quiet again.

"Apparently there's also a real fear that Zack could develop chronic respiratory problems."

"When will we know?"

"Not for some time." Peter's face was bleak.

"Oh, my." Georgia breathed hard and sat down. Her husband sat with her and reached for her hand.

"This is only the beginning," Peter said, as he slumped into a chair. "Of course, he might escape it all, but as of right now there's no way of telling."

"Will Zachary be transferred to Laurelhurst?" Liz asked. That was where Sean's babies were usually sent because the neonatal intensive care unit there offered the technology and expertise that would give little Zachary the best chance at life.

"Dr. Jamison is making the arrangements now," Peter said, tiredly rubbing the back of his neck.

"How's Julia?" Clare asked.

"Julia's resting... Naturally she's worried about Zachary."

Clare nodded. "Is there anything I can do?"

"Yes," Georgia cried. "Pray."

"Zack might...die?" Adam asked, as though the information was just now beginning to sink in.

"Yes."

"I want to see him," Zoe pleaded. Her voice was shaky. "He's my baby brother."

"You can't now," Peter said as he wrapped his arms around his two older children. "I don't know yet what the policy is at Laurelhurst, but I'll do everything I can to make sure you get to see him."

Clare drove Liz to the children's hospital, where she waited for Sean until after dinnertime. When he stepped out of the neonatal center and found her, he seemed surprised.

"I thought you'd gone home."

"Hey, you can't get rid of me that easily."

Sean threw his arm around her shoulders. "I'm glad you waited."

"How's Zachary doing?"

He exhaled sharply. "About as well as can be expected. He's a little fighter—I'll give him that."

"That's good, isn't it?"

Sean nodded. "Yes, but statistically he's the wrong gender and the wrong race."

"I beg your pardon?" Liz knew premature girls fared better than boys, but she didn't know about race.

"We're not sure why, but black girls are the most likely survival candidates, followed by white girls and then black boys. White boys are at the bottom of that hierarchy."

"What are the chances he'll survive undamaged?" From what Peter had said earlier, the baby's odds of survival sounded good. It was everything else they needed to worry about. "Fifty-fifty?"

He shook his head.

"Less? More?" She wanted him to give her something to focus on, something to diminish her worry.

"I don't give estimates," Sean said. "Too often, I'm proved wrong."

"The idea of strictly minding our own business is rubbish.
Who could be so selfish?"

—Myrtie Barker

33

CHAPTER

KAREN CURTIS

August 1st

I spent the entire day on a shoot. This commercial has the potential to get me a bit role on a sitcom, and I should be thrilled. Normally I would be, but so much is happening. I'm beginning to wonder if my head's screwed on straight.

Glen's been on my mind a lot. I can't believe I'm falling for a chemistry teacher. A brain, but he's so much fun and so levelheaded and just all-around wonderful. Last week he casually mentioned that the high school has an opening for a full-time drama teacher. That was all he said. He didn't urge me to apply, didn't give me any of the details, but he knew. He *had* to know.

The most fun I've had all year was the few days I filled in for the drama teacher. That includes *everything* else I've done, even the hair spray commercial that was shown nationally. Even the times Glen and I have gone out. I absolutely *loved* teaching that class.

I don't have the certification required for a full-time teaching position. Oh, there are ways around that, but I have to decide if this is something I really want to the exclusion of all else. I don't know. It was a point of pride with me, too. A teacher is what my mother always said I should be. I refuse to believe she knows me so well.

Last week, when Gwen called me to audition for a bit role in *Tom, Dick and Harriet,* a pilot for a situation comedy, I hesitated. Normally I would have leaped at the chance. I hemmed and hawed until my agent asked if I actually wanted this audition, because she had thirty other clients who'd die for the opportunity. I told her I wanted it, but I don't know if that's true anymore. I'm finally close to the goal I've been after for ten years—and I'm on the verge of saying no to it all. I wish to hell I could figure out what's wrong with me.

Perhaps it's all the worry about Victoria, who still isn't speaking to me. My sister's attitude has really got me down. I've tried to explain, but the minute she recognizes my voice, she hangs up the phone. I went to her house but she wouldn't answer the door. I sent her a letter, which she blatantly ignored. A week later I mailed her a schmaltzy card about the bond between sisters. I thought if anything would work on her, it would be that. Still, not a word. I wonder how long she intends to let this continue.

Fine! Whatever! If that's the way she wants to be, then it's her loss. I've done everything I can to repair our relationship.

Mom's having difficulties with her, too. My mother called me twice last week. Twice! Apparently, Victoria's embarrassed that Mom knows about Roger's explosive temper. It seems my sister had hoped we'd all blindly look the other way and pretend this is acceptable behavior. In your dreams, big sister—or maybe your worst nightmare.

It isn't just the falling-out with Victoria that's bothering me, or the job dilemma. The breakfast group is deeply involved with Julia and her baby. Little Zachary isn't responding as well as Dr. Jamison would like. It's tearing poor Julia apart. She's spending as much time as she can at the hospital. When she isn't with the baby, then Peter is. Julia's mother is retired now and thankfully, she's filling in at the shop. Georgia is there, too—she took vacation days to do this—and one of Julia's customers. An older woman whose name I don't remember.

Adam and Zoe finally came around. After months of claiming they wanted nothing to do with this baby, they're helping out at home and at Julia's shop, doing whatever they can. They've been incredibly helpful these last three weeks.

The situation is so intense. We all know it can go either way with Zachary. He might be all right; he might end up disabled. If he lives... Statistically, the odds for normal development aren't in his favor, and there's always that ten per cent who don't survive. Julia's in agony over it and blames herself, which makes no sense. We tell her repeatedly that she did everything she could, but she doesn't listen. She's going through this terrible guilt. If she'd eaten better, rested more, tried to do less... Everyone understands how she feels, although we know none of it is true.

Dr. Jamison has been wonderful. I remember when Liz first started seeing him and what a jerk we all thought he was. Our opinion of him has taken a one-hundred-and-eighty degree turn. He's been so kind to Julia and Peter, answering their questions, spending time with them. He hasn't minimized the dangers of Zachary's situation, and although it's painful, I know Julia wants the truth.

Last Thursday, we threw a baby shower for her. Clare gave Zachary Justin Murchison a silver baby spoon with his name engraved on it, plus three outfits. We all laughed because Zachary will probably be close to a year before he fits into them.

Liz knit him a cap and booties that look impossibly small and delicate, and she gave Julia a complete collection of Beatrix Potter stories. I found a store in L.A. close to the studio that sells clothes especially designed for preemies. My baby gift was the cutest little outfit that looks more like doll clothes. It was more than I could afford, but I don't care.

The baby shower lifted Julia's spirits. Mine, too, and everyone's. I never realized how strongly I'd feel about Julia's baby. My admiration for her grows all the time. In some ways, she's stronger than the rest of us put together. When she first discovered she was pregnant, I expected her to quietly terminate the pregnancy. I wanted to ask her why she didn't, especially when it became clear what an inconvenience the baby was going to be in all their lives. We would've understood and we certainly wouldn't have judged her. But she didn't do it.

Julia has taught me so much about inner strength and conviction. Even now, when the outcome with Zachary remains so uncertain, in my heart of hearts, I feel she did the right thing.

What with my own career, or lack thereof, my sister's problem and Julia's baby, I feel emotionally drained. This heat isn't helping, either. It's miserable, and just now that's the way my whole life feels.

* * *

Karen set aside her journal and took a sip from her glass of iced tea. She stretched out her legs as she tried to make herself comfortable on the patio chair—a cast-off she'd rescued from her parents' garage. At least this apartment had a balcony, tiny though it was. She sighed; her confusion seemed to be growing, until she felt as though she was walking in waist-deep mud. Every step forward was impeded.

Wiping away the sweat on her face, she got out of her chair, wincing as her bare thighs stuck to the vinyl cushion. She recalled summers as a child when she'd wait with her sister to hear the ice-cream truck come down the street. Then she'd race Victoria to see who could reach it first.

Her heart ached constantly over the estrangement between her and Victoria. In the past, weeks had often gone by, whole months during which they didn't speak, but that was different. It just meant they lived dissimilar lives, had dissimilar interests. It didn't mean they didn't care about each other. They were *sisters*.

"That does it," Karen muttered and without further thought, went inside to grab her wallet and car keys, then headed out. She made only one stop along the way.

Standing in front of her sister's door, she leaned on the doorbell.

Victoria appeared, looking frazzled and worn-out. She would've slammed the door shut if Karen hadn't put out her foot to prevent it.

"Remember when we were kids and we used to race to the ice-cream truck?" she asked.

"We're no longer children," Victoria muttered. Her hand was on the door, ready to close it.

"I usually won, didn't I?"

"Is there a point to this question?" Victoria feigned boredom.

Karen was tempted to remind her sister that *she* was the actress in the family. "Here," she said instead, and thrust out a chocolate-coated ice-cream bar with the wrapper peeled off. Unfortunately, in the late-afternoon heat, it'd already started to melt.

Victoria stared at it, as though she didn't know what to say.

"Go ahead, take it," Karen said.

"Do you seriously believe that offering me *ice cream* will wipe out what you did? You don't get it, do you?"

"No. Why don't you tell me?"

"No."

"I'm so sorry, Vicki. I never meant for any of this to upset you. I was only trying to help. I'm here now because I want us to talk this out."

The bar continued to melt and Karen caught the melting chocolate in the palm of her hand.

"Come inside and get rid of that before it leaves a mess on my porch," Victoria snapped. She opened the door wider so Karen could enter the house.

The foyer and living room were immaculate—even with a three-year-old underfoot all day. Karen's gaze fell on the coffee table and she was astonished to see that the magazines were not only in precise rows but stacked in alphabetical order.

"Throw that out." Victoria eyed the melting ice-cream bar and nodded toward the kitchen.

Karen discarded it in the sink and thought it was a real shame her sister hadn't eaten it. Victoria was thinner than she remembered. Too thin.

"Where's Bryce?" she asked. Normally her nephew would be leaping around her the minute she arrived.

"It's naptime."

Victoria didn't offer her anything to drink or suggest she sit down, so Karen stood with her back to the kitchen sink. A moment of stilted silence followed.

"How are you?" she asked. She searched Victoria's face and bare upper arms for bruises.

"None of your damn business."

Karen swallowed an angry retort, reminding herself that she hadn't come here to argue. "How's Bryce?"

Victoria shrugged.

"How many times can I say I'm sorry?"

"I thought I could trust you... I thought, I hoped, you'd be the one person in the world I could talk to."

"And then I blew it. Is that what you're saying?"

"How could you tell Mom? She's the last person I expected you to go to." Victoria's sense of betrayal seemed to overwhelm her; fears gathered in her eyes. "Do you hate me so much?" she cried.

"No, of course I don't hate you—"

Victoria didn't allow her to finish. "Now Mom's full of questions and Dad talked to Roger, and everything's a thousand times worse, all thanks to you."

"You don't actually think I could hate you?" Karen asked, close to tears herself. "You're my sister. The thought of anyone abusing you is more than I can bear."

"Sure, it is," Victoria taunted. "As I remember, you did your fair share of hitting me, too."

"We were just kids!"

Victoria turned her back. "Go away."

"No, I can't. I won't leave. Not until we've settled this."

Victoria shook her head. "Nothing you can say is going to make things right."

"You let your husband hit you."

Victoria whirled around so she was facing her once again. "He didn't mean it," she said heatedly.

Karen wanted to scream with frustration. How could her sister defend Roger? "Are you telling me it was an accident?"

Victoria refused to answer.

"You're furious with me because I said something to our mother. That was an accident, too, but you won't even give me a chance to explain."

"Roger loves me."

"I love you, too," Karen said. "You're my sister."

It looked for a moment as though Victoria was prepared to listen. Karen could actually see the indecision in her face—until they heard the sound of a car door slamming.

"Roger," Victoria whispered, and her eyes widened with panic.

A minute later, the door off the garage opened and Roger stepped into the kitchen. He hesitated when he saw Karen, and his lip curled with contempt.

"I didn't invite her," Victoria explained hurriedly.

"If you know what's good for you, you'll get out of my house," he threatened.

"Nice to see you, too," Karen muttered.

Roger set his briefcase on the kitchen table and Karen watched as the blood drained from Victoria's face.

"I want to talk to my sister," Karen insisted.

"She doesn't want to talk to you."

"Victoria can speak for herself, thank you," Karen said curtly, hands clenched at her sides. She wanted to hurt him the same way he'd hurt her sister.

"Fine, you tell her," Roger ordered his wife.

"It would be best if you left now," Victoria said, her voice low and pleading. "Please, just go."

Karen wanted to leave, but she was afraid of what would happen to Victoria if she did. She couldn't understand why her sister let Roger control her like this, why she let him belittle and abuse her.

"Shall I phone the police?" Roger asked no one in particular. He opened the refrigerator and took out a beer.

"Maybe you should," Karen said as calmly as her frantically beating heart would allow. "I'm sure they'd be interested in talking to me."

Roger slammed the beer down on the counter; at the violence of his action, Victoria cringed and leaped away. "Get the hell out of my house," he shouted.

"I'll go, but Victoria and Bryce are coming with me."

"No way."

"Victoria?" Karen stared at her sister, silently begging her to walk out the door and not look back.

Her sister wavered, and for a few seconds it seemed that she just might do it.

Hope surged within Karen and she smiled in encouragement.

"Fine, go," Roger stated calmly, as though bored by the whole scene. "But Bryce stays with me."

Any chance of her sister leaving was destroyed by those few words. "I'll stay," she whispered.

Roger's smile stretched from ear to ear. "That's what I thought."

"Courage is the price that life exacts for granting peace."
—Amelia Earhart

34

CHAPTER

CLARE CRAIG

When Leslie Carter unexpectedly walked into the Chevy dealership on a Friday evening early in August, Clare did a double-take. As general manager she had to oversee the sales staff and approve each deal. She was chatting on the phone with the head of the service department when she saw Leslie.

He had a luxurious tan from long days of sailing in the sun. He wore shorts and boat shoes and was so handsome it was difficult to take her eyes off him.

She watched as he approached the receptionist, who turned to shoot a glance in her direction. Clare swiftly ended the phone conversation, stepped away from her desk behind the glass wall and hurried into the showroom.

"Leslie, hi," she said, extending her hand. She felt a strong and immediate urge to hug him, but suppressed it, since this was only the second time she'd seen him. They'd talked occasionally over the intervening months and there'd been a couple of postcards, even some e-mail messages, especially after Zachary's birth. But she'd forgotten what he looked like. Absurd as it seemed, she'd forgotten he was this attractive, this downright good-looking.

Leslie stared at her extended hand, as though he was having the same thought—that this was too formal a greeting for someone who'd become a friend. He smiled warmly before clasping it between his own two hands.

"When did you get back?" she asked.

He peered at his watch. "About three hours ago."

He'd come almost directly to find her. His answer flustered and thrilled her.

"I thought I'd take you to dinner, if you're free."

"Let me find out." She already knew there was nothing scheduled for that evening, but glancing over her appointment calendar would give her a few minutes to gather her wits. With Michael living at the house now, she wasn't exactly free. But she didn't want to launch into a long explanation about her ex-husband or why he was living with her.

"Janet, would you get Mr. Carter a cup of coffee?" she asked as she disappeared into her glass office.

She made a pretense of looking in her book, then dialed the house. She couldn't very well announce that she had to check with her children before she agreed to a dinner date.

Alex answered on the second ring, his voice hushed.

"How's Dad?" she asked.

"He's sleeping."

"I'm going to be late, is that all right?"

Alex was silent. "How late?" he finally asked.

The boys took turns staying with Michael. He didn't want or need constant attention, but at this stage of his disease, no one was comfortable leaving him at the house alone. He was usually in a drugged state, and growing weaker day by day. Mick and Alex were with him during the days, and she often relieved them in the evenings.

"I'll be home before eight," Clare said. She and Alex reviewed the medication schedule for Michael, then she hung up.

Leslie was waiting for her. He stood when she returned to the showroom.

"When would you like to leave?" she asked.

"Is now too soon?"

"Now would be perfect."

Clare knew Leslie's arrival had stirred a lot of interest among the staff, but it didn't bother her. Her long hours had brought the dealership back to prosperity within a few months. With the staff's cooperation, she'd averted chaos and financial disaster. Her ideas had been welcomed and put into action, and all the employees had rallied around her. With some inventive, humorous television advertising, the dealership was reaching record sales.

True, the hours she'd put in were grueling. The reasons behind her renewed ambition, her drive, weren't entirely clear, even to her. Yes, the dealership was Mick and Alex's heritage, but there was more to it than that. Clare had something to prove to herself, and to Michael.

Living with her ex-husband wasn't easy; despite that, she felt the decision had been right. For Michael, for her and for their sons.

Clare didn't spend a lot of time alone with Michael. Because of her hours at work, she often didn't arrive home until he was asleep. But he remained in her thoughts—and in her heart. It had come as a revelation to discover she still loved him. Not the same way she had when they were married, of course. Now she loved him because of what they'd had, what they'd once been to each other. She loved him as the man who'd fathered her children.

"What's your favorite kind of food?" Leslie asked as he escorted her outside.

"Italian," she said automatically.

"Mine, too. Ever been to Mama Lena's?"

Clare nearly tripped over her own feet. "Yes." It had been Michael's and her favorite restaurant.

Some emotion must have been evident in her response because Leslie immediately said, "Someplace else?"

"Please," she whispered, not eager to explain.

"Luckily there's any number of good Italian restaurants close at hand. You choose."

Clare did, and before long they were sitting across from each other in an elegantly spare room, dipping warm bread into a small dish of flavored olive oil.

"I didn't know you were planning to get back this soon," Clare said, taking a leisurely sip from her glass of Chianti.

"I wasn't."

"Have you had a chance to check in with Julia and Peter yet?" she asked.

"I talked briefly to Peter earlier this afternoon," Leslie told her. "He was on his way to the hospital to relieve Julia, so we didn't get much of a chance to chat. He sounded pretty stressed so I didn't keep him long."

"I know." Liz gave her an almost daily update on the baby's progress.

"How is Zachary?"

Clare shook her head, unsure how to respond. "This is such an incredible baby. He wants to live so much. Julia and Peter are with him practically every minute. I talked to Julia the other day about his progress, and it's as though she's speaking in a foreign language. All these medical terms and procedures..."

"Little Zack's going to make it, isn't he?"

"We hope so. I gather that most of Zachary's problems have to do with his lungs. He isn't even supposed to be breathing air this soon, and it causes serious complications."

"Poor little boy."

"You can't imagine how small he is," Clare told Leslie. "Julia showed us a photograph at our baby shower, and he's barely as big as Peter's hand."

"Can they hold him?"

"They have." Clare wasn't sure how often. "Julia showed us another picture of Peter in a rocker with Zachary against his bare chest." Then feeling she should explain why Peter had removed his shirt, she added, "The baby needs Peter's body heat in order to keep warm. He can't regulate his own body temperature yet."

Leslie nodded.

"I pray every day that he survives." It was a prayer every member of the breakfast club shared.

From the subject of Zachary, they turned to talk of Leslie's adventure, sailing from California to Hawaii, and then the return flight home. The sailboat was berthed at Kauai while Leslie took a break from sea life. His crew of three had dispersed, two of them planning to stay in Hawaii, the other heading up to Alaska. He'd fulfilled his dream, achieved his goal and now had some decisions to make.

The meal was delicious; Clare had ordered a Caesar salad and her favorite eggplant dish. They lingered over a second glass of wine and then espresso. When they finished, Leslie drove her back to the dealership.

Precisely at eight, Clare arrived home, just as she'd promised. After dropping her purse on the kitchen counter, she ventured into the den, where they'd set up Michael's hospital bed.

"I'm back," she announced.

Mick sat at his father's bedside, the two of them watching television. Every time Clare saw Michael, she felt a sense of shock. He'd lost so much weight that he barely resembled the man she'd known. His skin held a yellowish tinge and his face was gaunt and drawn. The ravages of the cancer seemed more apparent every day.

"Who'd you go out to dinner with?" Mick asked. "Alex didn't say."

"A friend."

"Male or female?" Michael asked, turning his attention on her.

She hesitated, then decided there was no reason not to tell the truth. "Male."

Michael's eyes narrowed. "Anyone I know?"

She shook her head.

"I might," he insisted. "You can't say that until I have a name."

"Leslie Carter," she told him reluctantly. "He's Julia Murchison's uncle."

Michael frowned, and she could tell he was displeased. "Did you have a good time?" he asked.

"Yes." She wasn't going to lie, but she didn't intend to rub his face in it, either. This wasn't a revenge tactic. Her dinner with Leslie had been a pleasant outing and she refused to feel guilty about it.

Mick made a show of checking his watch. "I'm meeting a few friends later. Is it okay if I leave now?"

"Of course," Michael whispered. He closed his eyes, resting his head against the pillows.

When Mick left, Clare remained standing in the doorway. "Would you like a cup of tea?" she asked.

Michael nodded. "Please."

She made them each a cup and carried his into the room. Michael was out of bed, wearing his bathrobe and sitting in the nearby recliner. He rarely had much energy to move around anymore, especially toward nightfall.

"Can you stay for a few minutes?" he asked as she was about to leave.

Clare sat on the end of the bed. For a few moments, they both gazed at the television screen, as if a rerun of *Law and Order* was of utmost importance.

"I didn't know you were dating," Michael said in a casual tone.

Clare wasn't fooled. She opened her mouth to explain that Leslie was only a friend and that technically this was their first date, then changed her mind. She didn't owe Michael an explanation, nor did she feel at ease discussing this subject with him.

"When did you meet him?" he asked, again making his interest sound casual.

"Why?"

Michael still stared at the television. "No reason." He sipped his tea, then asked, "Do you intend to see him again?"

"Probably. Listen, Michael, I'm not comfortable talking about my social life with you."

"Sure," he said with an offhand shrug. "It's none of my business, right?"

"Right."

There was a pause during which they both watched the show. Then he murmured, "You might have waited."

"Waited," she cried, suddenly angry. "For what?" They'd been divorced for nearly two years, separated for three. He certainly hadn't waited to move in with Miranda.

He glared at her then. "I'm dying, Clare," he said in a low voice.

"Yes, I know. And I wish with all my heart that none of this—none of it—had happened. But you aren't my husband. *You* were the one who didn't want to be married to *me,* remember? Just because you live in my home now—"

"A house I bought and paid for," he shouted with more energy than she'd seen in weeks.

"Like hell," she tossed back. "I worked just as hard for this house as you did."

Michael clamped his mouth shut. "You can screw everything in pants for all I care, but I'd appreciate it if you'd—" He stopped abruptly and pressed his hand over his heart. His breathing came in deep, irregular gasps.

"Michael! Michael!"

He shook his head. His tea had fallen from the end table and spilled onto the carpet.

"Should I call for help?" Clare had already moved into the hallway, toward the phone. She didn't know what else to do.

"I'm all right... Just go."

Clare stood there in the doorway, irresolute. She couldn't tell if this attack was the result of their argument or a consequence of the disease. She started to leave, since that was what he seemed to want.

"No." He held out his hand to stop her.

She came slowly back into the room.

"I'm sorry—you're right," he said hoarsely. "Who you date is none of my damn business."

She nodded and turned away before he could see the tears in her eyes.

> "It is best to learn as we go, not go as we have learned."
> —Leslie Jeanne Sahler

35

CHAPTER

JULIA MURCHISON

August 24th

The last time I wrote in my journal was the morning of Zachary's birth. It's hard to believe that was nearly two months ago. From the moment he was born, everything in our lives has been centered on him.

I'll be heading out to the hospital soon, since I try to get there by eight every morning. I'm writing this at the kitchen table, with a cup of tea at hand. (Yes, real tea once again!)

I used to worry about the shop. I'd get into a state if I had to close an hour early, certain I was losing a sale. In the last two months, I've barely given my fledgling business a thought.

Thankfully, my mother, Georgia and—to my everlasting surprise—Irene Waldmann are taking turns filling in for me. I realize this isn't a permanent solution, but all three claim they're enjoying themselves. It's one less thing to worry about. Mom's fully retired now and she loves to knit as much as I do. She came to me recently and suggested she continue working half-days after Zachary's home. Then in the afternoon, we can trade places and I'll work while she stays with the baby. I haven't talked to Peter about it yet, but the suggestion sounds ideal to me. Mom isn't the only person wanting to care for Zack—my sister volunteered and amazingly enough, Adam and Zoe, too.

My one concern is that Mom not feel any obligation, but she insists this is something she wants to do. She's alone and after working all these years, she'd miss the routine and the companionship, or so she says. When I asked her about traveling and doing the things she's always talked about, she said she still wants to do them, but for now it's more important to be a grandmother. When Adam and Zoe and Janice's children were born, she was too busy with her job to really enjoy them as much as she would've liked. Zachary's giving her a second chance and she's not about to lose it.

I can only say I'm grateful.

Adam and Zoe have been wonderful, and I'm grateful for that, too. Neither Peter nor I have given them much attention lately, and I realize our being at the hospital most of the time is hard on them.

Adam has shown a level of maturity I hadn't seen in him before. Maturity and a willingness to help in any way he can. Luckily, since he has his driver's license, he can take Zoe to her tennis lessons and run other necessary errands. He's chauffeured me to the hospital every afternoon, and we've had more time to talk one-on-one than we have in years. He's shared his goals with me and his plans for the future. I'm thrilled that he wants to go into teaching, like his father. He's a natural with kids, the same as Peter, and would be an asset to any classroom.

Zoe's been a great help all summer, too. She's taken it upon herself to cook dinners and take care of the laundry. I haven't had the time or inclination for housework; when I get home from the hospital, it's late, and I'm exhausted and emotionally drained. Without my having to ask her, Zoe took over. Dinner is waiting for me, and the house is clean. I still can't believe the way my children have pitched in—after all those months of complaining.

Peter, my wonderful, wonderful husband. I've never loved him more than I have in the last two months. Whenever I get discouraged about Zachary's condition, he finds a way to raise my spirits. He refuses to allow me to give up, or worry about the expense. I don't have any idea what the hospital and doctor bills will be or how much will be covered by our insurance. It's frightening to think about. Frankly, I don't care if we end up going bankrupt. I want my son to live and to grow up a normal and happy child.

Looking at him now, seeing the tubes and needles coming out of his tiny, emaciated body, my heart is so full of love it actually hurts.

When I see him struggle to draw each breath, it's hard to remember how much I didn't want this baby. Now all my energy is focused on willing him to improve. He's not out of danger yet, but he's taken a turn for the better. If everything continues the way it is now, we might be able to bring him home close to his original due date in the first week of September.

I know why Liz fell in love with Dr. Jamison. His attitude toward women might be thirty years behind the times (although I suspect much of that's for show). But when it comes to dealing with preemies and their parents, he's a saint. What I like most about him is how deeply he cares. I've never had a physician as tender as he is, or as patient.

He and Liz are well-matched—in their intelligence, their sense of humor, their compassion. I know Liz delayed her vacation because of what's happening with me, although she denies it.

I've missed meeting the group for breakfast, but I didn't need to show up on Thursdays at eight to feel their support. At my lowest point, when I was sure we were going to lose Zachary, they threw a baby shower for me. I'm not likely to forget everything they've done. Their faith and love comforted me during my darkest hours.

Irene Waldmann came by the hospital one afternoon last week with the baby blanket she'd knit for Zachary. Peter was with him at the time so the two of us sat in the waiting area. Her gift meant a great deal to me—the blanket and helping out at the shop and all her concern for Zack and me. There was a time I thought of her as difficult. She's a bit prickly, but I should have seen past that. She mentioned the son she lost and tried not to let me see the tears in her eyes, but I did.

Peter and I decided to ask Irene to be Zachary's godmother. When I mentioned it to her, she grew extremely flustered and immediately left. But she visited again the next day.... Although she didn't come right out and say it, I think she's thrilled. Me, too.

Soon Peter and I will be making plans to bring Zachary home. I feel more confident than ever that our son will, indeed, be coming home.

* * *

Adam was waiting outside the hospital when Julia left at three-thirty that day. They ran into terrible traffic on the commute home, but she didn't mind; it gave them extra time to talk.

He dropped her off at the house and then went on to his part-time job at the neighborhood grocery, where he worked in customer service. When he got off at nine o'clock, he had instructions to come directly home for a celebration.

That afternoon, Zachary had weighed in at a whopping four pounds, and he was scheduled to be released within the week. Each and every one of those precious ounces had been reason enough to throw a party.

"Hi, Mom!" Zoe called out when Julia entered the house. "How's Zachary?"

"Fabulous." She hugged her daughter, then headed for her bedroom to change clothes. To her surprise, Zoe followed her and sat on the end of the bed while Julia shed her dress. She donned a pair of shorts and a tank top.

"I made spaghetti for dinner. I hope that's all right."

Zoe had developed her own sauce recipe that had quickly become a family favorite. "It's perfect."

"I added a can of sliced olives this time."

Julia had to think about that, then nodded. "Sounds good."

"I like cooking." Zoe drew up her legs and folded them beneath her.

Julia sat down next to her daughter. "Something on your mind?" It wasn't like Zoe to follow her around.

"I—I wanted to talk to you and Dad about Zachary, but it's been hard because either Dad was at the hospital or you were."

"I know." Julia hadn't seen as much of her daughter as she had Adam.

"I've...I've had these feelings and Aunt Janice said I should talk to you about them."

Julia took a deep breath, a little anxious about Zoe's concern and unable to guess what it might be.

"All right, let's talk."

Zoe was very quiet for a moment. "I'd better check on the sauce," she said abruptly. She hopped off the bed and dashed into the kitchen.

Although Julia was curious, she decided not to question her daughter. This had to come from Zoe voluntarily. She trailed after her into the kitchen.

Without being asked, Zoe poured her a glass of iced tea and set it out, with two cookies on a napkin—just as if she were serving her mother an after-school snack—which made Julia smile. Then, wooden spoon in hand, she lifted the lid to the simmering sauce and stirred.

"Do you remember when you told Adam and me you were pregnant?" Zoe asked conversationally.

Julia wasn't likely to forget. "I remember."

"I was really mad at you." She continued stirring the sauce, her back to Julia.

"You felt a baby would be an embarrassment to you in front of your friends." Julia spoke in a matter-of-fact voice, merely recounting Zoe's reaction, not judging it.

"I want you to know I don't think of Zachary as an embarrassment anymore," Zoe said in a rush. "I'm glad you had him. I'm proud of my little brother." She sniffled and rubbed her nose. "Mom, I'm sorry for all the things I said."

Julia left the table and Zoe turned, threw her arms around Julia's waist, and hid her face against her mother's shoulder.

"I was so afraid he wasn't going to live."

"That decision was in God's hands. It still is."

"I know..."

"There's something I have to tell you," Julia said, brushing the hair from her daughter's forehead. "When I first learned I was pregnant, I wasn't happy about it, either. I kept thinking of all the things our family would have to give up because of another baby."

"That's all I thought about, too," Zoe admitted, her eyes bright with tears. "I didn't once stop to think what Zachary would add to our family."

Julia was amazed at her daughter's insight. Zoe was right; Zachary had brought them all together again. As Adam and Zoe grew older, their family life had splintered, each member going in his or her own direction. They'd stopped functioning as a cohesive unit.

It was a process that had begun innocently enough as the children grew into their teens, and had escalated when Julia started her own business, since the focus of her energy and attention had gone into that. Even the things they'd once enjoyed as a family, like hiking and camping, had fallen by the wayside.

The kids had their own interests, which was completely natural. Equally natural, Peter and Julia appreciated having some time to themselves and the opportunity to see their friends. In the last couple of years, though, there'd been very few family occasions. She'd insisted on family dinners as much as possible, but too often they were rushed and perfunctory, a source of tension more than pleasure.

Until now. Zachary had changed all that.

"Adam and I talked it over, and we both want to share our rooms with Zachary." She looked quickly at her mother. "Once he's old enough to sleep in his own crib, I mean."

Julia nodded. "He'll be in the bassinet in our room for a few months still."

"Adam thought Zachary should sleep in his room because he's a boy, but I convinced him it was only fair that he spend time with me, too."

Julia smiled despite the tears gathering in her eyes.

"Don't you agree?" Zoe leaned back to look at Julia.

"Of course I do," she said seriously. "Of course I do."

"Adam said once he leaves for college, Zachary can have his room full-time."

"That's considerate of you both."

"I'll watch him, too, Mom. After school and whenever you need me to. I know I said I wouldn't, but that was before he was born and I realized I was going to love him. He's my little brother, you know."

Julia hugged her close.

"And he's very special. No one thought he'd even live, did they? And...and now he's all right, isn't he? That's what Dad said." She gazed expectantly at her mother.

"Yes," Julia whispered. "Yes, he's fine. We've been very, very lucky."

"It's because he's a miracle baby," Zoe told her solemnly. "Our very own miracle baby."

"Vitality! That's the pursuit of life, isn't it?"

—Katharine Hepburn

36
CHAPTER

LIZ KENYON

Liz had never purchased a vehicle of her own. Her car had been new six years ago; after Steve's death, she'd replaced the car destroyed in the accident with one identical to her husband's. She'd given her own car to Brian and driven the new one—for six years now. It had never occurred to her to purchase anything else. Never dawned on her that she might have distinct tastes and preferences.

Now she wanted a car of her own choice. She had the extras, the options and the color selected, but had yet to decide on make and model. The one person she could trust to guide her was Clare, who knew more about automobiles than Liz ever cared to learn.

They met at the dealership one hot August morning; Liz had stopped by on her way to work. Clare walked around the lot with her, pointing out the advantages of one style over another.

"So you're still determined to drive out to Oklahoma by yourself?" Clare said once she'd finished the tour.

Liz glanced away so Clare couldn't see her smile. She was astonished that a woman who managed an entire dealership, cared for her dying ex-husband, maintained a home and looked after two children, would ask such a question. "You seem skeptical. I *can* make the trip on my own, you know."

"You can do anything you put your mind to," Clare said, doing a quick about-face.

"Then why the concern?" They paused in front of a used two-year-old Seville in the very pearl-white color Liz preferred.

Clare shrugged off the question. "I was wondering if it's safe for you to be traveling alone, that's all."

"Why not? I'm not going to take any unnecessary risks. I have three weeks' vacation, so I've got the time for an extended trip. Besides, I happen to enjoy driving on the open road."

"What does your daughter think?"

"Same as you. She's afraid it's not safe. I haven't even pulled out of the driveway yet and already she's worrying."

"Well, maybe you should listen and just book a flight," Clare suggested.

"I could," Liz said as she strolled between the vehicles. She paused and looked back at the Seville. The sleek lines of the vehicle and the color were perfect, and the car had all the options she wanted; not only that, it was still under warranty. Liz sighed. She was definitely considering the Seville, but everything would be easier if she didn't have so many cars to choose from. The choices confused her, and every time she saw one she liked, it was more money than she wanted to spend or, if used, had too many miles to suit her.

"But you won't fly, will you?"

"Probably not," Liz agreed, walking back to the Cadillac Seville and looking inside the driver window.

"What does Sean have to say?"

So Clare was pulling her trump card, and far sooner than Liz had anticipated. "What does he say?" she repeated. "Actually, he hasn't said a thing."

Clare's gaze narrowed. "You haven't told him, have you?"

"Is there any reason I should?" Liz knew she sounded defensive, but she couldn't help it. To think Clare would suggest she submit her vacation plans to a man, any man, for approval! It was laughable.

"He isn't going to like it," Clare said, crossing her arms and exhaling slowly. "And you know it."

"Then he can take a number and stand in line like everyone else." She opened the Seville's door and slipped behind the wheel. Although the vehicle was two years old, it smelled of new leather. Liz adjusted the seat and placed her hands on the steering wheel.

"This is a beautiful car," she murmured. "And it's comfortable." She took a deep breath, relieved to have made a decision. "I'll take it."

Clare stared at her as though she hadn't heard. "Don't you want to test-drive it?"

"Not particularly."

"Liz, I can't let you pay sticker price. You're supposed to haggle with me."

"Why would I haggle?" Liz asked. "You're one of my best friends. If I can't trust you to be fair with me, then who can I trust? You're giving me a good trade-in value and this is a great price." She got out of the car. "Let me know what the total comes to and I'll write you a check." She headed toward her old car, which she'd left parked in front of the dealership.

"Where are you going?" Clare called after her.

"To work. I'm already late. Phone me when you've got the paperwork ready."

Clare hurried after her. "Think about what I said."

"Which part?"

"Just tell Sean, would you?"

Liz frowned. Naturally she'd tell Sean, but not until she was good and ready.

The office was buzzing with activity by the time Liz arrived. She breezed past Cherie, who was on the phone. Her secretary stuck out her arm with the day's mail. Liz took it from her without missing a stride.

When she entered her office, she was surprised to find Sean sitting behind her desk, his long legs outstretched, hands locked behind his head.

"About time you got here," he said, granting her one of his sexiest smiles.

"Is it, now? Have I kept you waiting long?"

"Yes, about six months, but we won't go into that."

Liz rolled her eyes; any reaction would only encourage him.

"I take it you have a reason for being here?" she asked, sorting through the mail as she stood beside her desk.

Cherie came into the room with a cup of coffee, which she handed to Liz. "Would you like a cup, as well, Dr. Jamison?" she asked hesitantly.

"Dr. Jamison is on his way out," Liz informed her secretary.

"Actually I'd love a cup," he murmured, but Cherie had already left.

Liz walked around to her chair. "Sean, I've got a million things to do and I can't do a one of them with you here."

"Hey, don't worry about my ego or anything," he muttered.

"You have a perfectly healthy ego."

"Aren't you going to ask me what I want?"

"Not on your life." Open-ended questions were his forte, and she'd learned the hard way to avoid them.

"A little birdie told me you're planning to drive to Oklahoma on your own."

"Clare?" The traitor! She'd never have believed her friend would go behind her back.

"Clare knows?"

"Who told you?" Liz demanded, in no mood for games.

"Your daughter phoned me."

"Amy?" Liz sputtered. "How *could* she?"

"And that isn't the only secret she revealed."

Liz could well imagine. "I apologize. Trust me, it won't happen again." She led him to the door and held it open for him. "Sean, please, I'm busy."

"Places to go and people to meet?" he said pointedly.

"Yes," she replied with equal emphasis. "Now get out of here."

"We're not through with this discussion."

They were as far as Liz was concerned. She playfully shoved him out the door and closed it. No sooner had she done so than the door opened again and Sean stuck his head inside.

He gave her a hangdog look and she laughed and leaned forward so they could kiss. And what a kiss it was. When they finished, Liz's knees were shaking and her head spinning.

"Dinner tonight?" he asked. "O'Shaunessey's?"

Liz needed a moment before responding. "Six o'clock?"

He nodded and was gone.

Smiling softly to herself, Liz tore into her day.

At five-forty-five, just as she was about to leave the office, Sean returned.

"I thought I was meeting you at O'Shaunessey's?" she said.

"You still can if you want," he told her, stepping toward her desk, "but I have something I want to discuss with you first."

"Fire away." She gestured toward the chair.

He remained standing. "I've been thinking about our conversation this morning."

Liz wrinkled her brow; she couldn't recall that anything of importance had been said.

"About you driving to Oklahoma by yourself," he quickly filled in.

Everyone was taking her to task about this, and she didn't like it. Before he could elaborate, she held up one hand. "Sean, don't even start."

"Too late, Liz," he said sternly, "it isn't going to happen. You aren't going alone."

Liz frowned at him.

"I'm coming with you."

Coming with her? "I beg your pardon? I don't remember inviting you."

"You don't have to. I've invited myself."

This took the notorious Jamison arrogance to a whole new level. "Sean!"

"Amy and I talked it over," he said, "and this seemed like the best solution. I haven't had a real vacation in ten years. If you want to drive, that's fine by me."

"You and *Amy* discussed this?"

He nodded, looking exceedingly pleased with himself. "I like her. She's a lot like her mother—smart, witty, beautiful."

"You've never met my daughter. How do you know what she looks like?"

"She sounds beautiful. Besides, how can she not be? She's your daughter."

All these months they'd been seeing each other and not once had Sean said she was beautiful. The compliment, although backhanded, robbed her of any witty reply.

"You know what else Amy suggested?" Apparently more relaxed now, he threw himself down in the chair. "She said she wished you'd marry me."

"She didn't!" If ever there was a blatant lie, this was it. Amy would *never* suggest such a thing.

"She did so," he said.

Liz stared at him, hardly knowing how to react. Then it dawned on her that he just might be serious. They'd never discussed making their relationship permanent. "Is this a proposal, Sean?"

The laughter faded from his eyes; her question appeared to catch him off-guard. He gazed at her a full minute, then muttered, "I don't know."

Neither did Liz.

"I hope you decide to let me take this trip with you," he said, standing now and heading toward the door. He seemed in a rush all of a sudden, as though he regretted introducing the subject of marriage.

Liz reached for her purse, locked up and followed him out. "The truth is, I didn't really want to go alone, but there wasn't anyone I could ask to join me."

"I'm volunteering," he said, taking her hand and placing it in the crook of his elbow.

"Then I'd very much enjoy the pleasure of your company."

He looked as if he were about to kiss her, then hesitated. "How would you feel about a small side trip?"

"Side trip?" she repeated. "Sure. Where do you want to go?"

"Seattle."

"Seattle?"

Sean slapped the side of his head. "This room has developed an echo."

Laughing, she lightly punched his upper arm. "I'd love to visit Seattle. I hear it's beautiful."

"I think it's time you met my daughter." He shook his head. "Actually I think it's time I met her, as well. It's been nearly eight years since I saw her. A lot has changed."

Which meant he had yet to see his granddaughter. Liz could tell this trip was going to be one grand adventure.

They started slowly down the corridor. Everyone else who worked in the administrative offices had already left. "Did you mean what you said about me being beautiful?" she asked shamelessly, wanting to hear him say it again.

He shrugged. "You're not bad on the eyes."

"Well, thank you very much. You aren't either."

"I know."

Liz groaned aloud.

"Hey, are we going to share a hotel room on the drive?" He waggled his eyebrows outrageously.

"I think not."

"You are such a prude."

Liz enjoyed their banter, enjoyed these conversations in which they both gave as good as they got. "Perhaps I am, but you love me, anyway."

Sean chuckled. "Yes, I suppose I do."

"People change and forget to tell each other."

—Lillian Hellman

37

CHAPTER

KAREN CURTIS

September 1st

I barely slept last night. Gwen had her secretary phone me Friday morning to ask for a meeting. When my agent calls, I'm there. Something inside me said she wanted to discuss my audition for the sitcom and I was right. The whole time I was driving into L.A.—and traffic was a bitch—I had this premonition that I'd gotten the role.

Any other time in the past four years I would've been *so* excited. But it wasn't excitement I felt. Instead, I experienced a crazy sort of letdown feeling. Get real! I mean, a television role is what I've wanted my entire life, what I've worked so hard to achieve, what I've sacrificed and struggled for.

By the time I found parking and made my way into Gwen's office building, my stomach was full of knots. That was when it hit me. My head was telling me I should be jumping up and down for joy, and my body was telling me something completely different. It took me a while to connect with my feelings and realize that I didn't want the role.

I stopped in the rest room, washed my face with cold water and stared at myself in the mirror. I don't know what I expected to see because the face that stared back at me wasn't any different. Somehow, I felt it should be....

A weekly television show is the opportunity of a lifetime and worth thousands and thousands of dollars, in fees and residuals. I didn't understand what was happening to me or why I'd hesitate.

Then again, perhaps I did.

The last couple of weeks with the drama class at Willow Grove High School have been *fabulous*. I love the kids and I see so much of myself in them. Myself, ten years ago, that is. Creative, talented, passionate and totally in love with the idea of self-expression.

It's more than just teaching that I've enjoyed. Since I've been at the same school as Glen, we've eaten lunch together every day. I love being around him, love the way I feel, or more accurately the way he makes me feel. It's as if I'm the funniest, wittiest, most attractive woman in the world. No man has *ever* made me feel as special as he does.

I remember when we first met and how I wanted to make sure he understood I was only interested in being his friend. No romance; I wanted fireworks. What I wanted—or thought I wanted—was a man just like me. Glen didn't seem passionate enough. Hard to believe I could have been that blind. Glen is so great. I really admire him. Not only is he brilliant, he's gentle and honorable and...I never thought I'd find this an attractive trait in a man, but he's humble. Yes, humble. We've gone out a couple of times since our movie date and both times I've been the one to suggest it. When I casually led up to the subject of getting together, he seemed genuinely surprised and pleased. Later, when I came right out and told him I'd welcome an invitation, it flustered him so much he asked me to chaperon one of the school dances with him. Then he decided that wasn't the kind of date I'd probably want and withdrew the invitation. It took me five minutes of teasing to make him believe I'd *love* to chaperon a dance with him. Any dance. Anywhere. Any day of the week. (Although I didn't mention that part.)

Well, to make a long story short, when I arrived at Gwen's office, her secretary ushered me into the inner sanctum where my agent awaited. All my worry was for naught. I didn't get the role. In fact, Gwen had viewed the audition tape herself and was disappointed in my performance. She suggested a series of classes for me. In other words I am no longer meeting her expectations. That was the reason she wanted to meet personally with me. I was being put on notice, so to speak.

I didn't sleep well on Friday, and now I'm afraid tonight's going to be an exact repeat.

* * *

The phone woke Karen out of a deep sleep. It took her a moment to realize the ringing wasn't actually part of her dream. Lying on her stomach, she stretched out her arm and groped blindly for the receiver. She opened her eyes just enough to glance at her clock radio and saw that it was just past 1:00 a.m. She hadn't even slept an hour and groaned at having her rest interrupted, especially when she'd had such a hard time falling asleep.

None of her friends would think twice about calling her any time, day or night. Okay, maybe not Glen, but then he was an exception to just about everything.

"This better be good," she muttered into the mouthpiece.

"Karen?" The timid voice was fragile and breathless.

"Victoria?" Instantly alert, Karen sat up, blinking rapidly. "Where are you?"

"Home—can you come and get me and Bryce?"

"Of course." Her response was automatic. Then it dawned on her that something must be terribly wrong if her sister was phoning her in the middle of the night, asking for a ride. "Are you all right?"

Victoria didn't answer.

"What happened? Tell me." Panic filled her throat.

"I might need you to take me to the hospital."

Karen was off the bed and pacing with the cordless phone in her hand. So this time Roger had gone too far. This time Victoria had had enough. She prayed her sister would press assault charges, prayed she'd leave him for good. "Where's Roger?"

"He's...asleep. Just hurry."

"I'll be there in fifteen minutes," she promised rashly. Never in her life had Karen dressed faster. She pulled on sweats, then shoved her feet into tennis shoes without bothering to tie them. Not until she was in her car did she wonder why her sister hadn't simply left on her own. There was something Victoria hadn't told her.

Coming to a red light, Karen stopped and looked both ways; she didn't see any traffic in either direction. Unwilling to waste time waiting for the traffic signal to proceed through its cycle, she ran the light. Halfway through the intersection, she caught sight of a police car.

"Great, just great," she muttered. A heartbeat later, the patrol car was behind her, lights flashing.

Karen pulled over to the side of the deserted street and reached for her purse, extracting her driver's license even before the officer arrived.

As he approached her vehicle, Karen rolled down her window.

"Good evening," he said politely. "Did you happen to notice that the light at the intersection of Universal and Sixth was red?"

"Yes." She wasn't going to lie.

"So why the hurry?"

"My sister..." Karen started to explain, then realized this could be the most opportune event of her life. "Officer, listen, I realize I deserve a traffic ticket." She talked fast, hoping to get everything out without stopping to answer a lot of unnecessary questions. "I won't try to talk you out of giving it to me."

He raised his eyebrows. "This is a refreshing tactic."

"My sister just phoned me and...and I'm afraid her husband beat her again. She asked that I come and get her...." Karen swallowed hard, knowing that if she involved the police she was going against her sister's wishes. Victoria wouldn't want her talking to the authorities. But she'd begged for help and this was the best way Karen knew to provide it.

"My brother-in-law is physically abusive," she continued, "and I don't know exactly what the situation is right now." Nor was she comfortable walking into circumstances that had the potential to be explosive. If Roger had no qualms about hitting his wife, he probably wouldn't hesitate to attack his sister-in-law. Especially a sister-in-law he considered an interfering bitch.

The young patrol officer asked her a few questions, returned to his vehicle for a moment and then walked back to her car. "The address you gave me is out of my area. A patrol car has been dispatched and will meet you there."

"Thank you." Karen was so grateful she felt like sobbing. "Can I leave now?"

He nodded, and gave her a written warning as well as a verbal one. She drove off immediately, careful to stay within the speed limit. She hoped she arrived at her sister's before the police did so she could explain to Victoria what she'd done and why. It'd taken tremendous courage for Victoria to call her, and Karen didn't want to destroy her fragile trust.

The outside lights were on when she turned into the driveway. As soon as she did, Victoria opened the front door. She held Bryce with her left arm, her right arm cradled against her side.

Karen leaped out of the car and hurried forward to help her sister and nephew.

"What happened to your arm?" Karen demanded.

"Daddy hit me real hard," Bryce sobbed, "then he pulled Mommy's arm."

So Roger had taken to hitting his son. Victoria had accepted the abuse for herself, but now that her husband had begun to hurt their child, she'd drawn the line.

"How bad is it?" Karen asked, wondering if she needed to get her sister to the hospital immediately.

"It doesn't matter. Let's go." Victoria's voice was edged with panic. "Please, it's all right."

"Mommy, Mommy?" Bryce started to cry louder.

"Everything will be fine, sweetheart." Victoria comforted him in soft tones. "Auntie Karen's here to take us to her house."

Karen ushered the two of them toward her car and was fastening Bryce's seat belt when she heard Roger's shout.

"What the hell do you think you're doing, bitch?"

"Go," Victoria cried.

"No." Karen turned to face her brother-in-law, who stood in the open doorway, his hands on his hips.

Swearing and clearly drunk, Roger stumbled down the steps and started toward his family. He was in a rage, his face red and twisted with anger. He stared at Karen, and then Victoria, who huddled protectively over her son in the back of Karen's vehicle.

"Stay out of this," he warned Karen.

"I wasn't going to say a word."

Her response apparently surprised him, because his gaze wavered from his wife and son to briefly clash with hers.

How dared he hurt her sister! How dared he strike a child! "You're a pitiful excuse for a man," she said contemptuously.

He swore again and lunged at her. Karen was quick on her feet and managed to avoid his swing. Victoria screamed. Unfortunately, when Karen moved, she gave Roger access to his wife. Cursing, he reached inside the car and yanked on Victoria's arm.

Victoria let out a shrill cry of pain.

Hardly aware of what she was doing, Karen leaped onto Roger's back, pounding him with both fists. Everyone was shouting at once, Bryce was crying and Roger was bucking and heaving in an effort to throw Karen off.

Out of the corner of her eye, Karen saw the patrol car pull up to the curb and released her frantic hold on her brother-in-law. That gave him the slack he needed to strike out at her. She didn't see the punch coming until it was too late. He got her square in the jaw, hitting with enough force to knock her to the ground.

Almost immediately, the two police officers had Roger in a tight grasp. They dragged him away, toward their car. Roger's demeanor altered instantly.

"Officers," he said, sounding completely sober. "I'm glad you're here."

"Sure you are, Roger," Karen shouted back, although her jaw ached just from talking and she still felt so dizzy she thought she might faint.

While one officer spoke with him, the second approached Karen. "Can you tell me what's going on here?" he asked.

"My sister..." Karen pointed to Victoria, who climbed out of the car, holding Bryce against her left side.

"This is all my fault," Victoria sobbed.

"It *isn't* your fault!" Karen yelled, afraid that now, with the police involved, her sister would change her mind.

"I should never have called you," Victoria said.

Then they were talking at the same time, each one struggling to be heard over the other. Karen was trying to explain why the police were there, and Victoria kept insisting she was to blame. Roger was shouting, too.

"Who's married to whom here?" the older of the two officers asked.

It took several minutes to sort out the details. As she listened, Karen couldn't help thinking that her brother-in-law was the one who deserved a career on the stage. According to him, Karen was a meddlesome troublemaker intent on breaking up his marriage. He wanted to press charges against her for a malicious attack on his person. While it was true he'd struck out at her, he said, he'd only been defending himself. When he finished, he demanded that the police haul her away.

For one confused and crazy minute, that seemed about to happen. Then Victoria stepped forward.

"I...I phoned my sister..." she said in a small, hesitant voice.

"All right, all right," Roger said, staring at Victoria. "I'll be willing to drop the assault charges against your sister if you'll agree to put this...this incident behind us."

"You've got to be joking," Karen yelled.

Roger ignored her. "I'll admit I did get upset with my wife earlier and I probably overreacted." He turned to the officers, laughing as if it'd all been a misunderstanding that had gotten out of hand. He regretted his annoyance, he said; the last thing he wanted was to turn it into a federal case.

"I'm sorry, sweetheart," Roger said next, looking at Victoria again and sounding eminently reasonable. "I really do regret this. There's no need to get the police involved in a family matter, is there? You don't want this, and neither do I."

Victoria bit her lower lip, her eyes cast down. She actually seemed to be considering his words.

Karen didn't know what she'd say or do if her sister decided to go back to this bastard. She noticed that the neighbors' houses were now blazing with light. Great—an audience.

"I'm sorry, too," Victoria whispered.

Roger relaxed and glanced toward the police officers again. "A man works hard all week. Is it too much to ask that his wife have his dinner ready when he gets back from a Saturday golf game with clients?" He made a good-natured question out of it, but Karen heard the censure. In his view, this *was* all Victoria's fault.

"I'm sorry," Victoria repeated, her voice stronger and more confident now.

"I know you are," Roger said in cajoling tones. "Why don't we let these people go about their business and get back inside? Come on, sweetheart."

Karen thought she was going to be sick.

"I'm so sorry it's come to this," her sister continued. She turned to face the two police officers. "I'll be pressing abuse charges against my husband. I believe my shoulder's been dislocated. This isn't the first time he's hit me—doctor's records will confirm a number of recent visits in which I've been treated for so-called accidents."

Roger's anger exploded and he started toward his wife, fists clenched, but the police restrained him. Within minutes, he was in handcuffs and in the back of the patrol car.

Victoria sobbed and Karen gently placed both arms around her sister, offering what comfort she could. At the same time, she held tightly onto Bryce. He didn't understand what was happening or why. He clung to his mother and buried his face in her stomach, not wanting to look.

It was dawn before Victoria was released from the hospital emergency room, where her shoulder had been reset, and a police report filed. Not long after that, Karen brought their parents fully into the picture. Victoria, along with Bryce, moved back into the family home that day, and Vernon Curtis made immediate arrangements to collect their clothing and personal belongings. He also provided Victoria with an attorney whose name Karen recognised—Lillian Case. Their father had always been a practical man, Karen thought now, something his daughters had never valued enough.

At noon, an exhausted Karen prepared to return to her own apartment. She'd been a heroine in her family's eyes, and she basked in their love and approval. Before she left, Victoria hugged her and with tears in her eyes thanked her sister.

But the one with real courage had been Victoria. Roger was a formidable enemy, but his reign of terror had finally come to an end. Karen would relish sitting in the courtroom when her brother-in-law faced a judge.

She didn't wake until nearly six that afternoon. She sat up, stretched her arms luxuriously and reached for the telephone. Although she'd never called Glen, she knew his number by heart.

He sounded preoccupied when he answered.

"It's Karen."

"Karen...hello."

The joyful surprise in his voice warmed her from the inside out. "You doing anything important?" she asked.

"Not a thing."

"I thought I'd invite you to dinner."

"Sure. What night?"

"How about tonight?" she asked, smiling as she spoke. "It's a celebration."

"What time? And what are we celebrating?"

"A job."

"You got the part in that sitcom?" he asked.

"No, they turned me down flat." She felt such rightness about all of this. "Actually, it's a little premature to celebrate, but I'm fairly confident the position of drama teacher is still open."

"It was the last I heard," Glen assured her. "Are you applying?"

"I do believe I am."

Her announcement was met with a shocked silence. "Are you *sure* about this?"

"Yes," she told him. "I'm very sure."

All her life, Karen had known what she wanted; she hadn't known nearly as well what she *needed*. Only now was she beginning to understand the difference.

May the road rise up to meet you, may the wind always be
at your back

—Irish toast

38

CHAPTER

LIZ KENYON

September 7th

In a moment of weakness I allowed Sean to talk me into coming along on
this driving vacation. Afterward, I had some reservations, but I have to
admit, I'm enjoying his company. We left early this morning. I had our route
all planned. The first night I thought we'd stay in Flagstaff. We could drive
farther, but I wanted to have plenty of time for stops and sightseeing.

One day on the road, and all my careful calculations went down the
drain. We're in Las Vegas. Sean's idea, naturally. I'd been here once before, years ago, with Steve. Has this town changed! We're staying at the
New York, New York. As soon as we checked in, I went to the video poker
machines and Sean headed for the blackjack tables. I didn't see him again
until dinnertime. He got us tickets to see Lance Burton's magic show, and
we didn't call it a night until after one. Tomorrow we hit the road again.
I almost hate to leave.

September 13th

I meant to document every day of the trip, but by the time I get to bed, I'm too exhausted to write. Sean and I ended up spending two nights in Vegas. We'll probably stop there on the way back, too, if time allows. Naturally it depends on our route. I asked him about visiting his daughter, and as best I can determine, he hasn't made contact with her. It's hard to keep my opinions to myself, but on the subject of his ex-wife and daughter, I'm doing exactly that.

Those two nights in Vegas were a wonderful start to this vacation. It's like an amusement park for adults. I came away a hundred dollars richer and Sean isn't saying, which leads me to believe he lost at the blackjack tables. We sat and played slot machines for a couple of hours during our last night there, laughing and joking with each other. The mood was light, energetic, *fun*. It's very easy to love this man. Far too easy.

The third night, we stayed in Amarillo, Texas, which made for a long day on the road. I was anxious to get to Amy and Jack's, and Sean seemed to realize that, pushing ahead. We arrived in Tulsa by nightfall. Amy had dinner waiting for us. She'd also prepared *two* guest rooms, one of them the den with pull-out couch. Sean offered to take that—an offer I accepted.

Andrew and Annie were all over Sean, and he's just great with kids. Both my grandchildren think he's wonderful and so does Amy. In fact, the four of them are getting along famously.

Yesterday afternoon Jack took Sean to play golf, which both deemed a success.

Amy and Jack have adjusted well to the move. Jack got a big promotion with the shipping company and enjoys his job at corporate headquarters. Amy loves being an at-home mom and is grateful for the opportunity.

Our second day in Tulsa, Annie wanted to have a tea party the way we used to when she lived in California, so we did. Sean was invited, too. I wonder if he realizes what an honor that was.

September 17th

Sean phoned his daughter this afternoon. He'd been putting it off and I know it's been on his mind since before we left. Amy and I sat on the patio with the children while he used the phone in the den. He didn't come out for at least twenty minutes, and the instant I saw his smile I knew the conversation had gone well.

After talking to Eileen, he was eager to head for Seattle, which we'll do first thing tomorrow morning. I've so enjoyed this time with my daughter and her family, but it's been a week now and that's long enough. They need to return to their everyday work and school routines.

Sean never did tell me what caused the estrangement between him and his daughter. Nor has he mentioned what caused his divorce—other than "fickleness" on his wife's part. What does that mean? An affair? It's not that I want to hear all the ugly details. It's a matter of trust. I want him to trust me enough to share his past, and I don't know if that's possible for him or not.

September 20th

We arrived in Seattle and the city is just as beautiful as I'd expected. I met Eileen, Sean's daughter, her husband, Ron, and their four-year-old daughter, Emily. The meeting was a bit strained at first.

Eileen looks a lot like Sean, but any resemblance stops there. She's quiet and soft-spoken and delicate. Her husband works for Boeing and is currently putting in a lot of overtime. He's not around much.

Wanting to give Sean as much time as possible with his daughter, I've gotten acquainted with Emily. She's a delightful child.

This evening, as we were driving back to the hotel, Sean finally told me about his divorce. His ex-wife had been involved in an affair with his former business partner—more or less what I'd suspected. As is often the case, Sean was the last to know. The divorce was messy, and because his daughter was in high school, Sean felt Eileen would be better off with her mother. The problem was that she wanted to live with Sean and he turned her down. Eileen was crushed by what she saw as his rejection and afterward refused to speak to him. Apparently his daughter's hurt and disappointment was fueled by her mother. Sean told me his ex has been married and divorced twice in the last ten years.

Sean admitted he'd played a role in the estrangement, though. When Eileen refused to answer his phone calls and letters, he gave up trying to communicate with her. He couldn't force her to let him into her life, or so he reasoned. He kept track of her from a distance, but rather than face continual rejection from the one person he truly loved, he buried himself in his work. It was during this period that he helped establish Little Lambs. Still, he sees now that he should have persisted in trying to stay in touch. He particularly regrets missing her wedding and the birth of his granddaughter.

After our talk, we walked along the Seattle waterfront to the hotel. I feel that the bond between us has grown. There's trust and commitment now. I'm happy, happier than I've been since Steve died.

While Sean was in his room changing for dinner, I stood on my balcony, which overlooks Puget Sound, and watched the sun set over the Olympic Mountains. This has been one of the best vacations of my life.

"The excursion is the same when you go looking for your sorrow as when you go looking for your joy."

—Eudora Welty

CHAPTER

CLARE CRAIG

October 22nd

I've been spending a lot of time at the hospital with Michael, doing what I can, which seems damn little at this point. The boys are here, too, as much as possible, although it's difficult for them to see their father like this. I'm proud of them. It isn't easy to watch your parent die and they're handling this with an inner strength I didn't know they possessed.

Mick and Alex both decided to take the first semester off from college; they didn't want to leave their father, knowing that Michael's time is very short now.

Because of the drugs, Michael's out of it most days, but every now and then, the fog clears and he's aware of who's with him and what's happening.

This evening was one of those times. He's so weak now. The fight is gone and with it the will to live. I always thought that when death came, it would be as "a thief in the night," stealing away what is most precious. I thought death would be resisted to the final moment, the final gasp. It's not true. Michael has accepted his death.

In those few moments of clarity, Michael told me he doesn't fear it anymore. After everything he's endured, the pain of liver cancer, the treatment, followed by the riptide of hope and despair—after all that, dealing with death seems almost easy.

We laughed about that. Until tonight I could never imagine laughing about death. But it was either laugh or cry, and I knew Michael needed the laughter more than my tears. Then he did the most unexpected thing.

He reached for my hand and without a word of explanation whispered that he was sorry.

He didn't need to elaborate. I knew what he was saying. He was sorry for the affair, sorry for the divorce, sorry for the grief he'd heaped upon me.

I remember when he first told me he was moving out. The shock of his falling in love with Miranda had left me speechless. I was stunned and bewildered long before I felt the pain of his betrayal. Perhaps that should have told me something. I remember that, as he was packing, he claimed I didn't need him and Miranda did. At the time that incensed me. Of all the ridiculous things to say! If he wanted a clinging, insecure little girlfriend instead of a grown-up wife, then he was welcome to her.

Only now do I truly understand what he meant. It wasn't that I didn't need him, because I did in all the ways that mattered. It was that I didn't let him know it. I didn't let him know I enjoyed his company and valued his opinion. I'd slipped into the habit of making all the important decisions when it came to our family. I was the one who handled the finances, dealt with our sons, the house and just about everything else. Without knowing what I'd done, I stripped Michael of his pride.

I'm not justifying the affair, but I'm admitting I played a role in what led up to it. It's easy to excuse Miranda. She was young, vulnerable and grieving her father's death. Because of that, she confused dependence with love and latched onto Michael.

As Michael coped with the cancer, he seemed to need forgiveness. He's talked to the boys, talked it all out with them, but not me. Not until tonight.

I forgave him, and then I asked him to forgive me. He held my hand, nodded briefly and turned his head away, but not before I saw the tears. I would have said more, but I was crying, too.

Death is approaching. I can feel it now, sense it. Everything inside me is screaming that it's too soon and Michael is far too young to die. But if he can welcome death, surrender to it, can I do less?

Who would have thought the end would come like this? I've hated Michael, and I've loved him. Now as death grows closer, I've discovered that my love is stronger than my hate

* * *

"Mom." Alex gently tapped her shoulder and Clare started, unaware she'd fallen asleep.

As she'd sat vigil at Michael's bedside, she'd drifted off. Her sons stood on the other side of the raised bed, looking at her, their eyes filled with dread and pain.

"Dad's breathing has slowed," Mick told her.

Clare chewed on her lower lip. This was exactly what they'd been told would happen. Michael was in the final stages of the disease and had, several days earlier, quietly slipped into a coma.

Her pulse racing, Clare glanced at the heart monitor and watched the irregular beat of his heart. She reached for Michael's hand, holding it firmly between her own as his body released its life.

"No..." Alex sobbed, his agony nearly undoing Clare's forced calm. Then there was nothing. A beat. One solitary beat, followed by a flat line. A nurse stepped into the room and stood with them, noting the time of death on a chart.

This was it? The end? Somehow Clare had expected there to be more as Michael Craig moved serenely from life to death. Then the reality of it suddenly overwhelmed her and with it came a flood of pain, the current so strong it threatened to pull her under, to consume her. Alex broke down and crumpled into the chair, his shoulders racked with sobs. Mick stood tall and silent. Clare wanted to reach out to both her children, but was lost in her own agony.

"We will always love you." She choked out the words and leaned down to kiss Michael's forehead. Kiss him goodbye.

"It's over," Mick announced as though this was the end when in some ways it was only the beginning.

Clare nodded and walked around to the other side of the bed. Her two sons hugged her, the three of them forming a tight circle. The same circle they'd formed the afternoon Michael had moved out of the family home. Only this time Michael was gone forever.

The funeral took place two days later, and the service was crowded with people from the business community, family and friends. The *Willow Grove Independent* ran a full-column obituary and the dealership closed for the day. Clare hosted the wake at her house.

Liz, Karen and Julia were all there, helping with the setup, seeing to the guests and lending Clare their love and support. She would never have asked them to help, but was grateful her dearest friends could be with her.

It was evening before the last of the relatives and business associates had left. Mick and Alex were in the living room talking with Karen and Julia when Clare sat down in the kitchen.

"It's about time you took a rest," Liz said, joining her. "How are you holding up?"

Rather than answer, Clare simply nodded.

"It hurts, doesn't it?"

"More than I ever thought it could," Clare whispered. "We were divorced. I assumed I'd done my grieving.... I didn't have a clue."

"I don't think anyone really does."

Clare looked away. She wasn't a woman who easily shed tears, but after a day in which she'd held back all the pain, she could no longer restrain her emotion. "I accepted a long time ago that Michael was dying," she said. "I was prepared—as prepared as anyone can be. Yet when he died, I felt as though someone had shot me in the gut."

Liz nodded, and they sat across from each other, their hands wrapped around coffee mugs.

"I remember when the police officer came to tell me Steve was gone. I heard the words, saw his mouth move and understood what he was saying, but I couldn't take it in. I just couldn't absorb it."

They were quiet for several moments, and Clare suspected her friend was dealing with the impact of her own memories.

"I'll say one thing for Michael. He was full of surprises right to the end," she murmured after a while.

"How do you mean?" Liz asked.

"Our attorney told me Michael altered his will during the last month of his life. He left the dealership to me." She almost smiled. As part of the divorce settlement, Michael had been required to buy out her half of the enterprise. And now...he'd given it back.

"He didn't leave it to the boys?"

"No," Clare said, still amazed. "He didn't give Fred any explanation, but I know what he was thinking. Mick and Alex have no interest in selling cars. Their talents and desires lie in other areas. Being stuck with Craig Chevrolet would be nothing but a burden. It's just not a career either of them wants."

"They could always sell it," Liz suggested.

Clare knew that was exactly what *wouldn't* have happened. Michael feared the boys would keep it out of a sense of obligation and misplaced loyalty. Despite their feelings, they would've held onto it in an effort to honor their father's memory.

"You love the car business."

Clare nodded. "Yes, and I'll make a success of it."

"You already have," Liz reminded her.

All Clare had done was pick up the pieces. Yes, she'd worked long hours, but she'd thrived on the challenge, just as Michael had known she would.

"How are Mick and Alex holding up?"

Clare wasn't sure how to answer. Like her, they'd thought they were prepared for Michael's death, but it had shaken them more than they'd expected.

"They're dealing with it, but they'll need time." As would Clare. She would go on, struggle forward and find her way through this grief, the same as her children.

"How about another cup of coffee?" Liz asked. "I made a fresh pot. Seems a shame to let it go to waste."

Although she'd had enough coffee, Clare felt the need for company. She didn't feel a need to talk, she realized; she just wanted someone to sit with her. Suddenly the thought of being alone seemed terrifying.

Liz poured their coffee and sat down at the table.

Clare tried to speak and couldn't. Then Liz, who seemed to read the agony in her heart, reached across the table and touched her arm. Clare tried to hold back the tears, but it was too hard. She hurt too much.

"Go ahead," Liz said softly. "You don't have to be strong anymore. Let it go."

Clare broke into sobs and felt the comforting arms of her friend around her.

"May the hinges of friendship never grow rusty."

—Unknown

CHAPTER

THURSDAY MORNING BREAKFAST CLUB

It was barely November, and already Christmas decorations were up. Clare pulled into the strip mall where Mocha Moments was located, noting that Liz Kenyon's Seville was parked out front. Knowing her friend, Clare suspected Liz had ordered her croissant and coffee, and had their window table secured.

The air was cool and damp this morning, with a breeze coming in from the Pacific, but Clare didn't mind. The Santa Ana winds had dried out the valley these past few months, and the moisture was a refreshing change.

Clare entered the coffee shop, waving to Liz, and read over the menu, although she always ordered the same thing. When the group had first started meeting, her double-shot espresso, bitter and strong, had matched her mood.

"Espresso and currant scone, right?" the young man behind the counter said, obviously proud of his memory.

"Normally yes, but I'm in the mood for something different this morning."

The teenager's face showed surprise.

"I'll have a pecan roll and coffee," she told him, deciding quickly. It was time for a change.

"Coming right up," he said, bouncing back with a cheerful smile.

When her order was ready, Clare joined Liz and was followed only a couple of minutes later by Karen. Julia arrived last, with Zachary in his carrier; she set him in the middle of the table.

They took turns peeking at the baby, wrapped in his exquisite hand-knit, yellow blanket. In some ways, this precious little boy belonged to the entire Thursday morning group. Like the other women, Clare had invested a great deal of emotion in Zachary. The infant's successful struggle for life brought balance to the loss she had so recently suffered. She was thrilled to see that he was thriving.

"It's almost time for us to come up with another word for the year," Liz said once they'd all sat down with their orders. "For next year, I mean."

"Already?" Clare protested. "You're as bad as these mall people putting up Christmas decorations before Thanksgiving."

"What are we supposed to do with the word from this year?" Karen asked.

"What was your word?" With so much on her mind, Clare had forgotten.

"Acceptance," Karen told her.

"Did you learn anything from it?" This came from Liz.

Karen took a sip of her peppermint-flavored latte and mulled over the question. "Yes, I think I have. A year ago, I was constantly arguing with my mother over which direction I should take. I was so sure I knew what was right for me. *She* thought I should be a teacher. Go figure." Karen made a mocking face. "Then there was Victoria." She paused, apparently thinking it all out. "When I chose *acceptance,* I wanted my mother to accept me for who I am. I wanted her to appreciate me."

"She apparently knows you better than you know yourself."

Karen nodded. "I never realized how much I'd enjoy a classroom, but I'm loving every minute of it. My mother has her annoying little habits, but then we all do. She only wants what's best for me and for Victoria."

Clare exchanged a look with Liz. This was Karen speaking? Wow, what a difference in less than a year!

"Over the last few months, I've learned that I needed to accept myself first. I wanted Mom to be proud of me, the way she was of my sister. At the same time, I resisted that feeling and tried to be as different from Victoria as possible."

"I don't know what Victoria would have done without you," Liz said.

Karen dismissed the praise and seemed almost embarrassed by it. "She's my sister."

"Get back to your word," Julia urged. "I want to know what you learned."

"What I learned," Karen repeated slowly. "Okay. I thought I wanted to act, to work in theater and film, and I do, but I don't need to look for my self-worth in a credit scrolling down some screen. I've discovered something better."

"Teaching high-school drama classes," Julia supplied.

"No," Karen teased, "regular meals."

They all laughed.

"Being on stage is great fun, but sharing my love of the stage with others is even more compelling."

"That's great." Clare was genuinely pleased for her.

"What's the latest on your sister?" Liz asked.

"Ah, yes," Karen said, frowning. "As you already know, Roger's serving a six-month jail term. Victoria's seeing a counselor and with the help of my parents and Roger's, she's back in her own home. She loves her job selling commercial real estate, and seems to have a real knack for it. Mom and I are both confident that she's going to be just fine."

"What about Bryce?" Julia asked.

"He's in a day care facility three days a week and my mother takes him on Monday and Fridays."

"Sounds like an excellent solution," Liz said.

"Is Victoria going to file for divorce?" Clare wanted to know.

"I don't think she's decided yet," Karen said. "She'd prefer not to go the divorce route, but she might not have any option. Naturally, the twit is saying all the right things—he would, with his job on the line—but Victoria needs proof that he's changed first. They'll continue living apart while Roger proves himself."

"I'd hate to see a repeat of the abuse."

"Victoria's being very careful. She's taking it nice and slow, and not making any major decisions until she's had time to work everything through with her counselor."

"Good for her," Liz said.

Karen heaved a sigh. "There's something else about *acceptance.* Glen and I are seriously discussing marriage."

"He proposed?" Julia cried excitedly.

"Well...yes."

"And you've accepted," Clare finished for her. Making the connection.

Karen's face beamed with happiness and she nodded. "He's perfect for me. It's amazing how well we balance each other. Oh guys, I'm so in love."

"That's the way it's supposed to be," Liz said. "When's the wedding?"

"May," Karen informed them. "I already have my new word. *Bride.*"

Clare exchanged smiles with Liz. It wouldn't surprise her if next year Liz announced that she was marrying Dr. Jamison.

"What was your word again, Liz?" Clare asked,

"Time," Liz reminded them. "Last January I hit a real low point in my life."

Clare remembered how lost Liz had been without her family around her.

"It seemed as if all the good years had somehow slipped through my fingers. I felt as though time was disappearing and taking with it everything I'd wanted to accomplish and never would." She frowned. "I suppose I was afraid of living the rest of my life alone. It was bad enough when I lost Steve, but then without the children around me, the loneliness seemed so much worse."

Clare would soon face that herself when both Mick and Alex left for college. The thought of coming home to an empty house every night filled her with dread, and yet the boys were so seldom there that in practical terms it wouldn't make much difference.

"Do you still feel lonely?" Julia asked.

"No." Liz's look was thoughtful. "*Time* is still a good word for me, but not for the reasons I assumed. This is *my time.* In the last twelve months, I've learned to relax and enjoy every single minute."

"You forgot to mention that it's also your time to fall in love."

Liz smiled. "Falling in love," she echoed. "I feel like I'm in high school again. Silly, isn't it?"

"No," Julia insisted with a wistful sigh of her own. "I think it's wonderful."

"And so unexpected," Liz added. "I always said I didn't need a man in my life and I don't."

"But it's certainly a bonus," Karen piped up.

"I think what stands out the most for me," Liz said with a glimmer of amusement, "is that it takes a hell of a man to replace no man."

"What?" Karen asked, frowning. "I don't get it."

"I do," Clare said.

"A hell of a man to replace no man," Karen repeated thoughtfully, then slowly nodded. "I understand now. You discovered that you liked your life, and Dr. Jamison sort of complements the…the *serenity* you found all on your own."

"I couldn't have said it better myself," Liz agreed.

"Well, I've discovered I like my life, too," Karen said, happiness shining in her eyes. "Who would've believed I'd marry a man my mother approved of? Certainly not me, and Mom's wild about Glen. She thinks he's the best thing that ever happened to me. Which he is."

"What about you, Clare?" Liz asked. "What was your word for the year?"

Talk about ironies. *"Faithful,"* she reminded her friends. "I chose it in anger on New Year's Day. At the time, I was trapped in bitterness. I remember thinking *I* was the one who'd always been faithful—to Michael, to our family and to myself."

"You *were* faithful—right to the very end." Julia's voice was so quiet, the others had to strain to hear.

"Yes," Clare replied, "but not in the way I'd anticipated."

"I can't tell you how much I admire what you did for Michael," Liz told her.

Clare looked away, embarrassed by the praise. A year ago she would've laughed in the face of anyone who dared to suggest she'd bring Michael back into the family home. Yet she had. She'd nursed him, loved him and together with her sons, she'd buried him.

"I did learn a valuable lesson this year," Clare said, struggling to keep the emotion out of her voice.

"What was that?" Liz asked.

She wasn't sure she could adequately put her thoughts into words. "I hated Michael for what he'd done to me and the boys. I mean, I *really* hated him. I didn't dare let any of you know how intense my anger with him was for fear you'd think I should be locked away."

Her friends silently studied her and Clare had the feeling that her confession hadn't come as any big shock. They knew and had always known.

"And I loved him," she said. "Deeply and totally. Despite everything. In the end I forgave him—and I forgave myself. In ways I thought were impossible, I *was* faithful—to both of us. To what we'd been and...and to the people we really were." Flustered, she waved her hand and looked away. "I'm not expressing myself very well."

"Yes, you are," Liz countered, reaching for her hand and briefly squeezing it. "You're making perfect sense."

Clare laughed, the sound deep and throaty, and the noise startled Zachary awake. Julia deftly dealt with her son, bringing him into her arms.

"I had an epiphany of my own this last year. My word was *gratitude* but it should have been *surprise!*"

They all laughed again, garnering interest from the people who sat around them.

"I remember the day you told us you were pregnant," Karen said, grinning down at Zachary who looked back at her with big beautiful blue eyes.

"A baby at this time of my life. Oh, pleasssse, say it isn't so."

The laughter rang out again.

"Our family's working as a team now," Julia said. "I'm amazed at Adam and Zoe and how unselfish they've become for Zack. What an incredible blessing he's been."

He gurgled as though to add his own comment.

"The last few months have been hectic," she continued. "It isn't easy having a newborn in the house, especially a preemie who needs a lot of extra care. Starting over with another child is a challenge, I'll grant you that—but I wouldn't change a thing."

"You said you had an epiphany?"

"Basically that's it," Julia said. "I realized that I *can* have it all. The big beautiful home, the husband and family, plus the career. Just not at the same time. I will return to my shop, but not until it's right for Zack."

"That is so wise," Karen said, as though in awe.

"You'd be surprised how smart we all are," Clare said, "you included." She wanted Karen to realize her contribution to the group.

So here they were, the four of them, each at a different place in her life. They could laugh together and cry together and often did, sometimes both at once. To everything there is a season, and these were the seasons of their lives.

Four women, all friends, who met every Thursday morning at eight.